SOLARPUNK

Ecological and Fantastical Stories in a Sustainable World

Anthology edited by Gerson Lodi-Ribeiro

Translated by Fábio Fernandes

World Weaver Press

SOLARPUNK: ECOLOGICAL AND FANTASTICAL STORIES IN A SUSTAINABLE WORLD

Published by World Weaver Press, LLC
Albuquerque, NM
www.WorldWeaverPress.com

Cover layout and design by Sarena Ulibarri.
Cover images used under license from Shutterstock.com.

First edition: May 2018
ISBN-13: 978-0998702292
ISBN-10: 0-998702293

Also available as an ebook

SOLARPUNK:
ECOLOGICAL AND FANTASTICAL STORIES IN A SUSTAINABLE WORLD

CONTENTS

PREFACE
Sarena Ulibarri – 1

TRANSLATOR'S NOTE
Fábio Fernandes – 5

SOYLENT GREEN IS PEOPLE!
Carlos Orsi – 7

WHEN KINGDOMS COLLIDE
Telmo Marçal – 49

BREAKING NEWS!
Romeu Martins – 65

ONCE UPON A TIME IN A WORLD
Antonio Luiz M. C. Costa – 83

ESCAPE
Gabriel Cantareira – 117

GARY JOHNSON
Daniel I. Dutra – 131

XIBALBA DREAMS OF THE WEST
André S. Silva – 155

SUN IN THE HEART
Roberta Spindler – 189

COBALT BLUE AND THE ENIGMA
Gerson Lodi-Ribeiro – 203

ABOUT THE TRANSLATOR
273

KICKSTARTER BACKERS
274

PREFACE
Sarena Ulibarri

The literary roots of solarpunk stretch back decades (at least), influenced and inspired by thought experiments such as Ursula K. Le Guin's *The Dispossessed* and Ernest Callenbach's *Ecotopia*. One of the clearest forerunners is perhaps Kim Stanley Robinson's *Pacific Edge*, the last of his "Three Californias Triptych." The first of these three possible futures for California, *The Wild Shore*, envisions a post-apocalyptic world ravaged by nuclear war. The second, *The Gold Coast*, is a dystopian tale of rampant capitalism. To round them out, Robinson presents a third vision, *Pacific Edge*, a quasi-utopian future in which income inequality has largely been deflated and technology and architecture have adapted to create ecological harmony.

Though the Brazilian publisher Editora Draco was not directly influenced by Robinson's triptych, the *Solarpunk* anthology had a similar genesis. First came *Vaporpunk*, an anthology of Victorian era alternate histories, showing a world run on steam power and clockwork. That was followed by *Dieselpunk*, alternate histories of the World Wars era, with the gritty aesthetic of gas-powered tanks and planes. When I asked editor Gerson Lodi-Ribeiro why he went with "Solarpunk" next, rather than some more established genre like cyberpunk, he told me, "after polluting Brazilian's fantastic literature biosphere [with coal and then petroleum] it was the right time to write stories in self-sustaining fictional civilizations—no matter if those were located in future Earths or alternate history timelines—greener and more inspiring futures or timelimes not troubled by pollution, overpopulation, famine, mass extinctions and anthropogenic global warming. After all, as a reader, I was feeling rather bored myself with all those old dystopian plots."

Weariness with dystopian plots, coupled with a growing awareness of climate change, has been a driving force in the renewed interest in ecological science fiction in the 2010s. The term "Solarpunk" was independently coined by about half a dozen different sources amidst a host of similar terms: ecopunk, hopepunk, brightpunk, eco-fabulism, eco-speculation, etc. While it is part of the larger movement of "climate fiction," the "solar" in solarpunk has come to represent not only the ecological aspect of this budding subgenre, but also the idea of brightness and hope. Fascinating discussions have developed about what the genre is or isn't, what it should look like, where it should stand politically, etc. Indeed, there is much more written *about* solarpunk than there is solarpunk fiction itself.

The limited cannon of self-proclaimed solarpunk fiction was one reason I thought it was so important for this anthology to be translated into English. When I negotiated the deal with Editora Draco, I didn't know if the stories would even fit what was being defined as solarpunk in the English-speaking realm. But I knew it was essential that these early examples not be erased from the conversation simply because they were written in a different language.

The stories in this anthology are far less utopian and pastoral than much of the English-language solarpunk I've read. There is quite a lot of death and violence in them, and several of the stories show that just because a corporation or government is "green" doesn't mean it's free of corruption. And, no surprise when you understand the context in which they were published, two are alternate histories: "Xibalba Dreams of the West" envisions a high-tech Mayan and Tupi-descended society, untouched by European colonization, and "Once Upon a Time in a World" depicts a world in which the industrial revolution was replaced with a sustainable one, leading to accelerated technology and relative world peace—but certain familiar figures still want to make their grab for power. I was particularly surprised by the amount of gothic influence, most notably the immortal monster in "Cobalt Blue and the Enigma" and the overlap of science and religion in "Gary Johnson."

All of these stories feature "sustainable" energy sources, but these energies aren't always shown in a positive light. Because renewable energy has become so politicized in the United States, Americans tend to associate it with liberalism and left-wing ideology—the very *idea* of a world run primarily on renewables is often dismissed as idealistic and utopian. Brazil is actually one of the world's leaders in renewable energy, with 76% of the country's energy in 2017 coming from wind, solar, and hydropower. Brazil's political landscape, however, is certainly not a liberal utopia. Far (very far) from it. Some of these stories reflect that dynamic and defy the notion that sustainable = utopian. The photosynthetic humans in "When Kingdoms Collide" are hiding a nefarious secret; "Soylent Green is People!" shows how some scientists' extracurricular experiments go very wrong; "Breaking News" covers a protest against a GMO greenhouse that takes a sinister turn; "Gary Johnson" is a Borgesian tale of an energy source that is just as unethical as it is abundant.

The two stories I think readers will most readily recognize as "solarpunk" are "Escape," which is a race against time to prevent a planned disaster, and "Sun in the Heart," a much more subtle tale about sacrifices and privilege in a world struggling with food shortages. But I hope you will read all of these stories generously and appreciate the rich and diverse worlds these writers have created. Many thanks to all of the Kickstarter backers who made this translation possible, as well as to the translator, Fábio Fernandes, who has been enthusiastic and diligent through this whole long process, and to the illustrator José Baetas, who has a brilliant eye for picking just the right scene to draw. Extra special thanks to Luca Albani for connecting me with Erick Sama and Gerson Lodi-Ribeiro at Editora Draco and therefore making this whole project possible.

And thanks to you, reader, for picking up this anthology, whatever it was that drew you to it. If you find these stories worthwhile, please tell a friend or leave a review. The world is connected through words, and yours matter just as much as anyone else's.

TRANSLATOR'S NOTE
Fábio Fernandes

It should come as no surprise that the first solarpunk anthology came from Brazil. The biggest country in Latin America also has one of the highest levels of insolation in the world, at 4.25 to 6.5 sun hours/day. Not to mention the punk side of the equation: we strive to make a living in a shattered economy in every way we possibly can.

But let's not forget that solarpunk wasn't born in a vacuum. Most of the stories here will remind the readers of cyberpunk. There are echoes of *Mirrorshades* in this anthology, and that made my job as a translator even more challenging. As in the seminal cyberpunk antho, the solarpunk stories featured here are variegated: there is noir, alternate history, hi-tech utopias. There is ecology and there is punk. As in all good anthologies, the stories in it aren't that easy to pin down or to pigeonhole—and that's quite a feat of the original editor.

It was also a hard task for the translator; I'm used to translating from English to Portuguese, and that was particularly difficult to do in cases like Burgess's *A Clockwork Orange* and Gibson's *Neuromancer*, to name a few of the books I translated to Brazilian Portuguese along the years.

It was a pleasure to translate not only my fellow Brazilians, but also my friends. The challenge here was two-fold: I had to translate not only the stories, but also the author's voices, so to speak. The Brazilian Portuguese colloquialisms and the very creative neologisms in virtually every one of these tales were a pleasure to read. I hope you feel the same.

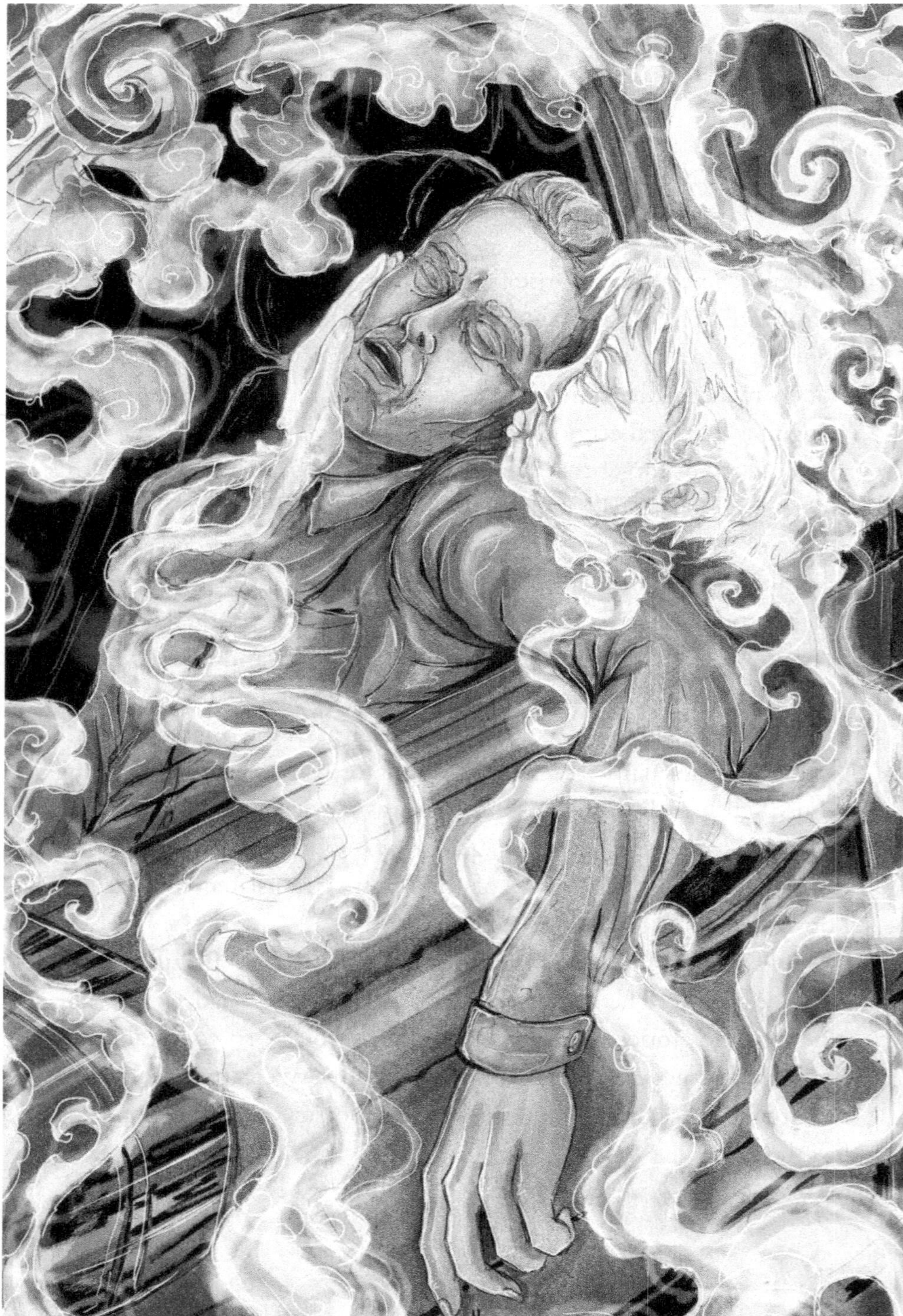

SOYLENT GREEN IS PEOPLE!
Carlos Orsi

When the police finally knocked over the garage door and found Raul's body inside the car, after the smoke subsided, everything pointed to a sad but reasonably simple case of suicide. It was only when the authorities began the always hard process of locating the victim's next of kin to give them the news that the plot, as they say in crime novels, thickened.

Raul Gonçalves da Nóbrega was an engineer at DNArt & Tech. You certainly have some product of theirs in the bathroom, whether it's a culture of bacteria to rub on the skin (DNArt holds the patent for an organism that uses UV rays for photosynthesis and secretes a golden pigment, acting as a sun block and suntan lotion at the same time), or the popular depilator-aphrodisiac hormone.

But I was talking about the next of kin. Raul was an only child, and even though he was over fifty years old, he still lived with his mother, a disabled lady of over ninety who, strangely, was not found in the house by the police officers who attended the incident. The house in which they lived had no employees, and residential automation was minimal and "dumb."

Now, I suppose some eyebrows have risen when the word "disabled" appeared in the paragraph above.

In fact, it is hard to imagine a condition, short of death pure and simple, that can't be greatly mitigated by some combination of gene therapy and cybernetics, and that these therapies are out of reach for a successful, single, childless engineer.

Besides, of course, ninety years is a long way from being a terminal age or something like that.

The reader probably already has the answer: Albertina Gonçalves was a member of the Church of the Puritans. Her faith allowed her to accept external aid to overcome physical weaknesses—glasses and a wheelchair, for example—but no more direct interference in the Inviolable Temple of the Holy Spirit that was her body.

Not even the replacement of her opaque crystallines did she allow, preferring the milky semiblindness of the cataracts; medicine and supplements, from a certain degree of technological complexity, had to be discreetly "smuggled" into her food, which her son lovingly prepared and served, every day.

For months, Albertina simply had not had lunch: she hoped Raul would come back from work so that he would make her a more substantial dinner and they could eat together, she in her bed, he sitting at the headboard.

The wheelchair (actually a maglev) was found in the room, floating beside the bed, but empty. There was a thin layer of dust on the seat, suggesting that it had not been used in ages. Her platinum-rimmed glasses, virtually useless because of the cataracts, but preserved as an icon of vanity, lay on a lavender piece of flannel on the bedside table. There were signs that someone had lain down and then got up—the bed was messed up, the cover pulled. There was a thin layer of dust on the sheets.

"Did she walk out there?" one of the two researchers there joked.

"Only if she was barefoot," the other replied, pointing to the slippers under the bed.

The search of the house showed no sign of the old lady. The garage contained only the car. Inside the car, an off-road biodiesel-powered model, just Raul's body. The wardrobes were full of Albertina's clothes, with few empty hangers. If she had decided to travel, she had left with little more than the clothes on her body. There were also three suitcases, open and empty.

Other rooms of the property, which was small and functional but still managed to be luxurious, also revealed few clues. Raul's room was in a better state than his mother's: neat bedding, the sheet stretched out like that of a barrack cot.

The kitchen was just a kitchen, albeit on a large scale: built-in cupboards, a solitary glass in the center of the sink with an inch of juice in it, a huge fridge-cellar-freezer complex connected to a hybrid solar/wind system on the roof.

The stove, a thing of brushed steel and synthetic ivory, connected to a biodigestor tank in the service area, a cylinder the size of an adult Labrador dog where patented bacteria turned potato and banana peels plus used soybean oil into fuel.

The service area looked out onto a narrow, but long, lush garden, where, in the middle of walkways paved with aged pink marble, there were some empty cages and bird feeders that did not seem to attract a large audience. One of the policemen noted in his report that he smelled beer somewhere between mulberry trees and ornamental bromeliads, but the observation did not catch anyone's attention.

* * *

That's where I came in.

Like the faithful Puritans, in her will and testament Albertina had left all her possessions to the Church if Raul was not alive when she died. The combination of a relatively long life, closed after decades past at the expense of a wealthy relative, and compound interest, is powerful. Therefore, to establish that the mother was dead and her son had preceded her into the Great Mystery became a matter of the utmost interest to the supreme leader of the denomination, the Archpriest Sérvio, who quickly put the considerable legal machinery of the Church to work toward this end.

I suppose the Archpriest would not have had any excuses to hire me right away—I can imagine him listing the various precedents of unworthy men called to serve the Lord's cause, such as disobedient Jonah, the adulterer David, or the cowardly Peter—but my agency certainly came into the case still well below the radar of his lawyers. Although my participation has ended up tied to the Church's demand, the fact is that I entered the investigation via another source entirely.

Sabrina was a tall, long-haired brunette, with brown eyes and skin a color between light brown and deep red, the exact shade of my favorite brand of bitter ale. Her lips and nose were too thin for the fashion of the time; her nose, without being protruding, was narrow like a razor, which gave her a cruel appearance that, honestly, did not bother me at all. I was sitting when she walked into the office in a short white dress. Her knees mesmerized me.

"Your secretary said I could come in."

My silence had probably made her uncertain. I shook my head a little to get back on the ground, smiled and pointed to one of the two empty seats I reserved for clients.

"My secretary" was a mediocre system of commercial automation that basically scanned visitors for hidden weapons or incompatible biological material (some types of mouthwash don't interact well with the bacteria I use to prevent oily skin, and dribbling splutters during the conversation is kind of boring), also making an anthropometric survey of the visitor in the social networks and in the Military Police and Federal Police files.

So, in the three seconds that Sabrina took to sit elegantly in the armchair, my desktop showed me her personal page on FaceSpace, her Currículo Lattes, and a "nothing" from the Public Security Bureau. To get a credit analysis I would need her Social Security number, which she would give me if I took her case, whatever it was.

According to "my secretary," her name was Sabrina Toledo: 48 years old, with half a dozen PhDs in areas such as medicine, genetics, organic chemistry, biophysics, and agrotechnology. She was an employee of DNArt & Tech's R & D department.

"Dr. Toledo." I leaned my elbows on the desk and steepled my hands right below my chin. "How can I help you?"

There was no more insecurity in her eyes, only a cold skepticism. I could almost see the glow of her brain cells firing as she tried to decide whether I was serious or a fraud, whether to tell me everything, or maybe just a little, or turn around and leave without opening her mouth.

"My husband." For some reason, she decided I deserved a vote of confidence. "He's dead."

"My condolences."

Sabrina reacted with a faint smile, as pasteurized and meaningless as my mechanical expression of sympathy.

"I would like to receive the inheritance he left."

"That's a matter for lawyers, isn't it? Why do you need a detective?"

"We were not *really* married." She sighed. "He made a point of keeping it a secret, because his mother depended on him, she had only him. Anyway, no one knew that we were married, and so the natural heiress is the mother, not me."

"Do you need to prove that there was a stable union?" That would also be a more appropriate case for a lawyer...

"His mother is missing."

It was my turn to take a deep breath and let it out in a long breath.

"Tell me everything."

* * *

She told me. It was there that I learned of Raul's death, the disappearance of Albertina, the movement of tectonic plates triggered by Sérvio in the forensic media. In addition to his mother's savings, the son's considerable fortune was also at stake, since Albertina was the natural heir of the engineer's estate, who officially died single and childless.

"I have lawyers working to prove that Raul and I had a relationship of the kind that guarantees me inheritance rights. For me, we were married."

She paused. I waited. Clearly she still had more to say.

"But the Church is sabotaging me. Some witnesses, co-workers who knew how Raul and I were…intimate, now refuse to speak in court. They're getting threats."

I let the expression on my face betray my disbelief. Just because you're paranoid doesn't mean they aren't after you, right, but still…

Sabrina read correctly what was happening behind my eyes and gave me a smile both sad and sarcastic.

"Come on, Detective. You are familiar with 'crying and gnashing teeth' tactics, aren't you?"

This was the name given to a purported network of intimidation created by the followers of the archpriest and dedicated to essentially pestering—or terrifying, depending on the case—the Church's adversaries. Journalists who wrote articles ridiculing its puritanism had their blogs hacked, or found dead rats in their mailboxes; politicians who refused to approve laws of interest to the Church suddenly became the target of ludicrous accusations of sexual harassment, or watched helplessly as long forgotten misdemeanors— bribes received decades ago, illegal campaign donations early in their careers—were brought ruthlessly to light.

A physician who had written a book denouncing the evils of the doctrine of the "Inviolable Temple" to public health was simultaneously prosecuted in twenty states. The work was seized the day after it left the presses. The digital edition, made available by a major international bookstore, had been contaminated by a virus.

"I know that urban legend," I said. "But it has never been proven."

Sabrina started to get up.

"If that's what you think, being a detective…"

Alarmed by the sudden movement of her knees and by the appalling prospect of them being taken away from me so soon, I gestured for her to stop.

"What do you want me to do?"

"Find his mother."

I made a face, as if I didn't understand. After all, if his mother was alive, the inheritance would continue to be open for dispute and Sabrina would still risk being left with nothing.

"Dona Albertina's body was not found," my client explained. "The Puritans' case depends on two things: one, that she is dead, and second, that she died after her son. I want you to *prove* that she's alive."

"Really?"

My cynicism was rewarded with yet another sad-sarcastic smile. Apparently, her stock of those was inexhaustible.

"Or at least set a reasonable doubt that my lawyers can use."

I understood.

"To raise hell with the Church. To distract it. To create confusion in the enemy field while you move forward towards the recognition of the stable union."

She pursed her lips.

"Right."

Then we started to discuss the details.

* * *

The first thing I did after Sabrina left was search for Albertina Gonçalves on FaceSpace. Puritans can be radically against cybernetic implants and recombinant DNA, but there is nothing in their credo that forbids interaction on social networks. From what my client had said, I knew that her mother-in-law was practically blind, but...

And the lady had a presence on the social network all right. Modest, as it were: she quoted her deceased husband, the executive son, posted a few sober and chaste pictures, Bible verses, and a calendar of religious activities that hadn't been updated in six months.

Even in the conservative pictures, I could see that Albertina had been beautiful, perhaps almost to the end. At 87, she still showed a vigorous face, where her (few) wrinkles looked more like marks of character than of age.

Curiously enough, the page was still active. It hadn't been converted into a memorial one. Maybe, I thought, only her son had the access level necessary to make the fateful update. That would be ironic, in a sort of paradoxical way.

Out of curiosity, I visited Raul's page. He had not yet taken the colors of mourning. He was "in a relationship", but Sabrina wasn't in the followers list and his "partner" link was inactive.

Among very lonely people, religious fervor is often linked to the need for companionship and social interaction: submission to doctrine is the "price" of having friends, support, and companionship. So, I wasn't surprised to see that, with the exception of Raul, all of Albertina's other followers were members of Sérvio's flock. I wrote down the three or four of the names and addresses that seemed most promising to my good old intuition and went out into the street.

Many people imagine that, in this world of networks, e-mails, and telepresence, all the detective work can be done from a desk. I'm not denying that much can be done like this. It's possible to learn and deduce a lot from virtual presence alone. But when it comes to interviewing reluctant witnesses, nothing beats the moral weight of physical presence.

And I had the impression that my Church-related sources would all be, at best, highly reluctant. If not hostile.

That said, I must say my conversation with the first person on my list was a pleasant surprise. I had decided to start with Olavo Pereira because he was the man who most often appeared in photos alongside Albertina in FaceSpace, was very close to her age (93, to be precise) and, incidentally, very similar in appearance to the late Raul.

Following the recommendation of my lawyer, I hasten to add that I'm not implying that Olavo was the true father of the alleged suicide. But if the son is like the father (which is a reasonable inference, actually), and after becoming a widow, the mother approaches a man like her son, this may indicate that, in fact, she is looking for a substitute for her dead husband.

Olavo was a tall man—more than a foot taller than me—and thin, but with an Olympic swimmer's chest. His skin had the exact leather texture and color of the boots I use when mountain trekking on the weekends. Under a pair of thick white eyebrows, intense blue eyes watched me as he opened the door to his apartment, a property that was comfortable without being luxurious, located near downtown.

It was in an old building that, I supposed, must have chronic problems with pipes and waste recycling, having been built before the era of urban biodigesters.

Before I appeared, I had sent an SMS explaining the reason for my visit—an investigation into Albertina's fate—and he had responded by making himself available. After a strong handshake, Olavo invited me in, and I made a generic comment about his healthy appearance.

He laughed, shaking his head.

"People tend to think that we Puritans are a lot of human carcasses, living ruins, because we refuse to allow technology to interfere with the physical abode that God has thought fit to grant our spirits, but the truth is just the opposite. We *take care* of the temple. Food and exercise, an active life. If people really cared about the health God gave them, prostheses and genetic implants wouldn't be necessary."

I thought about mentioning cases of hereditary cancer, type I diabetes, amputations, and, in general, the innumerable neonatal diagnoses of low life expectancy and other problems that could only be healed or circumvented through gene therapy or prostheses, but I stopped myself short of it. I had nothing to gain by harassing a source who was willing to speak.

"Did Albertina have a life as active as yours? You seem to spend a lot of time outdoors."

"I look like tanned leather, don't I?" He laughed again. "There's no denying it. As far as I'm concerned, this apartment is just a place where I spend the breaks between my outings and outdoor activities. My life is really in the mountains."

I nodded in acknowledgment that I understood him perfectly. The city lay in what could be described as the bottom of a bowl. The rim, encircling us on all sides, was the mountain range, a complex of gently sloping mountains covered by (almost) virgin forest, interspersed by streams and waterfalls, marked here and there by riverine pebble beaches and cut by parks and trails for trekkers.

"Answering your question," Olavo continued, "Albertina was as active as I was, even more, until about six months ago."

"But she was practically blind from the cataracts, and the wheelchair..."

"It's true that her legs no longer worked, but that 'wheelchair' *levitated* on rocks, rivers, grass, whatever there was! As for blindness, she was never alone and you have no idea what radar and sonar systems are capable of today. Albertina loved the countryside, the open space, the wind in her hair..."

"'Loved'? What happened?"

He shrugged.

"Suddenly, nothing else seemed to interest her. Things she considered easy to do became challenges that weren't worth facing. She was afraid to leave the house with her chair, as if the sonar in the machine was no more precise than the eyes of a guide dog. She...she..."

His eyes were wet. He brought the glass of orange juice in his hands with full force onto the tabletop. The noise was loud, disconcerting, but the glass top stood strong.

"I shouldn't tell you that," he spoke at last, his bombastic voice suddenly assuming an almost confidential tone. "But it's not exactly a secret. We almost had a fight about it in the Church. Before she quit going."

"Yes?"

"It was as if Albertina had *decided* to be an invalid. Just like that."

After an interval of silence, I asked, "She never talked about running away? Going dark? Going away?"

He shook his head.

"And leave her son? No way. The boy was her life."

"But what if she was to run away? If she suddenly got tired of her son, or if her son died? Who would she run away with?"

"With me. And I'm still here."

I thanked him and left.

* * *

Putting the car on autopilot, I called my client.

"Did your husband have friends at the firm?"

"Friends?"

"Friends. People whom he could confidently go out with at night to get drunk…"

"He had me. And in any case, in recent months his mother consumed most of his spare time."

Women. I took a deep breath before going on.

"There are things a man tells a bar mate he wouldn't tell his wife. Bride. Girlfriend. Mother. Whatever."

The line was quiet for a moment. I wondered if the call had dropped. Then Sabrina's voice came back, a little cooler than at first.

"We did not work together. Our areas were different; he was an engineer and I was working on pure research. But he was talking about this guy… Antonio something. From his department. Applications of Biofuel. They had beer sometimes. At least, that's what Raul told me."

"Did you mention him as a witness?"

"No. My witnesses are basically my friends and the HR and security people who record all the relationships in the company and…"

"Thank you. Can you give me the contact of one of these friends?"

She hesitated a bit—thinking that the Puritans had already made the "girls"s lives sheer hell, so on and so forth—but not much, and ended up giving me the data. In the end, I thanked her and hung up.

* * *

It wasn't too difficult to use the net to gather some basic facts about a certain "Antônio somethingsomething" (Kobaiashi de Toledo, actually), biofuel engineer for DNArt & Tech. We exchanged a few instant messages and he agreed to meet me for drinks and olives early in the evening.

It was almost noon, which left me with the lunch issue open. I called my police contact. It would be interesting to know what direction the official inquiry into the fate of Albertina was taking. But we were only able to arrange a meeting for the next day.

Then, unwilling to face other sources from within the Church before listening to the "other side" and, purely for lack of choice, I called Sabrina's friend. She answered right at the first ring. Her name was Cláudia, and she also had her half dozen PhDs.

After some reluctance and having me explain my reasons and goals in five different ways, she accepted my invitation to lunch, but made a point of choosing the restaurant and the time: Piccolo Cuoco at one-thirty. Stifling a grunt, I agreed.

The city had been developing quite a lot in recent years—hey, it was big enough for half a dozen private detectives already!—but among the pains of growth there were the inevitable fruits of the clash between ingrained provincialism and the desire for sophistication.

The Piccolo Cuoco was one of those fruits. Supposedly a traditional Italian family restaurant, it was actually owned by a Spanish man with an obscure past. The place had, on the outside, all the trappings of an upscale *cantina*—from the imported *mortadella* chunks hanging from the ceiling to the checkered tablecloth and the *mezzo* cheeky wait staff with a heavy accent—but the food was awful.

The last time I had been there for supper I had asked for a *penne* with cod slivers that had forced me to stay up until dawn, plucking fish bones from the gums and the roof of my mouth with pincers.

Despite her surname, Cláudia Abdala was blond and blue-eyed. Nothing that looked artificial, but so what? Nowadays, a good doctor can reprogram virtually any gene, including those responsible for pigmentation. There is an endless debate about the "futile" use ethics of retroviral therapy, but whoever has the money to pay does not usually pay attention to these things.

She was also a tall, beautiful, and elegant woman. Nowadays, however, they are all, except for some Puritans and others who choose to use their bodies as the basis for some kind of statement—though, even in those cases, the situation is ambiguous: I once met a poet who had a single red eye right in the middle of her forehead, and yet, or even because of it, she was sexy as hell.

But I was sure Cláudia would never do anything so unconventional. Her lips were full and her nose well-rounded, exactly what fashion dictated. In a crowd, surrounded by other women of the same age, income range, and social position, it would be impossible to tell her from the others. They would all be accidental clones.

I could see that, in a restaurant whose clientele consisted of dozens of other birds of a feather, the anonymity that her aesthetic options guaranteed didn't seem enough. My client's friend walked into the restaurant wearing a wide-brimmed hat and mirrorshades. She looked from time to time over her shoulder, like a bad actress in a bad spy flick. Her body language was confused and erratic.

I could only see her eyes, bloodshot and a bit yellow-tinged, when she finally sat down across from me and took off her glasses with a dramatic gesture. She was late: I was already enjoying my second glass of fernet.

I wrote that she sat down, but the most correct word would have been "collapsed." Her weight fell on the chair like an intolerable burden.

"You have no idea what they did to me." She emphasized the words "idea" and "me." "You really don't."

And she launched into a long soliloquy about indignities, real or imagined, suffered at the hands of the conspiracy of the Puritans. Her transgenic intestinal microbiota refill, essential for weight control, had been sabotaged, hence the swollen eyes and impaired motor coordination; her car had been stopped by a police officer exactly one day after the license expired, but before she had time to pay it, and the officer had been particularly insensitive as well as surprisingly honest. Finally, the only credit card in her bag to pay the cab fare, after her vehicle was towed away, was exactly the one maxed out.

"All this," she finished, pulling a handkerchief from her bag to wipe a tear trapped in a dimple strategically placed over the left corner of her mouth, "in the morning of the day I went to the notary office to file my testimony, you know, about Sabrina's relationship with that engineer."

I raised my left hand and counted off the events:

"Microbiota, police officer, card." I paused to thank the waiter who put a jug of sangria on the table and continued. "It would have to be a job for someone with access to your medicine cabinet, your documents, to find out the license expired and to tell the police, and your wallet, to make sure that only the maxed out card was inside.

"And to my electronic correspondence, to see, on the invoice, which card has maxed out," she finished with a look of contempt on her face. "What a great detective you are. Do you really think I hadn't thought of all this?"

"Oh well. So who was it?"

"My personal secretary." Pause. "I keep a human secretary," she added, incapable of resisting the opportunity to flaunt her status. "She's a Puritan. I hired her because of that: these religious fanatics usually work hard and…"

"…settle for little?"

Could the brief pause that followed be read as a symptom of guilt?

"More or less," Cláudia conceded at last.

"And the guard, was he a Puritan too?"

"I don't know. But I'm pretty sure I do. She must have called him directly. Just imagine, *collecting* my car because of…"

"And you fired her?"

Cláudia gave me a look of sheer horror:

"How could I *live* without her?"

"Then your assistant knows you're here."

"No." For the first time since the beginning of our conversation, something like a smile appeared on her face. The dimple grew larger, not without a certain charm. "Now I have a *secret agenda*."

The food arrived. No seafood for me this time.

"But you were afraid of being followed," I pointed out to her.

"The agenda might be secret, but my movements…"

"Right." I had a forkful of spaghetti, and then I decided it was business time. "So, what can you tell me about Raul and Sabrina's relationship? How long were they together?"

"Years," she answered without hesitating. "Not many, but at least a couple. They even talked about marriage, I think, about seven or eight months ago, but it didn't go well."

"Did they break up?"

"Oh, no. They just stopped talking about *living* together."

I chewed my pasta thoughtfully, digesting the information. Her food arrived next, a thing full of purple leaves and smelling of smoked fish. Silently, I hoped she was luckier with her salmon or tuna than I with my cod before.

"And what was it like 'being together' or 'staying together' for them?"

Cláudia gestured vaguely, turning the knife and resting the fork on the edge of the plate. It was as if she wanted to say, "Gee, I don't know, you know what I mean?" without opening her mouth. After reflecting a little and taking two short sips of sparkling water, she tried to explain:

"Well, they worked in different sectors of the industry. I think they met when Raul was instructed to try to create a process that gave commercial viability to a new yeast she had invented. They had a few meetings, he went to her lab, she went to his workshop, they started to meet at the cafeteria and, well… You know how it is. Birds and bees. The course of nature. Where do babies come from? Et cetera."

"Their dating was public knowledge, then?"

"Not exactly. The board certainly knew, with the kind of pattern recognition software that security cameras have today, that even says if the person who is going to the bathroom really needs it or it's just to kill time. But among colleagues, it was all very discreet. Sabrina is super quiet, she used to talk stuff with her friends… with me… but it seems to me that Raul wasn't like this. No one in his sector knew he was engaged. The two made a trip together to Europe last year, after much effort to synchronize some time off of work to which they were entitled, but the engineering team thought that Raul was on a working trip."

I raised my eyebrows slightly.

"And how do you know that?"

"I heard the boys talking then. It's the kind of thing that tends to catch your attention, even more to me, since I knew the truth."

"And they talked about getting married and living together."

"Yes."

"Did that happen right after the trip?"

"Good question. Yes, I heard Sabrina mention it a day or two after they came back, I guess."

"Are you still going to testify about her relationship?"

Since the beginning of the meal, Cláudia had calmed down quite a bit. The fact that she had arrived at the restaurant safe and sound and the food apparently hadn't been poisoned or sabotaged somehow was quickly rebuilding her sense of self-confidence.

"I'm thinking of going from here straight to the notary's office. As soon as we finish the dessert, I'll call the lawyer." The dimple grew large again, malicious, but then a look of fear formed on her doll face. "You were not followed here, were you?" If they know you're working for her and see us together..."

I thought about it a little. My previous interview had been with a Puritan. A nice fellow, but nothing prevented him from calling the Church right after I left, passing them the coordinates.

I shrugged. It was unlikely that some amateur could follow me without my noticing. And if Cláudia really had misjudged the secretary, I couldn't see we had anything to fear.

"I wasn't followed," I answered, sounding just a little more confident than I actually felt.

* * *

The fact is that I was not even taking seriously the idea of a "shock and awe" campaign against my client. Cláudia had described a sequence of unfortunate events—problems with her microbiota, her car, her bank account—but it was nothing that couldn't be attributed to an unfortunate confluence of coincidences.

Fiction is full of researchers who live by repeating things like "there are no coincidences" or "I don't believe in coincidences," but chance is a far more powerful influence than most people are willing to admit. Randomness and incompetence kill far more people than professional murderers and crime geniuses.

My predisposition to blame stupid, cruel fate, as opposed to hidden rational forces, for the vicissitudes of life was shaken, however, when I returned to the office after lunch, for there were still a few hours left before the interview with Raul's friend, and my secretary said to me, "Good morning."

It was a very simple part of the program, the machine saying "good morning", "good afternoon", or "good night" whenever the door opened, depending of the time of the day. Twentieth-century devices were already able to do this without difficulty. My software was cheap but not so cheap as to confuse the mid-afternoon with the morning period.

And that might just be my impression, but the synthetic voice was kind of creepy.

"Any messages?" I asked. Like everyone else, I walk with a phone plugged into my ear and I have a passive media screen in the lens of my glasses, but my number or privilege of access are off-limits to the general public. The desktop has a filter that defines when to pass the call to me when alerting me to the appearance of something interesting in FaceSpace.

Or when, simply, to jot down the message.

"Only a gentleman came here. He was identified as 'Archimandrite Serapião', speaking on behalf of the Puritan Church. Online search confirmed the identity and revealed that 'archimandrite' is a title reserved, by this denomination, to celibate brothers in the early stages of the priesthood..."

"Right," I cut her short. "Did he say what he wanted?"

"He just asked you to call as soon as possible. He left a phone number."

"Right."

"Shall I make the call?"

"In a while."

Leaving the antechamber and going to the office proper, I stopped by the coffee machine. The lunch drinks were starting to take their toll and the *cafezinho* in the restaurant hadn't been much more than hot water dyed black.

Looking at the machine, I felt a pang of guilt for not offering Sabrina a shot when she came here to hire me. Those knees had mesmerized me, no doubt about it. I missed a great chance to impress her.

The variety of bean I use is particularly good, and my obsession with keeping the machine well regulated is comparable to some guys with their car engines. It's no use having the best coffee beans in the world if the roasting point is wrong or, even worse, if the water pressure and temperature aren't well calibrated.

I set the machine for a *ristretto* and waited as usual. I was getting ready to put the cup in the base where the coffee should fall, when something made my eyes widen. I stepped back immediately.

I don't know exactly where the warning came from. It's possible that, almost unconsciously, I had sensed a faint, abnormal vibration of the great golden cylinder that formed the main body of the machine. Whatever the cause of my instinctive retreat, however, the device began to hiss like an angry snake. The sound came in a crescendo until it became a high gurgling that ended in a spurt of boiling water and steam, which jumped in my direction.

Scheduled to have my safety as top priority, the secretary remained silent. A few spatters had hit the sleeve of my shirt and the hem of my jacket. Where wet, the fabric produced a fine white smoke, small lint clouds.

It was water, only water, but at an absurdly high temperature, obtained thanks to the pressure inside the machine. If I were holding the cup under the spout of the coffeepot at the instant of the jet, my skin would probably now be loosening from my flesh. Nothing that a few days with restorative cream could not repair, but the pain would have been …

Just imagining the intensity of the pain sent a chill down my spine and I felt a cold wind on the back of my neck. The cup—I use the foam ones, which I prefer to old porcelain cups, not only because they diffuse the heat better, but also because they don't cut my hands when I crush them—was forgotten, in the clenched fist of my right hand. I suppose if I had a mirror in front of me at that moment, I would have seen a purple face of rage.

"Diagnostic mode," I commanded in a surprisingly calm voice. "Foreground." In response to the instruction, which deactivated all the functions of the secretary while the software was searching for defects or viruses, I heard some notes of classical music and the lights of the office suddenly became more intense, since, without the secretary, there was no one to control the smart dimmer.

Then I called Cid, a systems security specialist with whom I used to exchange favors now and then. He remotely accessed the secretary's program and gave me the preliminary report in less than fifteen minutes:

"Whoever did it was a smart guy."

"Did *what*?"

"Your secretary was disoriented with a data overload. Remember an old episode of a TV series, when the computer is disabled because they ask it to determine the 'last digit of pi'?"

"Don't think I saw it."

"Well, it was something like that. Your secretary seemed distracted and inattentive because she *was* inattentive, and *had been* distracted."

"By whom?"

"By someone who read the user manual of this model much better than you, I guess. Well enough to know how to use voice commands to define a high-level priority activity, capable of mobilizing most computing resources and leaving all other priorities behind."

"Including taking care of my safety and preventing tampering with the coffee machine."

"For example, yes, that. The origin of that order has been erased, but the order itself is still here: an analysis of the energy flow in M.C. Escher's *Waterfall*."

I was familiar with the image. There was, in fact, a reproduction on the wall of the antechamber. And I knew the task given to the secretary was impossible, since the water in the picture seems to rise and fall at the same time (I like Escher precisely because of the graphic paradoxes). Whoever the hacker was, he had worked quickly and with the material at hand.

"How long? How much money?"

"It's already done," he replied, laughing. "As I said, anyone familiar with the manual would know how to create the problem and also how to solve it. As soon as the secretary returns from diagnostic mode, it'll work fine. But I would give it an upgrade. As for the price, you buy me a beer later and we're even."

After thanking him and saying goodbye, I started to adjust the coffeemaker. As in the case of the secretary, the cause of the problem itself was not complex—a mere, so to speak, *malicious* valve manipulation—but, unlike the case of the program, the damage would cost me high: there were sealing rings to change, and at least one bronze tube was slightly deformed.

Then, my share of "unfortunate coincidences" already filled up for the rest of the week, I called the likely author of all the chaos around, the Archimandrite Serapião. Before freaking out, the secretary had printed the number and left the strip of paper stuck to my desk.

I was careful to keep the video off, so as not to give the bastard the pleasure of seeing my face purple with anger.

He picked up the phone on the first ring and then greeted me before I told him who he was. The archimandrite seemed to suppose that this foolish sleight of hand with the caller ID would baffle me.

"I suppose you have received...*my message.*"

The way he uttered "my message" reminded me of Bela Lugosi's inflection in saying "wine" in "I don't drink...wine" in the early scenes of *Dracula*. I had to hold back the urge to laugh. The guy really thought he was intimidating me. What kind of people are his kind used to dealing with anyway?

Olavo, the only Puritan faithful I had interviewed so far, didn't seem to me to be a complete idiot, but if he took people like Archimandrite Serapião seriously...

"My secretary told me that you called. What can I do for you?"

"Are you all right? Your health? How's business?"

"Very well, thank you."

An embarrassing silence. On his part. What did he expect me to say? "Actually, I just burned myself a bit..." or "How awful, my secretary fritzed"?

"Glad to know. May your future conduct allow you to continue like this."

And then I remembered something I had read long ago somewhere, how the original archimandrites—monks of the time of the Byzantine Empire—refused to bathe because they considered the concern with personal hygiene an unforgivable form of vanity. "The unspeakable filth of the saints covered several blocks in Alexandria, in an emanation of spiritual purity that offended the vultures of the sky," someone had written.

It wasn't that hard to imagine Serapião sweating and stinking a lot in some medieval alley.

"Thank you for your concern," I said in a neutral tone. "How can I help you?"

"Ah. Yes." He sounded rather mortified, perhaps for giving up the veiled threat game without scoring any point. "The Church would like to hire you."

"Ah, yes?"

"It has come to our attention that you are conducting a private inquiry into the passing of one of our faithful…"

"Disappearance."

"Beg your pardon?"

"It's not 'passing', it's 'disappearance'. There's no concrete evidence that the lady in question is dead."

"So you confirm your involvement in the case?"

I had to smile. The old man—the call was audio only, but I could only imagine him as an old man, and fat too—thought that by Machiavellian means he had extracted important information from me.

"Well, since at least one member of your church has talked to me about it, there's no reason to deny it, is there?"

"Indeed."

I noticed, once again, the mortified tone. My "at least one" had puzzled him. Perhaps there were relapsed Puritans out there, ignominious to the point of not communicating to the hierarchy the contact with this infidel sleuth? Oh, cruel doubt.

Cruelty, by the way, was something I was beginning to feel in the back of my throat, a metallic taste that leaves the saliva bitter. That fucker had sabotaged my office to intimidate me and, belatedly acknowledging the strategic error, was now appealing for indirect threats and childish charades. It wouldn't be long before he came to the bribe offer. I decided to encourage him.

"Since we have established, to our mutual satisfaction, my involvement in the case of Dona Albertina's disappearance, what, pray tell, can I do for you?" I made a point of giving an impudent tone to *you*.

To my surprise, the Archimandrite ignored the provocation.

"The Church would like to follow your efforts. I was allowed to mention the possibility of an incentive, a reward, so to speak, if the body was located."

"What if it can't be located?"

"Well, I suppose, for a man of your talent and creativity, it *really* should not be at all impossible to find a solution."

My patience was running scarce by the second.

"Is that so? And what solution would that be?"

I had a good idea of what that worm had in mind: that I should steal a suitable corpse or even kill a lady of reasonable likeness. It should be enough that the body was properly mutilated as to be unrecognizable, and they would surely know who to bribe for the DNA tests to provide the desired result. But my wish was to hear the son of a bitch say it. Request a crime. Deliver the body.

Of course, my anger had surpassed good sense: however rudimentary the means and techniques of the old Serapião, even he was too smart to propose a crime, explicitly, in a conversation that could have been recorded. As indeed was the case.

"If we here in the Church knew how to do that, sir, we would not need to offer incentives or rewards to professionals of your caliber," he answered in a glacial tone.

"Any idea of the value of the reward?"

"The archpriest's generosity is well known. Imagine your usual fees for dealing with a missing person case…"

"I don't need to imagine. I have the fee table here in front of me."

"…and multiply said value by ten."

It was good money. Not enough to guarantee me an early retirement, but still *very* good money indeed. There was the ethical question of acting in the same case having two clients with opposite purposes, Sabrina being infinitely more pleasant and, most importantly, Serapião having destroyed my coffee machine. Getting a piece of brass at a reasonable price to replace the deformed pipe would take weeks, maybe even months, in this world where everything is made of polymer and biomass.

"Up yours!" I said, hanging up.

* * *

Feeling lighter and spry, I decided to walk home. The plan for the rest of the afternoon was to ponder the information I had already obtained and put on a clean shirt before leaving for the bar where I would have a chat with Antonio, Raul's former co-worker, that night.

I lived in an apartment not far from the office, though most of the time I preferred to use the Light Rail Vehicle to get around. The place was only two stations away.

I was passing through the station door where I used to take the tram when I noticed a guy standing out from a small crowd that was watching a bipedal dancing dog show (hadn't such a modification been forbidden?) and started to walk in the same direction, but keeping some distance. I noticed he had put something in his mouth and, as he walked, he was chewing it vigorously. I had the feeling that it wasn't gum.

I started to walk faster, entered a bakery where the owner and the staff knew me and, without saying a word, asking for permission and apologizing by means of gestures and mimicry, ran to the back where there was a loading and unloading exit.

Outside, I walked in the opposite direction of my house until the first corner, and then I circled the block back, returning to the same stretch of sidewalk I had used when I left the office.

Then I saw the back of the gum-chewing guy a little farther on, standing at the entrance to the bakery, pretending to study the pastries in the display. He was obviously trying to find me in the middle of the confusion of customers jostling at the counter, balancing themselves on the poor little tables and making a noisy row at the cash register.

I had to admit that the chaotic interior of the establishment, the reflection of the sun in the window, the general smoke of fried bacon and water vapor that filled the bakery, all of this added to the fact that I was no longer there, made the task a bit hard.

I crossed the street and sat down on one of the small tables in a Japanese self-service restaurant that occupied part of the sidewalk, watching my poor stalker. He still stood, in a way that seemed pathetic to me, pretending to pay attention to the window for a few more minutes—trying to read omens and portents in the contours of the beaten egg cream and sugar covering the donuts, perhaps?—but then, with an attempt not at all happy to show dignity and indifference, he turned and walked away.

For a moment I was afraid he'd go straight to where I was, but instead he continued to walk in the general direction of my house. Interested, I followed him.

If my stalker really sucked in practice, at least someone had bothered to teach him the stakeout theory. Once you have lost sight of the person you should follow, the old masters say, it's best to go to a place where the target will be forced to go sooner or later and, if possible, resume the job from there.

The alternative is to close shop for today and try again the next day, but my mysterious chewer wasn't keen on doing tomorrow what he could do today. Following him I saw that he stopped very close to the building where I live, but at an angle that allowed me to observe the three broad steps of the main entrance without being picked up by the biometric camera of the electronic doorman. And he stood there, left shoulder barely resting on a light pole, waiting for me to appear.

I stood thirty feet behind him, and then I began to walk, fast and determined, in his direction.

I had a reasonable idea of what was going on. If I was wrong, however, what I intended to do with the imbecile would end up giving me a lawsuit for assault, maybe even bodily injury, if the D.A. had a migraine. But then I thought, so what? What's one more wound for a leper, after all?

As soon as I saw myself two feet away from his back, I raised my arm and, without slowing down, grabbed him by the shoulder, twisting him violently around the pole. Before he had time to recover from the surprise and loss of balance, I punched him really good with a left hook.

The impact caused him to spit a milky, rosy mass on the post, and with my right hand I grabbed him tightly by the nape of his neck and pushed his head up to rub his nose, brow and cheeks in the ooze. When I let him go, he hesitated for a moment, and I wondered if he would sit down, but no: he stood. Hysterically, he rubbed his face clean with his shirt. But it was too late.

In the meantime, I'd stepped back and watched, knowing what to expect. It didn't take long for the effects of the paste to manifest, as the saliva holding the virus inert evaporated: huge, grotesque and somewhat painful bubbles—judging by the moans and screams—began to erupt in his forehead and around his eyes. If any formed inside the nostrils, he would need medical help. If my mood improved, I might feel compelled to call someone.

The street wasn't very busy and anyway people in my neighborhood know the value of giving ample space and privacy to their neighbor, especially when said neighbor seems to be of the violent kind and the victim is no one you know.

I felt a rather morbid satisfaction as I saw the face of my pursuer getting disfigured at high speed. Much of this satisfaction came from the fact that I had been right in my conjecture: what the imbecile had been chewing on was a "Punk'd," a concoction made from a modified version of the papilloma virus, the same one that causes common warts. Punk'd is much faster, and creates much bigger and more fragile warts. It's also non-contagious and its effects usually disappear in ten days tops.

This is not to say that an attack using this biological version of cream pie on the face isn't humiliating, uncomfortable, and embarrassing to the victim, which is the whole point of the trick.

The product itself is illegal, but any anarchist with access to a backyard lab, any high school student with a penchant for bio-hacking is able to synthesize a few tens of milliliters in a few hours, like many snobbish It Girls, TV celebrities, police officers and even some especially photogenic senators have already discovered.

Noticing that he could still breathe, the stranger screamed in a soprano voice and ran.

"Tell Serapião I still owe him a kick in the ass!" I shouted at the fugitive, who was already turning the corner. Crying and gnashing my teeth. Bunch of jerks!

* * *

Antonio Kobaiashi de Toledo was a tall, thin man in navy blue trousers and a mustard-colored jacket full of pockets with buttons on his chest, sides, forearms, just as fashion dictated. His skin was dark like polished onyx. There wasn't a single hair on his head above his ears, but beneath it he sported a long, bushy white beard.

The overall effect of this appearance, supplemented by a pair of round gold-rimmed spectacles, was that of an old person, conventional enough to be trustworthy, but endowed with deep wells of wisdom. Which must have been exactly the first impression Antonio wanted to plant in the unconscious of all those who came into his orbit.

He was already sitting at the counter when I arrived. There was a mug of amber-colored beer next to his elbow and a plate of olives in front of him. I introduced myself, asked for a mug for myself, and sat down. We began talking.

The first thing Antonio told me was that it was his call to the authorities that had led the police to break down Raul's garage door.

"The guy hadn't been coming to work for a week, he wasn't even answering the phone. There had to be something wrong. Raul didn't miss a day, even if he was working at home, investing his free time in some new project."

"Busting down the door struck me as a bit radical," I pondered. "They had no employees or a virtual butler who could recognize the police credentials and open the garage?"

Antonio shook his head.

"The automation in the house was minimal, vestigial, even. The system washed and ironed the clothes, managed the water heating and vacuumed the floor, just that. His mother was virtually a Luddite, she didn't trust machines to cook or wash the dishes. On top of that, Raul was paranoid regarding intelligent automation. He was afraid of being hacked, especially when he was taking important projects home."

"And what project was that? If you can comment on it…"

He smiled.

"I don't think I could, if I was officially involved, but since it was something between him and his girlfriend, Sabrina's from the laboratory, I guess…"

That surprised me.

"Girlfriend?" I hadn't told anyone that Sabrina, who claimed to be Raul's fiancé, had hired me, but only that she was working for "interested parties" in the disappearance of his mother. And from what Sabrina's friend, Cláudia, had said, their relationship was kept secret.

Antonio swallowed two olives and gave me a look of amusement and guilt, more or less like married men exchanging glances as they enter a whorehouse.

"I bet a little bird told you that the lovebirds' courtship was highly classified, right?" He laughed. "Well, in a way, it was, but a bit clumsy. The rest of the engineering crew probably would have noticed if they'd bothered to pay attention. As for me, how could I not notice? Raul had invited me to be the best man."

"Best man," I repeated, attesting my mental slowness.

"Best man. For the wedding. They hadn't set a date yet, but they had decided on a kind of window of opportunity, an ideal period to tie the knot. They should have swapped vows a couple of months ago, but they gave up four months before that. When he told me my best man 'services' wouldn't be necessary anymore, Raul was very embarrassed..."

"Did he give you a reason?"

"He just said that the right moment hadn't come yet, something like that."

"Did he mention his mother?"

Antonio paused for one moment.

"No," he finally said. "I don't think so. At least not in that context."

I finished my mug and ordered another. While waiting, I commented:

"So he didn't show for a week, and then you called the police."

"Yes. I knew he was doing some informal testings off business hours, but as I explained, Raul was a straight arrow, and even if he was deep into some project at home, from midnight to 6 AM, he would never think of compensating overtime jumping out of normal business hours. He was dumb like that."

My draft beer arrived and the high foam collar smudged the tip of my nose. I wiped the beer off it and asked him again about the project. Antonio replied pointing to my glass:

"This very beer you are drinking is made of yeast that turns the barley's natural sugar into alcohol and releases carbon dioxide in the process."

"Okay."

"Much of the energy we use today in transportation, biodiesel, bio-kerosene, ethanol, is made in the same way. Yeast, or bacteria sometimes, turn biomass into precursor molecules that are then converted into the type of fuel that each specific vehicle requires. The old oil refineries turned into big breweries."

"Because of global warming," I suggested.

"Partly, yes. But the price of oil also had something to do with it." The mischievous grin of the father caught in the brothel reappeared on his face. "Planting cane is still cheaper than drilling the continental shelf. But it won't last forever. Because of the income."

"Income?"

He paused to swap the empty mug for a full, then went on:

"Generally speaking, more energy is extracted from a liter of oil than from a kilo of cane. And the global demand only increases. Soon we will reach a point where it will again make sense, economic sense, at least to extract and refine oil, as it was done in the twentieth century. Unless we can extract more energy from plants."

"Cellulose?"

"Cellulose, yes. Plants are made of things other than sugar, such as cellulose, fat, and protein, and there are biological pathways to convert all of those into fuel. The point is only about price and unwanted waste. Cellulose started to be a part of the scene in the beginning of the century. Animal fat has been used for decades to produce aviation kerosene. Protein is the new frontier, mainly because of waste."

"Waste?"

"Ammonia. Nitrates. In the old days, people thought that this wouldn't be a problem, that after yeast and bacteria finished turning the protein into fuel, the part with the nitrogen could be reused as fertilizer. A closed cycle: nitrates for soil, soil for plant, plant for nitrates. But then... Have you ever heard of nitrogen pollution?"

I shook my head. He swallowed three more olives.

"Bottom line, having loose nitrogen compounds in the soil, air, and water is not a good idea. Acid rain. Pollution of lakes and oceans. Bad, really bad. Not at first, but over time… Synthetic fertilizers had to be regulated almost to extinction some ten years ago. Hence, the golden dream of the protein biofuel was sent to the compost heap."

"Unless someone invented a process that could neutralize nitrogen," I added. "Which was what Raul and Sabrina were working on."

"Yes, this. She developed the organism, he was working on the reactor, digester or whatever the type of device he had built at home. If it had worked out, it would have been fantastic."

"Because the plants then would be fully exploited?"

"The animals too."

In the kind of literature I usually read, the sentence "I felt an icy fist closing in around my heart" appears with a certain frequency, but I had never understood its meaning until that moment. Something was taking shape in the back of my mind and it was not good.

"Animals?"

"Of course." The subject seemed to amuse my interlocutor. "Animals are fundamentally fat and protein. The fat processing is old stuff. In denser urban areas, restaurants can make good money by passing on leftover grease to mills. If you were to process the protein as well, it would be possible to reuse virtually all organic waste as a fuel source, the useless parts of animals slaughtered for consumption, carcasses of dogs and cats… In addition to creating a strong incentive for active pest control, such as rats and pigeons."

"What about the bones?"

"Bone is also protein. Collagen, especially. We'd need filters to keep the minerals, calcium and everything else, but still…"

His eyes took on a distant, dreamy glow. It was the engineer's brain, dwelling on speculation about an imaginary machine. I, on the other hand, could only think of the ending of a hundred-year-old movie, an old 2D production.

The protagonist, a famous actor of yore—not a good performer, but a fantastic screen presence all the same—ran down the streets shouting, "Soylent Green is people!", referring to some green cookies that formed the basis of diet in his world. According to that plot, people were cannibals and did not know it.

"And why—" I forced myself, not without some effort, to put away my cinematic reverie. "—was he working on it at home?" The project would certainly be of interest to the company.

"It was something he was developing along with Sabrina. I believe it had begun as an official mission of the company, but it evolved into a pet project of the two. I think they wanted to present the technology to the board when it was ready, or at least when they already had a functional prototype. Or, well… Look, you didn't hear that from me, but maybe they wanted to start a company. Their own company. If they could prove that all the development had been done outside office hours…"

"Got it."

My stomach was upset. I couldn't finish the second pint. An eloquent sign of declining health, in my case. After a few more lines of inconsequential dialogue, I excused myself and left.

On the way to the LRV station, hurriedly, I called my police contact. The voice exploded on the other side of the connection:

"Fuck, man, didn't I tell you I had today off?"

Major Adriana of the Unified Metropolitan Police—my sweet little sister, born two years after me, always affectionate with her older brother.

"Shut that fucking filthy mouth of yours, Dri." Whenever talking to Adriana, I always find it good to impose my authority right away. I can well imagine that anyone else trying to shut her up, including my brother-in-law, would end up with a nine-millimeter barrel stuck up in a nostril, or any other orifice. But being the big brother brings some atavistic privileges. "Shut up and listen to me. It's important…"

She had said she wouldn't have time to talk to me that day because of a party at my niece's school, but the fact that Dri had answered the call with a loud "fuck" was a sign that, at least for now, she was alone and could speak freely.

But I knew that wasn't going to last, so I quickly summed up the events of the day and the hypothesis that had come to me during the conversation with Antonio, who was still upsetting my stomach.

She listened to me with some exasperation at first, but, as the implications of each stage of the investigation became clear, she began to show a more pronounced interest. In the end, we engaged in a good talk about the case, and then I got a lot of the information I presented right at the beginning of this story.

As soon as we finished the conversation, I was already inside the train, and she promised to send me a team of experts to take a second look at Raul's house. With special emphasis on the car, which had been left in the garage after the removal of the body, and in the part of the garden where the policemen had smelled beer.

* * *

To my disappointment, the Archimandrite Serapião was neither fat nor old. He didn't even stink. The guy who came into my office the next afternoon was tall, thin, exuding a soft aroma of mahogany and citrus with a brief note of frankincense. He was dressed in a sleek chalkboard-gray suit with a jacket full of pockets (and epaulettes on his shoulders, something that anticipated the safari fashion of the next season), a Panama hat and, not to say that everything about him was beautiful and up-to-date, he had a curly goatee that looked like the tail of a dead sheep glued to his jaw with spit.

"Good afternoon, Your Reverence." The soft voice of my secretary greeted the newcomer.

His expression, which never was really pleasant to begin with, crumpled completely. The sheep's tail now looked like a storm cloud, ready to release lightning. As for me, I smiled the most beatific smile as I signaled for him to sit down.

"The system had a problem yesterday and hasn't returned to normality yet," I said, expressing a commiseration that, I hope, sounded as false as it really was. "She meant Reverend."

He grunted something as he sat down and, once settled, said, "I was surprised by your phone call. After the abruptness with…"

"But you didn't go, so nothing bad happened."

"Didn't I go?"

"Do as I suggested yesterday, before you disconnect the phone."

The archimandrite became livid. With almost clinical interest, I watched as the blood drained from his face. He would have gotten up and out of the office at that very moment. He might have tried to attack me, had it not been for the orders he had received directly from the Archpriest Sérvio, with whom I had spoken the night before.

It had not been very difficult to gain personal access to the supreme leader of the Church of the Puritans after I had escaped, for one of the stooges that served as the archpriest's shields in communication networks, my very good sister, UMP major, was interested in the Albertina affair.

The insinuation of the unlimited possibilities of manipulation of facts and testimonies through nepotism and traffic of influence within the police itself, which I had purposely left in the air, had intoxicated the Church. Enough, it seemed, to reduce the archimandrite to the most abject submission.

Exactly as expected: Before contacting the Church, I had spoken with my lawyer and he had told me that although it was possible in theory to untangle the Gonçalves da Nóbrega assets in the short term, the chances of that happening without Albertina's body were scant at best.

Laws about heritage and inheritance had changed a great deal in the last twenty years because of new possibilities such as cloning, uploading of consciousness, and asexual human reproduction, but it was still not so easy to declare someone dead.

If the Puritans really wanted to get their hands on the whole family inheritance, they desperately needed good evidence that you were really dead, and they needed it before Sabrina could prove the stable union.

"Reverend," I said with the happiness I always feel on the rare occasions when I know I have all the cards in my hand, "you had mentioned something like a payment of ten times my usual fees if a body were produced."

He leaned forward in his chair, anxious.

"Take me to the body."

"Pay me the money."

Serapião stepped back, suspicious.

"Come on." I felt so elated and lightweight I could almost feel my head floating above my shoulders. "I wouldn't fool you. I don't want pimps spitting papilloma in my face on every corner for the rest of my life."

He gave that a little thought. Then he took a notebook out of his pocket, typed something, and two minutes later I saw, in the desk terminal, the credit bar of my bank account change color—from orange to green—and going up, up, up.

"The body?" The Archimandrite was impatient.

"Here." I pushed a scrap of paper I had printed earlier across the desk. "This is the still unofficial content of the result of a detailed examination carried out on the automobile where Raul was found, and an experimental digester mounted secretly in the garden of the house. The police was there in the morning."

"Was the body in the car? Where? In the back? In the trunk? How these idiots did not notice that before…"

"No. It was in the tank."

Serapião fell silent.

"The details are there. Calcium precipitation in the fuel filter. Indication of corrosion by ammonia in the hose. The laboratory even found traces of mitochondrial DNA in the reservoir, which allowed a positive identification."

Adriana had passed me the preliminary forensic data shortly after ten o'clock. Slightly irregular, but blood is thicker than water. In addition, no one would have tried the tank if I had not suggested and, in the end, I also do my share of dirty services for the UMP, when the major whistles.

"I don't get it..."

"Raul was working on a process to extract biodiesel from animal protein. Human beings are animals. Albertina was a human being. You want me to draw a diagram?"

"Did he use his mother to produce the smoke that smothered him to death?"

"His mother's corpse. I don't think she was still alive when he shoved her into the digester, where, by the way, the cops found fragments of a sweater and also a few strands of hair, still with traces of genetic material in the root. Aside from that, a good synthesis. That was it."

"But that's...obscene."

"He lived with his mother to care for his mother. When she died..."

"She's really dead, then."

The bastard didn't even have the decency to hide the triumphant edge in his voice.

"Well, that's the good news," I continued, preparing my firecracker. "The police have evidence that Albertina is dead. The bad news, at least to you Puritans, is that the same proof shows that she died *before* her son. Since her body was the weapon of his suicide, there seems to be no other way out, logically speaking, unless his lawyers can prove that Raul invented the time machine, and yet the story is still complicated." I smiled, recycling my false pity. "Which means *he's* the heir, not you. And without it, her fortune goes to... Well, to someone other than you. I'm terribly sorry."

"No." The Archimandrite jumped to his feet, gritting his teeth in anger. "You are not."

"Yeah, I am not. And you know what I said about the papilloma urchins? It was a lie. I'll love to punch their faces when they come after me. One at a time or all together, whatever."

* * *

Sabrina came an hour after the man of the Church had gone. The coffee machine still had not been repaired. The work would have to be done by hand. Then I took out a bottle of bourbon from the drawer, two glasses the size of thimbles, and poured a dose for each of us.

She was wearing trousers and a turtleneck. Brown clothes, almost the color of her skin, but ample ones: the only notable curve was the elevation of her breasts, and yet more suggested than marked. No cleavage and knees this time.

I had sent her the police report in the morning. Now there was insecurity in her eyes: she wanted to know how much I had actually deduced on my own. If I'd hand her to the police.

"Raul stayed for a week without going to work, something totally averse to his character and his way of being," I said as she sat down. "But it was a workmate who called the police, not his wife."

"He called me, saying his mother was dead. And that he needed some time alone, to...to process what had happened, and then ..."

"And then you left the man of your dreams utterly alone, in a minuscule house and the corpse of his mother, for seven days, without saying anything to anyone, is that it? Until he went crazy with pain and loneliness and decided to kill himself too, is that it?"

"Saying it that way makes it sound so *awful*. But yes."

"But why kill yourself like that, choking on the smoke from your mother's body? Was it a sexual thing? Psychopathological? A message? What do you think?"

"I... I..."

She was scared. She knew that I knew.

"May I offer you an explanation?" Without waiting for an answer,

I began. "Albertina was an obstacle. A hindrance. Even blind and paraplegic, she was an active, lively, almost independent lady...until her son began to speak of marriage. Of bringing another woman to live in the house, or leave the house and leave her too, whatever. Albertina couldn't accept that. And what method did she choose to impose her will on her child? The time-honored method of mothers of only children: blackmail, no, emotional *torture*. Guilt."

My client swallowed.

"All the people who knew of your plan to marry Raul also told me that they were canceled about six months ago. Around the same time that, in the words of a friend and probable boyfriend, Albertina *decided to become* an invalid, blocking her son's escape route. But children of strong, assertive women tend to get involved with strong, assertive women, and I'll bet you're the type. Seeing that Raul would not marry while Albertina continued playing the role of disabled mother, you concluded that it was time to get rid of Albertina. I suspect that the idea of disposing of the body through the exhaust of the car was yours, was it not? With Albertina dissolved in the atmosphere, it would be possible to keep the illusion that she had recovered her good mood and decided to travel, go on vacation, move to another country. And you finally might be together."

"Interesting." She gathered her strength to build a mask of impassivity. But her eyes remained tense, haunted. "A bit morbid, though."

"The suitability of means and ends was so great," I continued, as if I hadn't been interrupted, "with the prototype installed in the garden of the house, and the fact that Albertina depended on Raul for her tonics and remedies made you forget the psychological factor of *guilt*. In the seven days Albertina's body fermented in the digester, Raul was slowly feeling dilacerated from the inside out. Until, in the end, he decided to apply a form of justice to himself: since he had allowed his mother to be killed, he would now allow her to kill him. So he filled the tank, locked the doors, lowered the windows, sped up... I wonder what would have happened if Antonio had called the police one day, or even an hour, earlier."

"I don't think we'll ever know, will we?" She was smiling. Not a fake smile, but something that accentuated the cruel aspect of her face: she had regained her composure. It's usually what happens when someone sees their sins exposed and, immediately, nothing happens to them. We all harbor an atavistic fear that the ground will open under our feet when some villainy we commit is articulated clearly in words. But if there are no immediate consequences, we relax and lower our guard. Some people even take great pleasure, exultation, from the effect.

Which leaves them more vulnerable than they can possibly realize.

"There's a glass," I said. "A glass with just a trace of juice, left in the kitchen sink of Raul's house. It must be in some police evidence cabinet now. I don't know what tests the authorities have done on it, or what further tests may still be carried out. Certainly fingerprints were collected and the rim scanned for signs of genetic material. I wonder if it wasn't your fingerprints, your DNA on it."

She shrugged.

"What if it is? It only proves that I was there one day. And why wouldn't I have been there? Raul and I were dating. In fact, there is no proof that Albertina's death was not perfectly natural."

"I wonder if there was poison in the glass."

"Poison?" She laughed a nervous laugh.

"The house was in perfect order except for two details: Albertina's bed and that glass. The bed where she slept for the last time, and the glass...maybe the glass from which she drank for the last time?"

Sabrina was shaking. The temperature in the room was 25° C.

"And if there's poison in the background, Albertina's DNA on the rim, and fingerprints... Would there be other fingerprints mixed with Raul's, I wonder?"

"You weak, stupid, sentimental, childish, invertebrate, idiot... Damn fool, *I can't believe you didn't wash the glass after I left!*"

* * *

"A good bluff, mentioning the glass."

I smiled. It's not every day that Adriana recognizes the merits of her older brother. Somewhere in the distance, my niece screamed, clinging to her father's neck. As far as I could understand, she feared being swallowed by a black hole, and the cervical spine of my poor brother-in-law was her last anchor in this universe.

As unlikely as it might have seemed, they were both having a good time.

"It was Raul's last drink, wasn't it?"

"Yes. He drank a mixture of milk, brandy, and mango juice before he got into the car and killed himself. He probably didn't see why he should have to do the dishes, if he wouldn't need them anymore."

"Makes sense."

"Totally."

In the distance, the gravity of the black hole had dragged my brother-in-law to the ground, and now father and daughter rolled across the grass. It was a sunny morning in the Sierra Park, and the lawn was still soft with the dew of dawn.

"Those two will have a hell of an itching bout later," I observed.

"It's all in the game," Adriana replied. "But how did you know that she had prepared the poison for Albertina?"

I shrugged.

"His mother wouldn't take a glass of juice from anyone other than her son. She probably didn't even know Sabrina was in the house. Raul had to bring the drink to her. But he could not have put the poison in his glass."

"In her deposition, Sabrina said he just walked into the kitchen when the mix was ready."

I nodded.

"Makes sense. So, without witnessing anything, he could keep the illusion that there was nothing wrong. Raul was the kind of man who would let a strong woman do whatever she wanted with him, but for

that very reason he was incapable of doing anything against a strong woman."

"Quite different from you, right, little brother?"

I looked up into the blue sky, pretending to think deeply.

"Fortunately, I don't have strong women in my family."

And I made myself scarce, running from the police as fast as I could.

* * *

Carlos Orsi is a writer and a journalist specializing in coverage of scientific topics from Jundiaí, São Paulo. He has published the story collections *Medo, Mistério e Morte* (1996) and *Tempos de Fúria* (2005), and the novels *Nômade* (2010) and *Guerra Justa* (2010). His works of fiction appear in anthologies such as *Imaginarios v. 1* (2009), and in magazines and fanzines in Brazil and abroad.

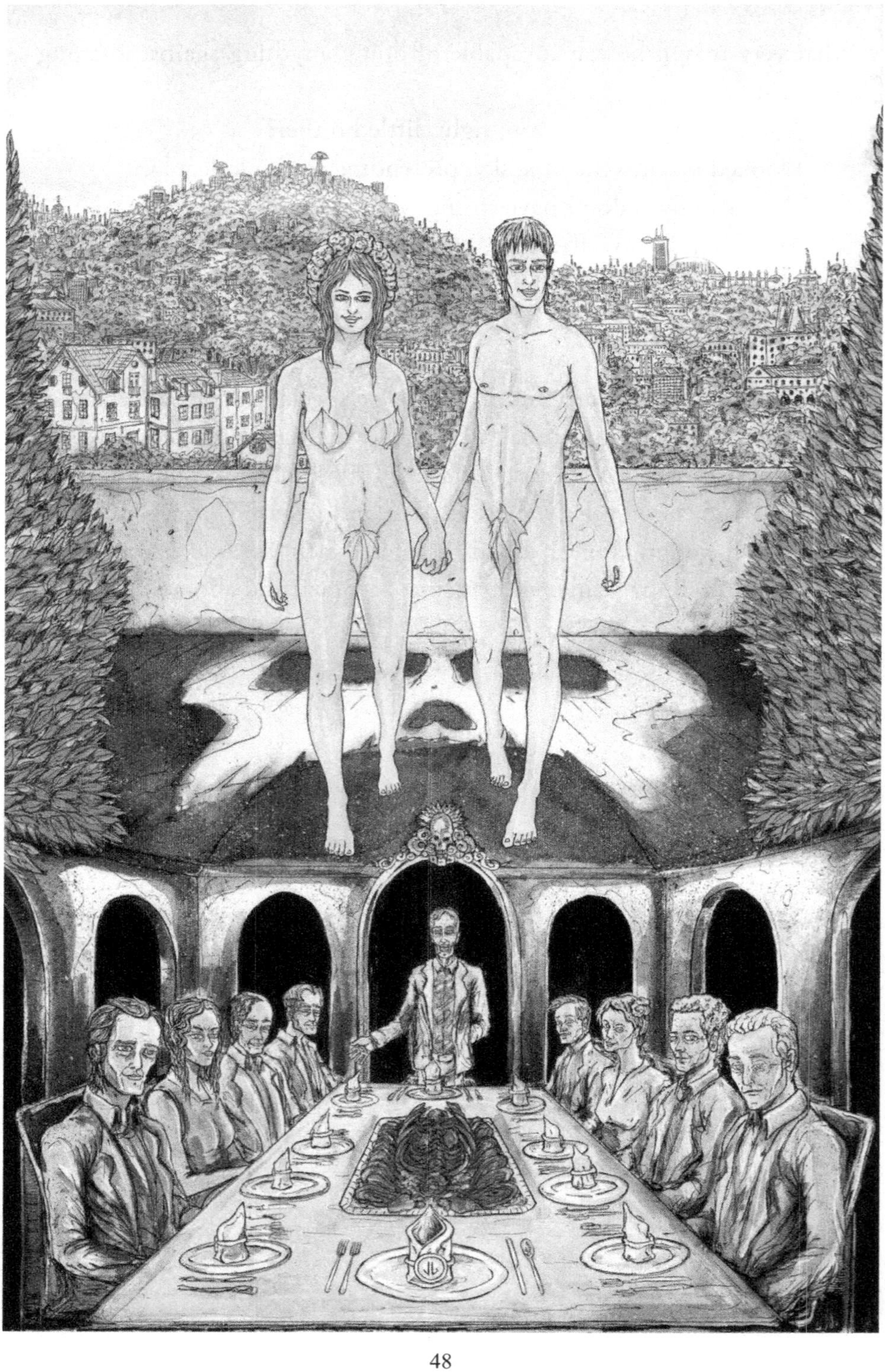

WHEN KINGDOMS COLLIDE
Telmo Marçal

I, for one, also mocked love then. I had fun with the imbeciles who shed tears watching TV, cooing over the passions of heartthrobs and starlets. I never thought those things could get me: the bittersweet anguish, the fires burning in one's heart, the dizzyness… It's because of love that I'm laying low in the mountain ridge, between the trees, keeping watch through the crosshairs of my gun. Searching for targets so I can have my vengeance.

I never felt any hatred towards the Kale Leaves. Even before I ever met one of them. Now I want them all to die: they murdered my girlfriend.

* * *

Once, when I was just a kid, we entered a hotel owned by the Greenies, me and two mates, both high-strung. Segregation was still to be approved, but it was already as if in place: everyone did what they wanted and nobody said a word; they were being led by the horns.

We couldn't care less about the doorman's scowling face. One of my friends was so cheeky that he told the man, in all seriousness:

"You have an ugly mug. You must be hungry. Want to go with us and grab a bite?" The guy was about to answer to this, but he only managed to gasp. He came with us, coughing, all the way to the desk.

The concierge told us something to the effect that that dump was reserved only for clorophyll people. That was exactly what we had wanted to hear.

"Reserved for what? For Artichoke Heads? Show me the line in the license where it says that. To me, this looks just like a hotel with a bar, where everybody has the right to drink."

They had to swallow that. But we couldn't swallow anything good. They only served vitamin and mineral-salt mixtures.

Why did the boss choose me for that mission? Maybe because of my previous experience?

Ages ago, I had a row with the Greenhouse Flowers. The message came when I was still washing the gunk from my eyes.

"Wakey wakey, sissy boy! Open your eyes! There's work to be done. Go and fetch me an Asparagus Sauce and go with it for a walk among the herd. Be very careful, so nobody gets bitten. Go now, move that ass out of bed!"

It's not always easy to get what the boss means. Fortunately, the mission specs always come in a formal tone. I was told to be at the gates of a palace at 9 AM, in the Village of Sintra, to escort the official delegation of the Kale Leaves to the Council Square. Nothing too complicated, if it wasn't for the fact that this rendezvous would happen in thirty minutes. I ran down the stairs, cursing.

But there was a limo and a motorcade waiting by the door. Everything equipped with internal combustion motors.

"Hurrah for such comfort!" I shouted, saluting them.

I sat shotgun and we rode on with full blasting sirens. No traffic lights seemed red enough for us to stop.

I only noticed there was someone behind me when we got in the fast lane. I didn't say a word; I just made a call to the boss, which he answered while lifting weights at the gym. The damned old man, well into his nineties, loves to torture his bones.

This time I got the message loud and clear.

"Very funny, letting a Neanderthal like you at large, among the

Cabbages. What you'd talk about? About the best bars to find cod pastries? You will remain outside, by the door, very quiet, while letting your colleague deal with everything. She's cute, isn't she? Prick up your ears, though: she's a bit loony, and very interested to go to the other side. The only thing keeping her from doing it is money for the therapies."

The old man is like me: he loves her in all colors, even green.

I looked at the girl again, and she said a very nice *Hi, good morning.* I had never seen her before, so she probably was a new acquisition. I know pretty much everyone at the service, we aren't so many. Lisbon doesn't have much to hide anymore.

Upon our return, my colleague and the Big Lizards chatted their heads off the entire way, with me having no place there. When we dropped the passengers off, I told the driver:

"Forget I was here." And moved to the back seat.

I put myself to the task of knowing better a wonderful girl named Rita. I think I fell in love with that first conversation.

She was a wonderful, but concerned girl. Very worried about all the madness in the world.

"Do you think it's normal to send special agents to guard the Greenhouse rulers?"

I told her something zany to make her laugh:

"Our mission is to assure that they wear their robes, otherwise they would walk around showing their tomatoes."

And she laughed, so nicely, so beautifully.

The truth was that there was anger in the air all right. Admiration for the solar beings had started to lose its appeal. Everyone here is living a shitty life, eating oatmeal and bathing in cold water, while those gentleman bask in the sun, far from the madding crowd, drinking juices and taking a healthy shit.

There were even people that, according to the reports, took this much too seriously. And, this morning, while I was falling in love, I got precisely such a message. *"A chance of provocation on the part of demonstrators; reinforce security measures. "*

Next stop was at the parrot cage, the São Bento Palace. There are always bands of crazy people, at the end of the staircase, demonstrating against anything. I stopped musing about love and activated the professional mode. I sent for a bigger vehicle to replace the limo, properly armored, with a water cannon on the top and yours truly at the wheel. She and her legs by my side and the Watermelon Heads crammed in the back, making faces.

Rita spoke low so they couldn't hear us:

"I hope they make it."

"What?"

"Don't you know what they are discussing today at the Parliament?"

How couldn't I know that? Everyone knew that. Even the foreign press was there covering it. The Grand Kale Leaf was going to make a speech to convince the representatives.

They were already convinced—bunch of fat bastards—to let the Greenies walk around freely. The reason for that was anyone's guess.

Rita had her particular view of the whys and wherefores.

"Everybody is entitled to privacy. They're tired of having curious people and tourists; it's understandable."

Do you know how I answered that, feeling very mushy inside?

"You're so right. I totally agree."

Wish fulfilled: the Special Charter for the Clorophylled People's Colonies was approved with a loud fanfare. Anyone who was ready to live without ingesting solid food was being voluntarily segregated from the rest of the society.

I invited my colleague to a night out, under the pretense of celebration. We went to the terraces of the Belém Commercial Center, the only place where you still can drink a cuppa in the dying city. I dared arguing a bit, not too radically, though; I didn't want to scare away my prey.

"Don't you think they went a little bit too far? In practice, the colonies will be totally autonomous now, as if they were sovereign territories. Institutions, the government, us, nobody has a say there..."

She almost convinced me that it was all to protect the way of life of the grafted people.

"But you don't think that the creation of ghettos might have a negative effect?"

"The beautiful village of Sintra—a ghetto?"

Yes, the beautiful village of Sintra, the Pilot Colony, where we wouldn't be able to stroll down and eat a good cheesecake, not anymore.

"The situation is not that dramatic. We aren't forbidden to enter the colonies," she tried to dial it down.

"Sure, but we have to get an authorization first."

Rita endeavored to explain it to me in simple terms.

"It's a good deal for both parts. The government doesn't need to worry about the clorophyllized people any longer. There'll be more to distribute. In return for that, we leave them alone. Nobody will go snooping around there."

I ended up agreeing with her, but only because I was drunk.

"Yes, yes. You're right. These people have very delicate noses. Imagine what their reaction would be if a savage got in there eating and having a beer and eating a ham sandwich!"

And she laughed again.

Such understanding earned me company for the rest of the night. Also the next one, and the one after that, and the one after, until we started to wake up together every morning.

* * *

One day, Rita asked me upfront:

"Don't you like pure clorophylls? They are so beautiful, so slender..."

And I lied.

"I don't know—I never tasted them."

53

The truth is that, on a certain occasion, I let myself be led by the ads. *"Come pick a flower."*

It was on the last floor of a building with a view of the Tagus at dawn. The terrace had been transformed in a greenhouse. They strolled leisurely among the plants, clothed only in their smiles, very green, very thin, offering refreshments. It was funny, even. But to get something from the little flowers one had to make a certain investment. The thing was rigged so these little things could get their money. The therapies to reach vegetal purity aren't cheap, no sir.

I chose one and asked for a private session in the solarium. Everything very delicate, songs to make you sleep, incense smoke. The rest of it was almost exclusively a massage, the chick wasn't going further. I had to shake the tree all by myself.

In my opinion, this eternal crisis is to blame. These little bastards get themselves into this clorophllyzation stuff because they're afraid of starving. They think, oh, at least the sun is an inexhaustible resource, unlike the rest. Damn, to each its own!

* * *

Things started to go south one day, when I was in the atrium of the headquarters, ready to go out, just waiting for Rita. My implant started to yell at me:

"Where are you going, jackass? Hold your horses and get your ass up here in the cabinet."

Friday, 5 PM, and the boss wasn't at the gym. Trouble for sure.

I trudged up the stairs until the fifth floor. We were right in the middle of the campaign *"A week without elevators,"* and public services to lead by example.

In person, the boss, wearing a suit and whatnot, looks at least as old as he really is. I think he pays good money to not retire. As good a way of investing his economies as any other. I like when he says:

"I wanna live until two hundred years old, work until one hundred and fuck all the women I can until one hundred and fifty.

A minute later Rita arrived, much calmer than I was. I was certain we would get scolded because we were dating, but it was something else.

"Aren't you tired of pampering these limp dicks and dry cunts? Do you want a real spy job? To be infiltrated? In disguise, the whole package? I have just what you need right here: vacations in Sintra, full expenses paid for."

I mentally smiled from ear to ear—imagining the Greenies in trouble—but I kept my poker face on the outside.

"Are they getting ill? Or the Great Leaf is plotting something?"

The old geezer frowned.

"They asked for our help. And you both are my more experienced agents in that area. I want full vigilance, but nobody can be the wiser. You're going to enter the Colony disguised as acolytes." And, to me: "This sissy boy here is going to become very slim!"

A week preparing. For Rita, it really was as if she had won a full vacation package all paid for; for me, the worst week of my life. They wanted me to be slim and dried out as a straw. They pumped my thyroid full of drugs until I had nothing but skin and bones, I spent hours with plasters on my skin so it could gain a bit of color, I was starved as a stray dog. With my girl, things went smoother: she had already begun her therapy before. Between transfusions, injections and radiation doses, they managed to change her species in due time. I couldn't get worse, but she made it through with flying colors.

* * *

I think of that a lot: after all, what separates plants and animals? Plants have clorophyll and produce their own food; that's what I was taught in school. But I know that there are dubious situations regarding those little things: beings that enjoy the best of the two realms. And now we do that with people. A new species.

But for me, nothing but a freak.

Rita was another thing entirely, of course. One must learn to distinguish edible from poisonous plants.

* * *

Finally, I was thin as a rail. I showed up at the checkpoint of the Colony with a concocted story: elementary school teacher, radical Greenie, recently arrived to Oporto, in search of a greenhouse to lay roots. I was led right to the representative himself, who was also part of the scheme.

The Greenbeans stood up from the lounger on the marquee and took the trouble of wearing a bathrobe to welcome me.

"I know you're not exactly an admirer," he probed. "But you disguise it very well."

Of course I did. And it cost me two weeks of my life. I was feeling like a reed in stale water. I didn't like to be reminded of that and I responded badly to it:

"I, for one, like to feed the old-fashioned way, with meat and wine, like the primitives. I don't feel like spending the rest of my life with heartburn."

He pretended not to take offense and started talking about practicalities.

"Mingle, keep your disguise and prick up your ears. Something or other will be said at the terraces, that's for sure. But be discreet..."

Of course! Nothing could transpire out there; the Greenies were the best, the Pilot Colony worked in perfect harmony.

But I had priorities. The first one was to have news of my colleague.

The fellow looked at me with a stupid expression.

"Your colleague... It's been two days since we last heard of her. I think this is another problem added to the basket..."

My blood froze.

I have yet to tell why they were so scared shitless at the herbarium. People were missing, that's why. Without a trace and without having ever passed through the checkpoints. No clues at all. And the Artichoke Head was telling me that bald lie, that he didn't know about Rita. It was all I could do not to turn him into soup.

And he kept on talking.

"Tell me what's your plan. How long are you staying? How are you going to survive without eating?"

But I could barely hear him now.

The boss thought everything was a misunderstanding.

"No one disappeared. This was all a bunch of newbies that go wherever it meets their fancy and don't tell anyone."

The thing is, he considered that sect just a dumb fad. But I knew better: to me, I was dealing with criminals. People who do such a thing to themselves are capable of doing anything. What the hell! They torture themselves, graft a lot of shit into their bodies, just to spend their lives doing nothing. I prepared myself to find corpses.

I told the representative that I wanted to examine the dumpsters and the sewers. I also told him that I'd send for special brigades, because more help was needed.

He was shocked. He even started to drool a little, probably wondering what would happen to him if those Neanderthals managed to get in there. He quickly remembered what he could do to help:

"There is a group of constituents, members of the solar community, who've been acting a little weird lately…"

He ended up giving me a small list with names, addresses and favorite terraces. I promptly started to stroll around up there, where the Lizards compete for space with photovoltaic collectors.

I listened to them talking. All of them youngsters. All of it bullshit. Hormonal therapies here, enzyme supplements there… To really understand them you'd have to be a pharmacist. I heard college kids talking leisurely about the advantages of removing such superfluous organs like the spleen and the liver.

"But it's a shame the procedure is so expensive," one of them complained. "I have to check if the bank can lend me the money."

To live without organs is not just expensive, but it's also impossible, as far as I know. But if this madness goes on…

The afternoon came to an end and I couldn't find any of the

people on the list. I decided to do a stakeout in front of the house of the nearest one. I sat on a bench in the Garden and tried to look innocent enough, while comparing the faces of the passersby to the images I got from the office.

I recognized the guy as soon I as saw him and went after him. We walked around there, up one street, down another, until dusk. He entered a dark alley. I waited half a dozen heartbeats and then I slithered through the same door I saw him going through. It wasn't locked.

Darkness and silence. I pulled my torch out. After the tiny hall there was a corridor. At the end, the kitchen. When I got in, the ceiling was suddenly illuminated.

Small kitchen appliances lined the bench: pots, plates, and cutlery, a stove with an open cover, and traces of fat over the burners. On a corner, a bucket full to the brim with stinky garbage. On another corner, a shovel and a broom for sweeping crumbs away. The most common of kitchens. As out of context as a one hundred dollar bill in my pocket.

My belly roared. I couldn't remember the last time I ate something.

I opened the door of the industrial freezer.

Rita was inside, her body chopped to bits disposed in plastic bags.

Armed, they came in.

"Gotcha! Raiding the freezer, huh? So you're a Eat'n'Shit! We were pretty sure of that."

I got my girlfriend's head out of a bag by her hair and walked right to them so I could rub it in their faces.

Then I saw the barrels of two guns raised to my chest's height. I remembered that the mission hadn't ended. There was no mystery at all in the disappearances, just a crime, but what I still didn't have was motive and details. I chose to have a momentary lapse of reason and animic force. I was ordered to go back through the corridor. I obeyed, and I was taken to the dining room.

An ample space, with a view to the gardened inner patio. In the center, a big table with a cloth, china, forks, and knives. There were roughly a dozen guests. They stopped talking upon our arrival. The man at the head of the table rose up ceremoniously.

"My dear Inspector, welcome to our social gathering."

What a horrible display of people. Black, burned, with no meat in their gums. Some of them were so crinkled they seemed like those fossils that appear in documentaries. One of the specters asked me if I wanted to eat. The others started laughing like crazy, like rattling corpses.

"You sons of bitches!"

They laughed harder, damn them! A few presented themselves, saying their names and ages. The one who told me he was fifty-five assured me he was the oldest of the company. He looked like an unburied skeleton.

"Then you are pretty fucked up, man. You look like you owe a few years to the Grim Reaper."

"It's the price to pay, boy," he said. "But it's well worth it."

I agree to dine with them. We had a lot to talk about. Who the hell could they be, and what could be the meaning of all that among those major league schizoids? They approved my decision enthusiastically.

"Excellent! Today we're going to eat fresh meat. I'm tired of the frozen stuff already…"

I told you before: sometimes I'm so slow I must look like a retard. I only came to my senses when I heard the next words:

"Prepare him for tomorrow. There will be time enough for him to bleed all night. For dinner tonight, we'll require just a few slices of the thigh." Only then I knew I was going to be the main course.

I felt so confused.

"But…but you don't need to eat!"

"No, we don't, but we like it," the fifty-five year-old decrepit geezer said. "We enjoy all the pleasures of life."

A lady of horrifying appearance mocked:

"We are carnivore plants."

Then, one of the other armed jackasses:

"It's hard to get the freezer properly stocked here. Our salvations are the stray secret agents who stumble upon us. The other one was more tender, but you'll do as well..."

There's not much to tell after that. I started punching them freely. When they were all down, mumbling and whining, I stopped and pondered: what should I do now with such fine gentlemen and respectable ladies? Maybe crush them like grapes, stomp on them, squeeze them out of their lifesap.

But when I lifted my boot to start the party, I heard noise in the corridor. I thought their reinforcements were coming. Fortunately, it was mine. And, ahead of them, the imbecile representative.

"It looks like we got here just in time to save your skin."

"Save? Me? Ten minutes more and I'd have wiped all the weeds from your garden."

* * *

I came back to the HQ in Lisbon that same evening, after lots of friendly pats on the shoulder. The murderers were still there, guarded by their peers. Not a single word of what had happened to the gossip-happy people of the newscasts. In my belly, I felt the full weight of fasting and failure. Why failure, if the mission had been successful? Just a bad feeling.

I still managed to get some dinner and then started to work in my office without sleeping. It was almost dawn when the boss appeared at the door, on his way to the gym.

"Couldn't get any sleep?"

I told him I wanted to dispatch the process right away. I was getting the evidence ready for Internal Affairs.

"Evidence? What evidence? What did I tell you to do yesterday? Go home, have some rest, take a few days off. I didn't tell you to prepare a process, right?"

Indeed, he had told me to get some sleep and present myself at work at nine o'clock sharp.

"And shut your yap! You look like a fish outta water."

I closed my mouth and sat down. I noticed that the old man was really pissed off, but I couldn't fathom why.

"Are you crazy, boss? I want to see those cannibals in jail, the sooner the better."

And then he dropped the bomb.

"M'boy! Things don't always happen the way we want them to. Take your nose out of that story if you don't want it cut off your face. Let the Greenies take care of this their own way."

"What? I had to face the representative and his stooges. All they wanted to know was if their pals were okay. They even threatened to sue me for excessive use of force… I'd rather gather a few friends and beat the shit out of them."

I had to hear a bitter scolding.

"The interests of the nation are more important than the interests of your cock. You're here to give your blood for the Homeland and also to do whatever the fuck I tell you to do. If I tell you to drop a bucketful of shit over your head, that's exactly what you're going to do. If I tell you to let go of something, you'll let go of it. This is a war between civilization and barbary. Your opinions are not welcome here."

Suddenly all the pieces started to fit in the puzzle in my stupid head. I couldn't avoid feeling sick. How stupid, how naïve! Those goons were all in cahoots. My boss included. They didn't want dumb people dreaming that they were being eaten by dumber creatures. They were going to hide the crimes to protect the scheme of the colonies.

Clorophyll humans aren't such a wonder, after all. Much less the next step, the great hope of mankind. They're just another crazy experiment. They managed to get free because they have friends in high places. Friends? I wonder! Just another pathetic plan to save the planet. A plan doomed to failure; just see the pitiful state of the fellas just a few years into the procedure.

I could only think of one proper answer to my dearest mentor:

"You can shove Homeland, civilization and your green friends up your hemorrhoids, until they come out your mouth."

* * *

The rulers of the world only see what they want to see. They create the truths that are fashionable at the moment and they believe strongly in them. They never admit making any mistakes, they don't run away even if the storm ahead of them is a big one. They drag us to the top of a cliff and tell us to jump, happily. There's so much stupidity, so much alienation, that nobody does just the necessary, no hesitations, no beating around the bush.

I am going to do what I need to do.

I'm a man. I have them in my target. I will have my vengeance.

They killed my love. They cut her to pieces. They ate her. These fucking Kale Leaves!

I'm sending quite a few down below to feed the soil. Me and my sniper rifle with telescopic sight. As many as I can. Men, women, children, old people, fuck them all! When the sun goes up. When they stretch themselves in the terraces.

After that, somebody will definitely come after me.

But they won't catch me. I'll run somewhere far, far away, leaving this lie behind. The only option left to a man without love is to disappear. Maybe I'll join some clandestine group. To the guys who are for nuclear power, for instance. If we had those powerhouses, working at full capacity, the world would be very different. Maybe freaks like this Cabbageheads sect would never be created in the first place.

* * *

Telmo Marçal is the pseudonym of a bourgeoisly restless forty-year-old, who writes disheveled stories with detached characters condemned to try to survive in worlds as absurd as family. His first short stories appeared in 2003, thanks to the dynamics of fanzines and electronic magazines in Portugal and Brazil. His work appeared in the anthology *Por Universos Nunca Dantes Navegados* and his first solo book, *As atribulações de Jacques Bonhomme*, appeared in 2009. In 2012, he participated in *Antologia de Ficção Científica Fantasporto*, published in Portugal and Brazil.

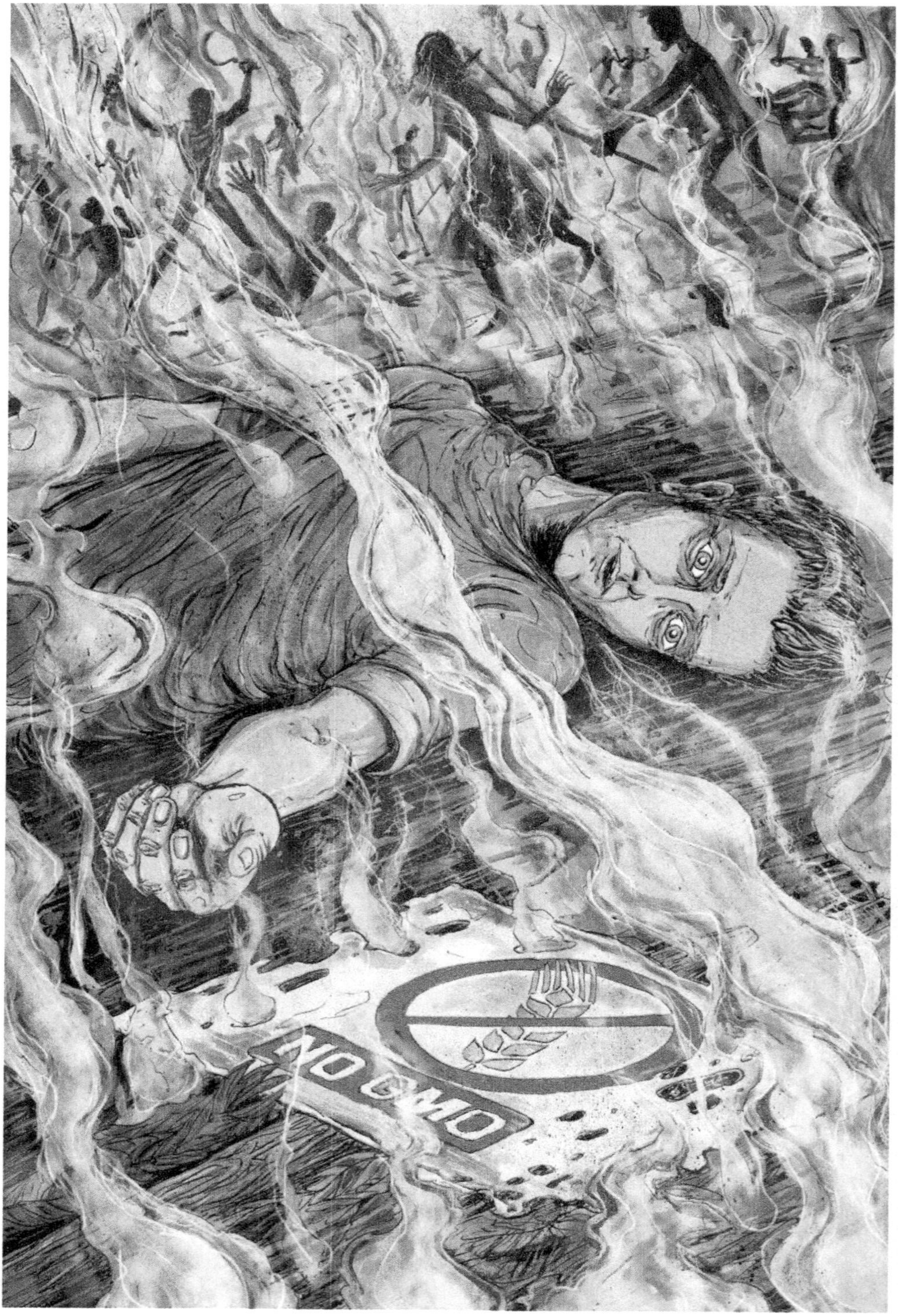
NO GMO

BREAKING NEWS!
Romeu Martins

[Anchor] It's eight-oh-one PM. Now that the Voice of Brazil broadcast has ended, your radio network, Tribuna Central, operating in Amplitude Modulada and surfing on the Internet waves, is back to the news.

[Jingle] *Teeeeeeee-Cee, Aaaaaaaaaay-Em! The radio that listens to you.*

[Anchor] And we are again reporting directly from the interior of Paraná, where the laboratory of a company in the agricultural research sector risks being invaded at any moment now by a mob of landless rural workers. Let's talk to reporter Helena Garcia, who has been tracking everything on the spot, since early afternoon. Helena, can you hear us? What can you tell our listeners throughout Brazil? Good evening.

[Reporter] Good evening. I hear you loud and clear, Herbert. I am here in the municipality of Telêmaco Borba, approximately 250 kilometers from the capital of Paraná, Curitiba. In front of me is the one that is considered the largest and most modern greenhouse in Latin America, used by the multinational TransCiência as a laboratory for growing genetically modified products. It is a huge

65

dome made of a special, transparent plastic. Right now, there are approximately one hundred demonstrators of the Rural Workers Movement shouting slogans and threatening to break into the company premises. They are people of the most different origins, I see descendants of Japanese, Germans, blacks, people from all over the state. I can also see people of all ages, from gentlemen and ladies with white hair to children, most of them young people, who are the front line at the entrance of the greenhouse. We are the only press team present in this live coverage of the demonstration. We can't get too close because this movement is very hostile to the presence of journalists, but I think you can hear them shouting on my cell phone. One moment, I'm going to adjust the TalkCel's directional mic to try to pick up the sound... There it goes.

[Crowd] *...with the lab food! We are not guinea pigs of the multinationals! Off with the lab food! We are not guinea pigs of the multinationals! Fuck frankenfood! Fuck franken...*

[Reporter] As you can hear, there has been an atmosphere of war since dawn, when demonstrators set up camp on the ground around the greenhouse. In the middle of the afternoon, they left their improvised blue canvas tents and surrounded the lab, blocking the access of researchers and staff. Although many of the company's resources were acquired through agreements with the Federal University of Paraná and Embrapa, the governor did not authorize the sending of Military Police troops to contain the demonstration. At this moment, only the security guards of the multinational are making a cordon to try to prevent the entrance of dozens of people, many of them armed with hoes, shovels, sickles, and machetes.

[Anchor] Helen, did you talk to any of the leaders?

[Reporter] No, Herbert, as I said, the Rural Workers are a very radical dissidence from the MST. Their main leader is a man from Santa Catarina who presents himself as Medina, but refuses to speak to the press... Wait a moment... Attention, studio, things are starting to get more intense here. Apparently, the demonstrators are advancing against the company's laboratory as we speak. Yes, they have broken up the cordon and are breaking through the greenhouse doors. With blows of hoes, and kicks, the crowd forced the entrance... They are in, the Rural Workers have invaded, right now, the largest experimental greenhouse in Latin America. Between screams and a lot of rushing, dozens of men, women, and even small children are destroying with sickle blows the transgenic plants of the place. Anyone who is not carrying a tool is ripping out stalks with bare hands or trampling the crops.

[Anchor] Hello, Helena, were there any employees inside the lab?

[Reporter] No, Herbert, the greenhouse was empty, and even the TransCiência security guards, who were trying to protect the place, remain outside. Meanwhile, more and more demonstrators enter the premises through the broken doors. It's very hard to get closer, but the environment is very well lighted, and we can see the movement of people through the transparent walls. They are destroying not just the plants, but all the equipment inside. Computers are thrown to the floor, tables are turned. I can see that even large gallons, probably fertilizer or other chemicals, are thrown against the walls. Chaos is widespread within what is the largest transgenic research laboratory in Brazil.

[Anchor] Helena, we were able to make contact with one of the persons responsible for the research done in this laboratory. Orson Wellmann is the CEO of the Brazilian branch of TransCiência and chief scientist of the unit being invaded right now. He's at the company's office in Curitiba. We will pass him on to your line, so you can interview him as you keep on reporting. Good evening, Mr. Wellmann.

[Scientist] Good evening, journalists, good evening, listeners and Internet users in Brazil and all over the world.

[Reporter] Mr. Wellmann, what do you have to say on the Rural Workers's agenda?

[Scientist] My dear, Helena, I'm the one who asks: what agenda? These people aren't interested in negotiating, they have no willingness to dialogue.

[Reporter] But the movement claims that your company doesn't just work with the creation of genetically altered foods. They accuse TransCiência of having links with military groups and claim that you experiment with weapons, don't you? What can you tell us about that?

[Scientist] These accusations, as you call them, are ridiculous. Where's the evidence? This is nothing more than slander and speculation to harm us, since we are a global company, a conglomerate with shares traded on the main stock exchanges in the world and with the participation of many investment funds. This lab being attacked in front of you is a good example of this. Do you see the large mirrored panels above the transparent polymer forming the walls of the greenhouse?

[Reporter] Yes, they form a kind of cover on the sides of the premises, but...

[Scientist] We call them electrical photosynthesizers, a technology capable of employing the principles of photosynthesis of plants for the production of electricity. These panels capture the sunlight so that the biophotovoltaic cells convert it into energy for the whole complex, making this unit totally autonomous. During the night, as now, the electricity used in lighting and to power the equipment is the same as that stored in the batteries located in the central part of the greenhouse. This technological innovation is one hundred percent sustainable and was fully developed by us. We work in many different areas in various industry sectors. However, all our research is guided by ethics and respect for the laws of each country in which we operate. It's not different with regard to our branch in Brazil.

[Reporter] How would you label the demonstrators' actions, then?

[Scientist] They use terrorist methods to hinder our work and the progress of science. Maybe your listeners have heard of neoluddites, haven't they? Neoluddites are people who, like what happened at the beginning of the Industrial Revolution back in England in the nineteenth century feared the advance of science and technology. They are afraid—indeed they are full of spite—for all that's new and try to prevent the march of the future. At that time, in the nineteenth century, the automatic weaving machines were their focus. Nowadays, the target of these intolerants are genetically modified organisms.

[Reporter] So, in your opinion, the Rural Workers are a terrorist and neoluddite group?

[Scientist] My dear Helena, I call these people Neolysenkists. I'll explain it for you and for your qualified listeners in Brazil and every part of the world who happens to be listening to us on the internet. Trofim Lysenko was a very important man in the former Soviet Union in the mid-thirties of the last century. He was the favorite scientist of the dictator Josef Stalin. He said he did not believe in genetics as it was taught in the West, because he considered it a bourgeois science, which would not be in accordance with dialectical materialism, the ideology prevailing in the Soviet state. His influence was so huge that any reference to chromosomes was banished from the textbooks of that country, begetting an incalculable scientific and technological kickback. But it was much worse than that: Lysenko claimed that his philosophically correct genetics would ensure greater wheat production for the Russians in the winter. Do you know what really happened, my dear Helena?

[Reporter] No, I've never heard of it…

[Scientist] The crazy theses of that man caused hunger and strife to millions of people in the fields and cities of the Soviet Union. They destroyed the country's economy and condemned many thousands of Russians to death and malnutrition. And that's what these people, these Neolysenkists, are trying to revive now, here in Brazil, in the twenty-first century. By stopping the work of genetic scientists, they are creating difficulties for discovering new medicines, new food sources, new products that may be fundamental for the future of humankind and for the Brazilian economy. The classic example I always mention is that of a type of genetically modified strawberry. Transgenic experiments allowed the use of salmon genes, a fish capable of resisting very low temperatures, to produce fruits with the same characteristics, a big economic differential.

[Reporter] But, if you'll excuse me, sir …

[Scientist] I've just told you, Helena, about the bio-electric technology we've developed to power the energy needs of our lab. Even more important than that are the improvements we have made in the plants grown there to better take advantage of their natural ability to turn sunlight into organic matter. Our country is privileged both for its natural genetic diversity and for the high rates of solar irradiance throughout the year, advantages that led TransCiência to decide on the installation of our greenhouse in Brazil. The same greenhouse that is being barbarically destroyed at this point. Another great Brazilian advantage is that we have some of the best researchers in this area of the world. Particularly among those working with plant genome sequencing, an area where national scientists are a well-recognized reference everywhere. It is one of the few cases where we remain technologically on par with any nation of the so-called developed world. We cannot lose these differentials that makes us stand out among the nations because of a radical group that insists on living in the past...

[Reporter] Mr. Wellmann, thank you for the interview, but I must interrupt to report that something strange seems to be happening inside the invaded greenhouse. The screams and the breaking noise have subsided. I can see that the movement of the demonstrators has changed from one second to the next.

[Anchor] Helena? Helena? This is the studio. What's happening? What can you see?

[Reporter] All right, Herbert. Yes, that's right! Several of the demonstrators who until a few moments ago were running and excavating the soil stopped moving. Little by little, more and more landless people are stopping their attack on plants and equipment. They're just standing there. It's as if they've forgotten what they were doing. They seem confused. Almost every one of them at this very moment stands still, and only a few go on... What's that? It's not possible! Those people started to attack each other! A man has just crushed a child's head with hoe blows... It's horrible...

[Anchor] Helena, I don't understand. Are the security guards of

TransCiência taking the lab, is that it? What's going on?

[Reporter] No, no, it's the rural workers who are killing themselves... They all dropped the plants and started attacking each other... Oh, my God! It's the most horrible thing I've ever seen! Men are hacking each other to bits, and also the women and children who came with them. Whoever isn't carrying a weapon is throwing objects upon the nearest person. Or attacks with punches, kicks, and bites. Many are lying on the ground, getting up... Everyone, even small children, attacks... blood flows everywhere.

[Anchor] But how is this even possible? Has anyone come near the greenhouse?

[Reporter] Nobody approached the place... Sorry, Herbert, excuse me, listeners, but it's very hard to describe what I'm seeing here. The level of violence is horrible. Even women, who are apparently the mothers of some of those children, are assaulting those by their side indiscriminately. Wait...did you get that in the studio, Herbert?

[Anchor] Did it sound like thunder...or an explosion? Grenades? Did the police or the Army decide to take action?

[Reporter] Hard to say, but I did see a glow and... Yes, a cloud of black smoke has begun to come out of the back of the greenhouse. I can see the flames, the place is on fire. That's right, the fire spreads faster and faster. It hits the plants and runs across the floor, among those gallons of chemicals with its contents spread... Another explosion, this time right in the middle of the greenhouse! Several people were thrown into the air... Oh my God, they still keep attacking! No one is trying to escape through the broken doors. Those people are still killing each other... Even those with their bodies covered by fire seem more intent in injuring their colleagues than in protecting themselves! It's not possible! An old man who had his arm ripped out and his clothes on fire came to the door, but instead of running out, he picked up a machete on the floor and returned only to attack a woman from behind... Nothing makes sense...

[Anchor] Helena, what was that noise? What happened? Are you ok?

[Reporter] More explosions, Herbert... The gallons of fertilizer are exploding everywhere... The black smoke is spreading, and is apparently toxic... Calm down, don't push me! I'm working here... The security guards are leaving the place and trying to make me leave too... The lights went out, the solar-powered batteries have just exploded. You can't see much in the glow of the fire. I can see that the ceiling is collapsing... The huge panels that collected the sunlight shattered into millions of pieces. Shards of glass fly through the skies. The metal structure supporting the ceiling and walls of the dome took a bad shaking. It just collapsed... Holy crap! The noise of the steel twisting is very loud. Tons of material crushed dozens of people. Even so, nobody tries to escape from that hell... I don't think anyone survived... Hello, Herbert, it's no longer possible to stay here. The security guards pushed me away from the greenhouse, only to see the fire, louder and louder, and a huge column of smoke that covers the moon and the stars...

[Anchor] Hello, Helena? Hello? They must have taken our reporter out of the place. We will try to resume the live link with our report. You from all over Brazil heard, here in Tribuna Central AM, the report of an invasion that ended in tragedy, in the interior of Paraná. Approximately one hundred demonstrators from the Rural Workers' movement may have died in an attempt to break into the laboratories of the agribusiness giant, TransCiência. More details after the commercial break, when we will continue with our exclusive, live coverage at the place where the news happens. With the support of TalkCel, the only cellular operator present in one hundred percent of the national territory, we are the station that listens to you.

[Jingle] *Teeeeeeee-Cee, Aaaaaaaaaay-Em! The radio that listens to you.*

* * *

"Only garbage now. We can turn it off and celebrate."

The speaker is a man dressed entirely in white, with hair as light in color as the social clothes he wears. He activates the remote control, muting the sound from the landscape in front of him, in a clearing 250 kilometers from where those events were being narrated.

On the other side of the huge room, still with the cellphone with which he gave the interview, the second occupant of the apartment gets up from the sofa with an enthusiastic expression on his face. Although he has darker hair, it is also much more scarce than his guest's, and his clothes less formal.

"Change the station, put some music on while I get the wine. We have a lot to celebrate; everything happened exactly as planned, or even better."

He heads for a side door while his guest looks over the musical selection available on the sound equipment display. The arrows on the small black monolith show the names of the artists, albums, and musicians on the screen that previously showed the Tribuna Central radio station's dial number.

"Did you have any questions at all, Orson? My organization gives a hundred percent guarantee on the services offered to the contractors. We said that you would at the same time achieve the experience you wanted with humans and all the publicity needed to launch the new product."

The answering voice comes muffled from the air-conditioned cellar.

"Sometimes your efficiency scares me, my dear Mr. Neves."

Amazed by so many options in the mp3 files, the white-haired

74

man ends up programming the shuffle mode on the jazz channel. Then Keith Jarrett's music begins to spread from the towering black boxes all over the room, sending piano chords around the place. Satisfied with the result, the guest drops the remote, pulls a cigarette box and lighter out of his pockets and, while lighting his cigarette, speaks louder to his host.

"What of it? The new weapon is all that your investigators have been announcing."

"Blessed was the day that I read that Royal Society paper about the possible impacts of an obscure protozoan on society's behavior." He sticks his head out of the door and points with his chin to a bookcase next to the stereo. "There's a hardcopy there, I was reading it again this morning. The London scientists gave me the idea of using *Toxoplasma gondii*, the cause of toxoplasmosis, as raw material for the hate gas."

Still sitting on the couch, Neves stretches his arm to the appointed spot and picks up a white folder with the TransCiência logo: the letters *TC* in blue surrounded by two gray bands simulating the DNA helix. On the same cover, the title of the six-page article appears in the English translation and in the Brazilian Portuguese translation: "Can *Toxoplasma gondii*, common brain parasite, influence human society?"

"Oh, so that was the original source of your insight."

"That's right. The UK Academy of Sciences was worried by the evidence that this simple parasite could affect people's brains and induce new behaviors in them. The protozoan has been shown to be able to traverse the membrane of our self-defense cells, invade the nucleus and simply fool all the immune barriers of the human brain. An authentic phenomenon of nature, it acted like a hacker who invades a computer, changes the software, and forces the hardware to function as it pleases."

Unseen by his interlocutor, Neves looks up at the ceiling as if instinctively reacting to a particularly boring lecture at a scientific seminar.

"A second paper, presented during an annual meeting of the International Society for Behavioral Neuroscience, stated that the microorganism had unveiled 'the vocabulary of neurotransmitters and hormones'."

"All in all, we're talking about a clever little bug." The guest flips through the paper without paying much attention. After all, the technical language in those few lines is indecipherable to laypeople like him.

The real expert on the subject finally returns to the room displaying a bottle of Romanée-Conti as a trophy.

"Really… Look, I'm going to open this precious thing as soon as I can find the corkscrew. The list of behavioral changes that our small biohacker is able to bring varies according to gender. It makes women more affectionate and men more conformist. It seemed capable of making people more sensitive to guilt. On the one hand, they become more predisposed to engage in dangerous situations, on the other, they become averse to change."

"A huge change in the brain chemistry, for sure." The expression on Neves's face while still leafing through the document doesn't display such certainty. "I'd buy a whole lot of this parasite if it could make my last mother-in-law, may the devil have her, a more affectionate woman… But I don't think that all the… *Toxoplasma gondii* of the world would be capable of such a feat, and I also believe the poor thing would fail if it tried to create in me such a sense of guilt."

"True, my friend, but you are a lost case of any kind of manifestation of the superego, as guilty or self-critical, as we well know." Orson Wellmann laughs at his own tirade as he opens and closes drawers in search of the corkscrew. Between one and the other he goes back to talking enthusiastically. "The point is that, worldwide, there are billions of people infected with toxoplasmosis. Billions of them. One detail that caught my attention is that the most affected country would be Brazil, with almost seventy percent of the population serving as a carrier to our friend. As a result, of course, of the indigent sanitary services in this country, which facilitate the contagion of the parasite. Isn't it ironic? Brazil may even have some of the best genetic engineers on the planet, as I told that bloody reporter, but it can't get plumbing to reach all the houses or end rodent infestations. Speaking of rodents, what really interested me was another Oxford experiment. This experiment proved that *Toxoplasma gondii* was responsible for an even more radical change in the behavior of rodents. The parasite simply induced these animals to suicide, can you imagine that?! In a maze, scientists marked a few corners with the smell of cat urine. Healthy people fled from there as if the devil chased them. But for the contaminated specimens, that odor had the same attraction as the smell of food. It is as if the animals, controlled by microorganisms in their brains, begged to be devoured!"

Sensing that the conversation might turn out to be a speech after all, Neves puts the British paper away as if he received an electric shock, straightens his jacket, stands up and goes in the direction of the owner of the apartment, searching for a shortcut to any subject that might be more in his domain:

"That's what I always say, if a thing like that can't be used as a biological weapon, what else could?"

"That's exactly what I thought. We just needed to figure out a way to take advantage of the skill of this lovely protozoan. In the TransCiência labs we detected, isolated, and enhanced the potential of the genes responsible for the production of the substances that induce behavioral changes in mammals. The next step was inserting this genetic code into some laboratory-modified plants so they could release a new toxin in the air along with their normal oxygen production. And then we have our hate gas. Where did my servant put that corkscrew, goddamnit?"

Before even reaching the counter where the bulky bottle of red wine is resting, Neves sees the opener waiting to be used in its proper place: the wall bracket.

"So many times all we need is an outside perspective, my dear scientist." With the same hand that holds his cigarette, he points to the opener as he speaks. "I suppose you have enough gas in stock to start industrial production."

"Merci, Monsieur Neves. Of course, of course, we now control the whole process and we can already synthesize the gas on a large scale, manipulating chemicals the way my beloved plants did with sunlight in the greenhouse. It was only a matter of doing the, say, reverse bioengineering of the toxin they released into the air. That's why the laboratory became expendable and we could destroy it from here, from the comfort of my apartment, triggering the explosives hidden in its structure. The hyperoxygenated environment and the amount of flammable substances helped spread the fire and put an end to all the clues that would compromise us. The fire will consume any traces of the gas and burn all the plants and human guinea pigs. Concentrated energy cells were charged with blowing up any clues that might remain of our experiments there, leaving a crater in its place."

Once the seal is cut, the scientist drills the thick cork of the bottle as he speaks, almost in the same rhythm as the music he continues to play.

"The precautions are not so much for fear of the police investigation, the idea was only to avoid industrial espionage. After all, the research of our private competitors is much more efficient than that of state agents. Now it's just trigger the insurance, put the blame on the landless, and recover the money invested. But that greenhouse served us as a field of evidence in the last necessary experience: the aerial application of the neurotoxin to humans in a real situation. To that end, those rabid workers that their organization manipulated to attack our solar laboratory of Telêmaco Borba were a bit useful."

Unmaking the knot of his tie, Neves dismisses the other's compliments with a gesture.

"That was the easy part of the plan. The technical expertise of your team of scientists wasn't even required. My organization specializes in finding creative solutions to the kind of problem you have presented us. It's not as if we lacked for manpower here. So, creating such a social movement in Brazil is as easy as opening an NGO or founding a new church. I speak of this from experience, believe me." While walking down to him, Neves picks up two glasses as he watches the other's effort to open the precious bottle. "Parasitizing the state and the parastatal structure of this country to make it work just the way we want is far more simple work than that of your protozoan changing behaviors of kamikaze rats. And the best thing is that, with all the dramatic advertising this episode will reach in the next few days, we will have the ideal advertisement to present the product to the several groups that have shown an interest in acquiring hate gas. The ETA and the IRA are no longer in business, but our network has already contacted Hamas and Hezbollah, along with the Farc..."

A dry noise interrupts him when the cork is finally removed from the bottle neck.

"Voila, and it's open! Yes, the experiment was proof that the toxin, when applied among a population predisposed to violence and with the necessary conditions to carry it out, can cause a remote control carnage." The chief scientist of TransCiência pours the drink for his guest, being careful with each drop. "And thanks to the diversity of the sample of peasants you gave us, we proved that the gas works in both sexes, in any age group and with different ethnicities. Couldn't be more perfect if we had asked for it! I almost cried out laughing as I remembered that even Darwin was not interested in parasites, did you know that? He said the creeping little creatures were just a deviation in the natural course of species evolution."

Wellmann hands the glass to Neves, who pulls a last drag on his cigarette and waits for the guest to finish pouring for himself.

"So old Charles had his day of—what's the name of that Russian you mentioned in the interview? Lysenko? Thank you, Orson. A good wine is always fine with these cold nights you have here in Curitiba."

The scientist is pleased with a third of his glass filled and lifts it in front of the visitor.

"Even geniuses are not immune to a few stumbles, my friend. But let's have a toast: to the *Toxoplasma gondii*, to my scientists and their human guinea pigs."

Having got rid of the cigarette already, Neves returns the gesture, which makes the crystal resonate when the glasses touch.

"They did their part well, of rats in the maze. To the future, that belongs to us. Cheers!"

Neves turns red, makes a face and declares:

"Very heavy. It's best to put it in the decanter for a while to rest."

* * *

Romeu Martins is a journalist, specializing in scientific dissemination, and an author of fantastic literature. He began writing fiction in 2008 for his own blog, *Terroristas da Conspiração (Terrorists of the Conspiracy)*, where he also published a few dozen other writers. Today, he has work in books by three national publishers, and an excerpt from his short story has been selected and translated into English for the *Steampunk Bible* by Americans Jeff VanderMeer and S. J. Chambers. With Editora Draco, he debuted as a short storyteller in *Sherlock Holmes—Aventuras Secretas* (2012).

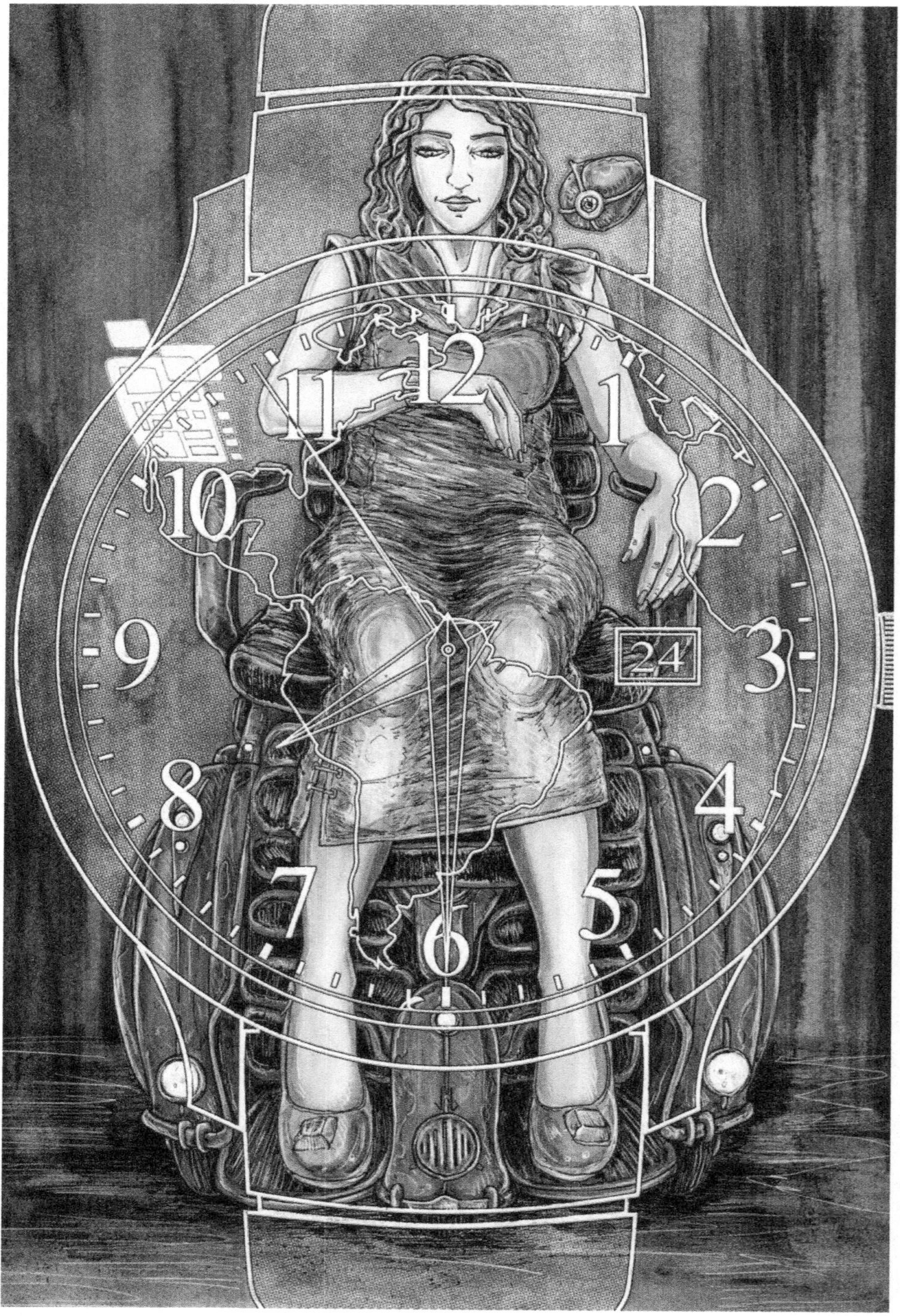
12
1
2
3
4
5
6
7
8
9
10
11
24

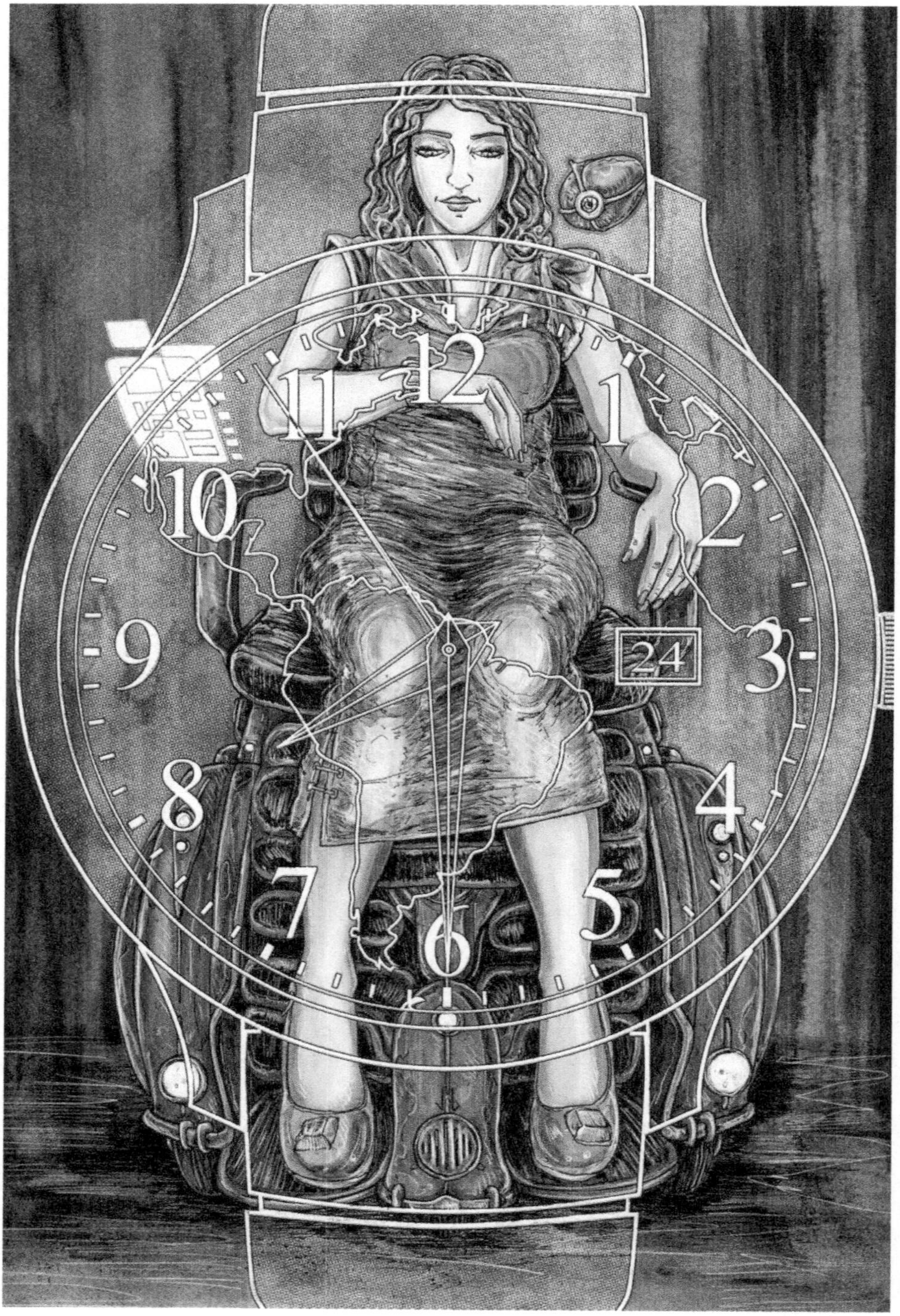
12
1
2
3
24
4
5
6
7
8
9
10
11

ONCE UPON A TIME IN A WORLD
Antonio Luiz M. C. Costa

"Patrícia Galvão, for the 'Abaporu', the *Anthropophagy*. Captain Luis Carlos Prestes and microbiologist Olga Benário announced they will tie the knot and live in Brazil next year, upon returning from Mars. In the following pictures, the couple thanks the well-wishes of the First Commissioner of the Union of Nations, Rosa Luxemburg, the German President Clara Zetkin and the Secretary General of Neogeia and President of Brazil, João Cândido."

The audience of the most popular program of Piratininga Jereré or Piratininga Network, if not of the whole Porandutepé or Brazilian Infohighway, reached a historical record. The young anchorwoman knew it instantly, for the data flowed through her visor in the form of three-dimensional charts that she opened and closed with the blink of an eye as she displayed a good-humored edition of the messages of cosmonauts and politicians. Almost a billion hits.

She recoiled, though she practically didn't allow fame to get into her head anymore. *Abaporu* was the most popular show at Poranduba Mytanga or Young News, which began the year before, almost as a joke. Journalism sophomores were hired for a year to create a news channel tailor-made by young people for young people, light and entertaining. It was the sensation of the year: agile and honest, talking about important things in a smart, simple way.

In the second year, the audience exploded, leaving behind the dour Aporanduba, World News, flagship network. Much of the secret was there, behind the attractive face of bristly hair and the gaudy, state-of-the-art display. The relevant, bold questions were asked there. Another part rested upon the scientific knowledge and the impeccable techniques of the partner, less known to the public eye but equally important: Avajoguyroá Apapocuva, the Guira.

The edited virtuality was already over; the live interview would begin in moments. The display warned that the guest was ready to be interviewed, or devoured, as she preferred. She tested the connection and maneuvered the microcameras in the environment to frame it and the holo alternately or simultaneously and turn the scene into a virtual experience that allowed the cybernaut to put himself in his or her place, or as a neutral observer. She crossed her legs, turned on the projectors, and the man in the white safari costume appeared with his chair.

Eighty thousand blocks away, in a parliamentary office in the capital of the Union of Nations, the hologram of the young woman appeared simultaneously, in all its splendor, one step ahead of the interviewee. She was savage, smart, and conceited, woe to those who underestimated her! And soft eyes, eyes that could hurt. Her slender body, umbilical and soft, possessed of a certain *je ne sais quois... How can I refuse to answer it? How could I be angry with her?*

She straightened up. She had to distract from her transparent blouse, the red shorts and everything they revealed and suggested. She glanced at the vast office window and looked at another equally magnificent but less disturbing landscape: the Council of the Union palace, the large artificial lake, the restored savannah in the heart of the Sahara, the flamingos flocking around...

"From Cosmopolis, Raul Bopp, chairman of the Commission of Science and Culture of the Council of the Union. Ready to go to the *moquém* and be devoured by our netizens, Deputy?"

"Certainly, my pleasure! I hope I'm tasty!" He smiled, trying to appear at ease.

"Well, the case of Olga and Luis Carlos has made the hearing of the monitoring of the Mission Ares an unheard-of success. It overcame the launch, arrival, landing, and discovery of living bacteroids in Hellas. In these two years, the public eye has been less interested in scientific developments than in the personal life of cosmonauts. I ask you: has the Union of Nations spent five billion credits just to create the most expensive romantic telenovela in history?"

The question was unexpected, but it wasn't aggressive, it was the provocative tone of one who really seeks compelling answers. It would be good if she could have them.

"Huh, Pagu, huh! I suppose the question is rhetorical, I don't believe you really think this." He looked as if he was going to stall, but suddenly he changed his mind. "Look, to put it another way, the mission costs a credit to every inhabitant of the planet, a day of minimum wage. As far as it concerns me, I give my part with pleasure, and I don't see the interest in their coexistence as a waste of time, not at all!" He gestured enthusiastically.

"Why, Raul? What good is it to observe and discuss what is happening every day and every moment with seven real people cloistered together, waking up, fighting, working, having lunch, dating? If they were in a house in, I don't know, Jacarepaguá, it would be a bit of dull, morbid fun, wouldn't it? Why it should be any different on a ship or on a Martian base?"

"Look, it's not any seven random people. They are people of remarkable courage, intelligence and competence, doing something extraordinary. Also, they are a metonymy, a synecdoche of humankind. The Martian base is a miniature of the Union of Nations, in which the public sees its future and its challenges, the problems and conflicts of the Earth and the power of fellowship to solve them so that all of them, all of us, can win. These people were also chosen to represent the seven confederations and their ability to cooperate…"

Pagu saw a breach to enter. "Infograph this, Guira," she subvocalized through the viewer to her associate, who made a map of the world associating the regions with photos and biographies to link to her page: Prestes and Neogeia, Benário and Eurasia, Zhou and Eastasia, Sartika and Oceania…interested people could consult this info on the network after the interview.

"But aren't there already a lot of joint projects, plus cultural and educational programs to promote peace and friendship between peoples? Did we need this one in particular?" She tilted her head, looking genuinely interested in the answer.

"It's something else. It's not a work of engineering, it's not a fiction, it is a spectacle of reality, a live adventure, true in all its risks and surprises. The involvement of people is much greater when the imponderable is at stake. We are human and this is how we get excited, with people with whom we share the perils of life and learn to identify ourselves with, even if they seem so different from us!"

"So the main benefit is political, Raul? That's not what you usually hear!"

"I think it's essential. I didn't live that, and you're even younger than me. But there are many people still living who fought in the Great War or suffered with it, and who didn't forget the post-war grudges and passed them on to their children. For example, I remember when I saw Santos-Dumont and Sinchi Yupanqui landing on the Moon. In the naïveté of my eight years of age, I felt so proud of my country: at last, the world bows to Brazil…"

"Link here, Guira!" Pagu asked for a link to a virtuality about the *Jacy 14-bis* landing on the moon, which she had put on the net in the morning to celebrate the 23-year anniversary of the feat.

"…in other parts of the world, however," Raul went on, "there was suspicion and spite: do Brazil and the Tauantinsuio plan to monopolize technology and the future? Who are these Pancolombians to call themselves representatives of humanity? Why go to the Moon when there are more important things to do on Earth? It was a mistake and this time the Union of Nations was keen to promote the active participation of all confederations, leaving no one out."

"Infograph this, Guira." She asked for schematics of the project with the contributions of each confederation: the *Tupá 8* launcher, the Xiuhtecuhtli accelerators and the Neogeia Ch'askawanp'u second stage, the Junrei robots and the Eastasia support satellites, the Ethiopian Mbombe exploration module, the Afrasia Jinni Robotic Plant, India's Svarga Habitat, Oceania's Garuda Take-off Module and Eurasia's Argos Return Module.

Pagu checked the remaining time and the netizens' questions. She used to focus on at least one of them, but this time there were millions to choose from. Most naïve or not to the point, but Guira chose two that were popular and reasonably pertinent.

"Raul, to wrap it up, two questions from the audience. Number one, asked by about twenty thousand, counting the variants: what's interesting about discovering bacteroids on Mars, if we've know that there is much more advanced alien life since the Samsa case in the last century?"

"Well, it's one thing to have a way of life of unknown origin and probably extraterrestrial at that. It's another to find an alien lifeform, a microscopic one, blooming in its natural habitat. Even more interesting is to find it on an inhospitable world. It's a sign that life is a much more common phenomenon than many people thought. Besides, we have discovered a different biochemistry and genetic code, which adds much to our knowledge of life. They would be interesting even if they were terrestrial."

"Number two, from over a hundred thousand: why don't we use robots to save money and avoid risking human lives? Wouldn't it be an example of global cooperation all the same?"

"We didn't have then—and we still don't have now—robots with the flexibility, intelligence and initiative of a human cosmonaut.

Maybe in the future, but I doubt it. Do you want to bet that we will have human cosmonauts exploring planets farther away than Mars before the end of the century?"

"I'll bite, Raul! But, geewhiz, if we live long enough for any of us to win the bet we'll be so old …what shall we bet, a caretaker robot?"

* * *

The freighter coming from Oslo that anchored in Fortaleza after twelve days was a typical vessel of its time, combining as it did millennia-old oars and sails with the last word in technology. In addition to three rigid mobile sails that were also solar panels, it had twelve fins configured to rise and fall with the waves and to move hydraulic machines. An electrolyzer converted spare energy into hydrogen for fuel cells, which was used when there was no sun or wind available. In this almost totally robotized ship, the commander's function was so solitary—except for the continuous access to Porandutepé—as it had once been that of a lighthouse keeper.

The *Solfisk* carried 13,000 tons of salted cod, smoked salmon, pickled herring, and *gravlaks*. Only three people at the Norwegian state-owned Norskargo, including Commander Vidkun Quisling, knew that some of the containers contained a very special cargo. Revolutionaries with old-fashioned weapons, but well-preserved and functional, discovered by the group in a secret World War arsenal, forgotten in a dark fjord cave.

How else could one arm a group of militants, with the world government prohibiting the purchase and possession of arms? What other way to dodge the surveillance of ubiquitous automatic cameras? Even after the containers were unloaded at the port by robot cranes, the fighters would have to wait until nightfall to open them and be protected by cloaks of invisibility and the complicity of the port administrator, a sympathizer named Gustavo Barroso. Agent Salgado would take them to the theater on a Sigma Turismo bus. It was traceable like any other vehicle, but it could take an unusual route and carry a group of strangers without drawing attention.

* * *

The interview ended in laughter, but Raul sighed with relief when he ended the call. He asked his fellow conspirator, who whispered data and suggestions through his headset:

"What do you say, Juca? How did you like our performance?"

"Awesome! He sounded like a statesman who knows what he's talking about. The comments on the networks are 76% positive. But some of our fellow commissioners might think you made a fool of them. For many of them, this argument will not sound so fantabulastic."

"Leave it to me. As someone said, 'when in doubt tell the truth: it will amaze friends and confuse enemies'."

"Speaking of surprising your friends, what's the big news in cosmonautics? You spoke with a confidence that made me realize that there is more than meets the eye."

"Oh, I really needed to tell you that." He rubbed his hands together. "A German physicist brought me a project that, if I have my say, will be built well before I need a robot caretaker. I just need the little toy we are going to inaugurate tomorrow to function properly so that I can present it to the Council. Here's the thing…"

* * *

Happy with the repercussions of the interview, Pagu exchanged ideas with Guira about the next program, put the visor in her backpack, and changed clothes. They were the last to leave the studio. The light-emitting diodes were turned off, the fans were turned off, and the doors locked automatically as their passage was registered by the cameras. She shared a robotaxi with her colleague, and the two-seat electric vehicle charged ten milis of each upon dropping them off at Lapa station, where they parted ways. Few people recognized her wearing a cap and without the visor, but the maglev did, and it deducted another ten milis from her upon embarking. Two chronos later, she alighted at Luz station and walked to her house at Barão de Piracicaba Street, where her companions waited. She celebrated her success with a threesome, delightful but without exaggeration. She had to wake up early.

* * *

The sun wasn't up yet, but, fearing some infrared-sensitive aero-robot, they took shelter under the panels of a solar plant surrounded by the thorn bushes of the Agreste, a few dozen blocks from their target.

"This is the Coaracytaba," the leader explained, displaying the plant with a holoprojector. "It's residence to the workers of the plant and also a base for visitors. The heliport, park, school, health center, social center, and hostel are here. Politicians will gather in the social center, journalists at the hostel. We will use the invisibility cloaks until the last moment."

He switched off the projection and went on:

"Franco's group takes most of the men and the best weapons, because they're going to invade the social center, and there might be some resistance there. Probably a not very effective one, for half a century reigning in peace over sheep made these people soft and careless. Luxembourg must bring up to six other guards and Cândido approximately the same, armed with stun guns and magnetic pistols. Eliminate the agents without hesitation, but you must capture the main targets alive. If not possible, at least one or two important representatives. Try not to kill civilians unnecessarily; we don't want to damage the reputation of our cause."

He paused and admired the impassive faces of his men, fierce, attentive and disciplined. A band that inspired respect. He went on:

"My group will take the buses of the visitors and take care of the journalists. Some are almost as valuable as hostages as the politicians. Even with the buses, the reds can reach the destination before us, because the convertiplanes are able to arrive from Palmares in five chronos. We need audacity, discipline, and hostages to complete the mission."

He turned on the holo again to display the symbol of the

movement, a fluttering black flag with a red hurricane in a white circle.

"Some of us will fall in this enterprise. The survivors will be thrown into the dungeons of the regime. It will be useless! Our coup will reveal the fragility of this decadent civilization and will initiate the economic and political collapse of the Union. Millions of brave people will know our message, follow our example and rely on us to lead the new world! Avast, heroes!"

"Better to live a day as a lion than a hundred years as a lamb!" his mate seconded him.

* * *

Early in the morning, Pagu said goodbye to Oswald and Tarsila at the airport and joined Guira in line. Upon seeing her ID, the Ybytukatu clerk looked at her surprised and whispered a request for an autographed holo. She smiled and electronically signed his visor.

They followed the other passengers along the long boarding bridge and settled into the seats of a Jubapirá, a subsonic airplane shaped as a stingray. While Guira distracted himself by creating colorful, three-dimensional curves with a holoprojector, she distracted herself by watching the sunrise and the movement of the hydrogen tankers until the commander gave warning of the takeoff. The vehicle took off and the solar roofs of Piratininga gleamed like gold in the morning sun. It would be a twenty-five-chronos trip to Palmares.

As soon as the robot picked up the breakfast tray, she ordered the visor to review information subprograms for the *Amanajé Mytanga's Young Messenger* special show, which she and Guira had prepared to later join or link to the final edition. In quick and funny animations, they told the story of the use of energy: the invention of fire, the water wheel, the windmills, the steam engine of Borba Gato, the alcohol and oil engines of Aimberê and Bartolomeu de Gusmão, Pedro II's large hydroelectric plants, Andrada and Silva's wind and solar generators and the lithium-water cells and the hydrogen plants of Gustavo Capanema. The pioneering nuclear reactor of Qarawayllu and the cooperation of the Tauantinsuio with Brazil and the Union of Nations in the Great War to launch the atomic bomb in Scapa Flow.

After the unification of the planet, the Rebouças brothers' study showed the dangers of greenhouse effect amplification for the climate and the planetary environment, after which UN resolutions increasingly restricted the use of fossil fuels. And also of nuclear energy, after its risks were evidenced when an earthquake followed by tsunami devastated the plant of Paramonga, in the Tauantinsuio.

Fifty years later, there were only thirty experimental nuclear power plants and three hundred small research reactors operating in the world, all under strict supervision by the Union of Nations Commission on Science and Culture. And coal, oil, and gas were being used only as chemical raw materials. Former mining and industrial centers disappeared in many places. Although the Union financed the substitution of renewable energy sources, the imposition aroused much resentment in Eurasia, where many saw the threat of global warming as a forged pretext to deprive them of their technological independence and subject them to the uniform and oppressive vulgarity of solar panels and wind turbines that turned magnificent landscapes in ugly things to behold.

Pagu looked out thoughtfully. They were flying over a sunny stretch of the Bahia backlands. Where there was once the Caatinga, regular lines of wind generators and the rectangular and circular compositions of solar panels alternated regularly and geometrically with crops and pastures. There were reserves of fauna and flora of that and other biomes, but it was a world much altered by the human hand, monotonically symmetrical and tamed.

Old hydroelectric plants still supplied 4% of the energy, geothermal another 4% and tidal and wind power plants 2%, but 3.8 million wind turbines generated almost half the energy used worldwide and the remaining 40% came from 40 thousand photovoltaic plants, 49,000 solar thermal plants and 1.7 billion solar roofs. All that covered 280 million quarters, more than the entire area of Greenland. The picturesque roofs of the past could now only be seen in old paintings and photos, save for a few historic buildings. A few plants, especially hydrogen-producing power plants, floated in the sea, but most had replaced ancient or bucolic landscapes. Majestic waterfalls and beautiful towns and villages had disappeared beneath hydroelectric lakes. And the future? What would things be like in another hundred years, with twice the population and four times the need for energy?

"Guira, isn't this too biased? This virtuality of how the world would be if fossil fuels continued to be used, for example, wouldn't it be exaggerated? Glaciers melting, hurricane multiplication, hunger from droughts and floods, people dying in cities, suffocating from the pollution... Doesn't that sound too propagandist for you?"

Her colleague looked at her, amused.

"Propagandist? These are quotes from a documentary organized by Professor Lacerda de Moura. You know her, right? She is more of an anarchist than you, but she thinks that if the World War hadn't abolished capitalism and imposed the energy conversion, we would be much worse for the wear."

"Even so, I wanted to give a more balanced account. When almsgiving is too much, the saint distrusts us and our audience, which is not stupid, as well. Let's show that there is another side, that this came at a price. Demonstrations against the pollution of rivers by quartz mining and solar panel factories... There was one in Minas last year and another in China. The cities abandoned by the closure of the coal mines in the Ruhr and Midlands, one hundred million birds killed every year by wind turbine blades, visual pollution, alteration of the wind regime..."

"I can do it, but what's the right measure of balance?"

"We'll see that when it's editing time. For now, I just wanted to have enough material available for this."

"Ok, I'll sort it out."

The plane arrived on time. As they emerged into the lobby of the airport, a beautiful *mestiça* approached them. Both recognized her: although they had not yet met physically, hers was a face almost as well known in Brazil as Pagu's.

"*Oxente*! You're Pagu da Poranduba Mytanga, aren't you?"

"Pleased to meet you! Guira, you know Anaíde Beiriz, from Quilombo Network, right?"

"Naturally…"

"Guira, what a riot to meet you!" She greeted him more than warmly and touched his bare chest. "I really like your work. *Coisa porreta, da gota serena*: damn fine thing!"

She kissed him on the lips, ever so slightly, and the boy returned it very happily. Only then did she kiss her colleague, who started to wonder. She acknowledged that Guira received a smaller than deserved share from the fame of the couple. Seeing someone give him his due usually pleased her. But that moon-eyed hellcat… Did she want to steal her partner? If she wanted to just bed him, she would be all for it, but something told her that it was more serious. Professionally serious.

"The gang who's going to Intirana is right over there," Anaide said. "Shall we?"

They nodded and followed her to where a hologram with the logo of the Nuclear and Energy Research Institute of the University of Palmares floated, a stylized atom with the Palmares coat of arms in place of the nucleus, hoe and hammer crossed over a book and a star. Brazilian and foreign members of the press gathered around the woman who projected him with her communicator, a black woman with braids and a colored dressing gown.

"Ah, the Piratininga gang has arrived, good morning!" she greeted them. And she turned to her colleague, a man of Mexican features. "Tlohtli, that's enough people to fill a convertiplane now. I'll take these people and you wait for the rest of them, okay? *Vo kinen me pos petin*," "follow me," she said in koina, the official language of the

Union of Nations.

"*Damn newspeak!*" a man's voice mumbled behind Pagu as they set off for the courtyard. She turned and recognized Tina Modotti from the ENN, *Euraziatische en Noord-Colombiaanse Netwerk*, beside a tall, thin, white man with disheveled hair. He wore black, from tie to shoes, a sign of a certain style of radical anarchism. She smiled without understanding and he was embarrassed, but Tina greeted her:

"*Lascia*, the trip left him in a bad mood. We boarded at New Amsterdam late at night, he was coming from London and didn't sleep well on the plane, you know…"

"More than seven and a half hours!" he complained.

"Huh?" said Pagu, not understanding, while stepping out of the corridor into the warm air and the northeastern sun of the concrete patio.

"It was a trip of one hundred and thirty chronos," Tina explained. "*Mi piace presentare* George Orwell, of the ENBC, who disapproves of koina and the decimal system and *molte altre cose.*"

Pagu noticed the old-fashioned wristwatch with hands.

"Bah!" he protested. "What bothers me is that there are privileged people who can do the same in two and a half hours."

Forty-one chronos, Pagu converted with the help of the visor as he pointed to the sleek commissarial supersonic of the Union of Nations, the *Aero Uno*, approaching like a gigantic heron for an elegant landing in Palmares.

"Why can *they* fly faster? Don't they say we're all the same? Or are some more equal than others?"

"*Più che sciocchezza*, Orwell!" Tina protested as she climbed in the convertiplane. "They travel the four corners of the world every day, they need a faster plane, but they still can't offer it to everyone, they have the constraints of energy, the environment…"

The argument continued until they sat down. Guira was still chatting with Anaide, and Pagu sat with Tina. The convertiplane fired the rotors and took off vertically. Upon reaching the appropriate altitude, the rotors moved to a horizontal axis and the vehicle gained speed.

As soon as she went on cruise speed, the woman who had guided them rose and spoke in *koina*:

"*Saluto! Me Mera nomines petin…*"

"Hi, call me Mera," she said in free translation. "Easier to remember than Almerinda Farias Gama, isn't it? I'm a professor of Plasma Physics at IPEN and a member of the board of the Neogeia Electroatomical Cooperative. We have a few chronos to get there and no onboard service, so we can spend time talking about the Intirana. It's a compound of 'Inti', 'sun' in Quechua and 'rana', 'similar', in Tupi, because it was built in cooperation with the Tauantinsuio nuclear research institute. It's similar to the sun for generating energy through nuclear fusion, even though the process is a bit different. Instead of fusing hydrogen nuclei, or protons, in helium nuclei, here the helium comes from the fusion of nuclei of deuterium and tritium, these obtained from the bombardment of lithium atoms…"

"And that will make the world depend more on the lithium of the Tauantinsuio," Orwell said. "Isn't that very comfortable for Cosmopolis, Cuzco, and the ruling party in both?"

Interesting question, Pagu thought. The guy was eccentric, but smart. It was worthwhile to further explore this line of thought and check data related to the matter, she noted.

"Look, friend Orwell," Mera replied, "it's a matter of physics before it's politics. This method is the most viable, the only one capable of generating useful energy with the technology available today. There are experimental units that don't use lithium, but consume more energy than they produce, or the reaction isn't sustained by more than a niche. And lithium is not so rare. In this reactor of three thousand and four hundred megaborbas, we used one thousand four hundred tons of lithium. If it were the case of replacing the world generation of seventeen teraborbas for similar reactors, we would need five thousand reactors and seven million tons, twice as much as we use today in batteries and fuel cells. The known terrestrial reserves are more than 100 million tons, but more than eighty percent are in the *kachikachi*, the Tauantinsuio salt marshes, but there are also 240 million tons in the oceans. And this is not a likely scenario. In ten or twenty years, before we generate 10 percent of the world's energy with fusion, more advanced reactors won't need lithium anymore."

"Mera," Pagu called, "I want to ask you another political question. Even assuming that lithium is not a problem and that the Tauantinsuio does not use it to pressure the Union, as it already did before…"

"Water under the bridge…" The physicist dismissed. "And we're about to discard the use of lithium in fuel cells." IPEN is developing various types of superconducting coil energy cells that only need carbon nanotubes plated with nickel and cobalt… and look, we have Tauantinsuians in this line of research, not only Brazilians and Mexicans."

"Whatever. But even so, isn't it a step backwards in the policy of decentralization, of making local governments more autonomous and self-reliant? I imagine that such an investment must be managed and planned by confederations."

Orwell looked at Pagu approvingly, and added, "In my country, the Isle of Wight, with just over one hundred square miles and one hundred thousand inhabitants, we have a community self-sufficient in energy with its wind and solar generators. Could it do the same with a nuclear fusion reactor?"

Mera stopped to get data with her visor and think of the answer.

"Hmm, no," she answered. "Today it's not practical to build much smaller units than the Intirana, because it's difficult to control a reaction with a temperature of eighty million thermograms. The investment of sixty million credits would be within reach of a state or a small country, but it has to be planned as part of a continental network."

"Then the communities will become more dependent on the confederations!" Orwell concluded.

"For now, yes, they will. But imagine a plant like this near the island. The energy goes to twenty millis per gigajuma, the same cost as wind power, or half the cost of solar power. If the island dismantles its generators and starts buying electricity from the reactor, it will save on average and free up space for reforestation, tourism, whatever you want. The Intirana is equivalent to four thousand quarters of solar panels or thirty thousand of wind farms. If I lived there, that would be my choice, as it was the people of this region."

"Why 'for now'?" Pagu intervened.

"Because when we can use muon-catalyzed fusion, we'll be dealing with much lower temperatures and scales. But we need to know more. Oh, look, from here you can see the Intirana …"

Tina and Pagu looked out the window. They could see a horseshoe-shaped complex: a large circular building in the center, reminiscent of an enormous gasometer or water tank, surrounded on one side by a semicircular pond and on the other by something that looked like a rectangular industrial complex. A little beyond, one could see the lake of the hydroelectric plant of Xingó.

"The cylindrical building is the fusion unit. You'll see later how it works. The two small buildings next to the reactor are engineering and support. There are cooling towers over here, then the deuterium-tritium pellet plant, and over there the steam turbines and the electric power substations. Let's stop at Coaracytaba, stretch out our legs, wait for the rest of the group and have a coffee before visiting the plant."

"I like your style," Pagu greeted Orwell when he stepped down from the machine.

"Freedom is the right to tell people what they don't want to hear." He smiled. "And journalism is publishing what some don't want to see published. The rest is propaganda."

The flags of the Union, Neogeia, Brazil, and the state of Palmares decorated the entrance. They were taken to the lobby of the inn next to the heliport, where a variegated breakfast awaited them. To keep Tina and Orwell at the table, Pagu took a glass of juice and asked the robot for tapioca, all the while glancing discreetly at Guira and Anaide.

"You really are going to tell me you don't have a pint in this joint?" Orwell grunted as he looked at the mugs for a draft of the machine.

"And what the *cazzo* is a pint?" Tina asked in line, eager to get hers. The hall was well ventilated, but not refrigerated and they were feeling hot.

"Blimey! Born in Europe and you don't even know what a pint is! A pint is half a quart. Must I teach you the ABCs?"

"I never heard of it," Pagu said as she consulted Porandutepé with her visor.

"A liter and half a liter, is what you have," Tina insisted. "These are the mugs in front of you."

"I like pints. I could very well have a pint. We didn't have this 'liter' garbage when I was a lad."

"You sound like you were young at the time we climbed trees," Tina complained, though she was probably a few years older than him.

Pagu laughed and Orwell blushed. But he poured himself a mug and sat with them.

"I could very well have a pint. Half a liter isn't enough, doesn't quench my thirst. And a liter is a lot, makes my bladder work."

"I checked the visor," Pagu said. "The old English pint was equivalent to 568 milliliters, 13.6 percent more. Does it make such a difference to you?"

"Of course not!" Tina intervened. "It's an English anarchist *rompicoglioni* thing." Almost everyone adhered to the international system since the end of the World War, but the State of England clung to its old ways and it was only eight years ago that the government of Secretary Ilych imposed decimal standardization and the right hand of traffic to the whole Eurasian and North-Colombian Confederation. In England, antique watches and measurements are the hallmark of radical chics like this *stronzo*!"

"It's not ideology," Orwell replied. "Ancient measures are natural, adapted to human needs by history. For example, if I say that my height is six feet three inches, you will intuitively perceive what I mean."

Pagu looked at him in astonishment, and Tina laughed.

"No, I don't understand," she admitted. "I had to consult Porandutepé to convert this into 19 modules to get a sense."

"You've been using the decimal system for two hundred years!" he protested. "You have adapted to the system, instead of using a system adapted to the people."

Then the second wave of journalists arrived. A man with a characteristic single eyebrow came to greet Pagu, accompanied by a tall, blue-eyed blond man.

"Hey, Juca! Tina Modotti and George Orwell, journalists from Eurasia…" Pagu introduced them. "This is Monteiro Lobato, Brazilian representative in the Council of the Union and member of the Commission of Science…did Raul come too, Juca?"

"A pleasure to meet you, call me Juca, please. Yes, he came on the first commissioner's convertiplane, but since there was no room for me there, I came with the reporters to keep company with this wise German with whom I was discussing ideas. Dr. Werner Heisenberg, from CERN, a sort of Eurasian IPEN."

"The TGCH of CERN in Geneva is the second largest particle accelerator in the world after the Pevatron of Palmares," Tina said proudly.

Pagu checked the data: The *Très Grand Collisionneur de Hadrons* accelerated particles to three hundred trillion electron-Veigas, the Pevatron a quadrillion. After, he would ask Guira to explain exactly what that meant. If he still wanted to work with her, that is.

"It doesn't matter," Heisenberg said. "The good thing about being a theoretical physicist is working with data from all over the world without asking about the particles homeland. I came here to discuss an enlargement of IPEN's muon accelerator to test a crucial point in my theory."

"At what cost?" Orwell asked, just finishing the beer mug.

"About forty million credits, divided between the Neogeia and the Union of Nations..."

"Some milis would come out of my pocket, then. I suppose I have the right to ask what it is for."

"Well, to extend the knowledge of the functioning of branes and the universe..."

"What if I think I know enough already and ask you for some practical use?"

"I can't foresee all the developments in theoretical physics in advance, but I set an example to the Commission. If I am right, we can create force fields with many interesting properties. We could control fusion reactions more potent than that of deuterium-tritium, such as the CNO cycle, which generates almost twice the energy per atom of helium and in nature occurs in the hottest stars..."

"After the Intirana we would have a Sirius-mirim!" Juca tried to explain.

"...and in addition we could create magnetic fields with a diameter greater than that of the Moon to draw hydrogen out of space and use it as fused material in a manned spacecraft."

That left Pagu confused. Oh, if Guira were with her instead of talking to that little bitch! She would understand what that meant and ask the right questions.

"Of course, after Mars the Union needs another bill of five billion to justify even more centralization!" Orwell protested. "For what? To plant the red flag on an asteroid?"

Juca laughed heartily.

"Not an asteroid or even half an asteroid, Mr. Orwell! Climb higher!"

"Saturn?" asked Tina.

"Higher!"

"Uranus, Neptune?" Pagu ventured.

"Up, girl!"

The three journalists looked at each other, flabbergasted. To go beyond Neptune? Juca approached Orwell and said with a dramatic expression:

"I'm talking about Alpha Centauri, Mr. Orwell! To reach the stars until the end of the century with the Heisenberg station! And it will not cost more than a trillion…"

"A trillion? Credits?" Orwell protested. "You are crazy! There will be a revolution!"

"Nothing will happen! The Intirana will break the limits of the environment and the production of energy that are chaining us down! Fusion and nanotubes will be tomorrow what oil and iron were a century ago, and it would be absurd not to use them to wake up the sleeping human genius! In twenty years the economy will more than double, in thirty years, triple or quadruple, so building the ship will cost less than one percent of the world product for ten years…"

At that moment, Mera asked for attention, for she would begin to explain the Intirana in detail. Then she projected in the middle of the hall a holo of the spherical chamber that was the heart of the plant, the *lonq'owasi*, as the Tauantinsuian engineers who built it, then cut it in the middle, to show the interior.

"The chamber sits inside a vacuum chamber, but inside it has xenon to absorb ions and radiation produced by the meltdown. Double walls, spaced a meter apart. In this space we have fused lithium, maintained at 900 thermograms. One day it will have to be dismantled and isolated, but its radioactivity will be harmless in just a hundred years, while the waste from a fission plant remains dangerous for more than a hundred thousand. In addition to absorbing the heat that will be used in thermoelectric generation, lithium captures neutrons that transform some of its atoms into helium and tritium, which is processed in the pellet factory along with the deuterium from the heavy water produced at the Piranhas plant. The deuterium of a liter of sea water contains energy equivalent to the burning of five hundred liters of alcohol or a thousand of liquid hydrogen..."

She showed the factory and explained how it produced more than one million deuterium-frozen tritium pellets per day. She followed the row of pellets to the *lonq'owasi*, where they were fired, one at a time, to the center of the chamber and there bombarded on all sides by hundreds of açaratás, coherent infrared beams that served as fuse for the fusion reaction—direct descendants, she explained, of the *doodsstraal* that had claimed Marshal Xavier nearly a hundred years ago. The pellet exploded like a supernova, disappearing and followed by another. There were 384 açaratás around the chamber, each with a power of one hundred kilojoules, and the merging of each pellet produced two gigajumas, the equivalent of two hundred dynamite sticks.

Slow-motion animation accelerated to the actual rhythm. The stars that turned on and off became a shimmering sun, and it was impossible to see the pellets, fired with the speed of a three-round revolver bullet, the cadence of a World War machine gun.

Then the people around began to scream, the holo faded and Pagu realized that real bullets were flying through the lobby. She threw herself beneath the table, not understanding, hearing explosions and smelling the acrid scent of a gas that stunned her and burned in her eyes and lungs. The attackers did not bother with this, they must have used some filter or antidote.

"You are under arrest, in the name of the future!" A bald man in a black uniform and gray mustache, who appeared out of nowhere, shouted in a megaphone in Portuguese with an Italian accent. "The old order dies here!"

"I can't believe it! *L'imbecille* Marinetti!" Tina growled through her teeth as tears streamed down her nose.

"Who?" Pagu whispered.

"An Italian writer who glorifies war in his fucking books and has created a fucking Futurist Party. He gave lectures in New Amsterdam last year. Another anarchist *pazzo*!"

"Hell, no!" Orwell protested softly. "That fucking bastard is not ours!"

"*Achtung*! Stand up, hands behind your neck!" A German with a mustache and a mad look shouted, wielding an obsolete but not at all harmless submachine gun.

Pagu obeyed and looked around. Several men in black uniforms, armed and nervous.

"Hail Marinetti, here are two famous ones!" the German shouted. "Tina and Pagu!"

"Bravo, Corporal Hitler! Put the handcuffs on them; this time these spokespeople of the system will have to hear the truth next to their bosses! Captain Mussolini!" He turned to a bald man who seemed to be the second in command. "Bring them here, they'll hear me better!"

Left with no alternative, Pagu let herself be arrested and driven, and, terrified, saw another group of men in black, led by a small, demented man, bring First Commissioner Luxemburg, President Cândido and some members of his entourage, also handcuffed.

"Bravo, Lieutenant Franco! He brought us the grand prize!"

Marinetti started to speak, both to his men and to the prisoners, throwing gestures, making faces, and striking poses, but nevertheless making his delusion more understandable:

"Finally mythology and the mystical ideal are overcome! We are about to witness the birth of the Centaur and soon we will see the first Angels fly! You will have to shake the doors of life to experience its joys and locks! Behold, on earth, the very first dawn! There is no match for the brightness of the red sword of the sun that fights for the first time in our millennial darkness! Let us come out of wisdom like one who breaks a hideous shell, and throw ourselves, like fruits spiced with pride, into the immense and twisted mouth of the wind! Let us give ourselves as pasture to the Unknown, not out of desperation, but only to fill the depths of the Absurd! We want to sing the love of danger, the habit of energy and temerity, we want to exalt the aggressive movement, the feverish insomnia, the step of running, the somersault, the slap and the punch. There is no beauty except in the struggle. No work that is not a violent assault can be a masterpiece. We stand upon the extreme promontory of centuries! Why look back, if we want to break into the mysterious doors of the Impossible? Time and Space died yesterday! We already live in the absolute, because we have already created the eternal omnipresent speed! We want to glorify war, the only hygiene in the world, militarism, patriotism, the destructive gesture of libertarians, the beautiful ideas for which one dies and the contempt for women! We want to destroy museums, libraries, academies, and fight against moralism, feminism, and all opportunistic and utilitarian villainy!"

He stopped to hear the applause and cries of *Hail!* of his men, but a thin, mustachioed sentry took the break for a warning, extending his right arm:

"Hail, Marinetti!" He had no foreign accent. "I saw a weird little thing fly through the window, it could be a Union spy robot!"

"Grazie, Sergeant Salgado! Let it record our manifesto for posterity! But we must hurry, to take the Intirana by assault before they can retaliate, comrades! With these hostages, they will not dare shoot! I already gave the message: they must evacuate the area in a radius of twenty blocks and we have to find the doors open, otherwise everybody will die! Mussolini, let's take Tina, Pagu, Luxemburg and Cândido. Choose two more expendable ones if we need to kill someone to get them to trade. Pound, Heidegger, lock the rest into the guesthouse. More than six hostages will only disrupt us."

Pagu, Tina, Luxemburg, João Cândido, Orwell, and Guira were pushed into one of the buses for visitors, accompanied by several men in black. More of them got on the other bus. The mustache cable reached the dashboard, turned on the electric motor, and chose the destination with a few touches on the screen.

"Can't you go faster, Corporal?" asked Marinetti.

"No, *mein Führer*, the machine will follow the normal programming."

"Could they not? Can the Union stop the damn engine?" he asked furiously.

"Rosenberg and Salazar were able to cut off the communication, the cameras, and the locks, but they didn't figure out how to take direct control without damaging everything."

"*Maledetto robot!*" he mumbled. "In the new order, vehicles will have steering wheels, brakes, and accelerating pedals. A machine is a woman, and it's not fitting for it to refuse a man's command!"

"Ah!" the First Commissioner burst. "Stupid, crazy executioners! Haven't you noticed that your order stands on sand?"

"Shut up, *sfacciata*! Your languid dreams of perpetual peace are the sickness, we are the cure! War is beautiful because, thanks to gas masks, scary megaphones, flamethrowers, and tanks, it establishes man's supremacy over the subjugated machine! War is beautiful because it enriches a flowery meadow with the fire orchids of machine guns. War is beautiful, because it combines in a symphony the firing of rifle, the cannon, the pauses between two battles, the perfumes and the odors of decomposition. The war has come, you have lost!"

"The direction failed," she admitted. "But this is not so important. The masses…"

Marinetti interrupted her with a slap.

"Hypocritical babble! The masses are clay and we will shape it! The destruction of the reactor will show how vulnerable this civilization is." Marinetti nodded. "The lithium cells are almost obsolete. When we show how fragile this machine is, the industrial complexes of Uyuni and Atacama will collapse, we will avenge the industrial centers of European coal in the last century and we will begin the crisis that will lead to World War II. The reactor is meant to convince the world that it needs to follow suit, united and kind to enjoy in peace the lithium of the Tauantinsuio, the food of Brazil, blah blah blah. Enough of this! Our only real need is to fight, it's health, life, and evolution! The strong will follow us!"

"Crazy," Tina whispered behind Pagu. "Completely *pazzo*!"

It didn't make much sense to Pagu as well. What was the use of kidnapping the First Commissioner? She was only a symbol, one of the members of the Council of Commissioners, one from each of the seven confederations, each of which rotated the presidency for a year. If they destroyed the reactor, so what? They would build another, with enhanced security. It would only be a brutal and empty gesture of performance art, even if it ended with the death of terrorists and hostages. But what if the Union was more fragile than it thought?

Mussolini called Marinetti to the back of the bus to talk, forgetting the hostages. Hitler was still ahead, but watchful outside.

Then a message appeared on Pagu's visor.

Guira @Pagu Hands behind your back. I'll cut the handcuffs. Without sound, pretend it's nothing.

Surprised, she obeyed. Her wrists felt hot and the link was cut off.

Pagu @Guira How?

Guira @Pagu Gambiarra with the holoprojetor, reprogrammed like an açaratá-mirim by the viewfinder. I've released Tina, I'm going to release Orwell. Take care of the front?

Pagu @Guira Rosa and Cândido? How can I warn them? They have no visors.

RLux @Pagu We have a visor, yes, in our contact lenses.

Guira @Pagu The projector password is $e \wedge (i * pi) + 1 = 0$, connect it to your visor.

Pagu received the projector, which looked like a flashlight. He cut the bonds of Rosa and Cândido's handcuffs as if they were paper. The kidnappers kept arguing back.

RLux @Pagu @Guira I need to talk to the UN, but there is a blocker here. Only the wireless works.

Guira @RLux The @Pagu visor can access special bands to activate remote equipment at outdoor work. If I can code it, you'll be able to talk to them.

RLux @Pagu @Guira Try please. Connection ComCon.un / Uno password Spartakus \ o / Bund.

Pagu @Guira The display password is Oswald <3Pagu <3Tarsila.

Guira made some adjustment on Pagu's display and said to try. She followed the instructions.

UN001 @Pagu @RLux @Guira Good they could call. Conditions?

RLux @ UN001 We 3 plus @JCndd, @ TMdtt, @GOrwll hostages and 10 elements. On the other bus, just terrorists. About 20 of them, total.

UN001 @RLux Ready to act. Any suggestions?

RLux @ UN001 Marinetti said he only wanted us 6. Can you check if there are no hostages on the other bus?

UN001 @RLux Recognition by cyberdragonfly, check. Total 19 enemy elements. Bus 2 carries guns and nitrate bombs, no hostage.

RLux @ UN001 Plane: detonates bus 2. Shock makes bus 1 stop, stuns elements, opens doors. We run, you cover. Approved?

UN001 @RLux Risk of some of you being machine-gunned.

RLux @UN001 I take responsibility. Best maneuver: unexpected & audacious turn.

Pagu followed the exchange of messages and understood what was going to happen. Tina sighed. They quickly exchanged messages about how to get away.

UN001 @RLux Cover almost ready, operation authorized. Countdown of 10 decanicts, on 1 you cover your ears and get down.

They were already arriving at the gates of the Intirana. Mussolini and Marinetti, with rocket launchers, decided to go back to the front in 5…4…3…

At the same time, the six hostages bent down and covered their ears. Perplexed, Mussolini noticed that they were free of the handcuffs. He shouted and reached for his holster, but at that moment a tremendous explosion shook the bus, shattered the back windows, and threw down those who were standing. The bus stopped and opened all doors and windows automatically. Adolf, bleeding from from the unexpected shock on the windshield, took too long to react. Pagu saw Rosa and Raul dribble over the fallen leaders and jump out. He then jumped, along with Tina, in the opposite direction until he found a corner behind the main building to hide. A plume of smoke rose from the rubble of the second bus at the end of the bridge over the semicircular pond. The Pagu display registered one more coded message:

RLux @ UN001 I and @JCndd are safe, the others?
UN001 @RLux Sighted @Pagu and @GOrwll outside the firing line, others not confirmed. Aerotroops in the air.

He heard the sharp sound of turbines. Soldiers from the UN rose from behind the Intirana, flying with dorsal jets, açaratás ready to fire. Marinetti and Mussolini grabbed Guira and Tina, using them as shields as they walked to the open entrance of the plant.

RLux @ UN001 Do not shoot. Try to negotiate their surrender.

Marinetti and Mussolini walked with the hostages toward the

reactor, looking up. Some of his men followed them with guns cocked, looking downtrodden, some visibly wounded. A megaphone told them to lay down their weapons, but the group went to the plant.

"We have to do something!" Orwell whispered. "I don't know how I can live without this woman!"

Pagu was astonished to realize that he was talking about Tina. How had she not realized they were lovers? It did not matter, she had her own reasons for grieving. Guira was a good friend and, if he were in her place, he would try to save her again. But how would he do it?

The leaders were already inside the plant when she remembered the projector. He told Orwell what she intended to do and he approved. Then she yelled, and the last latecomer, who was jabbering in his hand, looked in his direction. The visor widened and focused on the frightened face and directed the shot accurately into the blue eyes of the mustachioed German.

"Ach! Ich bin blind!" he shouted, dropping his weapon. They ran up to him.

"You've always been blind!" Orwell snarled, knocking him down and taking the submachine gun.

When the German fell, Pagu tried to take the pistol, but he jerked it away. Before he reacted, he took the pistol from his hands, thrust it into his own mouth, and fired. Fragments of bone and gray matter spilled onto Pagu, who turned, trembling.

"Chin up, darling," Orwell cheered her up. "We can't waste time!"

The others didn't come back to see what had happened, they headed for the heart of the reactor. Orwell and Pagu found a ladder for a tall walkway and ran. Bullets bounced off metal structures, but they were lucky. Then the Marines appeared, and the terrorists forgot about the pair to concentrate on preventing their entry with a barrage of shrapnel.

Pagu and Orwell reached the central area. Marinetti and Mussolini armed the rocket launcher against the vacuum chamber of the reactor. The hostages had their backs against a wall, hands at the back of their necks, watched by one of the gunmen in hand, the rest shooting at the military.

"Now what?" Pagu asked.

"You have more precision, point to the nape of the gun man's neck. I'll shoot the leaders. On three." He went back several steps to get a better angle and waved his hand: three, two…

Orwell fired, Pagu too. The guy watching the hostages gave a sharp shriek as he was burned by the açaratá. It was the Pound guy. Tina and Guira took advantage and ran away through a nearby corridor. Swept away by the Englishman's blast, Marinetti and Mussolini fell on their backs and the rocket launcher fired. But instead of hitting the steel wall of the reactor chamber ahead, it shot to the ceiling and struck a shielded tube. A fused lithium shower, radioactive and corrosive, rained on the terrorists like red lava cherries exploding in purple flames. The fiery breath of the pyrotechnic spectacle reached Pagu and everything went dark.

* * *

I'm still alive, she thought as she discovered herself on a hospital bed. She vaguely remembered the feeling of suffocation before they put on an oxygen mask. Then they boarded a military convertiplane. She regained her consciousness among atrocious pains as she landed on the heliport of a hospital and was soon sedated. She felt less ill now, but then she remembered the horrors of Paramonga. Would it be better to have died?

A robot whistled by her side and a doctor appeared in moments. Dr. Deré Lubidi, Radiotoxicology, said the badge.

"How do you feel?" she asked Pagu.

"Very sick, hard to breathe, headache, throat burning…" she spoke hoarsely.

"It's to be expected, don't worry. You are out of danger, everything is under control." She put a hand over her face. "You were very brave."

"And the others? Is Guira all right?"

"The Apapocuva? Yes, and Tina too. Orwell fell ill with the toxic vapors when he rescued her, but there is no risk either, he is here, look." With some invisible command, she made the room divider move to show him, and he waved uncomfortably from the other bed. "The terrorists, on the other hand, almost all of them are dead, and I don't know if we'll be able to save the two survivors. Unbelievable: one of them is a North Colombian poet and the other a German philosopher."

"What about the radiation?"

"It wasn't so bad. It's different from a fission plant, the radiation outside the reaction itself is smaller. You all absorbed some radioactive tritium from the lithium leak, not fatal, and received nanotherapy and gene therapy to minimize damage. The discomfort will last for another day or two and for four or five weeks you will feel sunburn and maybe the hair will fall off for some time, but we expect a full recovery. There is an increased risk of cancer and children with congenital abnormalities, but if you follow the annual screening program and the treatments you are entitled to under the health care system, your life expectancy and your children will not be harmed."

"Okay, I guess…when can I go home?"

"Whenever you want, we don't need to keep you here. The treatment can continue at home and this bracelet will monitor your health from a distance. But before you leave, I'd like you to speak to someone who waited to see you as soon as you could receive visitors." She spoke through the visor. "You can let him in, Galvão is able."

"Good evening!" the First Commissioner greeted her. "I'm here to thank you, for me, for the Union of Nations, and for humanity, and to give you President Cândido's thanks. He's at an emergency meeting, but he'll see you personally at the earliest opportunity." She shook Pagu's hand.

"Thank you for your kindness." Pagu couldn't think of anything better to talk about.

"To be honest," Orwell answered in turn, "I thought of Tina and Pagu, not of humanity."

"It doesn't matter. It was the part of humanity that was yours to protect. And I want to welcome this opportunity to invite you both to the re-inauguration of the Intirana. It must be two or three months from now, when the damage is repaired and you are in top form."

"Sorry," Orwell cut off, "but I've had enough nuclear reactors for a lifetime."

"Listen, this has gained a much greater significance, it is about reaffirming peace and solidarity among peoples, not only launching a new energy source. And the axis of the ceremony will no longer be the reactor, but you. I want to have the honor of giving you the Golden Stars of Union of Nations heroes. Guira and Tina have already accepted. And you?"

"I accept!" Pagu answered with youthful enthusiasm.

Orwell was slow to reply.

"I accept, on one condition: I want the opportunity to speak on behalf of anarchism and explain that our criticisms of the Union have nothing to do with Marinetti's cretins."

"You'll have as much time to speak as you want, Orwell. Freedom is always, fundamentally, the freedom of those who disagree with us. Will that be all right?"

"All right...my dear Ms. Luxemburg." He smiled. "Perhaps our points of view are not so irreconcilable. Count me among the ranks of loyal opposition to socialism."

"The state will one day be expendable, but at this moment the choice is socialism or barbarism, as the incident of today showed us. But I respect your position. And you, Pagu, what do you think?"

"I agree with each of you a little, but I'm not in the mood to debate politics."

"You're quite right, my daughter, I'm sorry. Can I help you get dressed?"

The First Commissioner and the doctor assisted Pagu and Orwell.

When Pagu started using the visor again, she had more than three billion messages in her mailbox accumulated in the last hundred chronos, and they kept coming. And the viewfinder pointed out several dear people in the hospital lobby.

She tried to stand on her own, but she felt sick and had to cling to the bed to keep from falling. The doctor ordered a robocycle, a combination of a wheelchair, a tricycle, and a robot.

"It works like a robotaxi," she explained. "It just doesn't charge for its use. Choose the destination on the screen and it will take you there. When you no longer need it, just return it to any health center."

His friend refused a similar device, managing to get along with a cane. But as she prepared to leave, the First Commissioner made a proposition to him:

"Orwell, Tina wants to go with you to take care of you and told me you hate long plane trips, so I thought... I need to go to Eurasia to discuss the inquiry about the Futurist Party with Secretary Gramsci and I can stop in London. Would you like to take a ride on Aero Uno? It reduces travel time to less than a third."

"Hmm... I can do that, it should be an interesting ride."

After saying their good-byes to Pagu, Orwell, Tina, and Rosa went by official car to the airport. Guira hugged and kissed Pagu, thanked her effusively for everything and promised that they would make the best show of all time. And she was so pleased to see her parents reconciled with her partners that she forgot the discomfort and promised an exclusive interview to Anaíde. They'd been fighting since she was eighteen, and had left her paternal home to live with the couple, but now they were hugging them and asking them to take good care of her daughter. Curious people and journalists broke through and Pagu left on the robocycle, escorted by Oswald and Tarsila, eager to sleep at Pousada Dandara before embarking for Piratininga.

"What is that on your wrist, my love?" Tarsila asked when they arrived at the inn.

"Oh, it's Orwell's watch. I was so curious that he gave me a memento."

"Interesting!" Oswald looked closer. "It's half past eight. And look, the date in the old calendar, October 24th, 1929. What a day! If you hadn't been there, our world wouldn't exist anymore!"

* * *

UNION OF NATIONS' UNITS OF MEASUREMENT

chrono = 3.6 minutes or 216 seconds. It's divided in 1,000 nicts of 0.216 of a second. A day has 400 chronos.

credit: the virtual currency of the Union of Nations. It's divided in 1,000 milicredits or milis. The per capita wage is 900 credits and the minimum monthly wage is 30 credits.

quadra=100 meters. It's divided in 1,000 modules (1 module=10 cm)

quarta = 1 square quadra = 10 thousand square meters or 1 hectare

borba = 0.99229 watt (unit of potential)

juma = 0.21433 joule (unit of energy). 1 gigajuma = 59.5 kilowatts-hour

veiga = 0.67779 volt (unit of electric tension)

termograde = 1 kelvin (unit of temperature)

liter and ton: same as in our reality

* * *

Antonio Luiz M. C. Costa has always enjoyed literature, fantasy and science fiction in particular, but he graduated in production engineering and philosophy, did postgraduate studies in economics, and worked as an investment analyst and economic and financial advisor before rediscovering his vocation in writing, journalism, and fiction. Today he writes about reality in *CartaCapital* magazine and about the imagination elsewhere. He published a collection, *Eclipse ao pôr do sol e outros contos fantásticos* (2010), and the novel *Crônicas de Atlântida — O tabuleiro dos deuses* (2011) in addition to collaborating with the means at his disposal for the development of speculative fiction in Brazil.

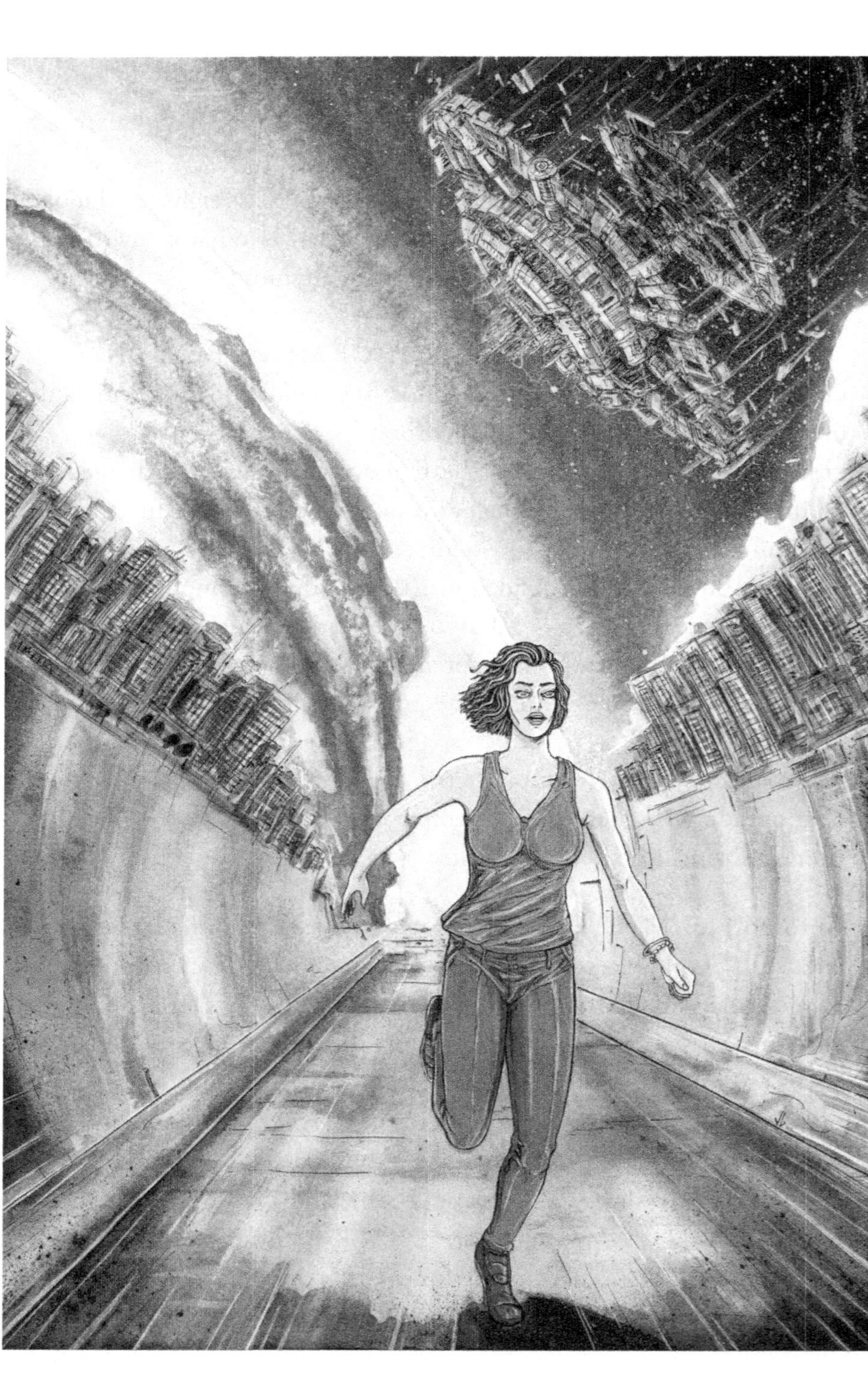

ESCAPE
Gabriel Cantareira

São Paulo. Thursday, February 20th, 2031 — 4 PM

Have you ever truly believed in something? So much that you had to risk everything, including your own life?

The immensity of white concrete and glass skyscrapers invaded the blue skyline, as if it wanted to reach the clouds. In the summer, at four o'clock in the afternoon, the solar panels that covered the buildings and followed the movement of the sun throughout the day lined up so that what light could escape from the matrices of photoelectric cells was reflected in the direction of the Cairo building. From there the impression was that the new Avenida Paulista had turned into a celestial pathway, surrounded by towers of light.

Mariana had always liked that view, but she had no time to enjoy it that day. She turned quickly and called the elevator impatiently. Some time later, the doors opened and she entered. She had to wait while other people walked in slowly, talking. She cursed softly when someone yelled for them to hold the door, and surprisingly the request was answered. Curious how the calm and patience of other people can sound like a personal insult when you don't have time to lose.

Nervous, she pressed her left hand, closed around the small

memory card, to her chest. Getting it out of the building shouldn't be so difficult, but making sure it arrived at its destination would be another story entirely. It didn't help that she felt as if all the occupants of the elevator were watching her, that she would be caught at any moment.

A few years ago, this task would have been easy. All she had to do was put the information on her PDA or mobile phone and the internet would do the rest, ensuring that anyone she wanted, anywhere in the world, would receive all the information contained in the card in a matter of minutes. Taking certain cautionary measures, it would be almost impossible to detect that specific data in the universe of information that was sent through the network every day. However, the internet was no longer what it used to be. Free flow of information is too dangerous a thing for governments and corporations.

Taking into account that virtually all non-sensitive information was transmitted via the internet and that it was possible to be connected at any time and from any place, the mere fact of carrying a memory card seemed suspicious. The card also had a security measure that ensured that the data was erased at the original source after a possible transfer to maintain the uniqueness of the information. That is, she also could not create copies of the content to increase her chances. Not without the proper equipment.

The elevator stopped at three more floors before reaching the ground floor. Finally, Mariana reached the main hall of the building, where busy people walked everywhere. She tried to blend in with the crowd and walk toward the exit. It would be difficult not to be recognized there, but the young woman hoped that when they realized that they should be behind her, she would be far away. As expected, some people greeted her, to which she just smiled and nodded nervously. Apparently, everything was still under control.

Home Sweet Home.

When she left the building, Mariana was greeted by the usual massive movement of the renovated center of São Paulo. The landscape from the top five minutes ago now loomed around her in detail: on the ground level of the imposing buildings covered with panels decorating the avenue, you could see the logos of the various corporations and companies that made their address: Solutions Solaris Technology, Advent Corporation, HSA Industries. Among the people on the sidewalks, dozens of armed guards with tactical equipment patrolled their beats. Luminous glass plates and OLED screens displayed advertisements of the city, large companies and their products. In one, a young black-haired girl appeared smiling while an HSA logo (which seemed to be the reason for so much glee) decorated the image. Mariana tried to ignore her surroundings and hurried to the Trianon-MASP subway integration station.

Beautiful, clean and elegant, the new center of São Paulo comprised a large region, including old areas such as Bela Vista, Jardim Paulista, and Liberdade. Planned to be safe and almost self-sufficient in terms of energy, the place was described as the throbbing heart that injected new life into a city that saw its glory vanish a few years earlier.

The third decade of the 2000s saw the world entering a new great war. The tensions generated by the nations' desire to control fossil fuel reserves so they could ensure their future development led to ever-widening conflicts that eventually reached global scale. However, the war was less spectacular than predicted by the great philosophers and Hollywood writers: within two years most conflicts had ceased and almost no weapons of mass destruction had been used. Globalization can be a problem for militarism, since a nation's civilian population will find it difficult to accept killing enemies who watch the same TV programs as they do.

Well, war indeed changes things.

An unpredictable result of the war was that the very fuel depots being fought over collapsed. The planet lost more than 70 percent of its known fuel reserves thanks to the development of Johnson-Cury technology, which allowed sabotage of oil and gas reserves on a permanent basis. Thanks to this, the nations had to focus their attention on alternative means of generating energy. Accidents at nuclear power plants during the war made most nations search for cleaner alternatives. Energy restructuring consumed much of the development effort over the next few years, so the technology advancement was a bit slower than previously seen.

Although Brazil had left the war in a favorable situation, the country had its share of destruction. With its infrastructure damaged during the conflict, São Paulo was abandoned by its population and its economy when the government showed no interest in rebuilding it. Slowly, the remaining buildings were abandoned and industries closed. However, the situation changed in the following years. Thanks to private initiative, renovation works began. Several corporations demonstrated an interest in reviving the pre-war metropolis, but with the structure and planning necessary to make it a cultural, economic, and social center, not the congested and deficient node that the city was turning into, even before the war.

Of course there was a catch. The signed agreement guaranteed that the involved corporations would exert total control over the renewed area, having the autonomy to put in practice any measures that they considered necessary. Combined with the corrupt nature of the government, this control meant carte blanche for the area to be managed as it pleased. Essentially, the renovated center would become a large private condominium for those who possessed sufficient resources. Corporations gradually became more obsessed with control and the established rules turned into oppression and censorship of anything the directors judged to be outside the desired standards.

And now this. Mariana still did not want to believe that they would really be able to do something like that. It was for this reason that she decided to act. She could not let them do as they pleased, not when human lives were involved. Although she knew she would not be able to do much, she found she was not alone. Thus it was possible to devise a plan to try to prevent what seemed inevitable.

All or nothing.

The station was not so full at that moment, as there were still a few hours until the departure time of the citizens who would fill the platforms. Driven by superconducting magnetism, the trains moved in and out of the station at a steady pace, moving to other parts of the city by means of an expanded rail network over the old subway lines and the city's rail network. Although the MASP building no longer existed, the station had kept its name by tradition. Its glass walls and white tiles displayed dozens of other colored panels and logos along the corridors leading to the underground platforms. Mariana walked down one of the corridors that led to a platform downstairs and entered one of the station's restrooms before continuing.

She washed her face and looked at her reflection in the mirror. A young woman with short, dark hair, green eyes, and a tired air stared at her with a nervous look on the other side. She wondered if it would be a good idea to try to disguise herself before moving on. Probably not. She sighed and tried to prepare for what she still had to do. Gathering her strength, she headed for the platform.

6 PM

The subway reached Paraíso Station. The people inside the wagon looked apathetic as good citizens should be, each too busy with their own affairs to notice the other individuals around them. For the first time in her life, Mariana considered this egocentrism a relief. Several screens arranged inside the vehicle displayed newspapers, notices or more advertisements. The images of a newscast caught the young woman's attention for a moment, making her bring her hand to her temple to synchronize the cellular device coupled to her ear with the sound transmission of the news.

"... This morning, the crew of the Ascension spacecraft returned home, in charge of maintaining the solar space station Icarus, responsible for 32% of the country's energy supply. Despite the indications that the

return trip could offer difficulties, fortunately, there were no problems."

Built four years earlier, the Icarus Station had been considered one of the hopes for the generation of energy for the next decades, along with other great works like the Berlin fusion reactor. The station consisted of a large network of stationary satellites that captured solar energy and transmitted it to the Earth's surface using microwaves.

That news had a direct connection to why it was so important that the memory card reach its destination. An obscure society composed of the owners of the largest corporations in the country had decided that the model developed in São Paulo was good, but it needed to be expanded. Control of the city was not enough when they could have control of the country and its population.

This was the other less publicized purpose for which the Icarus system had been conceived. A space station of gigantic proportions destined for the capture and transmission of solar energy that demonstrated all the progress and human development...until the eventual moment in which it would be sabotaged and would collide with the Earth, razing a great urban area in the process. The sabotage would be declared a terrorist attack, and the government, holding a country in panic with a third of its population and industries in the dark, would be grateful to relegate crowd control and security of territory into the hands of the companies who would kindly offer to help in such difficult times. To maintain security and progress, works would need to be done. People would need to be watched. Certain freedoms would need to be set aside to maintain order.

All for the greater good.

The memory card was so important because it stored details of that plan: which sections of the station would be sabotaged; what was the site of the fall on the Earth's surface; which people were involved in each stage of the project. Getting it hadn't been easy at all. It was the only hope of preventing the catastrophe from happening.

The station lights made her switch off the sound and turn her attention to the world around her. Before the train stopped, Mariana noticed a strange movement in the station and decided to go down as soon as the doors opened, afraid to be trapped in case something happened to the car. Her suspicions were confirmed, as soon as she left the train doors closed again. People who were still trying to leave the composition looked from one side to the other, confused, while those who planned to enter began to riot on the platform. The ads displayed on the station's dashboards suddenly popped orange, displaying a sign saying "WARNING: trains and exits are temporarily disabled. Thanks for understanding."

It made Mariana's heart race. She hadn't thought the siege would close around her so fast. Now it was for real.

Uniformed and equipped guards appeared in corridors and stairs at the ends of the station. She had seen more security than usual on the Trianon-MASP platform; She didn't know if it was really because of her, but she had managed to get on the train before she was forced to find out. The security guards at the Paraíso Station seemed to be looking for someone, this time with much less finesse, paving the way among the people trapped in the place. The way they came directly toward the train eliminated any doubt. She lowered her head and walked across the platform. Both stations also had dozens of cameras and sensors, and she was probably passing through all of them.

Locked doors: how to escape? Come on, think.

Mariana found what might be an escape route as she heard the security guards question passengers for information about a wanted terrorist who had a description uncomfortably similar to hers. The station was being expanded and there were several sections under construction, among them a new platform that connected to the one it was now. Apparently, the safety system of the corridor under construction had not yet been connected to the station's central hub, since the portals were still open. As soon as she heard a commotion behind her and noticed people pointing toward her, the girl passed through the tracks isolated by the construction without thinking twice and ran.

She ran as fast as her body allowed. She made her way to the platform under construction and continued to dart between debris and equipment left by corridors dimly lit by poorly placed white LED lights or spotlights. The path seemed strangely long. She could hear hurried footsteps around her, but she could not tell where they came from; it was as if they were everywhere. It made for a claustrophobic feeling: the white tile walls under construction suddenly seemed oppressive, and the tension grew at every turn of that maze of corridors, which could prove to be the end of the line, in a sudden merging with the owners of all those steps. Mariana felt a cold sweat trickling down her face from running and feeling nervous.

When she finally reached the hall with the stairs that led to the surface, the feared meeting took place. Several patrol guards blocked the entrances. The amount of equipment and weapons they carried left her worried. The thought that they probably believed she was a terrorist scared her even more. Her apprehensions were interrupted by the cries of the guards indicating that she had been spotted. The young woman ran again, this time back to the platform under construction. She almost panicked when she heard deafening sounds of gunfire echoing in the hallway as holes appeared on the walls around her.

Back on the platform, she hid as quickly as possible behind a large tiled box. The guards soon arrived and began to search for her. One of them issued orders and urged the others to undertake a search of the place and to move in for a siege. She remained silent and caught her breath, feeling the throbbing pulse as the guards walked around her.

She knew they would find her if she stayed there for a long time. So, as soon as one of the guards passed by and opened some distance, she took advantage of the opening and ran, going through all of them as fast as she could. She hurried through the corridors as she heard a new commotion behind her and crossed the now empty hall toward the stairs to the surface. She remembered leaving an electric motorcycle somewhere nearby in case of an emergency, and now was probably the time to pick it up.

8 PM

Mariana was still running. Her chest ached with the exertion, and her body offered more and more resistance to her commands. She knew she couldn't stop. She knew they were still after her. She was tired and afraid, but she couldn't give up while there was so much depending on her.

She had been forced to dump her motorcycle, and now she was in an old warehouse in an area far from the city proper. Under the sunset, the place looked rather bleak. The building was surrounded by a huge junkyard, filled with carcasses of old cars, unable to run without fossil fuel. She had come a long way since leaving the station. But though she was heading for increasingly difficult access, her pursuers remained ruthless in pursuit. She had kept them busy for some time in a game of cat and mouse among those relics of a bygone age, but now she felt that she could no longer mislead them. Her only option was to keep running while her strength remained.

The storage was gloomy, lit only by the light of the setting sun coming through the windows. Maybe that's why she hadn't seen anything. Maybe it was because she was exhausted.

She felt her body suddenly lose strength as she heard a muffled boom in the back of the shed. She collapsed on the dusty floor when her right leg refused to respond to her commands.

No. Please no.

Bullet wounds usually don't cause pain at first. Though she imagined what had happened, the gravity of the situation only struck her when she noticed that there was blood on her clothes and a small puddle under her. Leaving a trail of blood on the ground, she crawled to a wall, where she leaned back and stared at the dark, trying to find her assailant.

"You know, I swear I didn't want to do this, but you left me no choice."

The shape of a man appeared at the bottom of the warehouse, advancing toward her. He wore a formal black suit with yellow details, tactical combat glasses, and carried a pistol equipped with a muffler in his right hand. Certainly someone more important than the guards Mariana had missed before. He stopped to speak on a communicator, his fingers to his ear.

"Yes, I have everything under control now. I don't want anyone else in here."

The sounds she heard outside began to quiet down. Apparently, the guards were obeying the order. The man turned his attention back to her.

"You gave us a hell of a job, you know that? It has been a considerable feat to stand up to now, even more so considering you have no training at all." He bent down to check the wound on her body. The dark hole in her right thigh bled profusely.

"Let's cut a deal. I can help you, but I need the data you got. Where are they?"

"You'll never get them back," she moaned. "I'm sorry."

Now she was in pain. More than she could ever have imagined. The simple attempt to move her leg made her body shudder to a stop, and she couldn't breathe.

"You understand what's going on, right?" You were struck by a 9 mm bullet that probably passed close to the femoral artery. If you don't get help, you'll suffer septic shock in a matter of minutes and die shortly after. Come on, give me the card with the data!" He got annoyed and started fumbling at her clothes for the card. "If you have them, you know we'll find them anyway, even if it's at the autopsy." He frowned. "Unless…"

She laughed and her body trembled in the process.

"Right. I *never* had them."

A decoy. Her job was simply to keep them busy as long as possible to maximize the chances of the card getting to the right hands. In fact, it was she who had taken it from the Cairo building, but

Mariana had passed it shortly before entering the bathroom of Trianon-MASP, one of the few blind spots in the station's cameras. The original plan was for her to surrender the card and disappear, but as soon as the delivery was made she saw that it would not be enough. To ensure the escape of the true carrier, she should stage a flight. It was only for this reason that she had made a point of continuing to appear on the station's cameras, only to run when she had already been noticed. Once she realized she would no longer be able to foil the pursuers, she had tried to lure them into places of increasingly difficult access, even if it was obvious that they would not offer any way out. Watching how the mysterious agent seemed upset, the plan had worked perfectly.

"I can't believe you fell for such an old trick," she whispered weakly.

He brought his fingers back to his ear.

"It's not here! I repeat, the package is not here! Spread out and look around, she must have hidden it somewhere."

"...and to end your chances once and for all, you shot the only person you could interrogate to learn the whereabouts of the card. It will take at least half an hour until medical help arrives here, even if you call a helicopter. Unless one of your men is very good at first aid, I'll be dead by then."

She had no idea if what she was saying was really accurate. She had studied design, not medicine. But the important thing then was for the agent to believe what she said. She was trying her best to stay sharp, but things were getting harder and harder. He ended up calling medics by the communicator anyway, then he turned his attention to the girl's leg. He took off his jacket and pressed it with his hands against the wound where the hot blood continued to flow.

"Are you really willing to die for it?" he asked without believing. He kept pressing the wound and staring down at her face, which looked paler and paler.

"There's not much else I can do, is there?" She sighed. "Anyway, if it means saving thousands of lives, it's a price I'm willing to pay."

"I don't understand... You're on the good side of the scale. Mariana Souza, daughter of the president of the SSE...the company that merged with HSA two months ago and you became their advertising girl, turned the face of the company... You are beautiful, could even become an holovision artist if you wanted. People like you are the most privileged by the actions of this project."

The shapes began to fall apart. She could still see what was happening around her, but her perception was beginning to fail. It was scary.

"The population deserves more than that. I wouldn't be able to let you cause such a disaster knowing I could have done something about it. I wouldn't be able to let them manipulate people that way."

"The population *needs* to be manipulated. It's safer that way. To ensure the progress of society. People don't care that it's different. Have you noticed our politics? It's comical how the audience can watch the same show repeatedly and still laugh at all the scenes in each of the reruns. This is how it works... To be guided while thinking you are in control, otherwise there will be chaos. Sometimes someone needs to fall for the rest to go in the right direction. You know it's the best for everyone."

"For everyone or for the Golden Society?"

He stared at her with a surprised look. *How much does this girl know about all this?*

"The Society does its best to put the population on the right track."

"All I can see is a bunch of rich bastards who think they can dominate the world with their corporations. People should be able to choose their own destiny, have all the cards laid out on the table, and be able to make their own choices, according to what they believe. Sorry if I look too idealistic."

The process of stopping the bleeding wasn't working. There was blood all over the floor and the agent's hands were already soaked.

Her breathing was weak and she seemed about to lose consciousness. After all that, he realized that he didn't want her to die. Not just because of the mission. She was intelligent, unique, and could think by herself, something rare now. And she was willing to sacrifice herself to fulfill her purpose. In a way, he admired her.

"Mariana... I'm sorry." He looked in her eyes. Then he cleared his throat. "Probably all of this will be covered up, so your father will not see on the news that you were a terrorist or something. Would you like to say something to him?"

She shook her head slowly.

"You know, somehow it was nice to have talked to you. You can change, you know."

The pain was beginning to fade. Mariana felt her body numb and knew what was to come. She was more afraid than ever, but something inside told her that she had done the right thing, and now she could be at peace.

When paramedics from the emergency service finally arrived, they found the agent sitting with his head down beside the young woman, who wasn't breathing anymore.

The Next Day

Newscasts announced how the daughter of the president of one of the country's largest corporations had been kidnapped and found dead in a warehouse away from the city. Elsewhere in the city, in absolute secrecy, another group of people mourned what had happened and, with the information obtained on a small memory card, discussed how they could prevent a huge solar energy capture space station from falling from the sky.

* * *

Gabriel Cantareira was born in 1990 and lives in Itatiba, São Paulo. He holds a degree in Computer Science from USP and currently holds a master's degree. In addition to writing, he is interested in visual arts and music. Find him on DeviantArt: tioshadow.deviantart.com

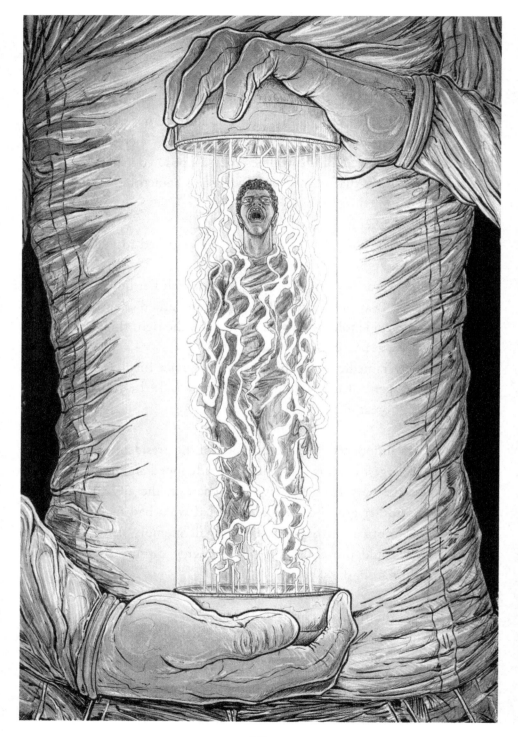

GARY JOHNSON
Daniel I. Dutra

Before starting, it's necessary to clarify that I have no concrete proof of any of the events reported in this document. This is only an attempt to organize in a text the information obtained, and I believe it will be of great value to the scholars to whom I will deliver this report duly followed by what I believe to be circumstantial evidence that will confirm my story. The best way to begin is by telling a little bit about myself, how I had my first contact with the journal of my great-grandfather Giuseppe Gagliardi, and how this led me to notice Father Roberto Landell de Moura and his scientific discoveries. Discoveries which, I might add, defy everything we know about the world and which I had a hard time believing myself, in part because of the lack of evidence to support my great-grandfather's account—perhaps the best evidence for the famed fire of St. Joseph's Church on August 15, 1909, a fact duly reported and whose occurrence still challenges attempts at rational explanation.

However, I am obliged to state that the main reason for my reluctance to believe the accounts found in my great-grandfather's journals is because, deep inside, I refuse to believe that something so impossible can be true. For if it's true, humanity will have to rethink its whole conception of life, soul, existence, and God. And most people are not prepared to take such a turn of events.

My name is Leonardo Gagliardi, I'm 25 years old. I was born in the city of Porto Alegre. I have a degree in Letters from the Federal University of Rio Grande do Sul. I am a descendant of Italians on my mother's side. My great-grandfather, the abovementioned Giuseppe Gagliardi, was born in the Piedmont region of northwestern Italy in the year 1878 and emigrated to Brazil at the age of five. His family settled in the colony of Dona Isabel, now known as the city of Bento Gonçalves, in Rio Grande do Sul. Giuseppe Gagliardi left home at age 22, moving to Porto Alegre in search of opportunities in the capital. He worked in a variety of professions, from public toilet cleaner to street vendor of nuts, until, in 1907, he got a job as a janitor in St. Joseph's Church. The priest in charge of that parish was a man called Roberto Landell de Moura.

I must confess that I had never heard of Father Roberto Landell de Moura before. A quick search in sources as different as Google and the public library of Porto Alegre revealed to me that Roberto Landell de Moura was a telecommunications pioneer in Brazil. A year before Guglielmo Marconi in Italy, Father Moura had successfully completed the first transmissions of telegraphy and wireless telephony. Unfortunately, the scientist-priest didn't get the recognition he deserved, but it's not my intention to talk about Father Moura's findings in the area of telecommunications. I want to talk about another discovery of the scientist-priest. A discovery that tends to be remembered as secondary by historians dedicated to rescuing the name of the inventor of radio from obscurity: this discovery is bioelectrography.

First, I need to talk a little more about myself so that you can understand how I got involved in this situation. I had been studying for two years in the Doctorate Program of Italian Literature in the Federal University of Rio de Janeiro. I had my application accepted in a cultural exchange program that offered me the opportunity to spend a year at the University of Bologna. I tried to get all the paperwork I needed to get my passport. That's when I discovered that, being a descendant of Italians, I could apply for dual citizenship. The official of the Italian embassy who answered me informed me that, in order to claim dual citizenship, I needed first of all to present my great-grandfather's birth certificate.

Having Italian citizenship would undoubtedly open many career opportunities for me. So I started the document search. I spoke to my grandmother, but she said that she didn't know where the certificate was, and wasn't even sure if it still existed, but that perhaps I could find it, or a clue that could lead to it, in my great-grandfather's diaries. Ensconced in an old handmade wooden trunk that was falling apart, the diaries consisted of a total of 58 notebooks—each recording a year of his life. My great-grandfather had started the habit at the age of fourteen and didn't stop, continuing to write until his death. It was in these texts that I discovered how the lives of my great-grandfather and Father Moura intersected.

I will now tell you about my great-grandfather's diaries. They relate all the details of his life, from ordinary, banal moments, such as the victory of the Grêmio team in the Porto Alegre City Championship in 1919 to historical events such as the Revolution of 1923, personal moments that marked his life, like the birth of his daughter, my grandmother, in 1928. One peculiarity of the diaries that made the comprehension of texts a real challenge was the fact that they were written in Italian. According to my grandmother, my great-grandfather wrote in Italian because, despite being able to speak Portuguese, he had never learned to write in this language. I say that reading the diaries was a challenge because my great-grandfather was writing in a dialect typical of northwestern Italy and, as if that wasn't enough, it was an obsolete dialect of more than a century ago. I forwarded copies of the journals to the Department of Neo-Latin Languages at the Federal University of Rio de Janeiro and I hoped that the experts would be able to decipher the passages beyond my linguistic ability. So, even though I am proficient in the Italian language, I found it very difficult to understand the writings and what I am reporting in this document is only what my knowledge in Italian has allowed me to decipher from its content.

My great-grandfather's work in the parish of St. Joseph's consisted of services as diverse as sweeping the floor of the nave, mowing the lawn, watering the plants, and repairing the church pews. In short, he was a real handyman. Father Roberto Landell de Moura had nothing to say about him but good words. Father Moura is described as a docile, gentle, and beloved man in the community. However, if my great-grandfather echoed those who appreciated Father Landell de Moura as a person, the same could not be said of the *scientist* Roberto Landell de Moura. The journals, especially those written between 1907 and 1909, are filled with notes on the experiments the priest held in his laboratory in the basement of the church.

It was during this period that Father Moura received the visit of James Paulsen. A visit that lasted for a period of two years. As far as I could gather, Moura welcomed Paulsen into his residence.

James Paulsen was an American engineer and physicist. Father Moura met him while in the United States between 1903 and 1905, to where he left in search of new opportunities, since in Brazil his inventions in telecommunications were simply ignored by the government. Father Moura met James Paulsen in a lecture by Professor Willem de Sitter, promoted by the Department of Physics at New York University.

The two worked in a laboratory set up in the basement of St. Joseph's church. There were numerous journal entries about how Moura and Paulsen entered the basement at dusk, leaving only at dawn, or even the next morning. My great-grandfather never had access to the laboratory, having seen it only at a glance. When it was necessary to have a word with the priest, he was instructed to knock on the door and wait for him to come out to meet him. All that my great-grandfather could see from the lab is what he described as an oval machine with a transparent cylinder at the top, plus several pictures hanging on a blackboard that, however, didn't appear to be photographs in the traditional sense, but pictures of dark figures whose contours resembled human bodies, wrapped in flames of various hues, some of an intense white, some gray or darker shades—the tones changed from photo to photo. At least that is what I deduced from my translation of the text. However, it may be that the lack of further information is due to the fact that my great-grandfather looked only at a glance at the laboratory, since Moura always closed the door behind him when he had to talk to my great-grandfather or to anyone else who dared to bother him in his lab. Attempts to question the priest about the nature of his work in the basement resulted in ⎣laconic⎦and fruitless answers, and my great-grandfather did not insist.

There are several excerpts from the diaries, identifying not only the day, but also the time when they were written, in which strange noises of machines and lights coming from the basement are described. One of the entries in the diary speaks of an intense blaze, which changed color constantly and would be very similar to what was in the photos, but multicolored, emanating through the cracks of the closed basement windows and illuminating the floor.

But what really puzzled my great-grandfather was what he witnessed on the night of August 1, 1909. A modest hut in the backyard of the Church of St. Joseph served as his home. It was a rainy night. The strong wind had knocked down a tree branch which, in its turn, broke a church window. My great-grandfather had to leave in the middle of the night to solve the problem. After removing the branch and covering the window with wooden planks, he saw a multicolored light shining through the crevices of the small rectangular windows in the basement, illuminating the paved floor that surrounded the church. As it was raining, my great-grandfather noticed a phenomenon that surprised him: falling and coming in contact with the light, the raindrops evaporated. He described what he witnessed as thousands of "coils of cigarette smoke" sprouting from the lit floor in plain darkness.

On August 6th of that same year, Father Moura gave my great-grandfather money so that he could buy a dog, a German Shepherd puppy to be exact. He was busy preparing the church for Sunday Mass, and for this reason asked Dorival—a black kid who lived near the church and could easily be found throwing a ball in the street—to go to the public market instead and fetch a pup. Dorival's arrival with the puppy coincided with that of James Paulsen, whom Father Moura was waiting for in his office. My great-grandfather took the dog, who was in a small cage, tipped the boy and, along with James Paulsen, went to see Father Moura.

James Paulsen's Portuguese was awful, much worse than my great-grandfather's, who had lived a big part of his life in the colony and never quite mastered our language. However, the American had the necessary fluency to make bigoted comments about the young Dorival. Comments that greatly annoyed Father Moura, who until then was unaware of the racist side of his friend and fellow scientist. Among his unpleasant remarks, Paulsen said that blacks shouldn't attend the same church as whites and shouldn't even be considered Christians, since they had no soul. He also made a comment to my great-grandfather, a tall, light-haired man with clear eyes, that the Italians were a privileged people because there were no blacks in their country contaminating the purity of the European race. Convinced of the superiority of the white race, Paulsen did not understand why Father Moura didn't pursue the matter.

On August 8th, the priest called my great-grandfather to his office and asked him to look for Dr. André Macedo, a veterinarian. The night before, the multicolored lights had appeared again and the seemingly unrelated events gained new meaning at Sunday Mass. After Mass, my great-grandfather could not help overhearing the conversation of two ladies sitting on a bench in front of the church as he cleared the front steps. The two ladies are identified in the diaries as "Dona Lorena" and "Dona Vera," the latter the wife of André Macedo. Dona Vera told her friend about the call that her husband had received at Father Moura's church. Macedo saw something that bothered him greatly. According to her husband's account, the priest had in his possession what appeared to be a German Shepherd pup, except that this pup, despite having the size and bone structure corresponding to a dog of his age, had all the diseases of an elderly dog, such as arthritis and cataracts. Father Moura asked the doctor if he could keep a secret, but he apparently didn't resist the temptation to confide in his wife. Looking back over the situation, my great-grandfather wrote that he had remembered hearing a cry or howling from a dog in the middle of the night, but that was of little consequence, believing that it was only the puppy's reaction to its first night in the new home.

The night of August 15th, 1909, was the night of the infamous fire of St. Joseph's Church. "Fire" was just one way of describing the event, for witnesses claimed they had seen no flame, at least not in the usual sense of the word. The church appeared to be wrapped in what witnesses describe as a multicolored flare impossible to face directly, producing temporary blindness, similar to that generated when we try to see the sun with the naked eye. The first time I saw anything related to this event was via documentaries on cable TV. The St. Joseph's Church fire is a popular topic on television paranormal investigation programs and internet forums. Mystics claim that the multicolored flare was the appearance of an angel. Skeptics, however, claim that the blaze that covered the church was produced by subterranean gases that had escaped to the surface. But what both skeptics and mystics were unable to explain was the state of the church's debris. The experts agreed that a common fire, no matter how high the temperature, would never produce enough heat to turn the bricks of the church wall into the amorphous mass it had been reduced to.

Testimony from eyewitnesses raised even more questions. Although the words and terms employed varied, the essence of the description remained the same. I found on the internet the testimony of a long-deceased man who witnessed the event. He describes how the multicolored flames melted the church walls like a flame melting the wax of a candle. Witnesses also found the event strange because of its absolute silence. There was no sound at all. On the contrary, instead of the burning wood crackling and walls collapsing, the flame that surrounded the church consumed everything in silence. There is also the question of the divergence of the testimony regarding the colors of the flames. Apparently, it produced colors unknown to human experience.[1] This conclusion is supported by the confused testimony and the witnesses' lack of vocabulary to describe what they saw. It is almost as if new words had to be invented to describe those anomalous colors.

From the back door of the church leading to the basement, my great-grandfather heard what he describes as "the most distressing cry a person could ever give." Trying to open the trapdoor, whose staircase led to the basement, my great-grandfather claims that his body went through the door as if it were "made of air." The bright, strong colors covered the walls and made his vision difficult, forcing him to cover his eyes so as not to go blind, just as someone would cover his nose so he would not suffocate in the midst of smoke. All he could see was a huge bluish blur in front of him, surrounded by indefinite shapes. In the middle of that scene he could not find words to describe, merely saying that it was like being plunged into a nightmare, he recognized the oval machine. What differentiated the machine from the other occasions in which he had glanced it was that the transparent cylinder at the top showed a tiny crack. The origin of the inferno of colors seemed to come from that particular point.

There was a man lying on the floor. The right side of his body was deformed. Looking at the squirming walls, giving rise to bizarre forms, my great-grandfather noticed a strange resemblance between the appearance of the walls and the deformation of the man in front of him. The man was James Paulsen.

Paulsen's lips twitched in pain, making no sound. He tried to speak, but no sound emerged from his mouth. Some sort of phenomenon seemed to have suppressed all the sound in that place. In his confused, shaky, and chaotic writing, my great-grandfather confessed that his first impulse, when confronted with the body of Paulsen devastated in that hideous and incomprehensible way, was to flee. Being a religious man, he also confessed that the only explanation that came to mind at that moment was that he was in Purgatory. However, he managed to control his emotions and, in an act of courage, lifted Paulsen in his arms and removed him from the church. Outside, at a safe distance from the church and with Paulsen lying in the garden, my great-grandfather watched the church being consumed by the silent flames. The light became gradually stronger; at the same time its size diminished, the church disappeared. After the phenomenon many compared to that of a melting wax candle, all that remained of the church was a pasty, gelatinous mass—or so it seemed to whoever was watching then—that glowed, though, after a few minutes, the glow had cooled until it completely disappeared, leaving only the amorphous shape of what had once been bricks and wood.

From that point on, my great-grandfather's handwriting became increasingly shaky and hard to read. By his handwriting, it was evident that the experience had shaken him greatly, leaving a trauma that was reflected in his scrawled writing, expressing his chaotic state of mind, with a shapeless frame expressing the feelings of a disturbed painter. However, the height of horror experienced by my great-grandfather was not seeing the deformed Paulsen, or witnessing the church being swallowed up by an unknown force. What caused my great-grandfather's writing to become shaky was the other body he found in the laboratory. Tied to a chair in front of the oval machine was a man. From his body came wires and tubes that connected to the machine. The man was apparently dead, judging by his inert aspect. My great-grandfather lamented that he had no chance of saving the man, for the light had become so intense and it sent such a strong heat that increased more and more, hurting those who approached, that the rescue of the second man was impossible. He was a very old black man, and it was at this point that my great-grandfather's writing was so shaky that I felt great difficulty deciphering its meaning. When I finally understood the last passage that contained the narrative of that fateful incident, I discovered what my great-grandfather had witnessed that had left him with ragged nerves. The black old man was young Dorival. Despite the wrinkles, my great-grandfather was emphatic on writing that he would have recognized that face anywhere.

From what my grandmother tells me, my great-grandfather was always a man of good nature, the kind who rarely lost patience, always preferring conciliation to confrontation. However, she also warned me that when provoked, her father could become an intimidating man. I believe Father Moura had the misfortune to know this unpleasant side of my great-grandfather. I make this statement for two reasons. The first is because what I will report next in the diary is written in a different handwriting. It was my great-grandfather's handwriting, no doubt, but it was no longer that shaky hand. Now his writing was clear and lucid—as if the vigor of courage had invaded his spirit. The second reason for my assertion is the way Father Moura, when asked by my great-grandfather, offered no resistance in bringing him abreast of what was happening.

I am convinced that my great-grandfather did not quite understand the story the priest told him. The reason for this belief is that, from this point on in the diary, the account becomes extremely confused. For me, at least, it is evident that my great-grandfather, in trying to reproduce what Moura told him, could not remember the terms used by the priest, or even manage to understand the explanation offered to him. We should keep in mind that Roberto Landell de Moura was a physicist from the University of Rome, while my great-grandfather was a semi-illiterate rural worker. So I think it is somewhat redundant to say that the intellectual gap between the two men made communication difficult.

For this reason, what the reader will see in the lines below are not my great-grandfather's words. Consider this my interpretation of events based on the little that my great-grandfather has been able to explain in his journal and Father Moura's letter (which I will reproduce in full at the end).

James Paulsen argued for the thesis that there were dimensions other than those known to science but that our cognitive apparatus did not allow us to see—just as a bat or earthworm does not see and interpret the world by sound and touch respectively, humans also would be limited by their five senses. According to his theory, the human soul was as material as the physical body and existed in another dimension, which he called "transdimension." Because it is condensed matter at a different energy level from which human consciousness is accustomed, we could not see or touch the human soul. The physicist claimed that the human soul would be a part of the human body, as real as the heart or brain, and from where our consciousness would emanate. In transdimension, the human soul, as well as the thoughts and feelings that are part of it, are as material as a leg or arm of the human body. James Paulsen wrote several articles on the subject and all were summarily rejected by academic journals. Considered an eccentric by colleagues in the scientific community, Paulsen immediately won the sympathy and friendship of Father Moura, not so much because he shared his ideas, which, from the point of view of Catholic doctrine, were heresy, but for understanding what it was like to be discredited by all. After all, when he said that his discoveries in the telecommunications area would allow communication with other planets, Landell de Moura was called crazy by President Rodrigues Alves.

However, the scientist-priest was forced to revise his view of his friend's theory upon discovering bioelectrography. When photographing an object with a photographic plate, subject to electric fields of high voltage, high frequency, and low current intensity, the result was the appearance of a luminous halo around the object photographed. Everything seems to indicate that the strange photos that my great-grandfather claims to have seen at a glance in Father Moura's laboratory were bioelectrographies. Initially, Moura believed he had established the scientific proof of the human soul. However, doubts arose when performing the same experiment with inanimate objects and obtaining the same results.

Moura sent the results of his research to James Paulsen who, in turn, began his own work, based on his discoveries. The two exchanged correspondence, describing the results of their respective experiments over the next few years. When they realized that their joint research had advanced to a point that it had become impossible to go on as long as they remained separated by distance, Paulsen came to Brazil. Once together at the Brazilian's residence, Moura and Paulsen began working on a means of proving the latter's theories. The duo's first attempt was to create a machine that enlarged the human senses and allowed the transdimension to be seen. However, as the research developed, Moura and Paulsen began to discover other possibilities. As the construction of a machine for such a purpose proved increasingly unfeasible, and in addition, such a machine would prove nothing, since there would always be those who would accuse them of fraud, the two scientists decided to go the opposite way. Instead of creating a machine that would allow us to see the dimension where the human soul existed, the two built a machine that would bring the human soul to our dimension.

Once the machine was built, the first experiment with the machine was a success. Moura and Paulsen were able to extract the perianth (the scientific name with which priest had baptized the human soul, given the similarity of the halo in the photographs to the petals of a flower) of a copper vase. The perianth of the vase was stored in the transparent cylinder. That's when Moura and Paulsen made another unexpected discovery: when brought into our dimension, the perianth became a powerful source of energy.

Faced with this unexpected turn in events, Landell de Moura decided to end the experiment (for reasons that will be explained by the author at the end of this narrative). However, James Paulsen was persuasive enough to convince his friend to perform one last experiment: to extract the perianth from a living being. Despite his moral conflicts, the priest finally agreed to carry out the experiment on a German Shepherd puppy, which resulted in the most terrifying discovery of all. Extracting the perianth from a live being caused brutal side effects in the body, aging it to a near-death state. The pup survived the experience, although in a later note in another diary my great-grandfather claims that the animal died of old age about two months later.

As for what happened at the dawn of August 15th, 1909, this is what Roberto Landell de Moura told my great-grandfather: according to the priest, Paulsen was eager to try to extract the perianth of a human being. After the first experiments, Moura and Paulsen discovered that there was a scale of energy level of the objects. In other words, a table didn't have as much energy as a dog. By this line of reasoning, it wasn't difficult to deduce that the perianth of a human had more energy than a table or a dog. Paulsen speculated on the possibilities offered by the discovery, how the perianth could revolutionize the transport industry and replace the known energy sources, such as oil and coal. Because it was an easy and inexpensive method of energy extraction—after all, the machine had been built by two men in the basement of a church—Paulsen believed they would both be millionaires with their invention.

The moral objection of Father Moura was more than understandable: how could Paulsen even consider reducing human beings to a mere source of energy? They knew the side effects of perianth extraction. Who would decide who lives and who dies? Paulsen's response brought great displeasure to the religious: he argued that blacks were perfect for this purpose. There were many of them out there. Negroes only caused confusion, robbed, raped white women; therefore, that would be the best way to give them some measure of usefulness. These words made Moura lock the basement door and buy a passage back for Paulsen on the next ship sailing to the United States.

However, his racist colleague did not give up. He kidnapped young Dorival, invaded the church's laboratory in the middle of the night and performed the experiment on his own. The tragedy occurred because the receptacle designed to hold the perianth was not large and strong enough to hold the energy of a human being. The phenomenon of colors that had consumed St. Joseph's Church and deformed James Paulsen had been triggered by the perianth of the young Dorival.

I must now present a brief account of later events, since seven years have passed between the St. Joseph's Church fire and the time when my great-grandfather received the letter from Father Moura. After being discharged from the hospital, Paulsen returned to the United States. Apparently everything had returned to normal, since in the ten years that followed I did not read in the daily reports of new bizarre events. From what can be inferred from the writings, Landell de Moura had lost interest in science, resigned to dedicate himself only to the priesthood. Thanks to Father Moura, my great-grandfather got a job in the new church to which the priest had been assigned.

The event I wish to report is an entry in the diary dated August 13th, 1919. My great-grandfather was painting the church wall when he heard a cry coming from the window of Father Moura's office. Knocking on the door and asking permission to enter, he found the priest visibly downcast. "The man was as white as the candles in front of him," wrote my great-grandfather, referring to the fact that Moura was kneeling before a set of lit candles, kneeling and praying with a bible open on a bench. He reported that he had called the priest three times until he had reacted, seeing the state of concentration he was in. The priest stood up, went to his table, and told my great-grandfather to sit down. The reason for the abatement was due to a dream he had had the night before. Initially, the priest ignored it as being only the fruit of the unconscious, for, being a man skilled in the sciences, he was privy to Sigmund Freud's theory of interpretation of dreams. However, a letter from James Paulsen had arrived in the mail that day. The two men had not spoken since the incident at St. Joseph's Church, and the content of both the letter and the dream had convinced Father Moura that what he had had the night before had been more than a dream. My great-grandfather did not know what the priest dreamed about, nor was Paulsen's letter content revealed to him. All Landell de Moura told him was that he would have to travel to the United States for a while and that my great-grandfather would take good care of the parish.

Now we finally come to the letter that my great-grandfather received from Father Roberto Landell de Moura—which undoubtedly is the strongest proof in favor of the story reported in this text. It was sent from the United States and reached the hands of my great-grandfather on November 20th, 1919. I am not a calligraphy expert, but, comparing the handwriting of the letter with that of the documents written by Father Moura, exhibited in the Porto Alegre Museum of Radiology, I maintain that it does not seem to me to be a hoax. In addition, the yellowed paper, with moth marks on the edges and a strong musty smell, which can be felt throughout the paper, make this hypothesis even more unlikely. I transcribe below the contents of Roberto Landell de Moura's letter. Please take note that I decided to transcribe the letter, adapting it to contemporary Portuguese, eliminating the "orthography" of the 1910s.

My dear friend Giuseppe,

I write this letter to you because you are the only one I can count on in this moment of distress. I am writing these words in the New York port. I'm sitting presently at a diner near the agency where I just bought a ticket on the Jennifer III, in which I'll embark to Europe in a few months. My destination is Italy. I have a meeting with Vatican officials. Unfortunately, my findings have had unpredictable and disastrous consequences and it is of the utmost importance that action be taken immediately to avoid further tragedies. It is to prevent the worst from happening that I come to ask for your help through this letter. I ask you, when you finish reading, do not tell anyone, not even to your wife Marisa, what I have confided to you here, and burn this document.

You must remember that afternoon of August 13th when I called you to my office and told you I was going to travel to the United States. The reason for my departure, as you may have noticed, was the letter I received. I think you clearly realized how shaken I was that day, almost on the brink of collapse. I must thank God, because my faith and many prayers gave me the strength to not succumb to evil and rise up. I do not need to tell you what happened here in the United States. I could only beg you to do what I ask you to do at the end of this reading without further explanation. But I've decided it's best to let you know the situation. I believe it will serve as an incentive for you to carry out the task that I will ask you to. You understand, my dear fellow, that I consider you a man of good heart, and therefore I believe it is only fair that you know all the facts. God help us.

As you know, I had told you that I had a bad dream the night before the day I decided to travel here. It's time to reveal the content of the nightmare. It is hard to put into words the visions that my dreams brought me, visions which, no matter how horrific, at first I thought they were only my imagination, but Paulsen's letter proved otherwise. As a man of science, I have thought of all possible alternative explanations, and I must confess, none of them are satisfactory, which leaves only one possible conclusion: *I had a premonition.*

146

Admitting this is very difficult. The Vatican is very strict in such cases, and priests are trained to face premonition claims with skepticism, whether they are experienced by others or by the priest himself. Contrary to what many believe, when it comes to supernatural phenomena, the Catholic Church acts with extreme scientific rigor. But it is no use denying the facts, and in my case, I am convinced that the dream was a warning from God.

When I began my scientific studies, my only desire was to prove to the world that faith was not the enemy of science. I believed that I would revolutionize the world with my inventions and change the view that the scientific community had of the Catholic Church. Of all my discoveries, bioelectrography—which I regret now—was at first the one that most excited me. If I could prove that the luminous halo that appeared in the photos was really the human soul, this discovery would renew people's faith in God. To prove the existence of the human soul was a step closer to proving the existence of God.

Unfortunately, my findings revealed sad truths under the human condition. Conditions that ended my faith in God and reduced my priesthood practice to mere bureaucratic employment. I imagine you noticed the uninspired way in which I led the masses after the St. Joseph's Church incident.

I will explain the reason for my spiritual apathy: Paulsen, and especially myself, believed that we were about to discover the essence of life. That which makes the human being unique and different from all animals. To our dismay, however, research has revealed the opposite of what we expected to find. As you already know, the luminous halo is only one part of the human body that exists in another dimension. But I realized that you, being a man of humble origin, did not understand all the implications of our discovery. Please do not feel offended, my dear friend. If I make such a statement, it is only because I wish to clarify your thoughts.

When we discovered that both living beings and inanimate objects possessed the luminous halo which I called perianth, the social, cultural, and philosophical implications perplexed me. Understand, my dear fellow, the human soul of which so many poets, theologians, and philosophers wrote about is a myth created to grant the human being more importance than he actually possesses. This property, of which our species so much prides itself, is only a form of energy that can be found in any dog, or even in a stone. If Charles Darwin shook the pillars of Christianity with his Origin of Species, my discovery would overthrow Christianity once and for all.

I have written several lines and I have not reported my dream yet. It is no longer possible to postpone this task. The best way for you to understand how the dream developed during my sleep is not to think of it as a dream, but as a story that passes before your eyes. Remember that time we met by chance at the opening of Odeon Cinema in Rua das Andradas in 1910 and watched the movie Revenge of the Innkeeper? My dream experience was like watching a movie projected on a movie screen.

The images I saw in my dreams were of a metropolis of unparalleled grandeur, with skyscrapers whose end you just couldn't see, walkways connecting the buildings with each other and lanes suspended for gigantic vehicles that traversed the bowels of the buildings. I felt as if I were inside one of the designs of the architect Antonio Sant'Elia. In this strange world, which I somehow knew was a future age, I witnessed the story of Gary Johnson. It was the name on his uniform, which was easily identified as that of a prisoner. He was standing before the judge in a place I thought was a courtroom from the way everyone was dressed, and especially from the opulent costumes of the court. Johnson was a relatively young man, said to be about 42 or 44 years old. After the judge pronounced the sentence— like a movie, there was no sound and therefore I did not know what words came out of his mouth—the guards took the prisoner into a vehicle that climbed an ascending walkway and entered a tunnel that crossed several buildings at great speed, that made me feel nauseated. His fate was a gray, windowless quadrangle flanked by two side columns. Gary Johnson was pulled out of the vehicle by the police and taken to an elevator. The prisoner's next scene unfolded in a corridor accompanied by two jailers. Along the corridor walls were a number of doors where many young men, mostly black, dressed in uniforms equal to Johnson's and others where old people were leaving, entered. Finally Johnson was led to the left, entering one of the hallway doors. Inside was a chair and another internal side door. The cops tied Johnson to the chair. I thought it was an execution. Since I did not know I was dreaming, I prayed to God that He would have mercy on Johnson's soul. I closed my eyes so as not to witness the horror of the execution. All I heard was the prisoner's cries of pain. I wondered how I had not been able to hear the judge's sentence, but it did not matter, because when I opened my eyes I saw what you saw that night of August 15th, 1909. Gary Johnson was no longer a young man but an old man who could barely walk. Before I could recover from the shock of seeing the prisoner in that condition, the inner door opened and from there came a man carrying an object that I would recognize anywhere: it was the cylinder Paulsen and I designed to contain the perianth.

The scene changed once more. Now I saw the city of clouds, as God sees it, and I discovered the source of energy that moved the vehicles, lifts, the unspeakable objects that flew through the heavens and, above all, that tortuous city. As if watching a documentary, I was shown the inside of those machines that infested the streets and how the perianth fed them. That world was a nightmare. Humanity had been reduced to fuel that moved the metal organs of that city.

I woke with a start. I sat on the edge of the bed and thought about what I had dreamed about. I concluded that my dream was just a way for my unconscious to deal with what happened to the young Dorival a decade earlier. But when I opened Paulsen's letter that morning all my certainties were shaken in a way that transformed me forever. I will not tell you what was in the letter, I will tell you what happened when I met him in the United States, since what I saw was exactly what was in the document.

To not take more of your time and get you to act promptly, I'll summarize what happened. Paulsen himself pursued his research with the perianth in the United States. Our machine had a serious problem: it could not contain large amounts of energy, which caused the incident in St. Joseph's Church. I will use an analogy so you can understand me. Imagine the cylinder containing the perianth as a dam and the perianth the water of a river. What happened on the night of August 15th was a breach of the dam, but not of the whole dam, only an insignificant hole from which a small splash of water escaped. In other words, what destroyed the Church of St. Joseph that night is but a tiny fraction of the perianth of a human being. I can scarcely measure the destructive power of the perianth in its entirety.

Well, Paulsen solved the problem of containing the perianth. The American government was funding his research and there was, even, an experimental submarine operating based on perianth. He began to lecture on the possibilities of the perianth, as he had done on other occasions, and how we were to revolutionize the world with a source of energy that would make solar power itself look like a campfire. I interrupted Paulsen and this is the appropriate time to say where this conversation took place: the address was a prison in the state of Arizona. Upon arriving at the scene, I was led by the guards to a laboratory set up in a decommissioned wing of the prison. That's when I found a disfigured Paulsen and knew he was using convicts in his experiments. I do not know what moved me the most, whether Paulsen's amorality or that of the American government—which I have always admired for advocating the ideals of liberty and equality—for sponsoring such an atrocity or Paulsen's undisguised preference for using black convicts as guinea pigs. He appealed urgently to my scientific spirit. He said that science was above moral issues, and when I objected to the use of human beings as guinea pigs, he countered with the racist theories of Herbert Spencer and

Francis Galton, who preached, among other outrages, that the progress of mankind was for the white race, and that Primitive races, like blacks, are destined to disappear. It was the law of survival of the strongest who, in Paulsen's prejudiced mind, justified his actions.

Paulsen called me for purely scientific reasons. He had solved the failure of the cylinder that holds the perianth, which he called the "transdimensional energy collector." The unfortunate man even gave a name to our blasphemy. The perianth could be safely used and was a more efficient and clean source of energy than is currently known. But there was a problem. The perianth could not be used to its full potential. By Paulsen's calculations it was only possible to use 10% of the energy of the perianth. He believed that the cause of the problem lay in the fact that the perianth did not belong to our dimension. According to him, bringing it into our world caused the dissipation of most of the energy. I gave him no chance to continue; he was not interested in the scientific questions of the perianth. I did not believe his boldness to ask for my help.

I killed Paulsen. With the same hands that write this letter, I took a microscope from a table near me and crushed his skull when he turned his back in a moment of distraction. I took advantage of the existence of inflammable products in the laboratory to set the scene on fire and leave before the guards appeared. The fire consumed Paulsen's notes and the prototype of the transdimensional energy-collecting machine, which was similar to the one you saw at various times in St. Joseph's Church.

I sent a letter to the Vatican describing what had happened. They want to hear my story firsthand and hold a conference behind closed doors to decide the next steps. I will be meeting in a few weeks with the highest authorities of the Catholic Church. They asked me to take my notes and project diagrams with me. It is precisely in this part that I need your help, my dear friend. All the documentation, which includes all the information on how to build the machine that brings the perianth to our dimension, is in a steel safe in my office.

You must have seen it several times, it's that gray vault next to the pedestal where I keep the Holy Bible. The password is 14-87-23-89. I want you to take the documents out of the safe and send them to the address: Hotel Marchant, 457 Street, New York. USA. I will deliver the documents to the Vatican. I hope they will keep them in a place where no human being finds them, for the good of both humanity and the Christian Faith, and I hope there will never be born a scientist as brilliant as James Paulsen, who will unravel the secrets of the perianth as he did. Although Paulsen was a despicable man, I am obliged to admit, unwillingly, that he was a true Leonardo da Vinci among the cavemen of our time.

I look forward to receiving the documents that I request.

Eternally grateful,
Roberto Landell de Moura

PS: As I said before, my belief is that my dream was an omen of the future that awaited humanity if James Paulsen continued his experiences. I also believe that God commissioned me to stop him, which is why I feel no remorse for the murder I committed. This morning I had an experience that further strengthened my faith already restored. After buying my ticket to Italy, I stopped at a bank and bought a newspaper. My shoes had to be polished. I saw a young black man, about eight or ten years old, on the corner working shine. I gave the boy a coin, sat on the bench, and he began his service. I looked at his face. He looked very familiar but I did not know where I knew him from. Then I asked the boy what his name was. His name was Gary Johnson.

* * *

Daniel I. Dutra is originally from Pelotas, Rio Grande do Sul. He holds a degree in Letters (UCPEL) and a Master's Degree in Comparative Literature (UFRGS). His Master's Dissertation gave rise to the book *Literatura de ficção-científica no cinema: A Máquina do Tempo — do livro ao filme (Sci-Fi Literature in the Cinema: The Time Machine — From Book to Film)*, a study on the work of H.G. Wells. In fiction he participated in the anthologies *Deus Ex-Machina — Anjos e Demônios na Era do Vapor* (2011) and *Erótica Fantástica v. I* (2012) from Editora Draco.

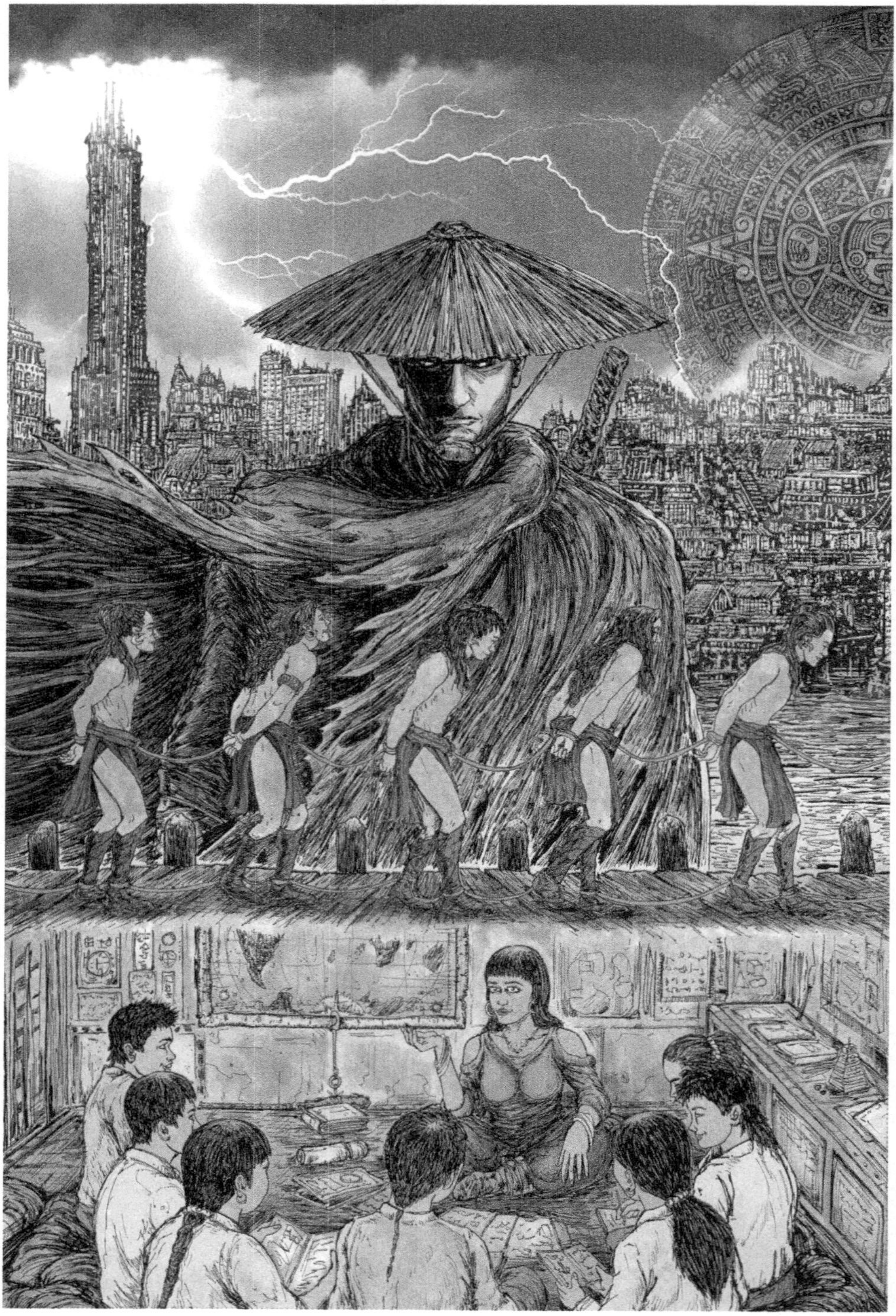

XIBALBA DREAMS OF THE WEST
André S. Silva

Come to think of it, it all began on a morning like this.

Maiara walked slowly from one end to the other of the semicircle of children. Seated on cushions on the floor, with the tomes of the day on their laps, the little ones watched the teacher with the eagerness of those who yearn to discover the world and trust her as their guide.

The topic of the morning was the same as the past few weeks. It really couldn't be any different when it came to Societal Studies. No event in recent history was so important. After all, Maiara and the children were on the verge of a historic event that would change the world forever.

"Who could answer me which city was chosen as Mark Zero?" A smile crept to the teacher's lips when dozens of little hands rose before she even finished the question.

"You can answer, Anirê."

"Xao-Kuna, teacher!"

"Very good!" the teacher congratulated her. "Your father has already visited the Silver City, isn't that right, Luc?"

Maiara knew the answer would be yes. She had asked the question over and over again. However, the children didn't care and she didn't either. Repetition was part of the learning and Maiara liked to share with her students this interest in the new, in still undiscovered things.

"Yes, teacher!"

"And he enjoyed the visit?"

"He loved it!" the boy replied, excited. "He said that everything seems to be made of diamonds, and that the bridges open and close all the time for ships to pass under, and that the whole city moves from side to side as if alive!"

"Where do they get the energy?" another girl asked.

"You moron, they have towers, just like ours!" a less than kind classmate intervened.

"*You* are a moron, beetleface…"

"Children!" Maiara exclaimed, gaining instant silence. "Actually, Iracema's question is a very good one."

Saying this, Maiara reached for a small copper ring that hung from the ceiling's support beams and brought it down, unrolling an old map of the world. She picked up an improvised plank of stone and twisted wire from the ground and hung it on the copper ring to keep the map in place. The presence of a huge star with a human face was drawing attention in the far east, beyond the Rising Ocean.

The letter was very worn, as was, in fact—Maiara didn't go a day without being angry about this—the whole system of education of her country. Educating one's own children seemed to be far from a priority for the High Priesthood.

Even so, now that she put the facts in perspective, it made perfect sense.

"Come here, Luc. We'll do a little Geography review."

The boy got up promptly and headed for the map.

"Point to us on the map where our city is."

The boy traversed the broad continental mass outlined over the blue infinity with his eyes. He wasted no time on the top of the map. He focused on the lands to the south and east and, with an uncertain finger, pointed to the coastal region where Guanabara was located.

Or close enough, at least.

Maiara took the boy's hand and shifted his finger a few millimeters to the right across the dusty sheet before continuing. "Yes, very good. Here we are, right at the tip of South-Tenoque. Now, let's find Xao-Kuna."

Under the attentive glances of the rest of the class, the boy went back through the map with the tip of his index finger, every inch going over hundreds of miles, heading north. It crossed the entire continental mass corresponding to South-Tenoque, passed through the Isthmus of Mexico, arriving then at the tropical expanse of Nahuá, the greatest nation and heart of all Tenoque. From there, he went on, skirting west by the Great Navajo Plateau, and finally reaching Xueiuá, the snowy lands at the north end of Tenoque.

At that moment, the boy stopped. His hand trembled and doubt cast on his face an involuntary grimace. The little eyes went rapidly from the map to Maiara, and to the map again.

"You can continue, Luc," the young teacher reassured her student. "You're doing well."

In fact, it was only a few miles away that the boy's finger transposed in a matter of seconds. To the west of Xueiuá, the map bore a peculiar design: two serpents, one winged, intertwined. The figure overlapped the territorial belt identified as the Dong-Dang Strait, popularly known as the Embrace of the World, the place where, many baktuns ago, West and East were reunited.

"Perfect. You may sit down, Luc."

The boy practically ran back to his place.

"As we can see, Xao-Kuna is the great link between Tenoque and our brothers in the west, the great Zonguá Empire. It's not quite a city, but several small towns, scattered along the entire strait separating our two continents."

The teacher pointed to the drawing of the two serpents. To the west of the figure, the territory identified as Zonguá had its geography considerably less detailed than the rest of the map. In fact, it was little more than a sketch of a border, with half a dozen cities identified here and there, which then disappeared into an empty, unknown wilderness as it advanced inland.

"Answering your question, Iracema, the energy that powers the turbines and allows the Xao-Kuna complex to function originates from the zonguanese side of the Strait. As far as we know, they get their energy the same way we do. After all, it was their engineers who brought to Tenoque the technology we needed to build our towers. But the truth is...we are not sure."

"See, see, see?" the girl turned, pleased, to her bully of a classmate. The classroom filled with excitement.

"But you're still dumb!" he said.

"Enough!" the teacher had to raise her tone again.

The fight ceased, but Iracema continued to display a conceited smile, thumbing her nose at the other. Maiara wanted to laugh too, but she restrained herself. She could almost feel in the girl the warmth of the discovery, the certainty of the settled mystery she knew so well. The experience that Maiara had been indoctrinated to never fail to look for.

"Well, now that we know where we stand, we can continue. As you know, we're very close to Transition Day. Our calendar and the Zonguanese calendar will merge when the bells of the fourteenth *baktun* sound. The heart of the Dragon and the Serpent will beat as one, and everything will start there, in Xao-Kuna. We're going to become more united. The Mayan *Popol Vuh* announces this moment as the beginning of a new era.

"Teacher, teacher!" A girl raised her hand euphorically. "My aunt told me it's going to be the end of the world! Is that true?"

"My grandpa said the same thing!" said another student.

"That's right, it's going to be the revenge of the Mayans for the Fall!" a third one said gloomily.

Thus, another confusion of voices began. Everyone seemed to have some different contribution to make to the mosaic of legends, prophecies and fears that made up the expectations surrounding the arrival of the new *baktun*, the cycle of the ages of the ancient Mayan calendar.

Maiara had to spend almost all the rest of the class to reassure the children, assuring them that these rumors were no more than misinterpretations of the ancient writings, and that they were indeed blessed to have the opportunity to experience such an important moment in history. Soon, the timecounts of Tenoquese and Zonguanese, for whom this was the Year of the Dragon, would become one, and a new calendar would begin.

"Have faith in the future, my children," Maiara sighed in a maternal tone. "There's always hope. And you know why?"

The class answered in unison:

"Because Quetzal-Tupá watches over us!"

"Exactly." The teacher nodded, pleased. "Quetzal-Tupá gives us everything and is responsible for everything around us. He brings rain and energy to us, and whispers good ideas to men in their sleep, allowing them to build something as wonderful as Xao-Kuna, and its bridges over the ice seas. There is nothing but kindness in our creator. He will always protect us, and this is..."

"The only truth!" everyone answered in a single voice.

Maiara smiled, sharing the same unshakeable conviction. The same innocence.

* * *

Children ran from one side of the avenue to the other, saying goodbye to their classmates and going to their parents. On the narrow sidewalk in front of the Institute of Education, a line of small ones formed, waiting for the last *xudá*, the collective electric transport vehicle, that would leave that same afternoon.

Embracing her tomes, and shouldering her linen bag, Maiara was on her way to the elevated platform at the end of the avenue, where the electric streetcar would take her home on the other side of the Bay in a few minutes.

When she walked by two students, the teacher couldn't help

listening to what one said to the other:

"I heard that the Mayans are killing the Zonguanese officers…"

The voices were lost in the noise of the avenue. Although the mysterious attacks were the talk of the moment, even among her fellow teachers, Maiara refused to pay attention to them. In her disinterested opinion, they were only political intrigues. Therefore, nothing new when it comes to the city-state of Guanabara.

Much more important, in her view, was the theme she had been addressing in her classes. The Day of Transition, the fusion of the computes, the beginning of the new era. Her father had talked so much about that day. She could hardly believe it was so close now.

If only her father had been alive to see it.

If only he hadn't ruined everything.

"Mama, Mama!" Luc's voice came out of the crowd as he ran past Maiara. A familiar face approached both.

Luc threw his school supplies behind him and grabbed the woman by the waist, almost knocking her to the ground.

"My dear." She kissed his sweaty forehead between his thin black locks. "You didn't get in trouble today, did he, teacher?"

"No." Maiara greeted her friend with a friendly smile. "A top-notch student, Tayanna, as usual."

"Did you hear, Mother?" Luc's eyes flashed with anticipation as he pulled the hem of his mother's dress from side to side. "I behaved good! Will I get my reward? Please please please!"

Noticing Maiara's curious expression, Tayanna disclosed the information:

"I'll take him to watch the sacrifice today."

The words caused an infectious blast of happiness in Luc. The boy began jumping and laughing, vibrant as if it were the greatest victory he had ever won in his life. He embraced his mother, his teacher, and even a complete stranger who walked past them.

"Today? Maiara asked, when the boy's excited shouts abated a bit. "Already?"

"The cycles are getting shorter and shorter," Tayanna argued. "It's really worrying, but apparently it's necessary. So many crimes... And now, this attack wave."

"Come with us, Maiarinha? Please?" Luc insisted, no longer seeing his teacher there, but the godmother he had known since he was a baby.

Tayanna gave Maiara a sympathetic look, aware of the discomfort that her son's invitation caused her. She tried to get her friend free of the nuisance, insinuating an excuse:

"Maiara has important things to do, Luc. Leave her alone, come now."

"No, that's fine," the teacher suddenly replied. "I'll go with you."

"Are you sure?" Tayanna asked, worried.

"Yes," Maiara confirmed as vehemently as she could. "I'll get something to eat and meet you in the cove."

Disguising the uncertainty that weighed on her chest with an affected smile, Maiara, more than a commitment to the boy, made one with herself. That would end today. The teacher would face and vanquish her personal demons. She was a woman, after all. It was time to leave girlish fears behind. She felt ready, she just didn't want to have to do it all by herself.

* * *

Many times Maiara had imagined her footsteps now on the wide paved sidewalk. The sky over Guanabara shone in a vivid, immaculate blue. The afternoon sun slanted through the treetops along the avenue, piercing its shadows with perfect light arrows.

It was a beautiful summer day, but soon Rain would come.

The peninsula was teeming with thousands of spectators, as happened with every sacrifice. In fact, a climate of excitement and urgency seemed to encompass not only that region, in the shadow of the so-called Loaf Mountain, but all of Guanabara. Port activity along the Bay had been temporarily suspended and its waters were free from heavy maritime traffic.

Maiara had no trouble finding Luc and Tayanna. It was a determination of the High Priest that children should have the right to preferential spaces during the ceremony which, for all those faithful to the Throne of the Serpent, was the supreme manifestation of justice. So, seeing the little one and his friend in the crowd in front of the port, Maiara went there. Passing through the cordon, she showed her teacher's ID to one of the ocelots, the Guardsmen, another condition that ensured privileged participation in official government ceremonies. A privilege that Maiara had never considered invoking until now.

"Are you all right?" Tayanna asked when she looked at her friend.

The exasperated countenance and sweat dripping from Maiara's forehead betrayed her nervousness.

"Right enough," she replied, intending to believe that for herself. She pressed the school tomes to her chest, at the same time trying to occupy her trembling hands and stifle the heavy pounding of her heart.

The boarding bay was open. From its damp darkness, a rusty bridge jutted to the quay like the rotting tongue of a beast, waiting to receive in its bowels the cohort of condemned men who, bound to each other by wrists and ankles, followed in slow steps along the wooden pier, to their own doom. Burned into their arms, the mark of the sacrifice, an undulating serpent, flanked by two circles, representing the twin gods of death.

A few steps ahead of the group came the Herald of Xibalba, as the priest responsible for the sacrificial ceremonies was called. Wearing a ceremonial costume adorned with representations of feathers and fangs in pure gold and silver, no one could see his face, for it was covered with a stylized snake mask.

The Herald ascended the pulpit in front of the audience and began:

"By order of the High Priest of Guanabara and under the blessings of the great Quetzal-Tupá, I begin the thirtieth-first ceremony of

Purge in this sacred year of the Dragon, thirteenth *baktun*."

As the priest read the accusations of the condemned, Maiara watched each of them. Her hands felt numb, the icy fangs of the monster called terror seemed to devour her insides. They were alone. There was no one there to say goodbye to, or to regret their departure, for the families of the condemned were forbidden to appear at the Purge, a decision taken to prevent commotions capable of jeopardizing the smooth running of the ceremony.

Perhaps, in the silence of a townhouse, far away, the daughter of one of the men looked at her home for the last time.

Maybe she felt as lost as Maiara had felt.

"By their crimes, these eight transgressors were condemned to the Purge," the Herald went on. "Their bodies will go through the waters to the Forbidden East, where they will be devoured by the servants of Xibalba. They will feel the weight of their sins in their flesh. They will bathe their souls with their own blood, and thus their torment will satisfy the will of the glorious Quetzal-Tupā."

Among the convicts were three young men who stood out. Not only by the huge holes in their noses and ears, but by the absolute hauteur of their countenances. Maiara saw no trace of fear, sorrow, or shame in them. The three of them stood impassive, their black eyes fixed somewhere in front of the crowd, but without addressing anyone in particular.

These were Sons of Palenque, as the descendants of the ancient Mayan Empire were called, who refused to accept the end of their people's sovereignty over South Tenoque and chose a life at the margins of society.

Maiara knew that these people were usually imprisoned in criminal acts of protest and condemned to the Sacrifice in the Purge. Yet she had never witnessed the notorious and disconcerting resignation attributed to the heirs of the fallen empire. For a brief moment, that singular demonstration stormed Maiara's senses, and she attempted to decipher it, unsuccessfully.

163

"May the Lords of Xibalba have mercy on their souls." The Herald's voice brought the young teacher back from her contemplation.

The ceremony finally ended. With a nod from the priest and the wild cheers of the audience, the ocelots made their way to the line of condemned men and, pointing their rifles, signaled for them to enter the barge. After the last climb, the boarding plank was suspended, sealing them in the darkness of the stern. From then on, there was no way to open the barge, bound to follow by the Rising Ocean, operated by its automatic system, to the far horizon, where the lights of Xibalba glowed. There, the demons of the underworld would rise from the black earth and devour metal and flesh, appeasing the divine hunger.

That was the price charged by the Lords of Death. Many *baktuns* ago, they fell when Quetzal-Tupá, furious with his ancient Mayan servants, lifted Xibalba in his arms, throwing it to the end of the ocean, bringing the great thunder of the ages, and with him, the storms.

Now the Land of the Dead stood alone in the east, its watchful gods waiting to exert eternal punishment upon those whose crimes— be they murders, robberies, or simple heresy—would tarnish the domains of Quetzal-Tupá.

Men like Ubirajara of Akangatu. Her father.

* * *

The gods were generous that day. Rain was approaching, and from the look of the clouds converging into the bay, it would be strong as it hadn't been for many days. The electric streetcar was right in the middle of the Mei-Long Bridge, where it rose before continuing to wind its way, disappearing between the glazed roofs of Maiara's native land, Arariboia, sister city of Guanabara.

A warning on the tram's internal radio system announced another news bulletin:

"Guanabara's security forces remain clueless on the whereabouts of the

criminal responsible for the death of Counselor Tseng last week," the metal voice said. *"However, evidence indicates that the killer might be the same one who was behind the attacks on the lives of three other dignitaries in the last two weeks. Nicknamed Anhangá by nearby sources..."*

The statement triggered apprehension in some passengers and a rumble about the mysterious wave of attacks began. But Maiara couldn't care less, whether it was the news on the radio, the passengers around her, or the stormy aspect of the Guanabara sky. Head against the window, the teacher was locked in her own thoughts. She couldn't get the resigned eyes of the Sons of Palenque out of her head.

It didn't make any sense.

Maiara didn't attend the sacrifices when she was a little girl. Ever since her father was sentenced to board the damn ship. Still, she remembered well that what was seen among the purged ones was shame, remorse, despair. Never haughtiness. After all, there were men and women doomed to leave family, loves and dreams behind, heading for an eternity of torment.

The tranquility of the young Mayan men was something that terrified Maiara, and she searched for an answer. Nothing disturbed her more than unanswered questions, and that presented a mystery which escaped all understanding. She had become accustomed to unveiling the world, to understanding it through persistent reasoning, and thus bringing knowledge to the surface. That was her obsession and, as a teacher, the reason she had chosen such a vocation in the first place. An obsession in her blood.

The first thunder was heard at the usual time. Maiara's gaze was drawn toward the cove to the south, right at the mouth of the bay. There towered majestically, like a colossal tree of glass and steel, the Guanabara Tower, the heart of the whole region of South Tenoque, where, once upon a time, her father had been a wise and respected researcher.

What would have been his reaction, the teacher always wondered? Had her father felt shame, remorse, fear? Or would he have remained silent and resigned, like those boys? Had he thought of her? Maiara would never know. This was her biggest doubt. The greatest of all her torments.

A bright light illuminated the sky. Drawn by the tower's powerful reactors, the storm swirled around her as if the clouds were a rough sea. Flashes of lightning lit up the sky, leaping through the clouds until they met in the whirlwind, bombarding the top of the tower with divine precision and violence. From there, the monumental structure began its crucial work, absorbing the energy, which for so many ages, had been wasted before the coming of Xibalba to transform the world.

Fortunately, by the grace of Quetzal-Tupá, the Zonguá brothers were able to cross the deadly ice waves in the Dong-Dang Strait, bringing not only the liberation of the Nahuá and Tupi peoples from the cruel Mayan dominion in Tenoque, but the knowledge necessary to build the Energy Towers. Thanks to them, the electricity that flowed in the skies was brought to earth to serve as food for the cities, from the smallest lamp to the vehicle engines, to the automated systems that managed whole buildings.

Blessed be the gods for their generosity!

This was the only truth.

* * *

The Rain ceased as abruptly as it had begun, and as timely as every day. Maiara had just arrived home, a small townhouse on one of the older streets of Arariboia, a house which had belonged to her family for generations.

She took off the pair of earrings, the bracelets and necklaces she carried, tossing them haphazardly over the dresser in the living room, now plunged into the orange glow of the setting sun. There was still an uncomfortable silence in the air, not only inside the house, but also in the street, something unusual for an evening.

The teacher felt uneasy. Shadows seemed to move in the twilight, perceived from the corner of her eyes, and the apprehension grew in her chest. She stood completely still halfway between the living room and her bedroom. For a brief moment, however, one of the planks of the wooden floor continued to creak.

There was someone else there.

Maiara didn't turn toward the noise. An instinctive impulse of survival hit her, and from where she was, she dashed to the door. But it was too late.

A huge hand covered her mouth and a muscular arm wrapped around her waist, pulling her close to the invader. Tears welled in her wide eyes as she felt the warm breath in her ear.

"I won't hurt you," the rough voice promised. "But I need you to listen closely."

Maiara's heart was pounding. She could faint at any moment, not only out of dread, but because of the nauseating odor that came from the bandage around the brute's hand. However, she forced herself to remain alert for a moment longer. She tried to focus her panic on her own instinct for survival, the same instinct that had told her to run before, and that now were telling her to simply wait—and listen.

"Everything you think you know about your life is a lie, Maiara."

For a moment there was silence. Maiara couldn't say what was terrifying her the most, the weight and the strange lucidity contained in the intruder's words, or the fact that he knew her name.

"I have very little time. You'll need to meet me later."

Now Maiara felt truly confused. Panic gave way to disorientation and she stopped struggling to disengage herself from the man. She only prepared for the worst, ignoring that nothing could prepare her for what would follow.

The invader pressed his lips to her ear and said:

"It's about your father."

Then, everything happened at once.

"Tonight, in the Lower City. It will be your only chance."

Maiara's mind was barely able to process what she had just heard when the door to the room opened with a crash. Two, three, many ocelots suddenly appeared, pointing rifles.

"Release her!" one of them shouted. "You're surrounded!"

The reaction of the other was immediate. He pushed Maiara forward, walking backwards to the back of the house. That was when she had the first glimpse of the man who would change her life forever.

An old beaten poncho covered the body of the man, who also had a large bamboo hat hanging from his back. There was something else, something that Maiara couldn't quite place, but that produced a silver flash, the moment he crossed the oblique light that fell on the house.

In one fluid movement, the intruder jumped out the bedroom window, bringing the bamboo hat to his head as he fell. He landed on the sidewalk next to three ocelots that covered the escape route. Without hesitation, he charged, disarming one of them of his rifle and using it to strike the next, right in the stomach. When he fell to his knees, out of breath, he jumped on his back, using it as a platform to fly over the third, striking him in the face with a sharp strike of the sole of his foot. Keeping the momentum, the man threw himself up, landing unscathed on the top of a *xudá* who was walking by.

At the same time, the other ocelots that surrounded the block gathered round. A few pairs rushed to their black combat *quexás*, while others mounted their individual autocycles, turning on the klaxons and firing toward the fugitive. The one who had been hit first still helped his fallen comrades when the radio around his waist sounded.

From its speaker, a commanding voice asked:

"Ground team, what's going on?"

"Perpetrator on the run, sir!" the ocelot replied. "Converging units, I think he's going to the bridge!"

"Engage command," the leader of the ocelots, a short, stout man of Zonguanese features, ordered from Maiara's room. "Block all access there. Get him!"

"Yes, sir!"

Sitting on her couch, Maiara stared at the scene with no reaction. The other ocelots left her home as suddenly as they had invaded it moments before.

"Are you all right?" the Zonguanese asked her.

Even if she could speak, Maiara wouldn't be able to answer.

"I apologize for our abrupt invasion, ma'am. I'm Officer-of-Arms Hwang."

Now that she was paying attention, Maiara noticed that his uniform was distinct from the others by details such as the darker shade of blue and the silver stripes that adorned the shoulder pads. He was an Officer of Weapons, also called a *lobo-guará*.

It was very common for command positions to be occupied by Zonguansese first, second, or third generation, both in Arariboia and Guanabara, and also throughout the rest of the continent.

"We received information that a wanted criminal would be hiding in this region. Our surveillance service saw him when he broke into your house. You were lucky we were around here."

"Yes..." Maiara felt disoriented. "Yes, of course. Thanks. But..."

The teacher couldn't think of anything. The rough voice continued to ring across her mind, like an ongoing echo.

"We believe he may have entered here after noticing our presence. Maybe he was hoping to get a hostage, or something."

Maiara said nothing. The lobo-guará peered into her silent face, noticing how she avoided looking him in the eye.

"Ma'am, what happened just before we arrived?"

Maybe it was the coldness in the inquisitive gaze, maybe it was the slightly aggressive and deeply distant tone of his words, but Hwang's presence made Maiara uncomfortable.

Afraid, she asked:

"Who was he?"

"As I said, a wanted criminal, ma'am. A killer," the lobo-guará replied coldly. "Now, please, answer my question."

Again, Maiara's instinct told her that there was something out of place. There were many criminals in the streets of Arariboia, but an ambush like that wasn't something you saw every day. In fact, Maiara had never witnessed such a thing.

Unless he wasn't just another criminal.

"It's the *Anhangá*," she said, regretting it at once. The officer's face became even more clouded, which she didn't even think was possible. In any case, she couldn't go back now. Nor did she want to. So she insisted, "It's him, isn't it?"

"We don't know his name, ma'am," Hwang snapped. "He's just another criminal to us, like so many."

Maiara didn't know what to think. The mere notion that a wanted assassin had been there, in her home, had already completely disturbed her thoughts. That this could also have any connection with her father, whatever the connection was...

"He grabbed me," she finally said. "And told me to shut up or he'd cut my throat. Then I...I just froze. I think that was when you came in. Sorry, I really can't..."

Maiara chose to lie. After all, the consequences of revealing that there was some connection between Anhangá and her father, considering his infamous past, were too complex to be measured at once.

It's about your father. The echo persisted in her mind.

At best, her life would be ruined once again. At worst, well, that was the problem. It was impossible to anticipate what might happen once the killer's puzzling words came to light.

For now, she had to remain quiet.

She needed to find out for herself.

But first, she had to get that man out of her house. Hwang didn't look away from her for even a second, like a jaguar watching his prey. He stared at her as if he could steal from her eyes the answers he sought.

"It's all right," the officer said at last. "If you remember anything else, please let me know. I'll keep some men on this block as a precaution."

Leaving these words in the air, the Officer-at-Arms left the house. Maiara felt the air returning to her lungs and, in a gesture of relief, buried her face in her hands, wiping the sweat from her temples.

Night came, but the teacher knew that trying to sleep would be useless. Her heart hadn't yet regained its normal rhythm, and the curious glances of passersby at her window only added to her anguish. The hunger for discovery turned her inside out. She had no choice.

She *needed* to know.

* * *

Lower City.

So Arariboia's southern outskirts were called. A part of the city not as prosperous as the port sector, it had become, over the years, a gambling den and a center for clandestine trades, bartering and prostitution. The region suffered from a lack of authority, and the energy grid, which had already been hampered by the decrease in rainfall in recent years, did not reach the homes of its most deprived population. Many ended up resorting to the illegal supply of batteries sold in Guanabara.

Maiara couldn't remember ever being there. Men and women of libertine aspect wandered through the streets, some of them crossing the teacher's path, silent like solitary shadows, others walking in noisy bands to and fro, disappearing into the darkness of alleyways that stank of garbage, cheap booze, and perdition.

However, the dirty atmosphere didn't frighten her. Her mind was oblivious to the unhealthy environment surrounding her. She could only think of the events of that afternoon, of the mysterious thug named Anhangá and her father.

For a long time, that had been an open wound in Maiara's life. The stigma of being the daughter of a purged man haunted her throughout childhood and adolescence. Maiara never knew her mother, dead upon her birth. Her father was all she ever had. Once a man respected for his wisdom and one of the brightest minds at the service of the Center for Climate Studies. One day, however, Yunru Zope, his great research partner, disappeared without a trace. Officers from all over South Tenoque were deployed to investigate, but they didn't have to look hard.

Maiara remembered it as if it were yesterday. The throng crowding at the door of their house, her father with his back to her, while the ocelots surrounded him. At last, the confession. Zope's successes in his work for the Center had piqued her father's envy and the two ended up fighting. Then one night her father had lured Zope to the beach, under the pretext of clearing up the quarrels. His plans, however, were different. That same night Ubirajara killed Zope, throwing his body into the high tide, making thus the ocean itself conceal the evidence.

Over time, Maiara's sadness turned into hatred for the one who should have been watching over her, but who, by his own actions, had been condemned to the most unworthy fate of all. She felt betrayed and remembered the good moments they had shared, the smiles, the walks, the puzzles, all this only increased her pain. So, she conditioned herself to keep only that living memory, the moment of betrayal. She tried to forget his face, but it was an almost impossible task. Even here, so far from home, Maiara stared at her own dark face in the reflection of a dirty windowpane, and the legacy in her eyes showed she was plagued by memories she'd rather forget.

She had already wandered for another hour, looking for she didn't exactly know what. For a moment she wondered, by the gods, what she was doing there. If, on the one hand, the teacher questioned how insane she would be to attend to Anhangá's request, on the other, she longed for a signal, something that would show that she had made the right decision and that she was now following a discovery, her great driving force.

Maiara didn't have a clue.

Suddenly she felt a hand on her hip and watched, out of the corner of her eye, a tiny figure disappear into an alley. A street urchin had stolen her money and run.

"Hey! Stop thief!" she shouted, running after him, but right then she chided herself for her naïveté.

After all, who would help her here? The drunkard in the gutter? The old man who showed her a malicious, toothless grin? A prostitute with her nostrils burned by opium? As far as she knew, that could be the boy's family.

The chase led her into an alley, where someone had abandoned a huge rusty battery. There was no way out, except for a small hole in the wall that looked like the back of an old shed.

"That's really great," she mumbled, trying to see something beyond the fetid darkness of the passage.

A snap behind her caught her attention. As she turned to the entrance to the alley, her heart froze. Half a dozen haggard-looking boys surrounded her. Each one wore bone earrings in their ears and noses, and displayed a disturbing austerity in their eyes, as if they were up to their necks in a very old grudge.

Sons of Palenque.

It was in places like the Lower City that a good many of the heirs of the Lost Empire congregated. For a moment, Maiara thanked the gods for not having any Nahua ancestry. She was a legitimate Tupi-Guarani and hoped that this would increase her chances of leaving this place alive. After all, her chances of escape were small. All she could do was bargain or die fighting. Surrounded, she was surprised at how naturally this last notion had crossed her mind.

That was when steps behind the wall of muscular Mayan youths announced the approach of someone. In his hands, the elderly man carried Maiara's stolen packet of bills, but she paid little attention to it.

"It can't be..." she whispered in awe. "You're..."

"Dead? Yes, my dear." Yunru Zope smiled.

His hair was gray, as was the thick beard on his face. Still, Maiara easily recognized him. How many times had she seen that face printed on leaflets, right next to her father's, illustrating the tragedy of a man's death at the hands of his best friend?

"How is that possible?"

"If you're here, Maiara, perhaps you already know the answer. Perhaps, deep in your heart, you always knew that your father could not be the terrible man your accusers claimed him to be."

Maiara felt her legs weaken. Chaotic winds were blowing in her spirit. It was impossible to think clearly. Countless questions were lost in the confusion of thoughts, in the revolution of infinite uncertainty.

"I know you're confused, that's good. It means that your mind hasn't closed completely yet. Otherwise, you would feel anger and not doubt, as the intolerant do."

"Stay away from me!" Maiara threatened, noticing the older man's approach.

"It's all right."

"What's going on here? Who are you?"

"All I can do is tell you a part of the whole. Ubirajara is innocent. At least he's innocent of the murder charge...of my murder. As for the rest, as to what is about to happen... Well, I don't know about that. It all depends on your idea of innocence, I think."

Old Zope's gaze seemed to be lost within himself. There was a deep fear in his words that made Maiara question the man's lucidity, as well as the reality of it all.

"Was my father innocent?" she asked, trying to placate her inner storm. "Was it all a lie, something to frame him?"

"Yes, it was. A scheme planned by your father. See, Maiara, Ubirajara wanted things to happen just like that. He wanted to be sacrificed."

This was incredibly absurd. Who in their right mind would

choose to be banished to Xibalba? Unless her father was mad, like that old man in front of her appeared to be.

"You're lying! Tell the truth!"

"I've already said that I can only tell you a part of the whole. The rest you will have to see for yourself. It's the only way."

"Way for what?"

"For you to believe. To understand why your father did what he did. The importance of what we discovered together. Which will change everything."

For a moment the wind ceased, and a clear sky opened in Maiara's soul. In this sky, she saw the face of her father, sharper than she believed she could ever see again. He smiled at her.

"What about you?" she asked when the clouds covered her again. "Why did you do this, disappearing like this... Letting my father be convicted of a crime he wasn't guilty of?"

"That was my share of the sacrifice." Zope nodded, serene. "I would have gladly gone in his place. But Ubirajara insisted. For you."

"Because of me?"

"Of course. After all, I had no one. I never had children. I'd have no one to trust to do what your father expects you to do. Now you must go. We acted as we did to make sure that nobody was following you. Even so, the ocelots are watching you. They won't take long to get here."

"No, no... I have so many questions. No one knows I'm here."

"They do. They've been watching you for days. Since *he* started."

Maiara stopped. It was obvious. A bamboo hat, a silver reflection. Anhangá. He wasn't the one the guard was looking for that afternoon, and it wasn't by chance that they came so quickly to her house. They were already there, waiting for him. Which could only mean that they knew he would seek her out. But why?

"What does all this have to do with me?"

"Your father's research, the discovery he sacrificed to protect, continues exactly where he left it. Waiting for you."

With that, Zope pointed to the east, where a powerful spotlight, shining white as a beacon, illuminated the pinnacle of the Guanabara Tower.

"They don't know what your father discovered. Ubirajara made sure his secret would leave with him for Xibalba. At least until you were ready for it."

"It's been so long…" Maiara stared at the Tower on the other side of the bay. "Whatever my father left is gone now."

"Ubirajara was a man of forethought, Maiara. Don't make the same mistake as those who condemned him. Don't underestimate him. Now go, before they find you here. Go, for your father, for me. For all of us."

In such a situation, many would say they felt the world revolved around them. For Maiara, it was the other way around. Everything around her seemed static, frozen in an ultimate moment of full lucidity. She felt like a lost child, and as such she longed for her father's hand to guide her in the next step.

Deep down, maybe that was exactly what she was doing.

"Wind activity," Zope whispered to her as he left the alley. "That's what you should look for up there. Don't forget it."

With her heart lost at the crossroads of fear and gratitude, she replied:

"May the gods protect us."

The old man just smiled.

* * *

All the time between the haunted farewell in the Lower City the night before and the end of that school day seemed to her little more than a lucid dream. The words she said to the kids in her class didn't sound like hers. Maiara felt distant, as if she had become a mere spectator in the theater of her life.

Her eyes reached the top of the Tower and the memory of a distant, sunny morning filled her thoughts. Her father had just opened the access door to the huge terrace and she, a little girl, had just had the best day of her life. She remembered the cold in her belly as she carefully traversed the walkways between the lightning rods and the cells of attraction, reaching the parapet of what at the time she thought was the top of the world.

This was the first time she had revisited those moments, for...a very long time. One last perfect day with her father. From then on, everything gave way to uncertainty, fear, shame. Now, however, everything had changed once more, and Maiara felt remorse for trying to forget how happy they had been back in the day.

Zope was alive. Alive. Anhangá had been right up to now. Everything she'd believed was a lie. But why? Why would Zope and her father plot such a thing? The former had told her that she needed to see it to believe it. Maiara didn't know if it was true, but there was no other choice.

With any luck, she'd be home before the Rain.

* * *

The security inside the complex was rigid. Half a dozen armed officers guarded the entrance hall, not to mention dozens of others scattered among the thirty floors of the Tower. Except for exceptional cases, that entry was used only by groups of visitors duly awaited and registered. Fortunately, for Maiara, she was an exceptional case.

Once considered a symbol of the progress and triumph of divine wisdom, the Guanabara Tower guarded within it the largest library of the city-state. As a teacher, Maiara had the right to study the tomes stored in there. Naturally the most delicate items were restricted to the High Priesthood. Maiara only hoped that the work of her father, a self-confessed *murderer*, wouldn't be included in such a category.

The panoramic elevator provided Maiara with a stunning view of all of Guanabara, its buildings and avenues blooming through the green of the woods, the gray of the hills and the blue of the sea. Once inside the library, it wasn't difficult to find the files she was looking for. Soon the teacher arranged her father's life work on the table right in front of her. She scanned the tomes, locating the one mentioned by Zope.

Wind Activity Bulletin said the cover. Maiara began to read it carefully, but was soon lost amid the technical jargon of the trials, analyses, and forecasts regarding the weather conditions in South Tenoque. She sighed, beginning to doubt the purpose of her visit, when she realized something peculiar about the tome: a subtle variation in the shade of black of the writing, more intense in certain sections of the pages. A close look showed that such patterns weren't random, on the contrary, they seemed to form perfect geometric figures within each block of text. Triangles, squares, trapezes, almost like in a...yes!

This was it.

The teacher's heart was pounding. She tried to control her shaking hands with excitement as she reached for a pencil and a few blank sheets of paper in her bag. Quickly, she began to transcribe each of the bold sections of the volume, which she now saw, were pieces of a jigsaw puzzle.

Coming from her father, it couldn't be any different.

It was a Zonguanese tangram, a jigsaw made up of distinct geometric shapes that, when correctly combined, resulted in a perfect square like the sheet of a tome. After copying the texts, Maiara began to fold and cut her leaves, finding the figures she had observed before. With the agility of a mind trained for years in solving puzzles, she organized the pieces, recombining passages at first glance incongruous, but which, once aligned, transformed themselves, acquiring their true meaning.

Maiara's eyes filled with tears.

Her father's secret message was revealed.

If you are reading this, it means that I left you a long time ago, and for this I apologize. I don't expect you to forgive me. I just wish my words could bring you some sort of closure.

The rains are almost through. Our measurements are perfect. Our ominous prediction of the near future is your reality. With each new cycle, the water is less abundant, the thunder less thunderous and lightning, the blood of our life, less brilliant.

Anticipating this fact was our job. That's what we did. We walked the path of the storm to its cradle. We followed the trail of the wind. But the wind has no voice. We prayed. And we prayed so much to be wrong.

What, after all, is the unit of measurement of faith?

What causes the gods to destroy one people to the ascension of another? Maybe the Mayans know the answer. After all, they have never stopped believing in their gods. For them, we live a lie. But if we don't believe, does it mean that they are the deluded ones?

The paradox persists. The gods must be imperfect, or not be at all. The possibility is real. What if we are not the dream of the gods? What if we are the dreamers? There is only one way to find out. I need to take the wind path.

Zope will wait for my signal. If you are reading this, then we were right. We certainly were not the first. Where will the others be?

I love you. I hope to meet you again.

The air was sucked out of the library. Even alone, Maiara felt surrounded, suffocated. It was cold. What was her father saying?

By the gods, what was he saying?

It couldn't be true. She had to get out of here. Run away, as fast as she could, and then forget the last two days had happened. She would beg for the protection of the guard so that Anhangá would be kept away and would again lock her father's memories in some dark and sad corner of her mind.

But then came the relief, when her heart refused to take on the terrified reaction her mind wanted. Because, contrary to all reason, Maiara rejected fear and embraced what could only be compared to the warm feeling of awakening.

It was still too early to be carried away by daydreams. There was only one place Maiara could go to if she wanted to get to the bottom of it. A sense of urgency rushed over her heart, like the Rain that would soon fall. But now it didn't matter to her. She needed to find Zope again.

* * *

The Lower City was more deserted in the hours before the Rain. Maiara announced her presence, waited, gossiped through blurred windows, and even through the fetid hole where the old man had escaped. There was no sign of the Sons of Palenque or Yunru Zope.

"Waiting for someone, Professor?"

She had fallen into the trap again.

Now, though, it was not the friendly, familiar face of Zope before her, but Officer Hwang's. There were no fewer than eight of his ocelots beside him, like watchdogs.

"What are you doing here?" Maiara asked, with all authority she could muster.

"I could ask you the same question. You're too far from home."

"I came to visit a…friend."

"Then we won't have a problem." The lobo-guará grinned. "Of course, if you're lying to me, you not only will have committed a crime, but also made the task of protecting you difficult. You know…"

Hwang moved slowly toward Maiara, who stepped back instinctively, reproaching herself again for her foolishness. Zope had warned her about the Guard's vigilance, and she had ignored his concern.

"…this is a dangerous neighborhood. If you're not completely honest with me, telling me exactly what you came here to do, and, most importantly, what you found on your short walk to the Tower, I'll have to go with my men. Hence, who will defend you?"

"Me."

The rough voice came from above. As if materialized from the air, Anhangá appeared on the roof of the shed that enclosed the alley, just behind Maiara.

"So I was right," Hwang said, appearing superior. "I just needed a piece of cheese to get the mouse out of the hole. This ends here, killer."

The ocelots engaged their rifles and pistols. Anhangá jumped, landing in front of Maiara with a somersault. He put his hand behind his head, pulling a *miao dao*, a Zonguanese sword with a wide blade, through a slit in the poncho.

The sky answered the first shot with the clamor of thunder. Maiara's instincts made her throw herself behind the abandoned battery the instant the first drops of rain and blood mingled in a brief red cloud. The ocelot screamed, clutching his torn leg through the *miao dao*, his mouth wide open, receiving the storm that seemed to rage against him.

Anhangá was a black spot interspersed between flashes of lightning. The ocelots tried to warn each other, but their voices were no match for the roar of the storm. So it was too late. The shadow was already rushing again, wrenching out a cry of pain from one ocelot, pulling another one from the fray. The arrows of water fell heavily and created a thin mist just above the asphalt. And Anhangá came running again.

Punished by the incessant flashes, Maiara's eyes saw a fragmented world. To her perception, Anhangá's blade swirled slowly, cutting through air and water, opening for a second a flap in the curtain of rain, an instant of dry, untouched air before the mutilated droplets could fall again.

In seconds, Hwang was all that remained of the squad. His ocelots were down, with moans, blood pumping in his arms and legs. They would survive, but they were no longer able to wield a weapon, much less oppose a killer with apparently superhuman reflexes.

Taking advantage of the moment, Anhangá went to Maiara. In shock, the teacher was cowering next to the battery. Anhangá was looming over her, crouched like a bird of prey, searching for some wound on her body.

"Are you okay?"

Maiara was so nervous she couldn't do more than nod, accompanied by an inaudible whisper. Anhangá raised his head slightly over the battery, aware of the approach of the lobo-guará.

That's when Maiara saw it.

At first glance, she thought it was a prank, something her frightened eyes played on her. She stared attentively at the figure, paying close attention to the details in the terrible crimson patch of burned skin on the murderer's arm. To his surprise, Maiara caught him by the wrist, exposing still more the signal that, in that brief moment in which he had risen, his old poncho could not hide.

"The Purge brand..."

Pieces of the puzzle fell gracefully into place. Maiara understood at last, and the sensation frightened her. The next question was impossible.

"Have you been to Xibalba?" Her sweet voice coincided with another thunder peel exploding in the sky. "You...you've met my father?"

"Yes."

"Is he alive? Dad...is my father alive?"

"The last time I saw him, yes."

Maiara felt a wave of numbness wash through her body. Stunned, she let go of his arm, without noticing it. Her parted mouth received the rain that flowed down her face until she managed to articulate a single word:

"How?"

Then Hwang's angry voice sounded:

"Surrender, assassin! Reinforcements are on the way, you won't be able to escape!"

"Your father is responsible for me being here. He saw what I could do and he chose me to bring the message to you. To them, even." Anhangá pointed at Hwang.

"Which message?" The noise of the storm forced Maiara to shout.

"A revolution is on its way. It has already begun, silent as a breeze, there, on the other side of the ocean. Soon it will turn into a storm that will once again sweep away the curtain of lies of the Nahua. But when it does, you must also be prepared here. The fourteenth *baktun* is approaching. The Transition. Your father thinks that's when they will act. We need to act sooner."

"But what is there?" the teacher asked, not sure if she really wanted to know. "In Xibalba?"

"A new world."

Hwang was moving. Anhangá could hear his footsteps splashing in the puddles. He tucked his bamboo hat over his head and flexed his body like a jaguar preparing his attack.

"The Zonguanese know it's all a lie. What fell in the east and brought the Rain was something else, not Xibalba. And it's happening. Soon there will be an energy shortage, unless they get another source. That's what they're looking for. There is a ruined land beyond the horizon and they are already there, allied with the Nahua elite, exploring the energy impregnated in the soil, using the purged as slave labor."

Suddenly Maiara remembered the look of resignation on those faces pierced by earrings of bone.

"The Sons of Palenque, they also know this..."

"They always knew."

Anhangá placed her hand gently on Maiara's shoulder and their eyes met through the threads of rain streaming from the bamboo hat. Despite his clothes, he had Tupi-Guarani features, such as hers.

"And now you know it too."

Her time was up. Suddenly, Anhangá jumped on the battery that sheltered them. The whirl of his body made the old poncho open, creating a curtain of water that confused Hwang's sight. Then the *miao dao* flew through the air through the rain in a swift turn until it reached the officer's hand in full, shredding the pistol he held and cutting off three fingers. The lobo-guará screamed, until he was silenced by a violent kick in the face.

When he came to, Hwang was half-buried in a muddy puddle. Sharp pain radiated from the mutilated hand and he felt something small and solid roaming the mass of blood in his mouth. He spat out one of his teeth.

"I have a message for your superiors," Anhangá growled in his ear.

Officer Hwang's eyes throbbed with hate, but he wasn't a fool. He knew he was beaten. It would do no good to react or rage, or say anything, even if his wounded mouth allowed him.

"Tell them their lives are now my indulgence. That, now, I am the only god to be feared. You've seen what I can do. Already they realize that there is no one that I can't reach. You'll leave the girl alone, can you hear me? She's only collateral damage. If I even suspect that you're pestering her in any way, I don't care who is responsible, I will kill you. You got it? Nod your head if I was clear enough."

After a moment of helplessly ruminating over all that hatred, Hwang obeyed Anhangá's command.

The killer slapped the lobo-guará again, turning to Maiara.

"Go away. Don't ever come back here. Go now...the rain is abating."

Maiara nodded. Her feet trod puddles of water and blood, and she had to go around the fallen ocelots to leave the alley. Before leaving the stage of the bloody battle, the teacher took one last look at the scene before her. Eight ocelots, in addition to their officer, overcome by a single man. Of all that Maiara had learned in the last two days, there was still the great question: who was Anhangá anyway?

She knew, however, that it was not yet time to find out.

For now, she had to trust him, and more than that, she had to trust her father.

* * *

The accounts of the following days served as additional confirmation of the lies told by their rulers. The official report of the High Priesthood reported that Anhangá was not acting alone and that he had actually received help from more than a dozen Mayan ruffians. According to the statement, were it not for the heroic performance of Officer-at-Arms Hwang in the Lower City, the lives of those valiant ocelots would have been lost at the hands of the killer and his new comrades.

This was the perfect excuse for an even greater oppression of the Sons of Palenque from that moment on. It could not have been more ironic, in fact, and in the days that followed, Maiara wondered if that had not been the intention of Anhangá all along.

It brought to mind the image of young Mayans being apprehended, day after day, for crimes they weren't guilty of, being condemned to damnation in the underworld of Xibalba. In their hearts, however, it would be certain that they were heading not for the punishment imposed by a god who had betrayed them, but for the opportunity of a new revolution.

A New World, where her father would be waiting for them together, to unravel what was perhaps the greatest of mysteries, or the greatest of lies. Anhangá had said that her father trusted her to be his eyes, ears, and arms on this side of the ocean.

But, after all, how to start changing the world?

Come to think of it, it all started on a morning like this.

Now quiet, Luc and his classmates watch their teacher with eager eyes, anxious to unravel the world and trusting her to help them. Young minds, fresh soil where lies had not yet been sown like weeds. Just alive and fertile.

"Are you all right, teacher?" one of the little ones asked as he noticed her silence.

Maiara smiled. She still felt watched, day after day, but she was counting on the threat of Anhangá to leave the sinister forces of Guanabara far enough away for her to do what she knew best.

To teach.

Maybe she couldn't change the world, but she couldn't be in a better place to begin.

For the Rains are abating.

And the fourteenth *baktun* is approaching.

* * *

André S. Silva is a carioca (native of Rio de Janeiro), a civil servant, and a student of Letters at UFRJ. He started writing fanfictions inspired by the X-Files series in the late 1990s. He collaborated with OTP Filmes in the screenwriting of short films and had short stories in the 2011 Literary Challenge and the Henry Evaristo Prize for Fantastic Literature 2012, both on the website A Irmandade (The Brotherhood). For Editora Draco, he participated in two anthologies, *Dragões* (2012) and *Excalibur* (2013). Find him on Twitter @andressilva.

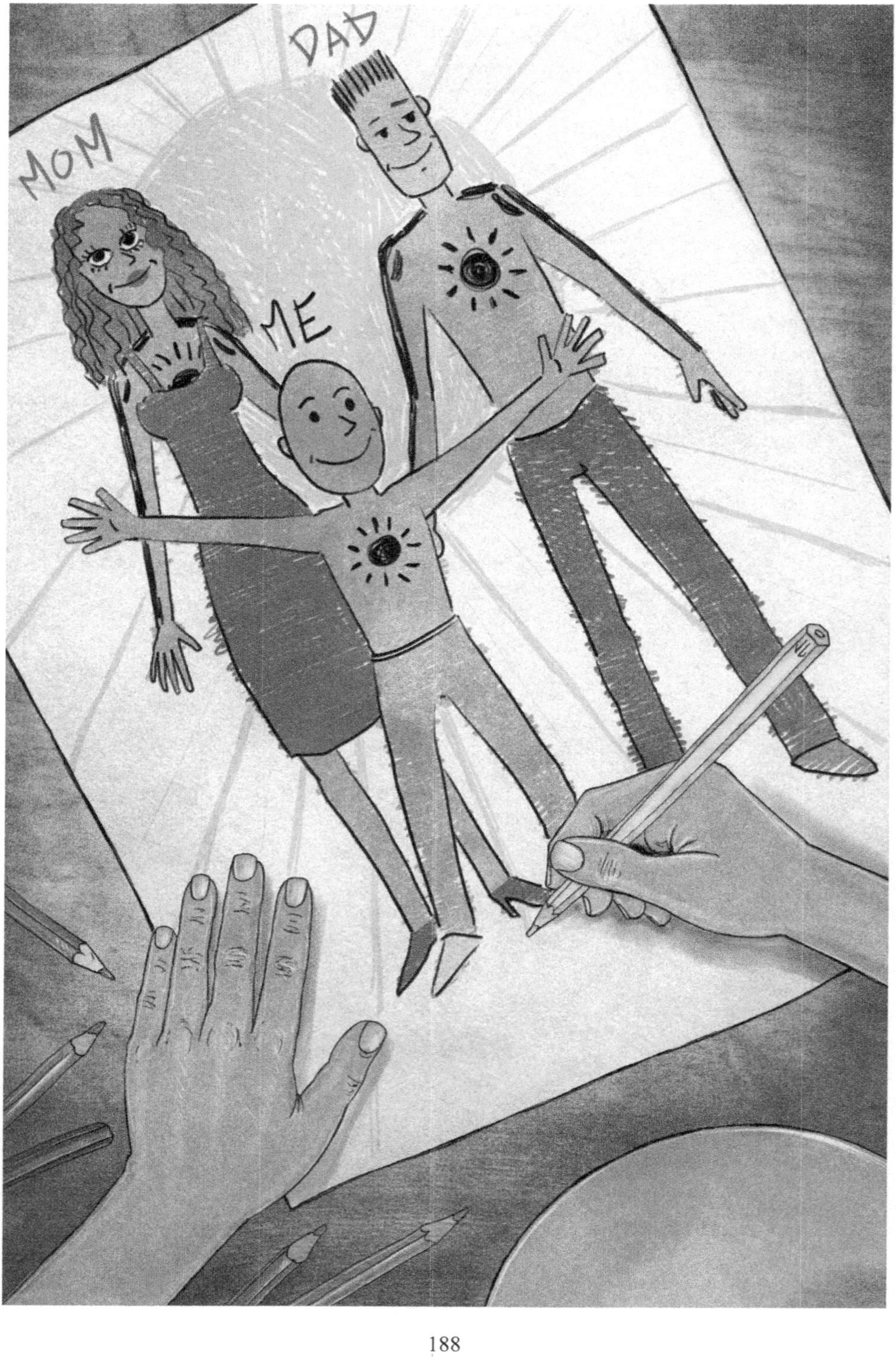
MOM
DAD
ME

SUN IN THE HEART
Roberta Spindler

He woke up to the persistent whistle of the old-fashioned digital alarm clock, vibrating on the bedside table. Slowly, he sat on the bed, stretched his arms and popped his joints. Through the wide window stretching across almost the entire wall, he could see the sunrise painting the sky with many shades of orange. But not even this beautiful panorama was enough to ease his restlessness. Sighing, he turned to the side and stared at the woman still sleeping under the covers.

"Wake up." He brushed the dark hair from her face and whispered in her ear. "It's almost time."

She frowned and shifted, drowsy, muttering some disconnected words.

"Let's go. If you lose the morning light, you will get weak."

With a single tug, he pushed the duvet aside and revealed his wife's slender body. He smiled at that sight and let his eyes wander across the tanned outline. Her skin was the color of honey, her muscles were sharp and well defined. He leaned closer and kissed her on the back, just above the biggest sun tattoo she had. The gesture seemed to wake her, because she shivered and let out a muffled laugh.

"Okay, okay. You win." She sat on the edge of the bed and stared out the window at the brightening sky. She took a deep breath, as if mustering the courage to get up. "Today is the big day. Are you nervous?"

He wrapped his arms around her, both covered by a thick black line that began at the wrists and ended at the base of her neck, and kissed the back of her neck.

"Terrified. You?"

Before answering, she closed her eyes and lowered her head, allowing herself to be distracted by that brief caress.

"I didn't want to wake up. Does that answer your question?"

Hand in hand, they walked to the spacious balcony and let the sunshine bathe their naked bodies. Relaxing, he closed his eyes and felt a light electric shock through the various tattoos that covered him. At the same time, he was much more willing, renewed.

"Do you think he's going to miss breakfast?" he asked timidly, still keeping his eyes closed.

"Since he abhors that watery porridge we force him to eat, I don't think he will," his wife said good-naturedly.

He tried to smile, but the tension made him stop in his tracks. He tightened his grip on her hand and watched her out of the corner of his eye.

"I'm scared, Laura. What if the surgery goes wrong and the implants don't work? Are we really doing the right thing?"

Laura silenced his questions with a long kiss. It was incredible how her simple presence could make him ignore any problem.

"Try to calm down, Lúcio," she said as they parted, sounding secure. She was always so strong… "Everything is going to work, and soon he'll be here with us. The sun will make him stronger, you'll see."

* * *

After the mandatory full hour of sunbathing, the couple left the balcony. While Laura went to the bathroom, Lúcio put on a pair of jeans and headed for his son's room. He opened the door slowly, afraid the hinges would make a noise, but found the little boy already awake sitting on the bed with his legs crossed.

"Hi, Dad, good morning," his son greeted him with his characteristic reedy voice. "Is it time to go?"

At the sight of his son, Lúcio felt a stifling grip on his chest. *Today, I could lose him forever.* He forced himself to leave behind any distressing thoughts and walked to the edge of the bed. The smile on his lips was insincere, but the boy didn't seem to notice that.

"We still have time, Élio. No need to get up so early." He stroked the boy's smooth head, completely devoid of hair, and carried him easily. In spite of being almost seven years old, he was a very light and thin child. "Are you so eager to get your first tattoo?"

The boy nodded agreement.

"I want a heart sun just like yours," he said excitedly, pointing to his father's chest where his largest implant was located. It was a black circle, the size of an enclosed fist, with short straight lines on the outside. Since he first saw the mark, Élio had been fascinated by its shape. He didn't take long to create that affectionate nickname.

Lúcio tenderly kissed his son's face.

"Sorry, but this time it will be a star, son." The star-studded implant was safest for children, and even so, in Élio's case, it was already a risk.

Élio frowned disapprovingly and hugged his father's neck tighter.

"Dad, I told the other boys that I was going to have a very special tattoo. Everyone has a star, even that dumbass Jorge."

Being the only boy in his class who hadn't gotten an implant yet was making Élio's life a hell of sorts. Lúcio knew the children could be cruel, but he had to restrain his anger and ask his son to accept the taunts passively. Sometimes it was painful being a father.

"Whoa! What does that mean, Mr. Élio? Your mother will be very upset if she hears you say those ugly words."

The boy huffed and apologized, but his heart wasn't in it. It was painful to be a good son too.

* * *

After being lucky enough to pick up the practically deserted *Expresso Solaris*—one of the oldest solar-powered Brazilian trains—they arrived at the hospital half an hour early. The doctor responsible for the surgery soon came to greet them. He appeared with his sophisticated tablet in hand, followed by two nurses. With sympathy, they managed to overcome Élio's initial mistrust and led him into the bedroom. They were going to prepare him for the procedure.

When she saw herself alone with the surgeon, Laura wasted no time. She greeted him with a strong handshake and then bombarded him with a tsunami of questions. The man smiled an amused smile that irritated Lúcio. *Don't laugh with the life of my son at stake, you bastard.*

"I understand your concern; Élio's case is quite special. The treatment for leukemia has weakened his immune system, but we can't postpone the procedure any longer. Since he is unable to catch the sun, I fear his body will not recover and thus will become increasingly fragile." He turned his attention to the tablet and ran his finger over the screen until he found Élio's medical record. He showed it to his parents, as if to prove his point. "However, I want to make it clear that my team and I are confident. Your son is a young man with a lot of will power, and we will do everything possible so that he can play again without fear."

Even though he understood the good intentions of the doctor, Lúcio knew that those words were empty. All the recommendations and specialist diplomas didn't make the famous Doctor Mateus Carvalho able to guarantee the wellbeing of small Élio. And that uncertainty was driving a worried parent into madness. Feeling an uncomfortable cold in his stomach, he decided to let his wife do the talking and walked away in silence.

Hands hidden in his pockets, he wandered aimlessly through the corridors of the hospital and watched the morning rush of the staff. He ended up stopping on a beautiful balcony in the waiting room on the third floor. Right there, many years before, there had been a cafeteria, now unnecessary for humanity's new standards.

In a few footsteps, he reached out and rested his hands on the concrete railing. He watched the skyline of the city of São Paulo, with its huge buildings of mirrored glass that reached right into a few clouds. In that open environment, the solar tattoos reacted almost immediately and sent energy to all the cells of his body. Even so, he wasn't feeling better at all.

A terrible fear overwhelmed his thoughts. Wouldn't it better to delay the surgery? Élio was already almost two years late, would he really need implants? He stared at the sun with a bitter look and cursed it in a whisper. Almost ninety-seven years had passed since the implants had begun to be used and they had already acquired the status of true salvation of mankind. But in Lucio's view, it was ironic that men depended on sunlight to survive, since the problems began when solar flares, already absurdly intense since 2214, tripled their strength three years later.

Little by little, the crops were dying, as well as the people, for the most part, victims of a devastating skin cancer. There was utter chaos; everyone was afraid to leave their homes, even at night, and all life on the planet hung by a thread. However, when all seemed lost, Brazilian scientist Ricardo Paes Nobre presented to the world his latest creation: nanomachines that could reverse the harmful effects of the sun's rays on the human body, preventing them from causing burns and tumors.

The revelation of the discovery caused a real confusion. Acquiring the new technology became a life-and-death affair and thousands of people were willing to spend all their savings to become guinea pigs in the early experiments. They didn't even know that Paes Nobre's discovery was not limited to just protecting people from the sun's rays. In fact, that was its least impressive feature.

As fruits and vegetables had become scarce and animals also struggled to survive, the renowned Brazilian scientist sought an alternative that would solve once and for all the problems that humanity would face in the long run with the lack of food. He established the concept of photonutrition, something similar to the process of the photosynthesis of plants.

That discovery marked the dawn of a new era and also the filling of the country's coffers. Brazil became a leader in the manufacture of solar implants and, in a short time, had already set its trade balance straight and was among the most important nations of the planet. Ricardo Paes Nobre was considered a hero of humanity and won several prizes, in addition to an important position in government. Lúcio never quite understood how a guy who claimed that his deeds were done for the good of the planet had managed to get rich so fast.

For some people, all that squalor was just a good opportunity to make some profit.

Over the years, Paes Nobre's technology had undergone improvements thanks to the help of research groups from other countries. The complex solar plates—which fed the nanomachines injected into the bloodstream—evolved, becoming no more invasive than a tattoo. After a short period of adaptation, improvements in the implanted population's quality of life were detected. They lived longer and almost never got sick. They also had no need to feed themselves and, depending on the kind of implant they were using, they could go for long periods without drinking water too. The notion that implants made their users stronger and healthier was established as unquestionable unanimity.

But it's also true that we became more and more dependent. We abandoned secular habits and we became..." Lúcio frowned in disapproval. *My grandfather died at the age of ninety-two, but now, for someone to be considered elderly, he must reach twice that age. Can we still consider ourselves human or have we become something completely different?*

"I finally found him," Laura's voice interrupted her husband's wanderings. In quick strides, she reached out and wrapped him in a tight hug. "The surgery will start in an hour and a half. What are you doing here alone?"

"I was thinking, remembering the past." He kept his eyes fixed on the numerous buildings of the metropolis of São Paulo. "As a child, before I got my first implant, I had a real fascination with peaches. At that time, we could still find some fruit in the market and I always begged my mother to buy some peaches, even if they were very expensive."

Lúcio paused and smiled sadly. Those memories always aroused a whirlwind of contradictory feelings.

"I remember crying so much the day before my surgery. I was so terrified that I would never taste my favorite food again that I even asked my father to let go of the procedure. Of course my pleas were totally ignored. After all, what does a five-year-old understand about life?"

Laura rested her chin on her husband's left shoulder and hugged him harder as she felt tears fall onto her arms.

"The funny thing is that today, even if I try hard, I can't remember the taste of peaches. I don't understand why it was so important to me." He turned to face the woman, his face filled with apprehension. "I don't know, Laura, but sometimes I have the feeling that I missed something very important that day. I believe that a part of me was taken away when this phototattoo was engraved on my skin."

They stared at each other for a long moment, until Lúcio had the guts to disclose what was troubling him.

"Could it be that in a few years, Élio will feel the same way?"

Neither of them was able to answer that last question. Finally, after an uncomfortable silence, Laura turned her face and sighed.

"Do you remember when I told you about my younger brother's death?"

"His name was Sergio, was it not?" Lúcio wiped the tears from his face, looking intrigued. "You never told me much about it."

"He was twelve when he died, and I was fifteen." She took a step away from her husband and decided to lean against the balcony rail too. "You know his death was something that struck me a lot, maybe because of that you respected my silence."

He opened his mouth to speak, but she didn't allow it. She went on, in a subdued voice.

"Please don't say anything. I want to tell you how it all happened."

Looking at the serious expression on his wife's face, Lúcio merely nodded guardedly. Talking about family was a taboo to Laura, so he thought it best to give her all the freedom she needed.

"I never told anyone this, but Sergio died because of me." She crossed her arms, visibly uncomfortable. "Remember that some fifteen years ago there was that very strong solar explosion that damaged several implants? Well, then, my brother and I were affected. I will never forget the pain I felt and my mother's cries of desperation..."

Moved, Lúcio tried to comfort her, but she escaped his touch.

"It would all be okay if my parents had had the money to pay for two implants, but our family had been experiencing financial difficulties since Sérgio's first operation. So even with the help of friends and close relatives, Mom and Dad could only get enough for one implant. So it all started to revolve around a single question: who should be saved, me or my brother?"

Lúcio's eyes widened, for he didn't know what to say. Of course he knew the government's unfair implant policy. Many people were left to die for not being able to afford the surgery and that always made him feel angry. Hearing Laura's assertion that she too had experienced such a tragedy, he felt even worse.

"Oh, my God, Laura. Why didn't you tell me?"

"Because you have such weird ideas in your head." The woman frowned. "You'd definitely want to get in a fight, or some kind of reparation."

Those last words made Lúcio tremble in anger. He just wanted the world to be a fairer place that people could choose. Was that weird at all? Proving that she knew him better than anyone else, Laura answered his questions without even hearing them.

"I don't want any trouble, Lúcio. As painful as it may have been, Sérgio's death is in the past. I just decided to disclose it to you now to make it very clear."

The look she gave him was so significant that all his anger evaporated. He loved his wife and child above anything and would do anything—even ignore his own convictions—to keep them happy and safe.

"When my parents chose me instead of my brother, I didn't dare ask why. I thought it was too cruel. But as Sérgio lay dying and my family started to collapse, I finally understood their motives." She wiped away the tears so hard that it left red spots on her face; she seemed angry with herself for such a display of emotion. "I was the strongest of the two. The only one capable of surviving that tragedy. And that's exactly what I did, I did what they expected of me. I…"

At that moment she lost her composure and burst into tears. It took her a few moments to compose herself, but she continued to refuse her husband's comfort.

"I know how you feel about this surgery, and in a way I even understand your fears. However, after everything I have lived, I can't help but find it childish." She pointed to his chest, right at his sun heart. "You question the validity of implants because you never had to live without them. Your family was rich, they could pay for anything the government offered or the damn Paes Noble invented. So you can't possibly imagine suffering, you have no idea what despair is."

"Laura, that is so unfair!" He couldn't control himself. "I live with our son every day, of course I know! That's why I wonder if this is the only way!"

"Sorry, Lúcio, but you don't know. You can't even know!" She hesitated for a moment, perhaps measuring her words. However, after all she had said, it was too late to hold back. "You have a fanciful view of the world, you still believe that we can go back to what we were before. Wake up! That time is over! We don't need food anymore, we don't need peaches! Implants are not something evil, they have not turned us into monsters. On the contrary, they are our only salvation and it is past time that you accept it!"

Distraught, Lúcio took a few steps back and stepped away from the rail. His wife's harsh words hurt him more than he'd like to admit.

"Unlike my parents, we can afford it. We have the power to make our son stop suffering. So I can't accept this resistance. The chances may be minimal, but who do you think you are to even think of denying this blessing to our son? Élio deserves this chance more than anyone else!"

To keep her from seeing him crying, Lúcio left the porch almost running and got lost in the corridors of the hospital. He reappeared only ten minutes before Élio was taken to the operating room. Facing the door to his son's room, he didn't know what to do. About to turn the knob, his hand stopped halfway.

"Aren't you going to talk to him?" Laura appeared behind him and startled him.

My God, woman, isn't it enough all I had to hear from you? Slowly and ashamed to show his red eyes, he turned to face her.

"I'd rather not have to say anything. If I get in there, it will look like I'm going to say goodbye. I can't think that way."

"Lúcio, I understand your concerns. Damn it, I feel lost too! But Élio is only seven years old. He needs to hear that it's going to be okay, he needs his father."

Those words hit him like a slap, forcing him to wake up. What kind of father left his son at the most important moment of his life?

Laura put her hand to his cheek and stroked it. She seemed totally recovered from the difficult conversation, her face showing no signs of crying. How could she?

"Sorry if I was too hard on you." Her voice sounded delicate. "With this whole situation, I'm in tatters. I ended up lashing my frustration on you and it was wrong."

He covered her hand with his and guided it to his lips.

"Don't apologize, I think I had it coming. My convictions have blinded me to what really matters," he admitted, embarrassed, and finally opened the door. "My son needs me."

* * *

It took two weeks for Élio to leave the ICU and one more for implant functionalities to be evaluated. After making sure that the kid's body hadn't rejected the nanomachines and solar panels, Dr. Mateus decided it was time to test the implant in a real environment. Then, at noon on a typical summer morning, the medical staff gathered around the boy and led him to one of the balconies of the hospital.

When he was released to leave the wheelchair, Élio looked at his parents with apprehension and only stood up when he received an encouraging smile from Laura. It was only normal to feel insecure, but the climate on the balcony was even more tense because of that. A nurse approached and removed the white shirt and bandages that covered the boy's chest, revealing two black triangles that, superimposed, formed a star.

With a hesitant expression, Élio took a deep breath and took his first steps toward the sun. It didn't take long and his eyes widened.

"I'm vibrating inside," he declared with a mix of fear and euphoria. "The heat is spreading through my chest!"

Dr. Mateus took a step forward and knelt to stay at the same height as the boy.

"That's normal, Élio. You may also feel something like little shocks, but don't worry."

The boy nodded quickly and turned his eyes to his father. Lúcio held his breath at the smile that was addressed to him.

"My heart beats hard, Dad!" Élio put his hand on the implant. "I feel much better already!"

That simple statement generated a small commemoration from the medical staff. Laura let out a small cry of joy and Mateus smiled with satisfaction. Everyone began to greet each other with pats on the back and sincere compliments, but Lúcio kept his distance. He could not look away from his son.

Élio seemed mesmerized. He kept his arms wide open, as if to embrace the light that strengthened more and more every moment. His chest rose and fell as the phototattoo shimmered discreetly. The smile on his lips was contagious, even if a solitary tear still stained his pale face. All Lúcio wanted was to hug him, but the first few hours of sunshine were the most important and shouldn't be interrupted.

Relieved, he breathed again. He put his hands to his face and rubbed his tired eyes. That last month had been unbearable, but it was finally over. Everything should get in place now and Élio would be able to live a normal life. However, something still didn't seem right.

I know I made the most sensible decision, but...

Suddenly Laura touched his shoulder and kissed him euphorically. He stared at her in surprise. Even after the apology, the couple was still distant. So it was only natural that they remained withdrawn during Élio's recovery, each one bound to his or her own fears. Now his wife seemed willing to forget her quarrels and start over.

"Still thinking about peaches?" she asked with an amused smile on her lips.

Instead of being offended by the joke, Lúcio smiled back. He shook his head and hugged the beloved woman, kissing her gently on the forehead. *Enough of discord in this family.*

"No, no peaches." He looked at his son again. "For the moment, being alive is enough."

* * *

Roberta Spindler was born in Belém do Pará in 1985. She graduated in advertising and currently works as a video editor. A self-confessed nerd, she loves comics, games, and RPGs. She has written since her teens and is passionate about fantastic literature. She has stories published in ebook and in several anthologies, including *Super-Heróis* (2013) and *Meu amor é um mito* (2012), from Editora Draco. She is the co-author of the novel *Contos de Meigan — A Fúria dos Cártagos* (2011). See her blog at www.rspindler.tumblr.com and find her on Twitter @robertaspindler.

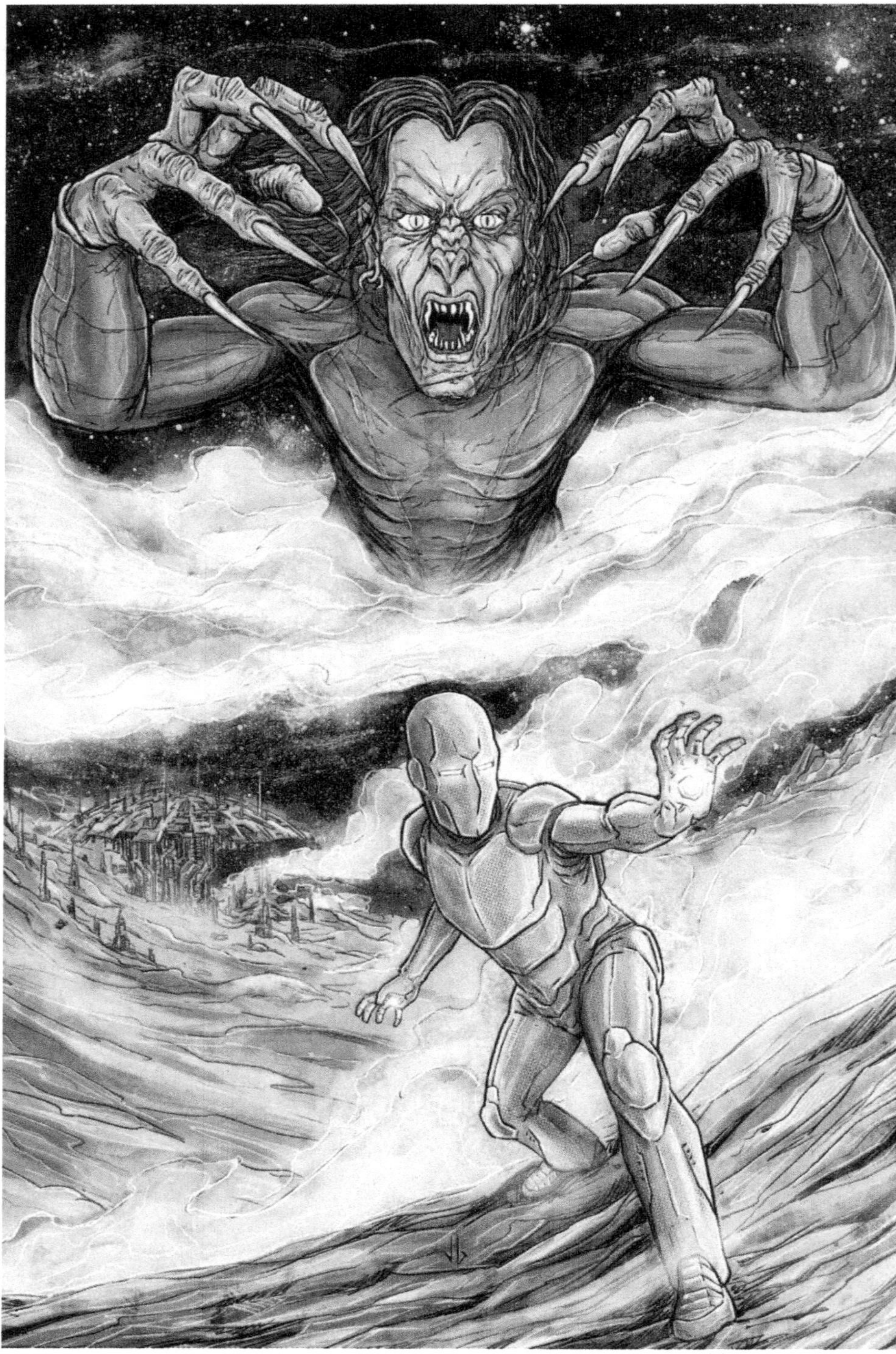

COBALT BLUE AND THE ENIGMA
Gerson Lodi-Ribeiro

1 PREMATURE LAUNCH

Under the approving eye of the gray general, the tall fellow takes three awkward footsteps in his metallic exoskeleton, until he stands on the shiny disk set on a raised pedestal in the center of the laboratory.

The general shakes his head in dismay. The individual supported by the computerized titanium apparatus pretends not to notice the bitterness of his hierarchical superior. He keeps the mask of cadaverous indifference buckled in his pale countenance. Until two years ago, he had been part of an elite command of military intelligence.

Before the accident.

Now, who knows, if all goes well and the project gets the green light, won't he be given a second chance?

Standing inside the titanium structure, dressed only in shorts, the very tall, thin man closes his jaws, turns his head with a certain effort to direct an inquisitive look at the superior.

"Go on." The general nods to the officer who still stands stiff on the disk. Then he stares at the stout scientist at his side, eyebrows arched in a tacit but emphatic interrogation.

"Just wake the VIB by voice command," the chief scientist of the project clarifies the obvious to the commander of the secret base. "Come on, Spider."

"Activate," the quadriplegic officer subvocalizes the standard command.

The voice recognition system of the armored smart garment sings the preliminary activation chord. The former member of the Brazilian Intelligence Service hears through the neurolink implanted in the middle ear:

"Positive recognition of primary content. Enter passcode in ten seconds."

Jonas Spider subvocalizes the three words that compose the current code. The tiny implant in his larynx captures the vibrations of the vocal cords and transmits them to the suit.

"Activation code correct. Completed vocal and retinal recognition. Prepare for activation."

The edges of the disc vibrate and rise, folding inward in a fluid motion, until it engages the user's feet. From there they spread, penetrating inside the exoskeleton, climbing up his legs.. At first, the diameter of the metal circle remains unchanged, though plates and pieces unfold from the main body of the disk, climbing and covering the lieutenant's body inside the exoskeleton, like a gigantic origami endowed with a life of its own.

As the origami pieces rise up through the untrammeled body of the tetraplegic, wrapping it and adjusting to each other perfectly, parts of the exoskeleton loosen and fall, drumming on the pedestal in a cacophony of strident clangs.

"Amazing," the general whispers at the scientist's ear. "As much as I watch this activation process, I still don't get used to the volition of the armor…"

"Assembling the exoskeleton again is usually the most work. But if the suit passes our tests today, our friend Spider won't need it anymore." The head of the project makes a vague gesture toward the titanium components scattered around the pedestal. He smiles thoughtfully as he gazes down at the officer's body, now clothed from the neck down by the self-adjusting suit segments. Four symmetrical concave plates emerge from the thick collar and merge into a harmonious whole around the quadriplegic officer's head, creating a mask resembling a glowing elm in the same silver hues as the rest of the metal suit. He can barely glimpse the wearer's blue eyes blazing through narrow rectangular crevices. "In any case, it wouldn't make any sense at all to make the user wear a biocybernetic suit whose operation is based on the integration of armies of nanobots as if it was an ordinary, everyday suit. We finally achieved absolute success in appropriating the pure science of Palmares, turning it into legitimate Brazilian leading edge technology."

"We expected no different from your team, my dear Cabezas." The general nods, smiling. "Even so, I confess I feel very proud of you. Finally, we formulated an answer to the enemy's supposed secret weapon advantage. An apparatus capable of transforming an incapacitated operative into a supersoldier."

"A secret enemy weapon whose existence has never been proven." Júlio Cabezas lets out a short laugh.

"You scientists and your categorical evidence..." The base commander crosses his arms over his chest full of medals, somewhat off-kilter in his rough campaign uniform. "The accumulation of evidence seems to have convinced most of our analysts."

"Full Activation," the smart suit whispers in the wearer's ear. "All systems operate within the programmed nominal parameters."

"That silver tone sounds a little conspicuous to me," the commander says wryly. A silly, derivative maneuver to change the course of the conversation. "Have the camouflage programs been realigned yet?"

"We completed the last tests this morning." Júlio caresses his goatee in amusement. "Show General Heinz, Spider."

The officer nods inside the suit and subvocalizes:

"Camouflage. Demonstration."

Before the captain's ecstatic gaze, the armor darkens gradually, until it becomes indistinguishable from a shadow. After a few seconds, it switches to a brownish-green shade. Suddenly it takes on the color of the clear sands of the Brazilian beaches and after that the bluish-green hue of the ocean. Finally, it stabilizes in a gray tint, more discreet than the original silver.

"Excellent, Cabezas," the general gives the scientist a friendly pat on the back. "You did it!"

"Note that these are only the primary options for demo mode." Júlio gestures, excited. "On a real mission, the suit is programmed to decide alone what camouflage to take, according to the conditions prevailing in the environment around it."

The base commander turns to face the lieutenant in the armor.

"Hey, Spider? Feeling better now?"

"Much better, General. Inside here I feel whole again." He subvocalizes so that the suit retracts the helmet. As if it had a will of its own, the VIB assumes the cobalt blue with gold stars characteristic of the Brazilian flag. With his face again visible, he smiles at his superior. "More even than before the accident. Almost like a superhero." Serious again, he gives him a perfect salute. "Ready to get back to action, sir."

"Very well, Lieutenant," the senior military man says in a low but excited tone. "Welcome back."

He can't decide whether to praise the officer who was reincorporated by the initiative or admonish him for taking too much liberty with the colors of the nation.

So this is it? Do we need a superhero, a Captain Cobalt, to take on the Secret Weapon of Palmares?

Stuck in this quandary, he merely smiles. He sighs deeply and changes the subject:

"What about power systems?"

"In addition to the conventional atomic battery for its own

emergency generation, according to the latest change in specs, we introduced an array of experimental quantum batacitors, capable of absorbing energy directly from compact fusion reactors and M-E converters."

"Splendid." Heinz gives the operative wrapped in cobalt blue a radiant look. Since, with the support of the United Nations, Palmares succeeded in banning the production of antimatter on a commercial scale from the Earth, direct absorption from a matter-energy converter would only become necessary in space. "Exactly what the SBI needed."

"I just don't understand one thing." Júlio shakes his head, puzzled. "Why this insistence on installing batacitors capable of extracting energy from converters?"

"In order to answer this question, maybe it would be better to leave aside the congratulations and begin at once the briefing of the first real mission on account of the project."

"First mission?" The scientist smiles uncertainly. "As far as I'm concerned, we haven't finished the last tests yet."

"Easy, Cabezas." The general rests his hand on the scientist's shoulder. "Under normal conditions, of course we would all like to continue with the tests and armor simulations, according to the approved schedule. Unfortunately, however, the homeland needs us as quickly as possible and far from here."

"What do you mean, Ivar?" Júlio turns to face his longtime friend.

"Infiltrated Palmarine agents are giving us hell in the moons of Jupiter again. This in itself wouldn't be big news, nor a direct concern to us. However, the latest reports confirm a terrible suspicion: the reappearance of an old acquaintance of our intelligence services, the mysterious operative codenamed Enigma, whose existence and real nature we have both discussed for a long time."

"As I mentioned earlier, the hypothesis using this creative, original codename is nothing more than speculation." Júlio caresses his goatee with a wry smile. "Probably an artifice, an excuse capable of justifying in one fell swoop most of our failures of the previous centuries."

"Speculation or reality, the fact is that we lost three of our best agents trying to fight an impalpable opponent in the Jovian system. The Minister of Security has practically demanded that our project act in the case, in order to contribute to…uh…to the solution of this problem."

"On the Jovian satellites?" Júlio frowns. "Project VIB is simply not ready to act…"

"More specifically, in the international scientific base just inaugurated under the auspices of the UN on Europa." An abrupt knife-hand gesture points out that Heinz admits no argument. "As I recall, the armored smart suit was designed precisely to deal with this kind of contingency, namely the superior power of the enemy operatives."

"We don't have the necessary means to …"

"Don't worry about the means. The Ministry of Space Defense will come up with the necessary funds."

"But, Ivar, the suit is not yet …"

"What do you say, Spider?" The base commander stares intently at the lantern-jawed officer, all wrapped in the beautiful starry cobalt blue glow. "Do you feel prepared to take down this Enigma guy on Europa?"

"I'm ready to take action, General. Thanks for the vote of confidence. You can count on me."

"If this mission is inevitable—" Júlio shrugs and nods toward the vast rectangular portal at one end of the laboratory. "—let's go to the last test, then. Reveal your *secret identity* to the general."

"With pleasure." Jonas flashes a happy smile before subvocalizing to his suit. "Civilian clothes."

"Perfect." Heinz exhales a satisfied sigh. Before his eyes, the quadriplegic wrapped in cobalt armor becomes a stocky, handsome fellow, a faithful copy of Lieutenant Jonas Spider prior to the accident. In the convincing simulation generated by the armor, the

military man wears a white and blue striped suit of the latest fashion. "It passes visual inspection, easy. However, you should avoid body contact."

"Evidently." Júlio nods. "We still can't disguise the metallic consistency of VIB."

"It doesn't matter." The general shrugs. "We deal with what we have. What about the metal detectors?"

"Show him." Júlio gestures to the lieutenant.

The civilian version of Spider heads in rapid, elastic steps to the rectangular portal at the edge of the room.

"Presence of circuit of detection of metallic objects." The suit whispers in his ear. "Intelligent deflectors activated."

The portal emits intermittent buzzing and pulses to indicate the activation.

Jonas steps under the device. The portal remains silent except for a discreet beep of approval. A green light comes on at the control panel.

"Excellent." Heinz rubs his hands together. "This detector is identical to those installed in the Galileo Base access hatches."

"So I guess it will be easier for Spider to pass as a new technician."

"That's the idea." Heinz stares at the scientist with a serious look. "The armor can handle the X-ray fine. But what about the infrared?"

"There's nothing like that on Galileo hatches, as far as we know." Julius smiles. "And once inside, the VIB will map the location of the infrared sensors and produce the proper pseudo-signatures."

"It's not the sensors and the hatches that worry me." The general frowns. "Not at all."

2 THE HIDDEN HISTORY OF PALMARES

"Fuck off, Pellê. I don't have any more time for your pitiful researches." The middle-aged fat guy turns in his chair, turning his back to his friend, a little older and gray-haired, but in better physical shape, sitting across from the multifunctional desk. "Unlike some others, I don't live off copyrights. I need to work."

"Damn, Fernandes. I thought I could count on you." Gilson replies, his tone deliberately friendly in the effort to captivate the journalist. Apparently, after all these years, he still has not forgotten the disagreement that culminated in the successful publication of *Brazil: Feet of Clay* in Palmares. "You're the only one I can trust for this kind of analysis."

"Look, there's no point in coming in with this 'old-time' chatter. I don't fuck with this shit anymore." Fernandes turns the chair back, facing his friend with his finger. "Fuck you, I won't be a sitting duck! Besides, if your suspicions are unfounded, it's going to be a fucking waste of time."

"You know very well they're not unfounded."

"Then it's even worse." Fernandes lets go an irritated sigh. "Because if what you suspect is true, then I want to be far away when the Palmares people come after you."

"I admit that the survey I'm doing carries some risk."

"Talk about fucking euphemisms, huh, Pellê! *Some risk* is a guy in my health condition eating what I eat and drinking what I drink. Some risk is crossing a busy street after drinking a lot." Fernandes laughs with contempt. "Some risk my hairy ass! We're talking a surefire risk here. Because in this case, as you are fond of saying, the order of factors changes the final result in the equation."

"Don't overstate it, Fernandes."

"Overstating it, me?" The fat man holds his hand flat against his chest in a studied dramatic gesture. "Who insisted that we deal with this investigation only in person? You've said it yourself that it wasn't safe for us to exchange information through the Network."

"All right, all right. I confess that I'm also afraid of what might befall us if the Palmares secret service finds what we have discovered."

"What you discovered. Or rather, what you claim to have discovered. Because I, my dear, want nothing to do with this."

"Too late. You already know almost as much as I do about this feast of mysterious deaths throughout the centuries."

"I wish I hadn't known anything," Fernandes murmurs softly. "Damned be the day when you came to me to reveal this basketful of absurdities."

"They're not absurdities."

"I wish they were." Fernandes shuffles uncomfortably in the ergonomic armchair. "Listen, man, you don't have any proof. Just a lot of empty conjectures. Let's put a pin in this subject…"

"I don't have any proof, that's true. But we have very strong evidence."

The fat man shakes his head with the expression of someone who would like to be somewhere else.

Because, if his old friend and fellow writer is right, the History of Brazil for the last three centuries will have to be rewritten.

On the other hand, it is hard to accept the fact that, ever since the wars against the Dutch, Palmares has always possessed a supernatural, mysterious, and infallible method of exterminating the Portuguese and Brazilian enemies who stood in their way.

Gilson Pellegrino seems to sense where his friend's thoughts are straying to, for it reminds him of the facts that the other would rather forget:

"Remember what I told you about the first mysterious death I discovered?"

"Fernão Carrilho, right?" Fernandes shivers. "Butchered at his camp on the eve of the Treason of Palmares."

"Exactly. I discovered another apocryphal account, a document more than three centuries old in the Tower of Tombo, in Lisbon. According to this account, the corpse of the Master-of-Field Carrilho was found without a single drop of blood."

"Apocryphal report, my ass."

"Anyway, I discovered a few days ago that Carrilho was not the first victim."

"Oh, no?"

"Negative. I found evidence of two killing sprees under mysterious circumstances. One in Salvador, the other in Recife, spread out over a few years before the War of Treason."

"Deaths in strange circumstances don't even get close to the Fernão Carrilho massacre. Even without this exsanguinated corpse bullshit, the disappearance of the main Portuguese-Brazilian military leader, a few days before that crucial battle in the shadow of the walls of Recife, made life easier for the first Zumbi."

"Changing the subject a little, remember that story of Diamantina that I told you about? Of that Devil Captain, killed by the Diamond Contractor?"

"The one who later escaped to Palmares with weapons and personal effects?"

"The same fellow. João Fernandes de Oliveira, a relative of yours." Gilson risks a smile. When he sees his friend is not amused, he goes on in a more serious tone. "Did you know I found a sketch, in fact a portrait, of that Devil? A hand drawing by a popular artist on the day of his hanging."

"A sketch?"

"Yes. Made with charcoal. Want to take a look at it?"

Fernandes nibbles at his lower lip. He shakes his head and snorts before nodding reluctantly with a sulky gesture.

"Show me, then." Gilson taps the indicator on the multifunctional desk top three times.

Fernandes nods, now more emphatically, in order to make himself understood by the equipment's routines.

The gray-haired man pulls out a tiny green cube from one of the multiple pockets of his pants and puts it on the table top. The black surface begins to blaze with bluish glints and emits the characteristic peep of the access release.

"The Devil Captain of the Geraes." Gilson grunts softly. He gazes impatiently at the violet veins radiating above the cube. When nothing else happens, he explains: "Sketch of execution day in Diamantina."

The face of a rough-looking man, with vaguely Amerindian-looking features, though he doesn't resemble a Tupi at all, floats over the black top. A slight gesture from Gilson's left hand and the misshapen face begins to rotate clockwise.

As the face turns to the journalist, he exhales slowly. The sketch depicts a horrendous individual. Gigantic eyes with yellow irises and pupils sharpened like those of a cat. Porcine nose with dilated nostrils, erected upright like a pair of dark caves; leathery lips; long hair with thick strands like an old piaçava broom.

"These colors, the skin, the eyes, how did your program extrapolate those from a simple coal sketch?"

"Artificial intelligence routines, of course." Gilson smiles. "They used the descriptions of the Devil Captain collected at that time to fill in the blanks."

"Didn't you say that the Palmares secret service had suppressed all descriptions of the criminal?"

"I was wrong. Apparently, João Fernandes himself took care of it. But there were descriptions of the Devil Captain before the time of his capture."

"This bastard is a real monster." Fernandes now looks at the nape of the holographic sketch covered by thick bristly hair.

"Really, beyond monstrous, and it also looks a bit like the description of a guy who has been prowling around the port of Boston for a decade or so, that is, three or four years before the start of the American Revolution."

"Are you going to tell me that your mysterious murderer painted the town red in the Yankee war of independence?"

"I have no proof of that." Gilson spreads his hands with a sly grin on his lips. "There is no timely sketch of the murderer this time. But if you want, I can ask my Simbaac to generate a holo constructed from the descriptions of the police authorities of colonial Boston."

"You don't have to." Fernandes giggles in pure nervousness. "I know very well how clever these self-conscious artificial symbiotics are at anticipating the expectations of the users."

"You should put your prejudices aside and start wearing one. It is a matter of quality of life."

"No thank you." As he shakes his head, the journalist manages to keep his angry stare fixed on the laid-back face of his technophile friend. *Pellê and his gadgets!* No way I will become a slave to a conceited conglomeration of A.I. routines. "I'm afraid to think about what the cyberneticists have programmed into these simbaacs..."

"I have already seen you harboring the same mistrust regarding other First Republic inventions." Gilson shrugs with a wry smile. "Anyway, do you remember that storm on the high seas that sank most of the British force sent to quell the insurrection at the port of Boston in 1775?"

"I may not use those smart symbiotics, but know that I take my doses of mnemonic enzymes all right." Fernandes glances suspiciously at his friend. "Come on, what's the wreck of that task force got to do with your so-called mysterious homicides sponsored by the secret service of Palmares? As far as I know, there were no Luso-Brazilians aboard those British ships."

"Indeed, I suppose there weren't. There was, however, an undeniable interest on the part of the Palmarine elite in fostering separatist movements in America."

"Nobody ignores this interest. This doesn't imply that agents or supernatural forces of the Republic caused those shipwrecks."

"What if I told you that your distant relative, João Fernandes, was in Philadelphia a few weeks before those fateful wrecks?"

"I would say that this is no coincidence." The journalist smiles innocently. "After all, we know that Palmares was negotiating the supply of arms and ammunition to the rebels. We also know that, at the end of his life, João Fernandes became a kind of informal diplomat from Palmares."

"You've got a point. But, what if I told you there was no storm on the night of the shipwrecks? You can check it by loading the weather conditions of all previous and later days in regions near and far from Massachusetts Bay. Then, just ask your systems to interpolate the data in a short-term climate simulation. There was no storm." Gilson lays his fingers on the multifunctional top. In the end, he knows that his friend, a technophobe, won't accept this suggestion. "Probably it was only a lame excuse from the British to justify the real reason for the claims."

"Okay, Pellê. And what would that be?"

"I don't know for sure. But I don't rule out the possibility of a Palmarine naval intervention."

"Against the *Royal Navy*?" Fernandes lets out a whistle and arches his eyebrow in a theatrical way to emphasize disbelief. "The guys held the greatest naval power of the day. Palmares didn't have by far the means necessary to meet them."

"Maybe it wouldn't take that many ships."

"It's all right. You served in the Navy, not me." The journalist winks at the interlocutor.

"I'm serious." Gilson peers at the ceiling thoughtfully. "Only one or two ships, with crew members with superhuman powers."

"There you go again." Fernandes offers his friend his best condescending smile. "What a huge obsession, eh?"

"There are times when I wonder if instead of several agents with superhuman powers we might not be dealing with a single individual..."

"Impossible. According to their own research, the mysterious murders have been occurring for over three hundred years."

"It's true." Gilson nods, intrigued. "However, the *modus operandi* is almost always the same and the few descriptions, spread over several countries and hundreds of years, coincide with each other."

"You're not suggesting that we're facing an immortal murderer, are you?"

"I confess that this has been one of my working hypotheses." Gilson shakes his head. "A hypothesis that keeps me awake at night."

"You look even crazier than I thought."

"Yes, my friend." The gray-haired man gives the fat man a defiant look. "It's just to check if I'm going crazy that I came here to ask you for help. I need you to analyze the data I collected in the last few months and the correlations and assumptions I have made between these data."

"I don't want to be involved."

"But you looked at the previous batch of data."

"And I bitterly regretted that analysis." Fernandes stares at his friend with an apprehensive look. "You were not the only one to lose your sleep. To this day I have nightmares about your conclusions."

"You're the only person I can turn to."

"It's all right. I confess I was overwhelmed by your conclusions." The journalist shakes his hands in disgust. "But there remains the indisputable fact that you have no proof whatsoever."

"Please help me find it."

"No, Pellê. Not this time."

"But why?

Fernandes releases a deep sigh before replying:

"Because I'm afraid." He raises his hand to stop the other's response. "Afraid of what will happen to us if this whole story turns out to be true."

"Look, Fernandes, I'm afraid too." Gilson stares at his friend with a straight face. "But I need to know." In view of his interlocutor's lack of reaction, he proposes as a last resort, "Let's agree on this: If my worst suspicions are confirmed, we only disclose the results of our study if we both agree on the terms of this disclosure, okay?"

"And you're going to resist the temptation to blow the whistle?"

"You have my word."

Carlos Fernandes stares his old friend in the eye. He doesn't answer immediately, and when he does, he doesn't give in:

"You're not going to leave me alone until I agree to help you in this madness, are you?"

"It's not crazy, and deep down, you want to know the truth too."

The worst thing was that Pellê was right.

* * *

First, Fernandes verifies the consistency of the information stored in the green cube his friend gave him.

As discreetly as possible, he follows in the footsteps of the renowned writer, getting roughly the same facts and figures.

Then the correlation work. Since he doesn't have the talent and patience to undertake the task himself, he turns to the intranet of *Voice of the Morning*, the news agency for which he works. Of course he takes every conceivable safeguard of secrecy. Because, in this respect, he is as paranoid as his old friend. He nurtures a deep conviction that the intelligence service of Palmares is able to infiltrate wherever there is a personal network, public or private, so it pays to be careful.

When the multifunctional's manager program announces the completion of the processing task and displays the results, Fernandes shoots to his feet.

In addition to the events written by his friend on previous occasions, even more: according to Sir Abraham Stoker's memoirs, a misshapen Indian associated with the Palmares embassy in London had influenced him in the writing of his masterpiece, *Dracula*.

"Son of a bitch! Pellê was right!"

Frightened, he says to the multifunc:

"Connect me to Pellê."

The program tries to comply with the order. It tries to comply for seventy-two hours, until it says, to the despair of its user, that Gilson Pellegrino is not connected to the Net.

"Disconnected? Not possible! Unless..."

No. Better not to even think about it!

Now that he has discovered that everything Pellê has suspected is true and that Palmares most likely has a superpowerful, immortal secret agent, he can't contact his friend.

Whereabouts unknown.

He feels terrified. Alone in the face of an unfathomable veiled threat. *Terrified, no. Creeped out.*

He gets really terrified when he finds out that that Pellê's simbaac hasn't connected at all in the last two weeks.

3 EVASIVE MANEUVERS

To reach Jupiter's orbit in record time, Jonas Spider boards in an unmanned high acceleration vehicle. With its antimatter-filled converter, the *Fulgurant* is able to maintain a constant acceleration of 25 m / s2. Although designed as an unmanned spacecraft to conduct high-priority loads to the Outer System, it has a tiny individual cabin and even a life-sustaining apparatus that has been concealed inside its secondary propellers. Of course, an ordinary crewman or passenger couldn't withstand a 150% acceleration higher than that of Earth's gravity for too long. Neither would it survive unscathed by the radiation emanating from the proton-antiproton collisions of the M-E converter, since the material annihilator shielding was kept to a minimum, in order to optimize the performance of the craft and increase its payload capacity. However, high acceleration and ionizing radiation don't pose insurmountable risks to the wearer of an armored smart suit.

Unlike most unmanned transports, giant spacecrafts that slowly move from Earth's orbit to the Outer System, taking months or years to reach their final destinations, a vehicle of high acceleration—because it shows urgency—draws attention to itself. That's why it's not fitting for Jonas to come to Europa aboard a ship of this class. What's more, it's an unmanned spacecraft. Hence, the need to stop in a discreet orbital station of Io, boarding there like a normal passenger for Europa.

* * *

Tied in his bed to prevent a sudden movement from hurling him into the cabin, Jonas Spider casts a puzzled glance at the hologram of

Jupiter slowly turning on the roof of the compartment. He smiles weakly. Even in this less-than-lunar gravitational acceleration, he would lay inert, if not for the protection of the suit.

A week in Galileo and no sign of the mysterious adversary. Worst of all was the feeling that this Enigma, whoever or whatever he is, got wind of his coming. Otherwise, how to explain that it had disappeared or, an alarming hypothesis, is hidden, undetectable to the sensors of the VIB?

It's most likely that Enigma has escaped from the international scientific base to some other place on Europa. Jonas doesn't even exclude the possibility that his adversary has traveled upward, to one of the satellite's three orbital stations. Although the launch logs don't indicate departures of manned vehicles after their arrival from Io in the *Oswaldo Cruz*, it is possible that the Palmarine intelligence has unregistered ships. He doesn't intend to commit the old naïve mistake of underestimating the enemy's ingenuity, responsible for many of the failures in Brazilian military history.

So much rush—the journey from Earth's orbit to Jupiter done in an acceleration of more than two gravities, provided by the new M-E converters and only bearable with the VIB compensation system fully activated—for nothing.

It's almost as if this Enigma had sensed my imminent arrival... In any case, at least there have been no casualties among the Service operatives since then.

The most senior agent, Vitor Machado, enters the stateroom he shares with Spider. With a rank equivalent to major, Machado is one of three operatives who survived the incursions of the Enigma and the only one informed about the mission and resources of Lieutenant Spider.

"Confirmed." Machado stands in front of the other, whispering huskily. "All the 212 Palmarinos residing in Galileo are normal human beings."

"So, as far as we know, they don't qualify as the Enigma." Jonas unties himself, raises his torso and sits on the bed to face his superior. *And if, contrary to what Intelligence has been stating for decades, our opponent turns out to be only a normal human, a subject whose extraordinary powers are provided by VIB-like armor? We wouldn't be able to detect him when he was out of the shell ...*

"Following the recommendation of the Service command, I checked the tomographic profiles of the other 397 foreigners."

"They're normal, too." At the agent's somber expression, Spider concludes, discouraged.

"Right. On my own, I checked the 59 Brazilian citizens residing at the base. As you may already guess, they are exactly who we thought they were."

"Enigma has left the base."

"How?" Machado frowns darkly. "We checked all the launches prior to the arrival of the *Oswaldo Cruz*. Our agents on other bases on Europa and on the other satellites have verified the identities of all foreigners who have come from here. We are pretty sure that Enigma did not leave Galileo this way."

"What if he used a surface vehicle?"

"Possible but unlikely. The pressurized tractors available here have a range of two hundred miles and the nearest station is more than three times as far away."

"Besides, it's a mere organic mining station of the Asian Consortium." Spider nods to his superior. "There are only five residents there."

"Unless our adversary is somewhere out there."

"You mean, out in the open?"

"That, or an improvised shelter near the base."

"We could throw a handful of microprobes to check this—" Spider breaks off as he remembers the obvious. "No. The probes' detection systems would interfere with the equipment that the several scientific teams have spread around Galileo."

"Yeah." Machado closes his jaws before proposing in a low voice,

"Would you be able to explore the vicinity of the base without disturbing the ongoing experiments out there?"

"It's possible. The suit has sophisticated camouflage circuits. It was designed for the purpose of being virtually undetectable."

"Maybe it's worth a search, then."

* * *

A new habitat for the True People. *Who would have thought? A son of the night under the light of Jupiter...* A whole virgin planet just for him!

He had never imagined that the Ebony would trust him so much as to allow him to leave Earth, a planet to which his ancestors referred to as the "Mortal World." Much less for Europa, the most exciting scientific frontier in the Solar System.

His Palmarine allies were ingenious, he gave them that. After all, the First Republic owes science not only for its very existence but, above all, for the opportunity to explore this world of exotic beauty. A satellite endowed with alien life, though microscopic and generally sealed under layers of tens of miles of ice more solid than any terrestrial rock.

However, there in Aurora Fault, those tens of kilometers are reduced to just over a hundred meters. That was why Galileo was erected on this site. For this reason, the scientific prospects of a humanity eager to find multicellular alien life are concentrated around the international scientific station.

The son-of-the-night extends the claws of his huge hands with a satisfied smile on his leathery lips. A normal person—a short-life— would die in seconds out there without a hermetically sealed space suit and an efficient life-support system. The problem is that space suits can be traced from a distance. However, as far as he is concerned, this insulated clothing and compact oxygen tank are enough to give him a modicum of comfort, although he could even survive without such luxuries if the mission required it.

He reminds himself that he shouldn't refer to ordinary people as "short-lives." According to the Elder's teachings, when among humans, one should not even think of himself as "son-of-the-night" or a member of the "True People." He must strive to think of himself only as a privileged agent of the First Republic. For the humans of this enlightened age are sensitive and indeed susceptible, and cunning by far. In this last respect, Palmarine masters are often even more crafty than other humans. Hence, it's not appropriate to discard the hypothesis that its sages have secret resources capable of foretelling, from tiny clues, their innermost thoughts and the way they consider their collaborators and antagonists.

Muscles tightening, he turns his left arm in a swift motion, sinking the sharp claws into the stone-hard watery ice. He reaches control of the skiff half a meter below the surface. Once activated, the device's atomic stack heats the cabin by sublimating the ice into water vapor.

If the decision was his to make, he would have preferred to remain in Galileo and face the Brazilian enemy. However, the Ebony's rulings were unequivocal and, as always, inflexible. He must keep the secret of his existence protected from the special operative sent by the Brazilian Intelligence Service. He will fulfill the order, notwithstanding the conviction that he would be able to defeat his opponent on Europa or on Earth.

Sullen, he crouches in the skiff, closes his eyes and prepares to hibernate for a few days. In his heart, independent of the postulates of the Way of Stealth and the doctrine that had been inculcated by the Ebony Circle, he stifles the impression that there is no honor in this evasive strategy.

4 DUEL IN THE LIGHT OF JUPITER

Jonas crosses the vicinity of Galileo in concentric circles of increasing diameter. The patrol has been going on for hours. No results.

It's not that there are no trails, tracks, and footprints around the base. Quite the opposite. Evidence of the wanderings of scientists and their pressurized tractors abounds in the vicinity. While most of the base's facilities are underground, the numerous sensors and equipment planted on the surface surrounding the Aurora Fault require the occasional presence of residents as well as their robots and vehicles.

As the sun passes the zenith in the region, there are times when a tenuous methane mist condenses out of the residual atmosphere of Europa. Nothing that compares to Titan's methane rains. However, enough to erase the tracks and footprints, making the plain adjacent to the fault recover for a few hours the smooth, pristine appearance prevailing before the arrival of the first manned expeditions.

For better or for worse, there had been no methane dew for days. Therefore, it's the profusion of clues and not its absence that confuses the sensors of the VIB. At a temperature on the order of 70 degrees absolute, the infrared tracker proves useless. In passive mode—so as not to interfere with scientific instruments—metal and electromagnetic radiation detectors would remain inert, unless they could pass close enough to access to their opponent's eventual lair. Under such adverse conditions, he would only discover the whereabouts of the Enigma in an extremely improbable stroke of luck.

Discouraged, he enlarges again the diameter of the concentric circle that he traverses around the base. Under the management of the VIB, the several active armor sensors automatically disengage at unpredictable intervals whenever Jonas passes too close to any more sensitive observation instrument. If, on the one hand, the safeguards reassure the Brazilian operative, confirming that he remains undetectable, on the other, this intermittent *blindness* disturbs the strategy he was trying to implement on his patrol.

When he completes six hours on the outside, he decides to abort the mission. Although he does not entirely rule out the possibility that Enigma is hidden somewhere in Galileo's vicinity, he concludes that it will be almost impossible to find him.

On the way to the nearest access hatch of the citadel, less than fifty meters from the aqueous ice bunker housing the hatch, the primary metal detector releases a sharp peep. The locator then projects an animated green arrow into his visual field to indicate direction. Then, the manager conjures the hologram of a rectangular brick encased in the ice. According to the indicators, the compartment is six meters ahead and lies less than one meter deep.

It's not an entrance. Apparently, this is a self-contained shelter.

He raises his right hand and subvocalizes the activation of the termolaser. Invisible to human vision, but not to VIB sensors, the coherent jet emerges from his open palm, bathing the ice sheet covering the brick. In seconds, the ice begins to bubble, evaporating by sublimation without turning into water. The resulting cloud of vapor rushes like whitish snow around what, with his magnified senses, he guesses to be a rectangular hermetic door.

Before the shelter door becomes visible to the naked eye, a silent explosion throws it upward in a dense cloud that expands and then pours out like droplets of liquid oxygen, while the nitrogen present therein remains gaseous.

Through the sensors, Jonas sees the bright figure jumping up into the cloud, an unbearably hot infrared blur.

The manager of the VIB superimposes a pulsating "310 K" in green flashes to the figure that moves in the cloud now totally revealed.

A human being. Enigma!

The temperature of the figure plummets as it comes in his direction.

Startled, he concludes that the subject is not wearing a space suit, not even a helmet, but only a flexible insulation suit and a climber's mask. Extremely wide boots. Fully visible now, Enigma presents himself as a stocky, medium-sized individual with large hands.

He has bare hands!

At this moment, he realizes that all the exaggerations that the Service has taught him about the Enigma fall far short of the truth.

Because if this guy can keep his hands uncovered at 80 degrees absolute without losing them by instant freezing, he's simply not human...

As if to corroborate this conclusion, the adversary raises his hands to face height and huge curved external claws glare yellow in the clear light of full Jupiter.

Enigma jumps with claws extended. A normal human being would have succumbed, overwhelmed by the ferocious attack. With the agility provided by the VIB, Jonas merely takes an elegant step to the side at the last possible moment. The opponent passes straight through without reaching him and now needs to consume precious seconds to regain balance in this typically lunar gravity.

Unwilling to take risks, the Brazilian fires a laser pulse through the palm of his hand. He misses the target, for Enigma seems to anticipate his intention and deviates, moving even faster than the Service's analysts estimated, despite the reduced gravity. He retries when the opponent charges straight at him and manages to shoot him this time.

The power of this second blast should be enough to kill an astronaut under the armor of his spacesuit. Enigma doesn't wear a suit. Still, though he is struck by an intense tremor, he stands still, and advances.

In the next second the Palmarine agent stands before Jonah and strikes a violent blow with the claws of his right hand. The Brazilian jumps again to the side, to sidestep and avoid the attack. But now Enigma anticipates the feint and strikes simultaneously with the crossed left of the opposite side.

The tremendous impact unbalances Jonas, causing him to sit and slide off the ice, until he stops a dozen meters from his opponent.

Enigma zig-zags closer to him to avoid another laser pulse.

Jonas shakes his head to get rid of the torpor. Hears the VIB whisper in his ear:

"Microperforations in the outer shield at four distinct points."

Impossible! With all these layers of flexible plasteel, not even titanium claws would be able to...

"Marginally compromised watertightness. Nanobot repairs in progress."

The Brazilian debates, struggling to stand up before the waiting opponent, gallant, claws extended.

"The primary content is not at immediate risk of suffocation."

At least, this!

Standing at last, he manages to deflect the enemy's blow with his left forearm. The fingers of his right hand grip his opponent's left wrist like vises when he, claws extended, seems about to unleash the deadly onslaught against his helmet.

They both stumble for long seconds, struggling over the slippery ice.

"Muscular amplification required in 62%," the VIB warns him. "Under current conditions, the maximum available power is 83%."

"Enable maximum power," Jonas shouts, staring at the sharp claws approaching inch by inch toward his helmet. "Now!"

"Maximum power available for 23 seconds."

He can stop the advance of the deadly claws, after all. Pull back the left hand and then use it to reach the enemy's chest with a jerk.

Enigma slides back. Jonas breaks the opponent's pulse just in time not to be knocked over by the other's impulse. He concentrates his efforts in maintaining the precarious balance on the treacherous ice in this lower gravity.

Without the help of the Brazilian operative, the VIB put the laser trigger in standby. When Enigma falls to his knees almost three feet away, Jonas sees him as a pulsating blue target on his helmet's visor. Below the bright bulge that struggles to stand up, it reads: **Emergency power available for continuous-flow shooting.**

When he raises his forearm to shoot, the enemy has already jumped on him with claws extended on both hands.

The shot hits him in mid-air. Stronger and longer lasting than the previous ones.

Jonas crouches in the last millisecond and the contender goes inches above his head to land eight feet behind him. The Brazilian jumps up. Ignores the warning hiss of the reserve batacitores and the right-hand laser override, advancing to engage against the opponent.

However, Enigma remains still. His body lies stretched out in the place where he landed.

The Brazilian approaches with cautious steps. It sweeps the inert adversary with its plethora of active sensors. *Fuck Galileo's instruments!*

He stood next to Enigma's corpse. He had almost been defeated on this hostile plain.

Then he observes the presence of vital signs in the corpse. Weak, but undeniable.

He's alive! Burnt organs and tissues... And yet...

"Preliminary metabolic analysis of the Palmarine agent indicates accelerated cellular regeneration process underway in the nervous and motor systems. Pulsation and oxygen intake show tiny but significant rises."

The SBI researchers were correct all this time, after all. Enigma has extraordinary regeneration abilities. No wonder the past reports insisted so much on the fact that he couldn't be killed...

But Jonas had been trained to handle this kind of contingency. He knows what to do.

In a determined gesture, he pulls the breathing ducts out of his opponent's mask.

"Process of accelerated regeneration of the interrupted agent," the VIB says in a satisfied tone.

Jonas takes a deep breath. He would love to take Enigma, alive or dead, back to Galileo and then find a way to smuggle his valuable body to Earth. Unfortunately, the plan is too risky. The scientific base is infiltrated by Palmarine operatives willing to fight like madmen to prevent Brazil from having this war trophy, the prey that the Service had dreamed of capturing for decades and which always slipped through their fingers. Until now.

Because there is a means of leading the prey safely to the earth. A safe method of making SBI unlock the secrets of Enigma's fantastic metabolism.

Jonas Spider smiles ruthlessly inside his helmet.

Who said Service needs the whole body? He ponders; the head probably contains enough information. After all, what analysts can't get out of the brain tissues, they will discover through examinations of Enigma's genetic material. *Yes, the head should suffice.*

5 VISIT FROM THE MAN IN BLACK

When Pellê fell off the map two months ago, Fernandes was sure he was screwed. He never heard from his friend again. He disappeared from his apartment without a trace. He hasn't been accessing his universal account, nor the Network. His simbaac can't be traced. The self-conscious symbiont is out of line or, perhaps, destroyed. Because even a technophobic zebra like him knows that nobody in his right mind would disable his simbaac. In his heart he fears the worst.

Why did I have to stick my hand in this gourd?

Apprehensive as he always is lately, two hours after he finished writing, late in the evening, he prepares to close his virtual office. At last, the old habit of working at home—a comfortable two-storey residence in the Botanical Garden—turned out to be sensible under the circumstances. At least, since he began to fear for his own life. After all, like every good paranoid who boasts, he has the last word in terms of a security apparatus and, therefore, feels much more protected at home than at the headquarters of the *Voice of the Morning*. Any attempt to violate the defensive perimeter of the residence will sound an alarm at the Gávea police station. Hence, if the worst happens, Fernandes knows that all he has to do is to keep calm, run to his armored panic room and stay sheltered there awaiting the forces of law.

This is why, alone in his spacious house in this tepid summer dawn, he feels a shiver of dread as he hears a deep voice greet him in his study:

"Good evening, Citizen Fernandes." The tall, blond, bright blue-eyed fellow materializes on the armchair on the other side of the multifunctional. He opens a smile intently reassuring. "Working late again?"

Palmares found me! It's him, the immortal bastard... He came to prevent me from revealing his existence...

"How...how did you get in here?" Fernandes stammers, rubbing his eyes, not fully believing the apparition.

The big man came out of nowhere! He checks the studio door to clear his conscience, confirming that it remains sealed. The alarms did not ring. A nervous touch with the tip of the indicator and the multifunctional informs him that the anti-invasion complex is still active.

On the other hand, this fellow bears no resemblance to that Indian with hideous features.

"Through the front door, of course. When you went out to the orchard to check out the robogardener's service."

"But that was yesterday morning..."

"Eighteen hours ago."

"Impossible. The house sensors would have beeped. My home manager has advanced routines of..."

"I rescheduled your manager to ignore me."

Eighteen hours in the presence of certain death and I didn't even know ...

"Who are you?"

"Call me Spider."

Fernandes contemplates the fellow's jovial expression. It would be better if he had the face of one who had few friends. *I hate friendly killers!* The impeccable black suit of the invader instills fear in him.

Comfortably seated on the anatomical armchair, entirely at will, the man in black scans every square millimeter of the pale countenance of his involuntary host with the air of a sci-fi telepath in a poorly written holodrama. Fernandes does not rule out the possibility that the visitor might really be able to search his mind. *With Palmares, you never know...*

Eyelids closed, he concentrates on the analysis of his alternatives.

If his inopportune visitor was black-skinned, dressed as he is, Fernandes would conclude beyond any reasonable doubt, that he was in the presence of an agent of the infamous and ubiquitous secret service of Palmares. Being very white, it is even possible that he is Brazilian. No matter if there are white Palmarinos. A few, but there are some. The fact that this Spider expresses himself in Portuguese without an accent doesn't reassure him. Portuguese is one of the two official languages of the First Republic.

"You seemed to come out of nowhere."

"Camouflage system. When I deactivated it, *voilà*! I became visible to your eyes."

Fernandes looks at the placid face of the visitor with a pensive expression.

"What do you want, Mr. Spider?"

"First of all, I need you to program your home system in absolute privacy. Nothing I shall say should be recorded." Jonas shrugs with a perfunctory smile of apology. "You know what this is, don't you? Let's play it safe."

The journalist steeples his fingers on the black top of the multifunctional device, and in his eagerness to conceal the almost panic-like fear he emulates a weary sigh before starting to talk again:

"Very well, Mr. Spider." He uses the name by which the other introduced himself. Certainly as false as the proverbial blue-eyed Banto. "We are isolated and, as you know, entirely alone. Can you now deign to answer my questions?"

"The only thing you need to know beforehand, citizen, is that I'm an SBI agent." Jonas extends his palm over the table top. The VIB assumes control and the multifunction activates, apparently on its own, to project the holocoat of arms of the Service, accompanied by holographic insignias and his functional agent identification. "Satisfied?"

"Very much," Fernandes stammers. "I thought…"

"You thought I was an operative at the behest of Palmares with the mission of silencing you, right?"

"Uh… More or less. Apologies."

"No problem." Jonas smiles sympathetically. "Let's say that, at this point in the events, it is not at all foolish to consider the visit of an aide to funeral matters."

"What?" The journalist feels a shiver on the back of his neck.

"Intelligence Jargon: operative endowed with executive authority to eliminate people that the Palmarine hierarchs deem inconvenient or harmful to their national interests."

"I understand." Fernandes swallows. "And the Service sent you here to protect me, right?"

"In a way."

"What do you mean?"

"As far as we know, Palmares has not yet reached its Herculean efforts to unburden certain information that the First Republic seeks to keep secret."

"Wait a minute. The idea was not mine."

"We know that the initiative came from the Citizen Gilson Pellegrino."

"He's…disappeared."

"Relax. Your friend is in good hands." The operative's blue eyes flickered with an ironic glow. "And yes, Cit Pellegrino has already received a visit from our staff. In his case, as is well known in Palmares, we think it best not to risk it."

"I understand." Fernandes nods. *Brazil: Feet of Clay* had not only sold millions of digital copies in the First Republic, but had also been transformed into an highly successful public and critical holodrama. "That explains Pellê's disappearance."

"Yeah. As for me, I was assigned to take care of your case."

"My case?"

"Work for your safety, Cit Fernandes."

"So you were actually sent to protect me."

"I'd say I'm here to advise you." Smiling, Jonas interrupts the retort about to emerge from the journalist's lips with an emphatic gesture. "Since Palmares has not yet noticed his investigative activities, so to speak, it is not necessary to protect him as we did with Pellegrino."

"Why are you here, then?"

"I have come to ascertain what the Cit has already discovered, and also to advise you to stop searching for this subject of the existence of a so-called invincible enemy operative."

"So-called my ass! We both found out that…"

"It's a grave matter, I agree. In fact, a matter of national security. Jonas nods. "We are fully aware of the situation."

"Are you sure?"

"Positive."

"How long have you known that…"

"We always suspected the existence of this special operative. As far as I know, at least since the end of the Empire." The officer is staring at the reporter. "Thirty or forty years ago, we were sure."

"If this is true, why didn't anyone ever do anything about it?"

"Who said we did nothing?"

"For god's sake! This guy, entity or whatever you rate it…"

"Enigma."

"Huh?"

"The entity was codenamed 'Enigma'."

"Very well. This Enigma seems immortal and, as far as we know, he has been acting for centuries, completely unpunished."

"Citizen Fernandes, please." Jonas holds his index finger to his lips. "There are issues that it is best to avoid addressing even in isolated and safe environments like this."

"But…"

"Believe me, we're taking care of this."

"How?"

"We have our methods."

"Apparently, these methods aren't working very well."

"That's where the citizen is wrong. Definitely, the Cit does not know what he's talking about."

"Oh, no? Enlighten me, then."

"I shouldn't even be mentioning this to you." The agent patted his chin with a thoughtful smile on the corner of his mouth. "Therefore, I hope you understand that everything you hear next is material classified unofficially."

"Of course."

"With the sole purpose of reassuring him, with the certainty of relying on his absolute discretion, I inform you unofficially that the problem to which the citizen referred was successfully solved last month."

"Solved, how?"

"Terminated."

"Terminated? From what I understand, that misshapen Indian can't be killed."

"Without going into unnecessary detail, I say again that we have developed the methods necessary to successfully complete this mission."

"You mean they exterminated the bastard?"

"Right."

"Where? Here in Rio?"

"No. Far from here."

"In Palmares?"

"Farther, Citizen. Off-Earth."

"Dammit!" Fernandes let out a shrill whistle. "Luna or space?"

"The fewer details the Cit knows, the better for his own safety." Jonas smirks. "The important thing is to know that the situation has been finally settled. Now we want the dust to settle. For this reason, the Cit needs to stop searching this subject."

"One last question, before I end this topic forever." Fernandes probes the calm countenance of the agent. In the absence of reaction, he takes courage to continue. "What was that creature, anyway? Certainly not human…"

Jonas Spider breathes deeply while elaborating the most innocuous answer possible:

"We still don't know what it was, but I promise we'll find out. But I can tell you that the Enigma was not human. However, the most important thing in this case is that the threat has been definitively nullified."

"Have you ever tested the genetic material of the corpse?"

"Citizen Fernandes, we should close this informal chat now."

"With pleasure." Despite his sad sigh, Fernandes rubs his hands, satisfied. "You brought me exactly the news I needed to hear. I'm going to sleep easier tonight."

"We're done talking, then." Jonas stands up and extends his hand in farewell. After shaking hands, he gestures to release the journalist's multifunc and open the door. "Farewell."

Fernandes realizes that the security system of the house stays on without taking notice of Agent Spider. He doesn't even appear in the holos of the rooms he walks through to leave the residence. He didn't know such technology existed.

It's as if had never been here…

However, despite the regrets, he feels happy. The threat that hovered over the existence of Brazil for centuries was eliminated after all.

As Pellê would say, "the homeland can sleep peacefully."

Fernandes shakes his head with a tired smile at the corner of his lips.

6 FATHERLY PAINS

No one had the courage or the dignity necessary to convey the bad news in person. Most probably, they were afraid of some violent reaction on his part.

As if ripping apart three or four mbundos could get my son back...

The fact is that the Ebony Circle is no longer what it was a century ago. The organization has many more agents now, and the vast majority of its current associates don't know the details of their past. Details that aren't included in the annals of the most secretive organization of the First Republic—incidents that he only dared reveal to three short-lives since the death of the last king of Palmares. The new members are unaware that, as a cub, he witnessed the massacre of his people by the elite Inca troops. The Last Elder of the True People fell beheaded before his terrified child gaze. However, the eradication of the last children of the night happened more than half a millennium ago. Long enough for the pain of loss to sink away from the surface of consciousness until it rests in the deepest recesses of his infallible memory.

However, it was one thing to lose his family in a childhood long buried under the weight of recent memories. Another, quite distinct, to be deprived of its seed, its future, in that stupid way.

Sharp Claws was just a boy... His firstborn. An impossible dream, materialized thanks to the arts of Palmarine gengineering. Little more than a century of life, with eternity ahead, and now...

From the beginning, he was opposed to the plan to send him to the moon of Jupiter. Notwithstanding the Ebony's optimistic predictions, deep down he believed that the young man wasn't ready to act outside the Earth yet.

"Well, what can go wrong, my ganga?" Caio Lumumba, the Ebony's senior agent, tried to reassure the troubled night-son. "Gamma-Alpha completed his training more than two decades ago. Trust the boy, he is well prepared. Moreover, in Jupiter's orbit, the Sun is little more than a bright star. I imagine your child will remain *connected* all the time."

"That's where the danger lies." Restless, Long Teeth entwines the fingers of enormous hands, a habit acquired from the short-lives. "Sharp Claws is too young to remain with his active gifts all the time. This is not healthy, even for an experienced hunter, much less for a young, immature son of the night …"

"The ganga is sounding somewhat overprotective. After all, as you told my predecessors, your people lived at the bottom of a complex of Peruvian caves." At the inquisitive eye of the senior protege, Lumumba shrugged, a confident smile on his lips. "It must have been very dark inside, right?"

"For you, yes. So what?"

"Then I suppose you were always connected."

"We left the caves in daylight. As you know, we are mostly nocturnal, but we hardly need sleep."

"This is true. Well, what effect does prolonged activation produce on the body of a night-child?"

"In some cases, it induces an unhealthy excess of self-esteem, a feeling of omnipotence, as with some humans when they drink too much alcohol."

"I see." Lumumba stared at the senior night-son with a concerned expression. "You're right. This mishap can compromise the Gamma-Alpha mission. I will make sure that the boy will be exposed to artificial solar radiation periodically during his stay on Europa. In addition, I will recommend that he hibernate, if the satellite situation allows it. Satisfied?"

"Calmer." Long Teeth rubbed his huge palms together. "Satisfied, if only you would put an end to this stupid idea of sending him to Europa."

In the end, his relative peace of mind did not save his child.

When the Ebony soba himself gave him the bad news from the remote security offered by the bottom of a holographic tank, he responded back in a roar:

"Bring the body back to Earth! If the corpse is in good condition, maybe we can reverse the process."

"That will not be possible, my friend. Not this time." João Negumbo gestured apologetically. "It seems the enemy knew who they were dealing with. They stole the boy's head..."

"No!"

"Therefore, we don't have the body unscathed to carry out the resurrection."

"Who did this?"

"Apparently, a special Brazilian operative. An agent endowed with high technology apparatus and unknown potential. An individual sent to Europa with the primary task of eliminating Sharp Claws."

"I warned you that it was too risky to operate so far from Earth."

"Your son had backup, my dear. There were two Ebony agents undercover."

"That support didn't help him when he needed it most."

"We didn't know that the Brazilians had such a deadly operation there..."

"I'm going to Europa to handle this case personally."

"Calm down." The gray-haired Banto gestured to the bottom of the holotank, trying to appease his protegé. "This is not the best time to think of revenge."

"It's not about revenge." Long Teeth smiled wickedly. "But, as the zumbis of the past used to say, of retribution."

Negumbo looked at his principal protegé with an uneasy look. After more than four decades of coexistence, sometimes he still felt uncomfortable in the presence of this superhuman collaborator who knew personally most of the zumbis of Palmares, starting with Andalaquituche, the Sage. Not to mention the kings of old, like Ganga-Zumba and Zumbi the Great himself.

Therefore, unwilling to butt heads with the mourning father, he told the truth in the guise of an evasive maneuver:

"It's very probable that his head is not there anymore."

"I'm not just worried about the boy's head," he lied cheekily. "My son is dead, and this time even the medical science of Palmares can't change that fact. Even if we got the head back, it's too late. I don't seek to find it. I'll go there to terminate the perpetrator of the feat."

"The head of a son of the night will provide Brazilians with a lot of knowledge about the nature of the True People."

"This is true. One more reason for me to act immediately."

"No way." Negumbo's hologram crossed his arms over his chest. "Besides, why do you assume that the Brazilian operative is still on Europa?"

"I see." In the gloom of his private quarters, Long Teeth sprouted out claws and protruding canines. He would love if the leader were still around Subupira. "What did Ebony find out about it? Did the kid's killer happen to have left the satellite?"

"Yes, he did."

"Did he return to Earth?"

"We don't know for sure. The operative that defeated Sharp Claws boarded a high acceleration craft in Io a few hours after the confrontation. Our best working hypothesis is that he's personally escorting the...head, protecting it for his return to Earth. The problem is that we lost track of the guy when his ship crossed the lunar orbit. There was a hint that he had been spotted in Rio de Janeiro a week ago."

"I understand." Long Teeth half closed his thick eyelids. "Tell me, did this high acceleration craft stop to refuel or something?"

"Not exactly. But it happened less than two hundred kilometers from the Fortress São Paulo."

"The Brazilian military base in geosynchronous orbit?"

"That one."

"Right on my doorstep, then." Long Teeth bared his fangs in a smile of anticipation. "One leap and I'll be there."

"No way. São Paulo is extremely well protected. Impossible to infiltrate there. Even for someone like you."

"We'll see about that."

"Leave it to us. We plan to approach any transportation from São Paulo to Earth."

"I'd rather handle this on my terms."

"Consider yourself strictly prohibited from ..."

Long Teeth never heard the rest. The Ebony soba imploded in a bright flash as he crushed the old-fashioned control panel of the holotank with his left hand.

He shook his head in dismay. It was foolish to warn the boss about his intention to move. He let himself be carried away by pain and acted again on impulse, as in times when he had been an ignorant and unruly predator roaming the streets of Recife...

Now, he must race against time. Before Negumbo closes its launch window, so to speak.

Fortunately, he has contacts inside and outside the Ebony Circle. Because to do what he plans, he will have to collect a good portion of the favors he has given to half a dozen good friends over the last half century.

* * *

Sharp Claws is dead forever. Nothing and no one can change this fact.

For centuries he longed for the company of other members of the True People. Now that he has succeeded in begetting his offspring with the aid of Palmarine science, he has suffered this terrible setback.

The most painful part of this loss is the notion that his eldest son died in the line of duty. He fell defending the interests of Palmares. Long Teeth shakes his head. His thick shoulder-length hair sways from side to side. *Short-life interests.*

Despite his criticism, it must be acknowledged that his son had been well trained. Too young and yet in full control of his hunting powers. He knew that very well; after all, he had personally handled much of the training. He was so well prepared that he has successfully performed several difficult and dangerous missions. *On Earth, not in the wilderness of outer space.*

However, with the human diaspora to the outer Solar System, Europa was far from being a wild and desolate place. Moreover, in this age of instant communication, his son never acted alone and helpless, as he himself had done in the early days of his long-lasting association with the Palmarines. *He was alone when he perished. Hidden in the frozen outdoors, where he was discovered, cornered, and destroyed.*

From the analysis of the decapitated corpse rescued by the Ebony, the only living coroner who could be considered to some extent a specialist in the anomalous biology of the True People, they had concluded that Sharp Claws had been knocked down by the continuous firing of a high-power laser.

"I didn't know they allowed weapons of this caliber on the international scientific base," Long Teeth joked, bitter.

Fearful, the coroner chose not to respond to the rhetorical provocation.

Apparently, the enemy who took the life of the young hunter has the necessary resources to camouflage his heavy weaponry from Galileo's civilian sensors.

Then the boy had been beheaded after his death, or at least after his metabolism had entered the state of latency peculiar to sons of the night struck by traumas that could kill a short-lived being. The decapitation removed any possibility of latent survival until an eventual resurrection attempt. He was forced to agree with Negumbo: the enemy knew who he was dealing with.

An enemy able to eliminate a son-of-the-night with relative ease...

Short-lives are neither fast nor vigorous enough to face a trained and prepared son of the night on an equal footing. The Incas themselves—successful in the secret war to extinguish the South American segment of the True People—learned that it was necessary to sacrifice hundreds of experienced soldiers for every hunter killed. Once in Victorian London, Long Teeth had faced a powerful alien, capable of defeating even a seasoned son-in-law. But Red Jack had been dead for over a century.

Unless this short-lived enemy has artificial implants to increase their strength, speed, and endurance...

It took nearly three days and his special touch to *persuade* Escura Mbutu, the director of one of Palmares' espionage agencies, to reveal everything she knew about a hypothetical secret project, the "Cobalt Blue," developed under the auspices of the Brazilian Intelligence Service. In order to leave no trace of his investigation, he induced Angana Mbutu to forget all the intimate and prolonged conversation they had.

Intelligent Armored Suits... So, SBI decided to endow their operations with superpowers?

Apparently, he would have to arm himself with more resources than initially thought necessary. Borrow some items from the Ebony's special arsenal. The worst is that he can't use the power of his touch of domination over there. Intended to safeguard the secrecy of the night-sons, Palmares' most secretive organization learned to make its agents immune to touch. Fortunately, the arsenal keeper is a good friend. Djogo will certainly understand the dilemma. Anyway, it will be another favor to charge.

* * *

Of all the events, passages and details lived during almost six hundred years of existence, Long Teeth remembers everything that is worth remembering. His birth in the Imperial Cuzco of Pachacuti Yupanqui, in full Final Dawn, the Time of the Fall of the True People. His childhood in the Ancestral Caves, after the flight to the west. The teachings given by the Ancient of the Caves, at a time when there was no longer any hope of redemption for the South American lineage of the sons of the night. The massacre undertaken by the armies of Prince Tupac Yupanqui and his desperate flight up the mountain range, and plunging into the warm gloom of the Amazon rainforest for almost two centuries, a time when he remained as a solitary predator around the villages of the short-lived Jê and Tupi tribes.

He was probably born around 1450. If this date is to be relied upon, then the massacre in the caves occurred around 1480. He was captured by the Palmarines in the Dambrabanga Mocambo in 1672. Hence the conclusion, much later, at a time when he had already come to care about the short-lived time count, that it took him nearly two centuries to cross South America from west to east, from the Pacific coast to a few tens of leagues from the Atlantic.

Nowadays, for the most part, he believes that his life actually began when he received the pardon of King Ganga-Zumba and began the long-lasting partnership with the Palmares intelligence services. For, if intimate and deep knowledge of the habits and mores of their prey forms an integral part of the existence of an experienced hunter, he must admit that he acquired little knowledge in two centuries as a nomadic predator in the Amazon. Only his coexistence with the Palmarine civilization—more sophisticated in its own way than that of the Inca Empire at its height—enabled him to become, himself, a civilized predator, a consummate master in the art of surviving and prospering in the great urban centers erected by short-lives who have settled in the Americas, coming from Europe and Africa.

Throughout more than three centuries of association with the political, military, and scientific elite of Palmares, he was protected so that he could perform several tasks relevant to the survival of the First Republic. He was a spy, secret agent, murderer, robber, naval commander, astronomer, engineer, diplomatic attaché, explorer, mountaineer and more.

When his old friend Andalaquituche returned from London in 1718 to take over the crown that had belonged to his half-brother, Zumbi the Great, a few months earlier, he decided to create the Ebony Circle to help the sons of the night in their missions and keep the secret of their existence safe.

It was an agent of this secret organization who, in the mid-nineteenth century, on an expedition to the former Transylvania in search of the shadow of truth beneath the shroud of medieval vampire myths, encountered two Thirsty Ones, females of the True People. Although buried almost four hundred years ago, Tenderdark and Blackmoon were still in a state of latent life.

When he listened to the report of their adventures, Long Teeth exulted like a cub from the caves on their first drinking night. Equally enthusiastic, the soba of the Ebony Circle issued a prior license for the protégé to go to Wallachia. After confirming the presence of the Thirsty Ones, he should arrange their immediate transfer to Palmares. However, an urgent mission delayed their departure and then came the message that they had already been shipped.

Impatient as a short-life, he barely endured the months of waiting, from the news of the discovery until the arrival of the cruiser *Negrume* to the naval arsenal of Ipojuca, with its precious cargo in the hold.

It did not matter that they were Thirsty Ones of European race. They were of the True People. And, more to the point, females with whom he could talk in the language of the spirit and procreate to produce new hunters.

Immediately upon landing, disappointment. The Thirsty Ones lay inert. Soba Kanjika and the agents of the Ebony sought to reassure him by stating that they knew how to act, and in fact succeeded in bringing them back to life in a matter of days after three repetitions of the amphora-and-cutlass ritual. Only they did not recover their sanity. Perhaps they had already gone mad when presumed dead by the time Vlad Tepes ravaged Transylvania. Or, perhaps, something had broken down in their spirits during Sleep. Long Teeth had never heard of anyone waking up, sane or mad, after a period of forced hibernation so prolonged.

Nor was he able to speak to them in the language of the spirit. His Wallachian princesses were only able to convey inarticulate feelings of atrocious suffering and deprivation. There were no coherent thoughts left in their broken spirits. No song that the South American hunter sung had the power to appease them.

The only human language they articulated was a bastardized version of the Wallachian of the XIV or XV centuries. It took almost a year before the Ebony found someone capable of understanding the few disconnected phrases stammered from time to time by Blackmoon.

Iphigenia Camarão, the greatest Palmarine geneticist of her generation, proposed at the end of the XIX century the improvement of techniques of artificial insemination to fertilize the Thirsty Ones with his semen. Long Teeth was reluctant at first. Adept of the Way of Stealth, he had always made a point of preserving the privacy of the True People before the excessive scientific curiosity of his short-lived friends. However, all attempts at a "natural approach" failed. If, on the one hand, Blackmoon and Tenderdark accepted with salutary greed the human blood that they were fed with, on the other hand they were not dazzled by his song of seduction, perhaps because they didn't understand his version of the language of the spirit.

The idea of collecting his semen and handing it over to Geninha disgusted him, despite the fact that he relied entirely on her. He took years consumed by this doubt before he overcame the repulsion. In the end, when he was able to overcome the moral barriers, he discovered that his seed was incompatible with the wombs of the two princesses. The American and European strains of the True People had been too long apart. According to the geneticist, perhaps they were no longer fertile among themselves.

Far from giving up, his friend declared that all was not lost. With the promising advances in the field of gengineering, it was assumed that, soon enough, Palmares would be able to combine his seed with the eggs of the European Thirsty Ones, manipulating them in order to generate viable embryos of hybrid children-of-night.

That promise did not materialize until a decade and a half later. From then on, although they had never recovered their lucidity, Tenderdark had given birth to four young girls and Blackmoon to

three others. In the pragmatic view of the Ebony, though insane, the Wallachian Thirsty Ones constitute "fulfilling matrices." Therefore, although he had never had the opportunity to fertilize his Thirsty Ones in person, Long Teeth became the father of three young hunters and four beautiful Thirsty Ones. Over six hundred years old, the undisputed leader of a tiny tribe, he sometimes delights in thinking of himself as an Elder.

However, what Elder in good conscience would have abandoned his firstborn at the mercy of the short-lived designs?

There is no denying that times have changed. There was a time when it might be possible for the True People to shepherd flocks of short-lives without the sheep even knowing who actually drove them. However, if such a feat was once feasible, it has become a suicidal strategy since the days of Pachacuti Yupanqui. The Palmarines demonstrated to him centuries ago the precariousness of his position. Today, short-lives are not just the lords of the Mortal World. They are also the protectors of the last remaining handful of children-of-the-night.

A handful, where a little more than a century and a half ago we assumed there was only one specimen... Not worth deluding. We only persist because of our association with Palmares and will only remain alive as long as we are useful to the interests of the First Republic.

On the other hand, he has just lost his firstborn. As the Palmarines themselves taught him, it is necessary to start searching for just retribution.

7 FRONTAL APPROACHES

According to the latest report from the Republican Information Agency, graciously transmitted, albeit involuntarily, by Escura Mbutu, the Brazilian operative codenamed "Cobalt Blue" returned to the São Paulo orbital fortress.

Finally, the Ebony understood his purpose. However, at least so far, he has managed to stay one step ahead of the opponents.

First, he appropriated the equipment he felt was essential to the execution of his plan. He then tricked the ground crew from the Palmarine launch base in Alcântara to climb to a low orbit aboard a cargo hauler. Then, the riskiest part of the scheme: boarding as a clandestine in the *Caloji* VIII, a general service ship equipped with mixed propulsion. He overpowered the three crewmembers with ease, tied them unconsciously and bound them to a small shuttle, and programmed the life-support system to wake them up twenty-four hours later.

By that time, Djogo must have already been compelled to report the invasion of the Ebony arsenal and the removal of certain special prototypes. Therefore, halfway to São Paulo, he is not surprised when the *Caloji* VIII master program announces in its characteristic placid tone:

"Encrypted transmission of Headquarters in Subupira. Priority grade: absolute black."

Long Teeth smiles. The Ebony's private priority.

"Decode and open in the holotank."

The miniature of a well-known Banto shows an involuntary smile on the holographic tank in the *Caloji's* control cabin. André Angoma, second-degree cousin to the current zumbi and third in command in the Ebony Circle, despite the fact that he has barely entered his fifth decade of life.

"Agent Delta Comma, you are in the illegal possession of an interplanetary vehicle of the First Republic. Return immediately to low orbit."

He couldn't pretend it wasn't about him, not anymore. Angoma has just referred to him by his code name, in force for the other secret services of Palmares.

"Activate holotransceptor." He decides to open the directional channel. "Keep encrypted transmission."

"Holochannel activated," the master program confirms the execution of the order.

Now, *Gana* Angoma can also see him with a delay less than a tenth of a second.

"Greetings, André. I did not know that you had returned to the HQ."

"We know what you want, L.T."

"Of course! I made no great secret of my intentions."

"Give up while it's time." Angoma stares at the holocamera with a heavy look. "Come back now, and we'll forget the whole thing."

"Who guarantees me that?"

"Promise of the Soba Negumbo."

"And where is our soba now?" Long Teeth smiles an amused smile as he senses the probable answer.

"He was summoned to the Mussumba Palace."

The confession catches him off-guard. He never supposed that in this age of ubiquitous telepresence, His Negritude, the Zumbi, summoned the Ebony soba personally to give clarification on his conduct. At least not so soon.

"If he continues in the current course, the São Paulo garrison will take him down, not without first warning the Brazilian high command."

"You're right, André. Caloji is a bit of a conspicuous vehicle."

"So. There is no chance of approaching the citadel without being noticed."

"I know. In fact, to be honest, I hope that the São Paulo garrison and command will be very concerned about my approach."

"That makes no sense, L.T. You risk causing an incident of serious proportions. We don't want to start a war with Brazil."

"Yeah, times have changed. But you can rest easy." he declares phleghmatically , fruit of decades of daily practice. "I only want to recover an item that Agent S.C. left behind."

"We will make sure that does not happen."

"Don't play the fool. You know as well as I do that Palmares does not have fast vehicles in the vicinity of São Paulo."

"Come back or suffer the consequences. You and yours. That's our last warning."

"I doubt that very much. The Homeland needs us as much as we need it."

"Don't you dare…"

"Close channel." He shakes his big head with fatalistic determination."

He always knew that this fateful moment of ultimate rebellion would come. He just did not suppose it would come so soon and so far from Earth.

* * *

"Commander, the Palmarine vessel remains silent."

The grizzled officer of aristocratic profile examines the trajectory of the invading ship in the holotank of the combat operations center. Her gray eyes peer into the stream of data trying to anticipate the opponent's intentions. Apparently, it's a civilian general-purpose spacecraft, a *Caloji*. According to the database of the citadel, Palmares has seventeen units of this class in activity. They have no weaponry. Unless, of course, the enemy has refitted the vehicle.

"Ma'am, the vessel has activated the bow searchlight." The service communications officer in the C.O.C. turns in the armchair to face the superior officer. "It is transmitting pulses in international standard code."

The information is superfluous. The Commander Prisca Didonet doesn't need help to decode by herself the luminous pulses in Mbuto Code:

"Explosion on board. Faulty transmission system. Antimatter nodes: unstable configuration. Safety measure: automatic deactivation of main propulsion."

"Commander, the *Caloji* is on a crash course. Impact against outer hull minus fourteen minutes, thirty-four seconds, max."

"Whose idiotic idea is this to come so close to us?" Prisca shouts through her teeth. *The kicker is that they chose just the worst imaginable moment to show their faces...*

* * *

"Activate equatorial batteries," Prisca orders, struggling to appear more calm than she feels. Shooting salvos of plasma cannons against the *Caloji* is definitely not a good idea. Even if they manage to destroy the unruly ship, the wreckage will continue toward the fortress with roughly the same kinetic energy as before the shots. However, there is always the hope of being able to divert its trajectory with a warning shot. "Concentrate fire on the upper end of the target."

"Ma'am, the Palmarine vessel..."

The commander looks away from the main holotank trajectory to the service cube that displays the ship's holo in maximum magnification.

The Caloji began to unfurl her sails. Carbon fiber rods start protruding from the main hull, unfolding over and over again, until their ends are tens of kilometers apart from each other. Then the thin films that constitute the sails unfold, fixing themselves to the neighboring rods, until the surface of thousands of square kilometers is complete.

Good thinking! Prisca rejoices. With the São Paulo between the Sun and Earth, the pressure of solar radiation on the gigantic sails will push the ship in the opposite direction, acting in practice as a braking system. *Will it have enough time?*

"Last form." The commander closes her jaws. Anyway, it's worth taking the risk. "Suspend preemptive strike until second order."

"Commander," the detection officer says, amazed, "the target seems to have regained some of the maneuverability."

Indeed. In addition to losing speed, the *Caloji* begins to position the sails to guide, drifting little by little from the São Paulo. The main holotank blazes with the reproduction of the Palmarine civil vessel that, once the sails have been unfurled, has become much larger than the fortress.

"Invading vessel reducing speed." The detection officer keeps her gaze nailed to her service holocube. "Angular deviation of two, now three degrees in relation to the original course."

That's not enough. Prisca frowns. With the sails fully unfurled, the ship now displays an oversized crash section. If it does not spin faster, it will sweep the southern hemisphere of the fortress with part of the upper canopy. Although they have very small densities, the sails will clash with the external structures of the São Paulo at a speed of several kilometers per second.

"Holy shit!" The commander's eyelids clench, dazed.

The blazing light explodes in the holotank, illuminating the hitherto obscure C.O.C. in a fiery glow.

"Detection Officer!" Prisca buries her face in the crook of her elbow. "Report."

The subordinate lets out a piercing groan before replying:

"Just a second, ma'am."

"Damage Control here." The deep voice echoes in the C.O.C. "Pulse of ionizing radiation from the target."

"Preliminary interpretation." The commander blinks without seeing.

"Most likely hypothesis: explosive decompression of the protective wrapping of one or more antimatter node."

"Ma'am?"

"Proceed, Detection Officer." The commander tries to focus on the holotank. The Palmarine vessel seems strangely displaced from its previous course.

"Explosion in the disperser of the primary propulsion of the invading ship."

Prisca shakes her head, bewildered. She contemplates the figure of the spinning space ship, slowly moving away from the fortress. *At least we're not at risk of collision anymore…*

"Damage control report."

"Radiation from the explosion returning to normal levels.

Emission levels poses no risk to us."

"Understood." Prisca let out a sigh of relief. "Boarding party, in their stations."

"Commander, depressurization on deck four." The Damage Control Officer calls back in a surprised tone. "Apparently, a loose piece of the *Caloji* struck the side. Repair team on the way to the site."

"Roger, CAV. Keep me posted on this action." Prisca sinks into her chair. "Boarding party, authorized departure. Proceed with caution. Seize the survivors of the *Caloji* and bring them aboard."

"Understood, Commander."

* * *

If everything went according to plan, obfuscated by the alleged overload of an antimatter node, the detectors of the São Paulo shouldn't have recorded the tiny emissions of the jets in their suit.

Long Teeth synchronized his advance toward the fortress so as to emerge from the shadow of the *Caloji* VIII at the moment of the blinding blast. It took him several minutes to reach the emergency hatch in the São Paulo section where he had landed. He thought most likely he had gone unnoticed. Made of smart material capable of absorbing incidental radiation, the suit must appear invisible to the fortress's sensors.

A short-life wouldn't have been able to force entry through the security seals of the watertight chamber, but he'd broken into it without much difficulty.

He tries to seal the internal hatch of the invaded chamber when the shrill alarm announces throughout the fortress the lack pressurization of the deck. Annoyed, he steps away from the chamber.

Have they found me yet?

He hopes against hope that he won't show in the internal surveillance circuit.

As he passes in front of the open hatch of a photonic laboratory, he stops and throws a stun grenade inside. He closes the hatch and destroys the opening control. He expects the amusement is enough to divert the enemy's attention.

* * *

"Micro-robotics to…Command…" The voice stops in a coughing fit. "…under attack…"

"Repeat, MR." Prisca turns in the chair to face her subordinates, as stunned as she is. *A Palmares double agent? Someone coming from outside? No.* The commandant shakes her head with a wry smile on her lips. *That kind of thing only happens on cheap spy holothrillers…* "Command on the line. Micro-robotics, repeat your last statement."

Another coughing fit tells the commander that something wrong happened in the micro-robotics lab.

"Security, send an armed squad to deck four." Prisca stares at the communications officer. "Internal circuit in laboratory seven."

"Affirmative." The lieutenant activates three commands on the virtual keyboard. "On the holotank."

The four technicians fallen on the floor of laboratory seven are not an enlightening picture.

* * *

"Commander Didonet, this is Lieutenant Spider."

"Go on, Spider." Prisca turns in the armchair to face the side holocube. She tries to stifle the expression of ill will. *What the hell does this prick want now?*

"Ma'am, I am convinced that the São Paulo is suffering enemy infiltration."

"There's a squad on the way to investigate the incident."

"If my suspicions are correct, the security of the fortress is not fit to deal with the problem."

"Oh no?" Prisca is already fed up with this conceited operative. First, he dropped that ultra-secret scientific payload in São Paulo. He then returned from Earth with orders to make a reservation of the most modern biological analysis laboratory in the habitat in order to "prepare ground" for a special SBI team which, he says, is about to board the ship. *Go figure...* "It would help a lot if you spoke in plain Portuguese, Lieutenant."

"All I can disclose now is that said infiltration is probably related to the cargo I brought onboard."

Great! The commander shakes her head in irritation.

"The mysterious cargo you smuggled here without my permission." Prisca gave a hostile glance at the agent's thumbnail in the holocube. "The one who you insist on protecting in person and that..."

"Commander, please." The little man in the cube gestures impatiently. "I'm just following orders. It's a matter of national security."

"It's what you intelligence types always say, for everything and nothing." The commander looks away from the hub to follow the squad's advance in the holotank. "Very well, Lieutenant. So what is it you want?"

"Authorization to deal personally with this focus of infiltration."

"Commander, report of the boarding party." With the fingers of his right hand pressing the headset, the communications officer turns in the chair to face the superior officer. "They did not find anyone on the *Caloji*."

Out of the corner of her eye, Prisca thinks she sees a dark figure moving very fast, next to the three members of the security squad, in the long corridor that goes to the hub of the laboratories. The holo blurs when the camera turns to try to keep up with the movement. Someone mutters a muffled expletive via audio. Then they hear screams and a kind of hoarse meowing. Then the holotank blanks out.

"Security, what happened?" Prisca swallows. *Either I'm wrong, or that blurred shape hit the astronaut who carried the microcamera...* "Safety, report situation."

After five seconds of ominous silence, without the military in service in the C.O.C. listening to the squad sent to the MR, the SBI operative returns:

"Commander, I'm afraid the enemy has intercepted the security squad."

"Spider, get off this fucking line!"

"Ma'am, I request permission to engage with the enemy."

"What?"

"Believe me, I am fully able to deal with this problem."

"How? Alone?"

"Affirmative. I have training and special devices. Besides that..."

"Commander, look at that!" The service ensign on the internal communications console points to the holotank. Apparently he managed to trigger a surveillance camera down the hall.

At first, Prisca doesn't understand what she is seeing. Red smudges dot the floor, the bulkheads, and even the hallway ceiling. *This can't be blood!* Then she comes across the corpse whose heart was ripped *through* his breastplate ...

"Increase resolution," she orders the lieutenant in a firm voice, despite the nausea rising in her throat. "Turn the camera around until we find our boys."

"Or what's left of them..." Someone lets out a hysterical laugh, which then turns into a series of uncontrollable sobs.

Another fallen body appears in the holotank. An astronaut with his skull crumpled, stretched out on the floor over a pool of blood. Three yards ahead, Prisca stares at what appears to be a torn arm, still in combat uniform, creepily poised on the top of an access panel.

"Who the hell—" she stutters, unable to link together her reasoning.

At that moment, the C.O.C. hatch slits open to let Jonas Spider enter. The astonished operative watches the dantesque scene in the holotank, as if mesmerized.

"It's not possible," he murmurs, finally. "Enigma is dead. I did it myself..."

"Who is this Enigma?" Prisca closes her jaws, fighting the urge to vomit. "Do you happen to know who did it?" She points to the terrifying scene in the holotank.

"I thought there was only one…" Jonas stares at the commander with a frightened expression. "I could swear I had rid our country of this torment…"

"Lieutenant Spider, I'm just going to ask you one more time." Prisca leaps to her feet, standing taller over the operative. She glares at the officer and drums with her index finger on the officer's chest. *Strange, it looks like an armored suit…* "Who killed my astronauts in that hallway?"

"Enigma…"

"Who or what is this Enigma?"

"An agent from Palmares. The worst enemy Brazil has ever faced."

"Did you already know him?"

"I already defeated him at Galileo Base on Europa. I mean, that was another Enigma…"

"How many of these monsters are there?"

"Until now we thought there was only one."

"Can you face it?"

Jonas swallows before answering:

"It's my duty. He came after the head of the other Enigma."

Great. The secret cargo is a fucking human head. Shaken, Prisca takes a step back and collapses into her ergonomic armchair. "What can we do to help?"

"Evacuate all corridors and accesses. Order the crew to remain locked in the compartments they're in until second order."

Prisca rests in a sullen silence. It makes sense. When fewer people circulate, the less chance of new massacres.

8 COBALT BLUE VS. ENIGMA II

Jonas advances through the labyrinth of corridors of the São Paulo laboratory hub with all sensors activated. It is no longer a matter of announcing his presence in a loud and clear tone, but of not being surprised by the enemy.

With a garrison of 382 military astronauts and scientists, the fortress is immense. Spinning on its own axis, it produces acceleration of a standard gravity in most living modules, arranged in a concentric ring around the power modules and supplies. The largest Brazilian orbital habitat. A self-sufficient world in Earth's orbit, stationary on the geometric center of South America, watching and protecting the homeland from all evil from the surface or from space, ready to retaliate definitively if the worst happened.

The point is that Enigma could be anywhere in this gigantic complex.

The motion sensors don't indicate anything abnormal. The corridors seem empty and the compartments next to the itinerary that he decided to take also show no signs of anomalous activity.

He never imagined there could be another Enigma. By its unique characteristics, all past and present analysts have always believed that it was a single supposedly supernatural operative. *We've always been wrong. How many of these heinous monsters does Palmares still have to throw at us?*

In principle, the current Enigma probably ignores his existence. However, also in principle, the mysterious entity should also ignore the location of the head of his colleague, and yet came straight here, infiltrated the fortress easily and already caused seven casualties, three of them fatal.

I need to stop this freak. Jonas reaches a junction of eight corridors. The VIB sweeps all directions with the sensors at maximum, looking for movement. *Again!*

* * *

Long Teeth walks through the tangle of the São Paulo corridors. Apparently they have already discovered his presence. Everything as planned.

There are no more crewmen circling between compartments and corridors of the fort. Well trained, they disappeared less than thirty seconds after the klaxon announced "hold current posts."

The corridors are plunged into shadows, lit only from time to time by feeble lights that flash in a blood-red comforting to his sensitive eyes.

Despite the capture of Sharp Claws, the Brazilian intelligence still doesn't seem to have discovered much, judging by the light intensity reigning here. For if they had studied the boy's eyeballs, they would have concluded that the night-children are nocturnal creatures, and that as such they may be dazzled by faerie light.

He hears the worried pulsations of sheltered short-lives in the nearby compartments. The frightened scent of their pheromones in the corridors makes it clear they already knew the lesson of the security squad.

The commander of the fortress certainly plans to capture him in some way or another. Apparently, she forfeited the direct confrontation. At least, for now. Probably she'll want to gas him out or even expose him to a vacuum in a sealed compartment. *If they only knew how long I can survive without breathing...*

He concentrates on the noises of the more distant corridors. It may not mean anything, but he thinks he's heard things four hundred yards ahead. Unfortunately, this rubber-coated floor stifles sound propagation. Even so, he notes that it is a single person.

Why does a solitary astronaut wander aimlessly about in a habitat under lockdown? Probably to be killed.

The pace doesn't indicate caution or fear, but determination.

Cobalt Blue? Long Teeth accelerates the pace towards the solitary short-life. *I can only hope.*

* * *

Jonas hears the high beep of the true motion sensor. Then the VIB opens the schematic holo of that section of the fortress. A presence suspected a deck below, two hundred and thirty yards ahead. Take the next access ramp to get off. Right now, he prefers relying on elevators.

"Access to surveillance cameras on deck three," orders the VIB.

Another transparent holo opens next to the first. The agent looks down the long corridor. The tenuous, scattered lighting creates a host of shadows. Enigma could be hidden in any of them.

"Infrared sensors?"

"The corridor only has fire sensors."

Jonas closes his jaws. He will have to reach the hall to use the suit's IV.

* * *

Footsteps approach. Cobalt Blue or not, whoever is approaching is on this deck, seventy-five feet from his current position.

He commands the retraction of the helmet and bares his fangs in a rictus of pleasure. Exposes the retractable claws of his hands and creeps into a denser shadow within the gloom.

* * *

The MV sensor has cleared the holo. Enigma noticed his approach and hid himself.

VIB activates infrared vision without having to sort. One can imagine that the enemy has a costume clever enough to suit his thermal signature at room temperature, but you never know.

The sonar exhibits a random anomaly that dissipates in less than a second.

"Analysis."

"Enemy generating destructive eco-interference. See now."

The echo of a figure appears again, now leaning against the side bulkhead of the corridor, less than twenty yards away. So close! Then it disappears again, when the enemy generator emulates the new frequency pattern.

"Request normal lighting."

Three seconds later, the hallway lights up. At that moment, the dark figure appears in front of him.

* * *

He moves faster than I do. Jonas stares at the ugly fellow in a black-fitting suit, apparently capable of absorbing incident light. *Even with VIB, he moves faster. It should have faster reflexes as well.*

"Cobalt Blue, I presume." The opponent grins fiercely, displaying protruding canines the size of an adult man's thumbs.

The Brazilian looks at the entity with huge eyes. The yellow irises fills almost the entire space between the eyelids. The pupils are nothing more than slits, like those of a feline on a clear day.

"So this is my code name in Palmares?" He never imagined he would talk to this nonhuman creature one day.

"The analysts of our intelligence communities don't excel at creativity in the christening of operatives and agents. They thought it simpler to take the name of their project."

Jonas shakes his head, grinning reluctantly.

"You have something that belongs to us."

"I can't imagine what that might be."

"Then I will clarify this pretended ignorance. The head of the other Enigma. Deliver it to me willingly and I promise to leave without causing more casualties in the São Paulo."

"I'm sorry. Whatever you came looking for here, it's not with us."

"In that case, you will not mind me rummaging through the fortress, will you?"

"Unfortunately, I can't allow you to do that." Jonas swallows hard. "To be honest, my primary mission is to fight and destroy you."

"What are we waiting for, then?"

Imbued with a peculiar sense of humor, of its own accord, the VIB abandons the matte gray camouflage and assumes the cobalt blue color, dotted with glowing golden stars, without its bearer even giving the order.

* * *

Jonas leaps back, raises his arms and shoots laser pulses with both hands. Anticipating such an attack, the opponent dodges to the side. The wrists open holes in the bulkhead at the curve of the corridor, from where sparks begin to emerge.

Long Teeth advances and counterattacks with a right-hand swipe. The sharp claws reach the opponent's flank at the level of the ribs, without being able to pierce the armor of the suit.

"Superficial microperforations in the outer shield. Repairs in progress. Occurrence alarms disabled."

From the confrontation with the previous Enigma, it was more or less established that the opponent's terrible claws can't produce significant damage to the VIB. With a relieved sigh, Jonas fires a continuous laser jet at point-blank range. Although struck in the chest and thrown back, the Palmarine agent doesn't seem mortally wounded.

This Enigma has defenses. In his own way, his suit is also an armor...

The son-of-the-night rises from a leap, deflecting at the last moment the new laser bursts that the adversary fires at maximum power with the palms of his hands.

"Batteries charge at less than 72%," VIB alerts Spider.

This strategy is not working. He's too fast and I'm wasting energy too fast...

With another jump Long Teeth hits the operative's torso with both feet, knocking him down. He rises and strikes the Brazilian's helmet with both hands. Although the piercing claws don't penetrate the enemy's skull, he feels dizzy with the intensity of the impacts.

The son-of-the-night rises to his feet and raises his opponent still dizzy by the neck. He growls in an angry tone:

"Did you think it would be as easy as it was on Europa?"

Am I imagining things, or is this one stronger and faster than the other?

Jonas recovers with the massive dose of noradrenaline that VIB releases into his bloodstream. He raises his arms and throws twin punches against his opponent's uncovered face.

Surprised by the adversary he thought defeated, Long Teeth falls to his knees. The Brazilian's kick hits him hard in the chest, hurling him against the hatch of the laboratory, giving in to the impact.

Jonas crosses the broken hatch portal to capture the opponent, but it rolls back from a set of benches, disappearing from view.

"Charge: less than 65%."

He is winning the mortal duel, but he must finish it soon, while he has the energy to overthrow this Enigma.

He runs to one end of the compartment and begin to cross it, scouring the spaces between benches, consoles, and panels with the active sensors buzzing at full power.

Perched on top of a tall bench, Long Teeth jumps over the opponent, knocking him over. The two of them get bogged down and, with the impact, they go rolling around. They reach a raised panel, which slopes and falls on them, causing an avalanche of equipment and consoles.

In the midst of the fight, the son-of-the-night realizes that the armor of the enemy performs a frenetic—and pathetic—attempt to mimic the mutating chaotic patterns of the fallen wreckage around them. Maybe it could fool him, if he saw as badly as a human…

Stunned, Jonas tries to throw punches and kicks at the opponent, but only manages to hit consoles and devices that fall around him and now lie as obstacles between the combatants.

A cascade of noise in the midst of the collapse indicates that Enigma was able to rise from the debris of the panel about ten feet away.

Jonas scours the confused environment in search of the entity and finds it nowhere. VIB activates the infrared sensors to plot the residual heat of the opponent. He follows the resulting trail with his gaze, but before he can locate the enemy, he hits him in the back, knocking him down again.

Enraged, he turns his body and shoots the laser non-stop, setting fire to part of the debris of the equipment scattered on the floor.

"You fool." Jonas hears the accusatory grunt in Enigma's ringing voice.

When he finally infers the direction from which the affront came, the other is no longer there. *Enigma is a master at this type of action.* Jonas shakes his head, angry with his own stupidity. *He must have centuries of experience...*

"Charge: less than 40%. Overload on the right hand thermolaser. Nanobot repairs in progress."

That was all that was missing! I need a new strategy...

He stands in the midst of the flames. Does not start the fire. The clothing will protect him from the flames and their reserves of air will prevent him from suffocating with the smoke that surrounds them.

When sweeping the smoky compartment with the IVs, he notices the sneaky approach of the entity and commits the attack. When he notices his opponent's momentary loss of balance, he aims a punch in the face, but ends up striking his left shoulder. Enigma falls and disappears again in the smoke.

Amazing! No matter how many times you knock him down, he's always on his feet...

At that moment, the compartment's fire-fighting system decides it's time to release dense jets of carbon dioxide over the main outbreaks.

Distracted, Jonas does not notice the IVs in time as the car comes flying toward him. The motion sensor alerts him too late. The armchair Enigma throws knocks him down like a bowling pin.

He rises, scared, and dodges another heavy armchair at the last moment, thrown against his head. A long metal rod emerges from the smoke and spins to strike from behind.

"Generalized electrical pane in right leg micro-scanners. Repairs in progress."

Shit! Not now...

He tries to rise, but the opponent hits him again with the massive shaft, now on the trunk. Gracelessly, he twirls his body to sneak behind a knocked-over bench, but Enigma anticipates the move and takes another blow on the head, and then another.

Can't get up. The failures mentioned by the VIB must be more serious than he thought. He sees the enemy emerging from the smoke. He no longer bears the metal club. In a leap, he crouches beside him and grabs him by the shoulder, while he raises his left arm with claws extended to deliver the *coup de grace* against his visor.

Without alternative, he holds the forearm of the entity and releases the most powerful electric discharge that the suit is capable of producing.

Long Teeth is cast away. Reaches the bulkhead at the opposite end of the lab and lands on the floor with a bang.

Jonas struggles to lift his torso by leaning on his elbows. Through the cloud of smoke, he observes through the infrared the opponent's inert body lying at the other end of the room.

"Charge: less than 10%. Severe risk to content survival. Available resources allocated for emergency repairs."

Doesn't matter. I beat him. Jonas rests his head on the floor covered with debris and fragments of battle. He breathes in while the VIB makes the necessary repairs. *No one survives with roasted neurons. Not even Enigma...* Comforted by that thought, he slips into unconsciousness.

Then, seconds or hours later, he awakens to a moan of agony, like a hoarse meow, out of the depths of smoke and debris.

No. It's impossible... I must be dreaming...

But the nightmare is real. The entity is crawling. First on his hands and knees, then on his knees, and finally standing up, walking hunched like an old man, but stronger and more whole with every step. Then, he stops in the middle of his stumbling advance towards the defenseless Brazilian.

Jonas shakes his head in disbelief. His sensors must be crazy. Because he can swear that the half-destroyed suit of the other is *smoking...*

"Enough of this." Long Teeth huffs with clenched teeth. "I've wasted too much time on you."

The son-of-the-night draws a long, thin artifact from a thin pocket camouflaged on the side of his thigh. A stick or rod. He tilts his torso and spears the rod in the opponent's chest. He closes his leathery eyelids to avoid the actinic glow emanating from the gun.

"No..." Jonas exclaims without strength. "It will disable the VIB."

"That is the general idea." Long Teeth displays a protruding canine smile. "I hate to appeal to such high-tech contraptions." He slowly cuts a circle in the chest of the armor, being careful not to burn too much of the meat underneath the suit. "It's a bit like cheating, but apparently I can't pierce your armor with my claws."

When it's over, the son-of-the-night removes the metal disc from his opponent's armor. The glowing circle squeaks in contact with the palm of his hand. The Brazilian must have tremendous self-control because he doesn't seem to feel pain. Just grief.

"Please don't do this." Jonas's helmet splits open, showing his reddened face and his teary blue eyes. "You don't understand..."

Fed up with the enemy's whimpering, the son-of-the-night rips off his scorched glove and rests his palm on the Brazilian's chest, half-free of armor.

"Sleep now."

"What?"

"It's not working..." Long Teeth contemplates the enemy's blue eyes. *A short-life immune to Domination? Wait a minute...* "You don't feel anything, do you?" *And here I am, taking damned care not to burn him...*

"I'm quadriplegic." Jonas smiles weakly. "I imagine your legendary touch does not work on me."

The son-of-the-night frowns. For a moment, the Brazilian almost comes to regard him as human, intuiting traces of piety in the countenance of his victorious opponent.

"I'm sorry." Long Teeth nods gravely. "It will be the hard way, then. At least you will not feel pain."

"How will it happen?"

"Like this." He sinks four sharp claws into the exposed chest of his son's killer and only removes them when he confirms that the heart has stopped beating and the brain will not work again.

Exhausted, he puts the plasma needle back in his pocket, standing up. *A quadriplegic. Who would have thought...* He still has a mission to fulfill in the São Paulo.

9 SABOTAGE IN THE ANDURO COMPLEX

He returned to the *Caloji* VIII and maneuvered the hybrid spacecraft away from the São Paulo.

At last he managed to find Sharp Claws's head in a safe installed in the late Cobalt Blue's own cabin, easily located by the olfactory track of the Brazilian agent. Full of bitterness, he used the needle to disintegrate it. When escaping from the fortress, for the sake of his own safety, he thought it best to disable the batteries of his defensive surface.

As soon as he left the São Paulo, the master program alerted him to encoded holing with absolute black priority.

"Show it in the holotank."

The utterly black face of Negumbo floats life-size in the control cabin. Notwithstanding the phlegmatic and proverbial self-control, he perceives in the semblance of the Ebony soba a subtle note of restrained irritation, mixed with a hint of disappointment.

"Contrary to our explicit assertions, you invaded the orbital fortress of a friendly country, risking not only your own life, but also bringing about a diplomatic crisis of interplanetary proportions."

Friendly country? Long Teeth grins a cynical smile. If there is one thing he has learned from his long association with the Palmarine intelligence community, then, in an extremely meritocratic society like the First Republic, all's well that ends well. What really matters is that he has managed to derive from the enemy vital biological knowledge about the nature of the True People. In addition, he verified the suspicion about the existence of the armored smart suits and developed an effective strategy to combat enemy operatives wearing those suits.

"Immediately transfer command of the craft to the flight program transmitted on board during its absence. We regret to inform you that you will be judged by the Ebony. If found guilty, you must prepare to give up many of the privileges that you now enjoy in Palmares. Best regards."

Apparently, this time he was wrong.

Fortunately, before leaving Earth, he made arrangements for such an eventuality.

"Don't enable this piloting package."

"The order to enable it has high priority."

"I strictly forbid this package. Absolute black. Confirm vocal pattern and retinal signature."

"Order confirmed. Previous order revoked."

"Excellent. Optimize positioning of the engines to reach the contingency target in the shortest possible time period. Add thrust of the conventional propulsion at maximum power and keep it until we surpass the lunar orbit."

"The selected destination lies far from the plane of the ecliptic and out of the holomap of the Solar System."

"Just follow the order."

"Understood. Executing."

Two hours later, Negumbo re-materializes in the control holotank. Now he makes no attempt to hide his irritation.

"If you don't start maneuvers to return to low orbit within the next fifteen minutes, we will render your ship unusable and then send back a special command to approach it. This is our first and last warning."

The Ebony soba goes off in a bright spot without a word of farewell.

Long Teeth has already deduced what they will do.

This time he won't bow his head. Both he and Ebony went too far to turn back. If he could return to Earth without retaliation, he might reconsider. However, the way things have gone, he has no choice.

The truth is that for decades he has had enough of this bondage to short-lives. It is possible that the fact that he is no longer the only son of the night wandering around the Mortal World has something to do with this feeling of annoyance.

Therefore, in deciding to avenge his son's unexpected death, he planned an emergency exit in case he had to face a threat of Ebony's punishment. An exit that, if successful, will give him a long vacation.

After more than three centuries of living with the Palmarines, it is not difficult for him to anticipate the strategy. After all, how to stop the escape of a spacecraft in full throttle, with the canopy fully unfurled? Simple: letting go of the sails. Palmares does not have warships or fortresses in the neighborhood. The treaties themselves for peaceful use of space signed by Brazilians and other short lives ensured that this was so. However, Palmares does not need plasma ships or batteries to knock down a spacecraft near orbit because it has the Anduro Station.

Recently inaugurated in a circular orbit around the Sun, a fifth of Mercury's average distance, the vast complex of solar-powered multilayer batteries has been severely criticized by other nations since the time when it was only a controversial project presented by Palmarine astro-engineers to the international scientific community at a symposium under the auspices of the UN.

The First Republic asserted that it would never employ Anduro for military purposes. Although it can drive coherent beams concentrated for hundreds of millions of kilometers beyond the Solar System, the real purpose of the complex is to propel automatic probes of the solar gravitosphere to the nearest star systems in a considerable fraction of the speed of light. Automatic probes and, perhaps in the future, manned spacecraft in the form of large space sailboats.

Like its past counterparts at the end of 2012, these early third millennium palmarine strategists think of everything and think big. Hence, despite solemn promises and legal safeguards, Anduro was prepared to act as a weapon. Not that there were plans to employ it as such. Just for an eventuality. Therefore, the same batteries capable of propelling the gigantic sails of a ship, continuously accelerating it to as many as a hundred or two hundred astronomical units away from the Sun, if employed in concentrated focus at point-blank range, so to speak, could perfectly destroy these sails.

Anduro is well positioned for the masterstroke. The senior son-of-the-night would be given one more lesson. Of course, strategists would not resist the temptation to use the new toy in a show of strength through the Inner Solar System.

Intuiting such facts, in the final favor of one of his best short-live friends, he managed to insert certain subtle instructions into the premises of artificial intelligence that Anduro manages.

When Ebony managed to persuade the Palmares Space Command to use the station's multi-stage batteries to stop the rebellious son-of-the-night's escape, they operated promptly, but not as expected. The laser beams hit the *Caloji's* sails with diffused focus, just as they had to do to accelerate it rather than cut off its wings. When the Anduro technicians attempted to clear the lasers, the manager revoked the order. Intrigued, the commander of the station determined the temporary deactivation of the systems housing the A.I. However, taken by Brazilian invaders, the technicians sent on that mission were put out of action by the defensive apparatus at the disposal of the manager.

When a high speed accelerated Palmarine warship especially of the terrestrial orbit finally managed to dock in the Anduro and its crew resumed control of the situation, the Caloji VIII was already outside the destructive ray of action of the batteries and, in addition, it had already jumped out of the gravitosphere. Too fast for anyone to do anything to stop it.

* * *

"My ganga, why were agents Djogo and Uiara not punished in exemplary fashion?" Lumumba sighs, depressed at the starry splendor unveiled through the holographic lookout of the Amalamale orbital habitat. "In my opinion, they deserved a treatment similar to that applied to João Anduro one hundred and seventy years ago."

Negumbo cast a stern glance at the subordinate. In four hundred years of history, since the establishment of the first mocambos in Serra da Barriga, you could count on your fingers the number of traitors for the cause of Palmares. In compensation, these few were treated in an exemplary manner.

"John Anduro betrayed his most sacred oath," the soba retorts with his eyes again nailed to the stars.

"But Uiara betrayed her country. What can be more sacred than…"

"What did you swear when you accepted the summoning of Ebony?"

"That's not the point, my ganga. What I meant is…"

"What did you swear, Lumumba?"

"To defend my protégés with the sacrifice of life and even of honor." The younger agent feels the hairs on the back of his neck rise as he understands the implications of the words he had begun to recite in automatic mode. "Guard the secret of the existence of my protégés with my own life, even from the most probable and eminent citizens of the country."

Negumbo smiled as he remembered that his predecessors used to swear an oath on the "protégé" in the singular.

"So, young man. Uiara and Djogo betrayed their oaths?"

"No, Ganga. No. But they…"

"They protected Long Teeth."

"…they betrayed their country."

"In a way." Negumbo sighs in despair. *The ever-crucial ethical dilemma of divided loyalties…* There are times when he feels much older than his well-to-do seventy-two years. "In order to preserve our protégé and keep his oath, Uiara introduced a Trojan horse into the Anduro to accelerate to Caloji instead of stopping it. Thus, it wounded the interests of the homeland."

"Is that not treason, Master?"

"Imagine that he acted differently."

"He would have acted correctly, then. The same bargain shipped the order to bring Long Teeth back by any means available."

"It is true. Even so, preliminary psychological analysis indicates that Uiara felt he would put his oath at risk if he fulfilled my determination to the letter. After decades of indoctrination to put the interests of our protégés above all and to ensure their well-being, it is understandable that Uiara felt compelled to act as he acted. I was wrong, of course. For this he will suffer the appropriate sanctions. But he respected his vows, and so it is not a question of betrayal."

Lumumba contemplates the fixed and immutable stars that scratch the sky. He remains silent for a long time, before expressing his doubts to the soba of the Ebony Circle:

"What shall we do now, Master? What will become of Ebony?"

"What we've always done. Our mission survives. There are still night-sons to protect."

"But Long Teeth?"

"Why, he's alive, is he not?"

"I suppose so. But unobtainable."

"It's true." Negumbo smiles. "At least for a long time."

"How long, my ganga?"

"At that speed, we estimate it takes about two hundred years to reach Alpha Centauri."

"But then, when he finally gets there—"

"I know. It is very likely that our children and grandchildren will be there waiting for him."

"Did he know that when he made his decision?"

"Of course. Long Teeth has a refined scientific background, even by current standards."

"Does the ganga believe he will arrive at his destination alive?"

"Certainly."

"Two hundred years, Master."

"He's spent three months at the bottom of the sea and didn't die. Three weeks deep in the waters of the São Francisco River and survived." Negumbo shakes his head with an amused glance directed at the triple Alpha Centauri system. "What are two centuries of hibernating inside a comfortable ship for a son of a night as experienced as he?"

"Ebony will need to have people of ours in the Alpha Centauri colonies when the right time comes."

"We'll be there."

"And what will it be like when he wakes up?"

"A new beginning, who knows? For him and for us."

* * *

Gerson Lodi-Ribeiro had two novelettes published in Brazilian *Asimov's*: hard SF "Mythic Aliens" and "The Ethics of Treason." The latter was the first alternative history story in Brazilian and Portuguese science fiction. His alternative history novelette "The Vampire of New Holland" won the Nova Awards 1996, while his SF novelette "The Daughter of the Predator" won the Nautilus 1999. His main short fiction collections are: *Other Histories…, The Vampire of New Holland, Other Brazils, Taikodom: Chronicles* and *The Best of Carla Cristina Pereira*. Gerson has published four novels so far: *Xochiquetzal: An Aztec Princess Among the Incas, The Guardian of Memory, The Adventures of the Vampire of Palmares* and *Strangers in Paradise*. He has edited eight short fiction anthologies so far: *Phantastica Brasiliana, How Lustful my Alien Girl Was!, Vaporpunk, Dieselpunk, Solarpunk, Fantastic Erotica 1, Super-Heroes,* and *Dinosaurs*. Beyond the science fiction borders, he published *Vita Vinum Est!: History of Wine in the Roman World*.

ABOUT THE TRANSLATOR

Fábio Fernandes lives in São Paulo, Brazil. He has published two books so far, an essay on William Gibson's fiction, *A Construção do Imaginário Cyber*, and a cyberpunk novel, *Os Dias da Peste* (both in Portuguese). Also a translator, he is responsible for the translation to Brazilian Portuguese of several SF novels, including *Neuromancer, Snow Crash*, and *A Clockwork Orange*. His short stories have been published online in Brazil, Portugal, Romania, the UK, New Zealand, and USA, and also in Ann and Jeff VanderMeer's *Steampunk II: Steampunk Reloaded, Southern Fried Weirdness: Reconstruction* (2011), *The Apex Book of World SF, Vol 2*, and *Stories for Chip*. He co-edited (with Djibril al-Ayad) the postcolonialist anthology *We See a Different Frontier*. He is a graduate of Clarion West, class of 2013.

THANK YOU TO THE KICKSTARTER BACKERS
WHO MADE THIS TRANSLATION POSSIBLE!

_Lasar Liepins
A Samuels
Aaron Feild
Abraham Martínez
Azuara
Adam Flynn
Al Billings
Alan S. Bailey
Alex Blott
Alexander F. Burns
Alexandra Weber
Allison Walters
Amanda Nixon
Amanda S.
Amber Brookshire
Amy Louise Brennan
Andrew Hatchell
Andrew Taylor
Andrew Wilson
anne m. gibson
Anonymous
Anonymous
anonymous
Ariel
Arkady Martine
Ashley Thames-Fung
Ben Vickers
Bjorn Wijers
Blake Rothwell
Bobbi Boyd
Brittany Murphy
Brontë Wieland
Burkhard Kloss
C Biondolillo
C.C. Finlay
Catherine Jacobs
Cathy Green
Cathy Laughlin
Caz Granberg

CG Julian
cheezopath
Chris Adams
    (@mrchrisadams)
Chris Brant
Chris Lay
Chris Xu
Christo Meid
Claudie Arseneault
clive tern
D Franklin
Damien Ryan
Dan Summers
Daniel Chant
Darrell O. Troth
David Andrew
    Cowan
David Mortman
Diana S
Dianna Sanchez
Djibril al-Ayad
Douglas Mota
Drew Shiel
Elias Kron
Elion Caplan
Ellis Cameron
Emily Dare
Emily Mah
Emma Schaper
Eric Brown
Erik T Johnson
Erin A. Bisson
Erin Subramanian
Felix
Filip Dedic
Finbarr Farragher
FoAM
Francis
Fraser Simons
Fred Herman

G. Goodman
Gabriel Rodriguez
Gerrit Niezen
Gilbert Podell-Blume
Greg Conant
Greg T. Sadownik
Greg Young
Gregory Scheckler
H. Rasmussen
Heather Jade Deura
Heather W Britton
Hel P
Helen Barford
Hessie Sheldon
Hilary D.
Hugh Platt
Ian Fincham
Ivan Andrus
J Corwin
Jack Pevyhouse
Jacob
Jasmine Ang
Jason Schindler
Jay Springett
Jenny and Owen
    Blacker
Jess Draws
Jess Gofton
Jesse Wolfe!
Jessica Eleri Jones
John Parry
John Snead
Jon Christian Allison
Jonas Bjärnstedt
Jonna Gjevre
Jose Rubio
Joseph Ulibarri
Justin Pickard
k. bird lincoln
K. R. Kemp

THANK YOU TO THE KICKSTARTER BACKERS
WHO MADE THIS TRANSLATION POSSIBLE!

Katrina Long
Katy Manck
Kayla Forshey
Kelly Robson and
Alyx Dellamonica
Kerri Regan
Kirk Mitchell
Kristyn Willson
Laura Wilson-
Anderson
Lauren C. Teffeau
Lauren McCormick
Lauren Skelly
Laurie J Rich
Liam Carpenter-
Urquhart
lindsay watt
Luca Albani
Lukas Dettlinger
Maggie Love
Margaret St. John
Marie Blanchet
Marissa Lingen
Mark Carter
Mark Newman
Mark Redacted
Mary Woodbury
Matt Jones
Matthew David
Goodwin
Maura Lydon
Mayara Barros
Michael Krawec
Michael Lipkan
Michelle Gibbons
Mike Cotton
Mordechai(Darth
Hamster)Levinson
Mx Roo Khan
Navarre Bartz

Ned
Niall Harrison
Nikki H.
nodejs
Patrick C.W. Archer-
Morris
Patrick Tanguay
Patti Short
Paul Clarkson
Paul Czege
Paul Miles
Paul Sittig
Paul Stephen Evans
Pedro Valente
Penelope Schenk
Peter Nowell
Phoebe Wagner
Prudence and the
Crow
R. J. Athaclena
Rachel Pennington
Rae Knowler
Ray Cornwall
Red
Regis M. Donovan
Rhel ná DecVandé
Rhys Williams
Robert
Robert Claney
Robin Moxie
Roxanne
Ry Feder
S.M. Mack
Sam Haney Press
Samuel Goldstein
Sarah Goslee
SeanMike Whipkey
ShadowCub
Shel Graves
Shelley Streeby

Sonia Reed
Stephen G. Rider
Steve Freeman
Steven Lauterwasser
Steven Shaviro
Steve & Sally Gilbert
Su J. Sokol
Sue Burke
summervillain
talkendo
Tasha Turner
Taylor Jones
Terry D. England
Theo Karner
Thomas Bull
Tom Cassauwers
Tomer Gurantz
Tony Gatner
Trysh Thompson
Ulrik Hogrebe
Upper Rubber Boot
Books
V Shadow
Valeria Vitale
Victor Okpe
Vida Cruz
Will Davies
Zachary Weeks

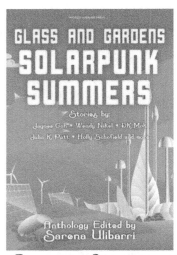

GLASS AND GARDENS: SOLARPUNK SUMMERS

Anthology

Edited by Sarena Ulibarri

Solarpunk is a type of optimistic science fiction that imagines a future founded on renewable energies. The seventeen stories in this volume are not dull utopias—they grapple with real issues such as the future and ethics of our food sources, the connection between technology and nature, and the interpersonal conflicts that arise no matter how peaceful the world is. In these pages you'll find a guerilla art installation in Milan, a murder mystery set in a weather manipulation facility, and a world where you are judged by the glow of your solar nanite implants. From an opal mine in Australia to the seed vault at Svalbard, from a wheat farm in Kansas to a crocodile ranch in Malaysia, these are stories of adaptation, ingenuity, and optimism for the future of our world and others. For readers who are tired of dystopias and apocalypses, these visions of a brighter future will be a breath of fresh air.

Featuring stories by Jaymee Goh, D.K. Mok, Julia K. Patt, Holly Schofield, Wendy Nikel, and more.

FAR ORBIT
SPECULATIVE SPACE ADVENTURES
Edited by Bascomb James

Featuring stories by award winners **Gregory Benford, Tracy Canfield, Eric Choi, David Wesley Hill**, and more, with an open letter to speculative fiction by **Elizabeth Bear**.

"Put aside all of your preconceived notions of what 'sci-fi' is—whether you think you love it or hate, it doesn't matter—pick up this book and get to reading!"   — Good Choice Reading

FAR ORBIT APOGEE
More modern space adventures
Edited by Bascomb James

Far Orbit Apogee takes all of the fun-to-read adventure, ingenuity, and heroism of mid-century pulp fiction and reshapes it into modern space adventures crafted by a new generation of writers. Follow the adventures of heroic scientists, lunar detectives, space dragons, robots, interstellar pirates, gun slingers, and other memorable and diverse characters as they wrestle with adversity beyond the borders of our small blue marble.

Featuring stories from Jennnifer Campbell-Hicks, Dave Creek, Eric Del Carlo, Dominic Dulley, Nestor Delfino, Milo James Fowler, Julie Frost, Sam S. Kepfield, Keven R. Pittsinger, Wendy Sparrow, Anna Salonen, James Van Pelt, and Jay Werkheiser.

World Weaver Press
Publishing fantasy, paranormal, and science fiction.
We believe in great storytelling.
worldweaverpress.com

Made in the USA
Middletown, DE
10 August 2022